Happy Birthday

Marg. I hope you find the time to relax and read this Passing Time

R Roy

Happy Birthday

Mavs I
hope you find
the time to relax
and read this.

Love

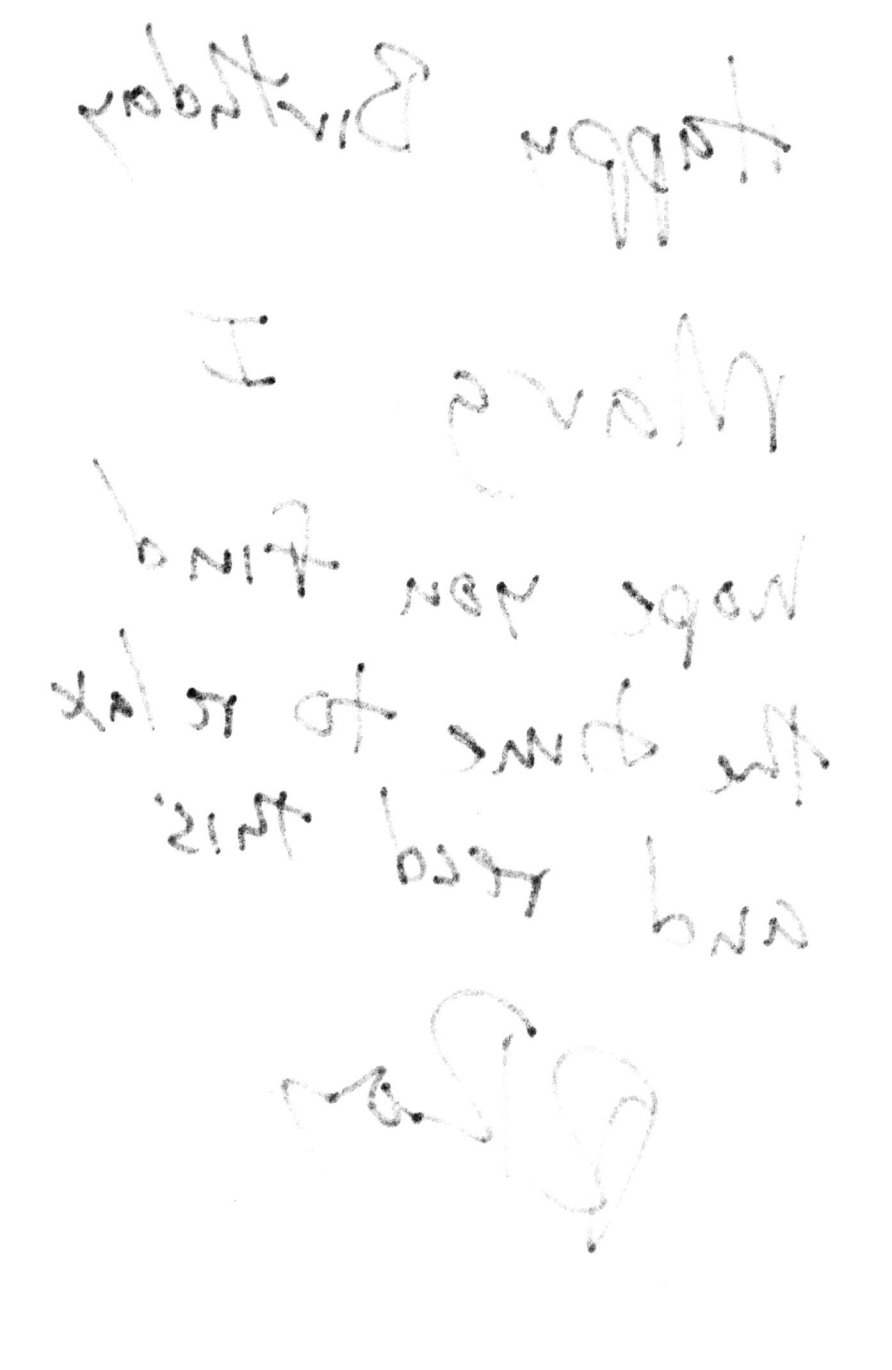

Ron Roy

Passing Time

Blue Cubicle Press

Passing Time

Copyright © 2011 by Ron Roy

Published by
Blue Cubicle Press, LLC
Post Office Box 250382
Plano, Texas 75025-0382

ISBN 978-0-9827136-1-7
Library of Congress Control Number 2010917207

Printed in the United States of America

LS Edition

This book is a work of fiction. Names, characters, incidents, and places are the product of the author's imagination or are used fictitiously. Any resemblance to actual events, locals, or persons, living or dead, is coincidental.

No part of this book may be reproduced or transmitted in any form or by any means, electronic or mechanical, including photocopying and recording, or by any information storage and retrieval system without the prior written permission unless such copying is expressly permitted by federal copyright law. Address requests for permission to make copies of the material to Permissions, Blue Cubicle Press, P.O. Box 250382, Plano, TX 75025-0382.

Cover photo courtesy of the Moffett House Museum & Genealogy Center in Berlin, New Hampshire.

Acknowledgements

Many thanks to the first readers of *Passing Time*: Josh Roy, Nick Clary, Pat Vaughan, Mike Tessarollo, and Carol Rita Henrikson. Thanks also to The Writer's Garret in Dallas, Texas, the Continuing Education Creative Writing Program at Southern Methodist University, and David LaBounty.

To my mother and father,
who taught me everything I know about work.

He plunged through the doorway and into the corridor as it stretched before him for what seemed like miles. Brick walls and machinery gave way to excess paper in the warehouse, rolls six feet in diameter and ten feet wide, stacked to the ceiling, canyon walls clear to the exit, where the lights of the parking lot glittered, promising safety and sanity and a dozen other things that he'd always taken for granted, that he'd always expected to be his very own.

He walked toward the light, holding himself back, trying not to run, dragging the stick along the wire-mesh that stood between him and the rolls. At first, he took comfort in the tiny jolts that ran through the foot-long wooden dowel and up his arm, but when he reached the first sign: BETTER SAFE THAN SORRY, these were not enough. He smashed his lunch box on the sign, splattering the remnants of his supper across the bright, orange metal.

And then he ran.

Signs flashed by him as he sprinted down the corridor. MORE CARE—LESS HASTE. HEAVY EQUIPMENT. He ran past a security guard who stuck out one hand as if to stop him, but then he seemed to think better of it and backed away.

At the first junction, he caught a flash of red out of the corner of his eye—MOVING VEHICLES—but plunged across the aisle, anyway. Propane filled his nostrils. A horn sounded, and he dodged out of the way as the forklift brushed against his leg. "Are you fucking crazy?" the driver screamed, but Gene left him far behind.

The PINCH AREA sign showed a stick man caught between two gears, but he couldn't read the last one, its thick, black letters blurred by his tears. He remembered it, of course, the first one he'd seen on his first day: DANGER: MEN AT WORK. Back then, he'd thought the danger was in the WORK itself, but now he knew that it was in the MEN.

Chapter One

Gene had never planned to cross the river, never wanted to work for The Company. College was his way out. He wanted to be an engineer, but when he failed calculus for the second time, he knew it was time to take a step back, to revaluate.

As he headed to work on his first day, he paused on the riverbank and studied his new home. Though he'd passed it every day on his way to school since he was six years old, this would be the first time he'd ever stepped inside.

A narrow, metal footbridge stretched across the river channel. A hundred feet below, its waters surged down a sluiceway of granite slabs. On the opposite bank, the buildings of Great Northeastern Paper rose like an extension of the stone.

He took a deep breath and inhaled the odors of paper processing, the thick sulfur that he'd smelled his whole life. Streams of black discharge spilled from a dozen pipes embedded in the granite walls and disappeared into the white water below.

This was his step back, his chance to stop worrying about the future. For the next few months, he'd be a robot. Somebody would wind him up and point him in the right direction, and he would do his job.

"How do I get to the Number Five paper machine?" he asked the guard who sat in the shack by the gate. "Just follow them," the man said, nodding toward the workers streaming over the footbridge. "You'll know it when you see it."

He fell in step. The men were paired off or in small groups. They hit the bridge, and their steps resounded off the metal. Mist swirled around them.

When they reached the other side, a ramp climbed to a loading dock at the end of a long, low building. Inside, rolls of paper, each ten feet high and six feet in diameter, formed a paper canyon that stretched as far as he could see.

Signs plastered the wire fence that separated him from the paper. They had thick black letters on bright fields of red, green, or orange. DANGER: MEN AT WORK, HEAVY EQUIPMENT, PINCH AREA.

The next sign said MOVING VEHICLES, and as if on cue, a forklift tore around the corner. He looked ahead and dozens more darted in and out of the narrow aisles that branched off from the main corridor.

Then he saw a door. It was twenty feet across and thirty high with a giant #5 painted in bright red on flat gray. In the lower corner, there was a smaller, man-sized door. He looked both ways and sprinted toward it.

He ducked inside. Fifty feet in front of him, two swirling, spitting piles of metal stood side by side, each of them the length of a football field, twenty feet wide and twenty high. Countless metal cylinders twirled in constant motion, sitting on thick, green metal frames, steam pouring from them as they turned. Their heat washed over him, and their vibrations rumbled up through the floor and into his bones, caressing everything on the way up to his skull.

"Are you the new guy?"

He turned to a stocky man with short blond hair and a neatly trimmed mustache. His white T-shirt and jeans were spotless, but his boots were scuffed and worn.

"That's me," Gene said. He held out his hand. "Gene. My friends call me Geno."

The man kept his hand by his side. "What's your last name?" he asked.

"Wheeler."

"I'm Hawkins. I'll be teaching you today." He looked Gene up and down. "How old are you, anyway? I swear they must be recruiting in the grade schools these days."

"I'm nineteen."

"Old enough to drink and vote, huh? Blair doesn't usually send us the raw recruits. He knows better than that. He must be pretty hard up if he's sending us a greenhorn like you."

Gene didn't like the greenhorn comment, but he rallied at the mention of Phil Blair, the guy who'd hired him. Phil Blair wanted him here, regardless of what this guy thought.

"Mr. Blair said the boss down here was Dale Supry," he said. "Maybe I should talk to him, first."

"Mr. Blair, huh?" Hawkins laughed and shook his head. "Mr. Blair told you to talk to Mr. Supry, and you sure don't want to go against Mr. Blair, now, do you?

"Let me give you your first lesson, kid. Supry is the foreman, but you don't have to worry about him. We only have one boss here." He pointed at one of the machines. "Tonight, you don't answer to anyone but her."

Hawkins glanced at his watch. "Come on," he said. "I'll introduce you to the guys."

Gene followed him toward the machine. With each step, everything was magnified: the heat, the sound, the vibrations in the floor. He wondered how people could work in this.

Hawkins stopped at the front of the machine where a sheet of paper flowed from the cylinders twelve feet wide and wrapped itself around a swirling metal drum, creating one of those giant rolls that formed the canyon walls he'd passed on the way in.

Two guys stood beside the roll. One seemed to be measuring the roll with a foot-long wooden dowel, while his buddy stood back, watching him.

They were an odd pair. One was handsome, too handsome, out of place in these surroundings. His sideburns were long and trimmed razor-sharp. He had olive skin, high cheekbones, and slick, black hair.

The other had shaved his head military-close, and his pale skin was ravaged by acne. He was one of the ugliest human beings Gene had ever seen.

The good-looking guy nodded, tucked the dowel under his arm like a riding crop, and turned toward Gene. He frowned when he saw Hawkins, then noticed Gene and smiled.

"Well, well," he poked his friend with the stick. "Look what Blondie brought us, Devo. Fresh blood."

The ugly guy shook his head. "Goddamn fucking rookies," he said, but his friend jabbed him with the stick again, harder this time.

"What the fuck, Ben?"

"You want to scare the new guy off first thing? At least give him a couple hours before he figures out what a bunch of assholes he's stuck working with."

"Wheeler," Hawkins said and pointed at the good-looking guy. "This is Bennett."

"Just call me Ben." He thrust out his hand. Gene took it. "Wheeler? Is that what you want us to call you?"

"That'll do," Gene said, not wanting to confuse things but grateful that Ben had given him a choice.

"And this is Devoid," Hawkins said.

"Don't mind my boy, Devo," Ben said. "He's not the friendly type. You wouldn't be either if you had a mug like that."

"Fuck you, Ben," Devoid flashed Ben the finger and stalked away, but something seemed wrong with Devoid's middle finger, as if half of it were gone.

A kid came toward them dragging a thick slab of paper behind him like a gigantic tail. Hawkins stepped on the slab, pinning it to the floor.

"Cut the crap, Hawk," the kid said. His hair was held out of his face by a red bandana and tumbled, shoulder-length, out the back, where it was captured in a thin, black net.

Gene recognized him. They'd gone to high school together, though Gene had been college prep and the kid was mechanical arts. Those were two different worlds at Cumberland High.

"Wheeler," Ben said, "meet The Hood."

Of course, Gene thought, Gary Hood.

"Jesus-H-Christ," Hood said. "Wheeler? Eugene Michael Wheeler? Cumberland High Class of '75?"

"You ladies know each other?" Ben asked.

"Sure we do. Wheeler was a big-time college prep guy. A goddamn whiz kid. What the hell are you doing here, man?"

"Working," Gene said.

"No seriously, man," Hood said. "What the hell happened to college?"

"It didn't work out," Gene said. It was bad enough he had to explain this to his parents and teachers and friends. He hadn't expected it to be an issue here.

Passing Time

"Come on, man," Hood said. "Give us the whole, sad story."

"Who cares," Hawkins said. "It doesn't matter why he's here. He's got a job to do, so get out of the way and let me teach him. We'll take care of this for you. I need to show Wheeler the pulper."

"Knock yourself out," Hood said.

"Wheeler," Hawkins said, "follow me."

Gene nodded, grateful for the reprieve. Hawkins bent over, grabbed the slab of paper, and dragged it toward the machine. He disappeared into the side of it, and Gene followed him.

A narrow corridor ran between two stacks of cylinders. Steam blasted Gene's face. He stepped back and felt the spinning of a cylinder inches away from the back of his neck. There was a strong odor. Formaldehyde? His head swam. He closed his eyes. When he opened them, Hawkins pointed down.

A three-foot-wide opening in the floor ran to the other side of the machine. It was guarded by three metal railings, and beneath this mouth, it opened up into a huge metal vat, a steaming cauldron filled with a lumpy white substance. The surface roiled and bubbled. Hawkins waved for Gene to come over beside him.

He slid the slab of paper along the length of the pit and then let go. It got stuck on the bottom railing. He stomped down, and it came loose. It tumbled down to the churning, white whirlpool. One end jutted into the air like a flailing arm, and then it was gone.

"Jesus," Gene said, but when he turned, Hawkins was gone.

Gene walked back out into the open. Hawkins stood beside Ben.

"I hope Blondie told you to watch yourself around the pulper, kid," Ben said as he nodded toward the pit. "That's no fucking place to get careless."

Hawkins smoothed down the bristles of his mustache. "I figured that goes without saying, Ben."

"For Christ's sake, Blondie, all the kid can see is a bunch of white mush brewing in a metal vat. He can't see what's underneath."

"What is underneath?" Gene asked.

"Blades," Ben said. "Blades that grind the excess paper so we can pipe it back into the mix. Of course, they'll do the same to you. They'll grind you into little pieces before we even notice that you're missing. You'll end up as shitty red streaks in the paper."

Gene studied his face. Was he serious, or was he just trying to scare him?

Hawkins must have picked up on his doubts. "You have to watch yourself around all these machines. To them, we're just so much raw material."

Ben winked at Gene. "We're not sure, but we think that's one reason Blondie loves the damn machines so much, because they share his utter disregard for humankind." He tapped Hawkins in the chest with his stick. He seemed to think the thing was an extension of his arm.

"Don't start with that, Ben," Hawkins said. "It's old."

"All right, all right," Ben said as he nodded sadly. "As much as I hate to admit, Blondie's right this time." He used the stick as a pointer, aiming at a frayed tangle of ropes that spun around the edges of the cylinders.

"You have to be careful around these nasty she-bitches. Respect them and you'll be all right—"

"But if you drop your guard," Hawkins said, "you could lose a finger just like that." He brought two fingers together in a snipping motion.

"You're just trying to freak me out," Gene said.

"You think so?" Hawkins stuck the same two fingers between his lips and let out a shrill whistle. Devoid had gone over to a smoking area. His head jerked up at the whistle. Hawkins waved for him to come over. Devoid made a face when he saw it was Hawkins, but when Ben nodded, he crushed out his cigarette and came over.

Devoid eyed Hawkins suspiciously the whole way over, like a stray dog that expected a beating.

"Give me your hand," Hawkins said.

"What the hell for?"

"Just give it."

"Fuck no."

Hawkins grabbed Devoid's wrist. He spun him around, pinned one arm by his side, and held the other hand right in Gene's face. Gene cringed as the glimpse he'd caught before became clear.

Half the fingers on Devoid's right hand were missing pieces. His pinky was chopped off to the last joint, as was the ring finger. The tip of his middle finger was gone, as well. Only his index finger and thumb were intact.

"Jesus Christ," Devoid tore his hand away from Hawkins and swung a fist at his head. Hawkins danced away. Ben wrapped his arms around Devoid.

"Be cool, Devo," he said. "Be cool."

"What am I, a fucking freak show?" Devoid asked.

"No," Hawkins said, "a visual aid. Wheeler didn't believe how dangerous this place can be. I couldn't think of a better way to show him."

"Touch me again, and I'll break your fucking arm," Devoid said as he stormed back to the smoking area.

"How the hell did he do that to his hand?" Gene asked.

"It's a long story," Hawkins said. "And a short one. All you need to know is the short version. He got careless, and the machine doesn't like to be taken lightly. She is one vindictive bitch." He made the snipping motion with his fingers. "Don't ever forget that."

Ben nodded. "Sad but true. Just check out some of the older guys. There isn't one of them who's got all ten fingers. The worst ones only got about five or six between both hands."

Gene didn't need to see anyone else. Devoid's mangled fingers were enough. He shuddered.

"That's good, kid," Ben said. "You've got to give these nasty bitches their due."

Gene looked up into the rolls. The rattle tore at his ears. Steam blasted his face. He pictured the slab of paper in the pulper flailing up like the arm of a drowning man. He wondered how anyone could ever get careless around these things.

Hawkins glanced at his watch. "How much time we got, Ben?"

Ben glanced at the roll of paper at the front of the machine. He shrugged. "Maybe twenty minutes."

"I'm going to the can," Hawkins said. "You think you can stay out of trouble for that long, Wheeler?"

Gene felt Ben's hand on his arm. "Don't worry about Wheeler," he said. "He can hang with me until you do your business, Blondie. What do you say, kid? Does that sound okay?" He winked as Hawkins studied Gene's face.

"Sure," Gene said. "I'll hang with Ben, if that's all right with you."

Hawkins hesitated, but then he shrugged. "Ten minutes," he said, and then he was out the door.

As soon as Hawkins was out of sight, Devoid came back over, saluting the door with both middle fingers. Gene tried not to stare at the mangled one.

Ben leaned over. Gene thought he was going to shout in his ear, some comment about Hawkins, no doubt, but Ben tapped it with his finger, instead. "Didn't Blondie give you earplugs?" he asked.

"Earplugs? He didn't say anything about that."

"Hard to believe," Ben said.

"He's usually so fucking efficient," Devoid said.

Ben pulled a small plastic bag from his pocket with two small, bright bits of yellow foam in it. "Pinch these and stick one in each ear," he said. "They do wonders."

"Yeah," said Devoid. "Wonders."

When Gene squeezed the plugs and stuck them in, the noise faded, even though he could still feel vibrations coming up through the floor. "Thanks," he said.

"Don't mention it," Ben said as he sat down on a bench beside the machine. "Have a seat, Wheeler."

"Thanks."

"So," he continued, "now that we don't have Blondie breathing down our necks, we can get acquainted. Have you been working in The Company long?"

"This is my first day."

"No kidding. What do you think of the nuthouse so far?"

"It seems pretty easy, actually. I'm not complaining, but are we ever going to do any work? It seems crazy that we're just sitting around and nobody cares."

"It's not so crazy," Ben said. "We're here to make paper." He pointed toward the machine. "Actually, she's the one who's doing all the work, we're just here to help her along. As long as she's running smoothly, then we've got it pretty easy."

He pointed back across the room to a smaller machine that Gene hadn't noticed when he came in.

"That contraption over there is the winder," Ben said. "When this gets big enough," he nodded toward the roll in the front of the machine, "I'll break it off, and then you guys will run it through the winder and cut it down to a size that some other companies can use. That's really all there is to it.

"The more paper Number Five turns out, the more money The Company makes. Some nights, we do have problems and we have to run our asses off. Trouble is, The Company doesn't make as much money on those nights because less paper is going out the door." He nodded toward the corridor. "Tonight, The Company is cleaning up. They're happy. We're happy. Most important," he said as he stood and bowed in the direction of the machine, "she's happy. Everybody wins."

"That ain't no fucking lie," Devoid said. He got to his feet. "I'm going to take a leak."

"Say hi to Blondie for us," Ben said.

"Fuck you, Ben," Devoid said without looking back.

Ben leaned over and measured the roll again. He nodded. "We've still got about fifteen minutes," he said.

More time to wait. Gene figured he'd make the best of it.

"So, how does this thing work?" He pointed toward Number Five. He refused to refer to it as a woman.

"That's a long story," Ben said.

"We seem to have time on our hands," Gene said, stretching his hands out, palms up.

Ben tapped Gene's outstretched hands with the stick and drew it back as if to club him on the side of the head. Gene ducked.

"Hey, hey," Ben said. "Nice move." He wagged the stick in Gene's face like a giant finger. "Follow me." Ben turned and walked down the long corridor between Number Five and the machine on the left. As Gene stepped between the rows of spinning cylinders, the heat clamped down as if a door had been slammed behind them. The air scorched Gene's lungs.

The stacks of cylinders stretched for a hundred feet on either side, row upon row, stacked on a thick, green metal frame, its surface chipped and cracked as if it had been repainted a hundred times. It reminded Gene of an old car that was held together by putty and baling wire.

Ben had gotten ahead of Gene, so he walked faster, trying to catch up. He glanced at the huge bolts that anchored the frame to the floor, like spikes embedded in the spread paws of a giant animal.

Gene looked up into the stacks and saw the sheet of paper that wound through the cylinders, intertwined like ribbon candy, touching every one. Steam rose from the swirling rolls into a metal hood that covered the entire machine, funneling everything into a vent at the top.

They reached the end of the cylinders and the harsh, dry heat was gone. Here the air was thick and wet. Ben turned toward him and twirled his arms as if doing the backstroke. Gene was just happy to be away from the heat.

Suddenly, a tongue of hot air caressed the back of his neck. He wheeled around, but there was nothing there.

Ben stood with his arms outstretched when Gene turned back to him. The swimming motion had stopped. He held his palms up, opened as if to say, "What's up, Wheeler?"

Just going crazy, Gene thought. "What happens down here?"

"It's better if I show you."

Ben walked past several smaller stacks of cylinders. Each of these had a wringer at the top like an old-fashioned washing machine. Next came a huge conveyer belt. Finally, there was a giant metal vat. Ben walked over to it and climbed a ladder on the side. Gene followed.

At the top of the ladder, a catwalk stretched across the vat. Beneath them, white mush bubbled just as it had in the pulper. Ben squatted down and motioned for Gene to do the same. He spoke into Gene's ear.

"We're the tail-end of the paper-making process. The guys in the other departments grind the logs into chips. They cook the chips, bleach the mix, and add the proper chemicals. Our job is to make the sheet and get the water out."

Gene pointed back toward the rows of cylinders. "It takes all that to get the water out?"

"Hey," Ben said. "This is the twentieth century. We're not the goddamn Egyptians laying stuff out to dry in the sun."

He scrambled across the catwalk and down the ladder. He paused by the conveyer belt. "This is the screen," he said. "The

Passing Time

pulp mixture gets sprayed out on this. At the same time it goes forward, it moves from side to side. That causes the wood fibers to mesh." He locked his fingers together. "That makes a sheet." He nodded toward the screen. "When the mixture hits the screen, it's ninety-seven percent water." He pointed at one of the small stacks with the wringer on top. "After the first press, it's sixty-seven percent." Ben walked to the borderline between the wet and dry air. "Those do the rest," he said, pointing at the swirling cylinders. "By the time the sheet gets to the end, it's only five percent water. That's the difference between soggy cardboard and notebook paper. That's why the stacks are so fucking hot." He glanced at his watch. "That's enough for today. It's almost time to turn up the roll."

Gene took one last breath of wet air and followed Ben back through the stacks. He kept an eye out for hot tongues.

When they got back to the front of the machine, Ben measured the roll again. He nodded and pulled out his comb, slicking his hair down.

"We've still got a couple minutes," he said. "What's this about you being college prep?"

"That's what I was. I went to college, but I flunked a course."

"Just one? I thought you had to screw up more than one to get bounced out."

"I flunked calculus. You have to be able to do math to get into engineering."

"Engineering, huh? What do you care about trains, anyway?"

"Trains? I don't want to be that kind of engineer—"

"Gotcha," Ben said as he flashed a wide grin, forcing Gene to smile, as well. "You can't possibly believe I'm that stupid, can you, Wheeler?"

"No. Of course not."

Ben tapped him on the chest with the stick. "If you ask me, Wheeler, college is overrated. You can't learn about machines in a book; you've got to work with them." He waved his hand toward Number Five, taking in the stacks, the steam, the smells, and the motion. "Math won't help you much around this crazy bitch."

"I guess that's right."

"Of course it is," he said. "One thing you're going to have to learn about this place is that I'm always right."

He threw his arm over Gene's shoulder.

"Maybe you lucked out with this math thing. It saved you from wasting three more years at school. And even if you do decide to go back, for now, you can make a little money, learn some stuff about real machines, have some fun. Things could be a hell of a lot worse."

"Yeah," Gene said. He studied Ben's face. It was as if the guy had read his mind. Ben was the first person who didn't think he was crazy for being here. If only he could get everyone else to understand.

Chapter Two

When Hawkins returned, he waved Gene over. He stood at a control panel and turned a knob. "This is the winder. First thing you have to do is start it up."

It had three cylinders, one in the middle with some kind of circular blades pressed to it, and two others in the back, at the base of a metal arch. As he turned the knob, all three cylinders began to rotate slowly. Gene studied them, trying to gauge the speed.

Behind them, a whistle blasted. Amazingly, the sounds from Number Five intensified, as if someone had floored an accelerator. Gene turned. Air blasted and paper rose behind the roll like a breaker at the beach, but just when he thought it would crash over and out onto the floor, Ben leaned out and slapped it with his stick. There was a loud crack, the wave disappeared, and the roll spun free, sliding down a long rack. The sheet flew from the front of the machine again, wrapping itself around a new spool.

"We're on," Hawkins said. "Just watch me this time. Try not to get underfoot."

Devoid and Hood stood on each end of the free roll, hooked it with a winch, and carried it across the room, setting it in a stand just behind the smaller machine, the one Ben had called the winder. Just behind them, Ben, red-faced, wiped his forehead with a towel, his hair sticking out every which way. He pulled out his comb and smoothed it down. Satisfied, he nodded and headed back toward the front of the machine, twirling the stick like a drum major's baton.

Devoid pulled a box cutter from his pocket. He dug the blade into the side of the roll and jerked it up, splitting the top layer of paper. He tugged at it, and the top few inches fell to the floor in a solid slab.

Hood went around to the other side of the roll and tore the top sheet of the roll away at an angle. He rotated the roll, and Devoid grabbed the end of the sheet as it came off the bottom. Gene looked for Hawkins and saw his boots sticking out from under the winder, but when he squatted down to see what he was doing, Hawkins scrambled back out, shoved past him, and ran to the back, where Hood already waited.

How had Hood gotten past without Gene seeing him? They pulled the sheet out the back. It ran across the entire width, but when Gene tried to get between them, Hawkins waved him away. He took a step back and collided with Devoid. "Jesus Fucking Christ," Devoid grumbled as he pushed past Gene, twirling him around. He might as well have been a revolving door.

Hawkins had walked back to where they'd started the roll. The slab of paper that they'd cut off the top was the same size as the one they'd taken from Hood and dumped in the pulper. There must have been a hundred sheets of paper, each one three feet wide and twelve feet long. It seemed crazy to waste so much. "Why did we just chop this off?" Gene asked. "Why aren't we running this through?"

Hawkins rolled his eyes. "You ask too many questions, Wheeler." He nodded toward the machine. "Do you think you can get this stuff to the pulper, or do you need for me to hold your hand?"

"I got it covered."

Gene grabbed the edge of the slab. It tore into his hand like a hundred razor blades. He jerked back.

Hawkins grinned and shook his head. "Jesus, kid," he said. "You never heard of paper cuts?"

Gene rubbed the edge of his palm. The tiny cuts crisscrossed his skin. He squeezed and blood oozed up. He stuck it in his mouth and sucked it out. He spit on the floor by Hawkins's feet.

"You could have warned me," Gene said.

"Some things stick with you if you learn them the hard way."

"Oh really? Then why did you warn me about the machines? Wouldn't I learn better if I lost a couple fingers?"

Hawkins tilted his head to one side. A smile flirted with the edges of his lips, but then it faded.

Passing Time

"So what's the verdict, Wheeler?" he asked. "Can you find your way back to the pulper, or are you going to stand there licking your wounds for the rest of the night?"

"I can find it."

"Good."

Gene grabbed the slab on the outside edge this time, smearing it with his blood. He dragged it to the pulper and dumped it in. He wondered, once the machine tasted his blood, would it want more?

When he got back, Hawkins sat at a picnic table beside the winder, reading the newspaper.

"Have a seat," he said. He nodded toward the bench beside him. Hood was across the table, but he didn't seem to notice when Gene sat down. He stared off into space. It was as if he were still back in high school study hall, and he was just marking time until the bell rang.

The roll of paper in the winder was being pulled through at an incredible pace. The roll on the back side grew as the one in the front shrank.

Devoid stood at a control panel beside the winder. His hand rested on the dials and gauges. The stumps of his missing digits hung off the edge. He glanced over and saw Gene looking, left the controls, and came over.

He pushed Hood aside and sat down on the other side of the table. He spread his hands out before him. "You got questions about these?" he asked.

"It's none of my business."

"Damn fucking right."

Gene glanced at Hawkins, desperate to change the subject. "You know, when I got dizzy in the pulper, I'd swear I smelled formaldehyde."

"You did," Hawkins said. "So what?" He glanced over at Devoid and rolled his eyes.

"Inquisitive little cocksucker, isn't he," Devoid said. Oh great, Gene thought, they finally found something they could agree on.

"Why would you need formaldehyde in paper?" Gene asked.

"What did I tell you about questions, Wheeler?" Hawkins asked. "You don't need to know why there's formaldehyde in the paper. All you need to know is that the smell is strongest where the paper comes off the roll, so you won't be sticking your face there and passing out on us."

He got up and headed to the winder. Devoid glared at Gene. "Fucking rookies," he said. He walked away.

They stood over the rolls and each put one hand on the surface, their fingers resting lightly on the new rolls as they grew atop the cylinders. Devoid used his good hand. Hawkins leaned over and spoke in his ear. Devoid nodded and smiled. Gene blushed. This was too much. One minute they hated each other, and now they were laughing at him? Why did they figure they were so much better than him, anyway? He hadn't been stupid enough to lose half his fingers or rude enough to start waving them in someone else's face. What was wrong with these people?

Devoid went back to the controls and guided the roll to its end. It ran out, and the paper exploded off the shaft. The frayed edges of the sheet flapped wildly as Devoid slammed on the brakes. A metal table rose up out of the floor behind the winder. Hawkins and Hood pushed the rolls out onto this.

A metal shaft held the rolls together while they were running through the winder. Hood went to the other side of the rolls and Gene could see his hands moving, as if he were loosening something. He held a metal collar above the rolls and waved. Hawkins grabbed the end of the shaft. "Catch it when it comes out," he said.

He backed away from the machine, almost running; Gene held his hands under the shaft. The end popped out before he expected. The weight tore through his fingers as if they weren't there.

The end of the shaft hit the floor with a wild, metallic twang. "Jesus Christ," Hawkins said, tossing his end away. The shaft bounced, first one end, then the other, like a deranged teeter-totter. The guys scattered. When it finally stopped bouncing, Devoid walked over and nudged it with his foot. "I think it's dead," he said.

Hawkins walked over to Gene. "It's heavy. Be ready next time."

Blood pounded in Gene's ears. Why hadn't Hawkins warned him how heavy the shaft was? What kind of teacher was he, anyway?

Hood climbed up on the table, got behind the rolls, and nudged them off. They tumbled down a short ramp and out into the hallway. Hawkins followed them, labeling each of them with a large red crayon when they stopped rolling. "Lot forty-seven, a, b, c. That's it." He turned away.

What was this? Gene remembered what Ben had said about nobody caring if they sat around, but this was too much. They'd worked twenty minutes, and now Hawkins was just going to walk away. Maybe he was setting Gene up so some boss could come along and ask him why he was goofing off.

"What do you mean 'that's it'?" Gene asked.

Hawkins stopped and turned slowly back toward Gene. "I mean that's it for now. Take a break, get a soda, have a smoke. Do whatever you want, just stick around this area."

"But we just started. We only worked twenty minutes. What are the bosses going to say?"

He shook his head slowly. "Come here," he walked back into the room and pointed toward Number Five. The roll of paper at the front of it was about half the size of the one that they'd just run. "See that roll?"

"Yeah."

"Our job is to run the rolls that come off Number Five through the winder so they'll be a size more suitable for shipping. Thing is, though, the winder runs a hell of a lot faster than she does. All we can do now is wait for her to catch up."

"But don't the bosses—"

"What did I tell you about bosses?" He tugged at his mustache.

"You said the machine was the only boss."

"And did you think I was just talking, that I'm full of shit?"

"No, I just—"

"Trust me, kid." He glanced at his watch as if he had some place else to be. "I know it's hard to understand at first, but around here, we have only one rule that counts. We move when the machine needs us to move. Everything else is bullshit. Give her her due, and you'll do just fine. Forget that, and she'll make your life a living hell. You got that?"

Gene shrugged.

"You . . . got . . . that?" He got right in Gene's face. Gene looked at the floor.

"I got it."

17

"Good. I'm going outside to get some air. I'll be back." He dropped the crayon into the pocket of Gene's T-shirt. Obviously, he was dismissed.

Gene walked back to the table. Hood sat on the winder with his back against the metal arch and his legs stretched out across the rolls. He read a paperback novel, some kind of spy thriller, its cover a splash of lurid colors, as a tape recorder by his side spewed harsh rock music that tore at the tiny speaker, though it seemed like a whisper amidst the din of the machines. Ben and Devoid straddled a wide bench in the middle of the room, smoking cigarettes and jawing back and forth. Gene ducked out through the door and into the hallway. Anything to get a break from the noise and the heat.

He noticed that there was a bathroom just across the hall and figured he'd better take this chance to use it. He'd be out of luck if he needed to take a leak when the machine decided she wanted him.

He stood over the urinal and wondered why Hawkins had been busting his chops from the minute he'd walked in the door. What had Gene ever done to him? One look at Gene, and he'd been off to the races.

He turned to wash his hands and saw his reflection in the mirror just above the sink. He frowned. He'd gotten his hair cut to apply for this job. He'd forgotten how young he looked with short hair.

Maybe that was it. He looked like a kid to Hawkins, and when he asked so many questions, it just made it worse. He might as well have been on a grade-school field trip. Maybe if he kept his mouth shut, Hawkins would get off his case. It was worth a try. There had to be a way to get out from under the mountain of crap Hawkins seemed determined to bury him beneath.

It was fifteen minutes before Hawkins came back. He frowned when he saw Gene, as if he'd expected him to disappear while he was gone. He sat down at the table and spread a newspaper out in front of him, as if Gene wasn't there.

"Hawkins," Gene said, but he didn't look up.

"Hawkins!"

He sighed, marked his place on the paper with his finger, and looked up.

"What is it, Wheeler?"

"You've got to help me out here. I know you said it's okay for us to hang around like this, but what's going on with the bosses? Why don't they fix it so all the machines run at the same speed? Don't they care if we're sitting half the night?"

Hawkins smiled. "Believe me, they care, and they've tried to change things, but luckily for us Number Five has a mind of her own. Any order that they run, there's only one speed she'll go. Every time they try to speed her up, all hell breaks loose. We have to run our asses off, but there isn't any paper being made, and that's the whole point." He looked down at the newspaper.

"What does that mean 'all hell breaks loose'? What happens?"

Hawkins glanced at his watch, then at the new roll growing on Number Five. "You know, Wheeler, I'd really like to read my paper while I've got the chance. Why don't you go chew the fat with Ben and Devoid for a while?" He pointed toward them. "In this department, the sewing circle is over in the smoking area."

"Sorry I asked." Gene couldn't get away from Hawkins fast enough.

As he got close to Ben and Devoid, he realized Ben had been watching them. "You and Blondie still going around and around? What was it about this time?"

"More of the same, really. I can't help feeling like I'm supposed to be doing something."

Ben grinned at Devoid. "Don't you love them when they're young and innocent, Devo? So eager beaver, so out to change the world?" Devoid grunted. Gene blushed. He was getting tired of doing that.

"Hey," Ben said. "I'm just playing with you, kid. I don't mean it in a bad way, not like Blondie, anyway." He poked Devoid with the stick. "And don't think I didn't see you and Blondie yucking it up about Wheeler at the winder, Devo. You need to cut that shit out."

"Jesus, Ben. I was just playing with the kid."

"With Blondie as a partner? You know that cocksucker will turn on you the minute Wheeler walks away."

Devoid blushed, the blood filling in the white patches of skin between the red bumps of his acne.

"A man has to know who his friends are, Devo, and Blondie is nobody's friend."

"Look," Gene said. "It's no big deal. Hawkins is getting on my nerves, though. Next to him, Devo's all right."

Devoid smiled.

"Blondie does have a talent for messing with people's heads, kiddo," Ben reached over and messed up what little hair Gene had left.

"I'm not surprised you don't trust him about all the sitting around we do," Ben said. "But you know you can trust me, right? Like I said before, the smoother the machine runs, the more money The Company makes. The easier we have it, the better it is for them."

Gene glanced up at the clock. "Don't you guys get bored?"

Ben grinned. "We have our little tricks." He tossed his stick in the air as if to illustrate his point. It was almost as thick as a juggler's baton. "We read and play cards and shoot the shit. The old timers even got a name for what we do between rolls, they call it passing time. They swear that it's just as important as what we do when we're actually running the rolls. They say that having a good way to pass time keeps you sharp, otherwise, you get sloppy."

He winked at Gene and took his eye off the stick. It glanced off his palm and hit the floor, rolling under the front of the machine. He got down on all fours and fished it out. He held it up like a trophy when he found it.

"And what do you say about that?" Gene asked when Ben turned back to him.

"I say the old bastards are full of shit, but I still have a lot of fun between rolls. Just enjoy it while it lasts. Tomorrow we might have to run our asses off."

Gene stayed with them, and the time did go by quickly. They seemed to get along pretty well. Devoid didn't say much, but Ben seemed happy to carry the load. He was easy to talk to.

Finally, Ben glanced at his watch and headed over to the front of the machine. He measured the diameter of the roll and nodded. He sounded a horn, looked down toward the other end of the machine, and waved the stick in a circle over his head. He stepped back in and started the whole thing again. The machine accelerated, the sheet rose up behind the roll like a wave. He raised the stick and cracked the sheet with one easy motion, threading it down behind a new spool.

"You need to start the winder," Devoid said. "Blondie's waiting."

Hawkins stood beside the winder. He looked annoyed. What else was new? Gene thought.

"You know what to do?" he said when Gene got over to him.

"Yeah," Gene said. He looked down at the controls. He could feel Hawkins's breath on his neck.

"What's the trouble?" Hawkins asked.

"I saw you start it up the first time, but I didn't see what setting you had it on."

"But you saw how fast the drums were turning, didn't you?"

"Yeah."

"So just do it."

Gene turned the dial and the drums spun crazily. Too fast. He backed them off until they looked okay. Hawkins reached over his shoulder and turned the dial another quarter-inch. "I guess you'd better just set it at twenty-five."

When they reached the others, Devoid had already stripped off the top part of the roll and had some rolled-up sheets of paper in his hand. Hawkins stooped to get under the winder, but waved Gene away when he tried to follow him. "The samples have to go to Ben." He nodded toward the stuff Devoid was holding. "Run those over to him." Ben stood at the front of Number Five. Gene ran over and handed him the samples, then sprinted back toward the winder and slid in beside Hawkins. Lying flat on his back next to Hawkins, the drums spinning a foot above their heads, his teacher's impatience was as real as the vibrations of the machine rising from the concrete.

Hood's fingers poked down between the drums. Hawkins reached for the end of the paper that Devoid held out to them, but Gene brushed his hand aside, grabbed the paper, and slid it up between the rolls.

He couldn't get it up high enough, though. The rolls twirled around his fingers, the paper went limp in his hand. Hood grasped only air. "What the fuck's going on down there?" he yelled. Hawkins took the paper from Gene and shoved his hands between the rolls, the metal brushed his fingers and Gene cringed. Hood grabbed the sheet and pulled it through.

Hawkins crawled out, and Gene went up with him, but he didn't get between them. After they pulled the paper out across the machine, Hood cracked the edge with his flat palm, and Hawkins balled it up and held it out to Gene. When he grabbed it, Hawkins wouldn't let go. "I know I told you to be careful around the machines, Wheeler, but you don't have to be totally chickenshit. You'll be okay as long as you don't stick your fingers in the wrong place. The goddamn machines aren't going to reach out and grab you."

Gene tore the paper from his hands and walked away.

In the pulper, he leaned on the metal railing, staring at the cylinder spinning in his face. He closed his eyes, but all he could see was Hawkins's pinched, impatient scowl, his smug grin. How was he supposed to keep his eye on the machines and Hawkins at the same time? He took a deep breath, and the formaldehyde gagged him. He stumbled back out into the open, coughing and gasping for air and ran right into Ben.

"Whoa." Ben wrapped his arms around him, holding him up. "You okay, kid?"

"I'll live," he said as he pulled out of Ben's grasp.

"Looks like you've got more on your mind than sucking in formaldehyde," Ben said. "You got a problem?"

"I can handle it."

"I'm sure you can handle the job, kiddo. It's that fucking asshole Blondie that will probably bring you down."

Gene studied his face carefully. How did he know that?

"I've been working with Blondie for years, kiddo. He does this to all the new guys. It's like you're in his own private boot camp. He wants to make you or break you real quick. He'll get you so you won't know whether you're coming or going. Ignore the petty cocksucker. It's your only chance."

"Thanks," Gene said. "Maybe I will."

He tried not to let Hawkins get to him after that, concentrating on the job, instead. They got a roll from Number Five every hour. They ran it through the winder in twenty-five minutes and waited for the next one. He passed the time between rolls with Ben and

Passing Time

Devoid, laughing and joking.

He helped pull samples with the guys and ran them to Ben. He passed the sheet through the winder, always mindful of where his fingers were. He dragged the broke to the pulper. Once they'd run the roll through, he pushed the rolls into the hall and marked each one. Not exactly rocket science, although it might as well have been for Hawkins. Whatever Gene did, Hawkins gave him one chance to get it right. If he was slow or messed up, Hawkins shoved him aside and did it himself.

They were taking samples on a roll at nine-fifteen, when Hawkins pinned Gene's hand to the roll. He heard Devoid snicker behind him. Just past Hawkins's shoulder, he caught Hood's eyes, just as he looked away. Gene glared at Hawkins.

"Let go of me," he said.

"You were—"

"I don't give a fuck what I was doing, let go."

Hawkins pulled his hands away.

"Don't touch me again," Gene said. "I don't care if I'm about to stick my head in the fucking winder. Keep your hands off me."

"Calm down, kid."

"I'm not a kid. I'm not much younger than you are. You've been ragging me all night. If you'd get the fuck out of my way and let me work, I'd learn this job a lot faster."

Hawkins backed away, his hands held up before him. "Whatever you say, Wheeler." He turned, plucked the newspaper from the picnic table, and disappeared out the door.

Gene turned back to Devoid and Hood. Devoid looked away, but Hood gave him a thumb's-up.

They ran the roll, and he fumbled his way through. When he forgot exactly what to do, Hood came over to help him out. They got another roll, and that one went better. Hawkins didn't showed his face again.

"Well," Ben said at eleven o'clock. "Any minute now our relief will be showing up. Another day, another dollar. You did okay, kid." He pulled a mirror out of his lunch pail, checked his hair, and ran a comb through it, even though there didn't seem to be a hair out of place.

"Thanks."

"And you sure set Blondie straight."

"Damn straight," said Devoid.

"How come he never came back?" Gene asked. "Doesn't anybody care that he went home early?"

Ben flipped the metal lid of the box back into place. "Actually, he's probably upstairs in the locker room reading."

"Maybe taking a nap," said Devoid.

"Maybe jerking off." Ben made the appropriate gesture.

"Doesn't anybody care that he's not working?"

"I don't care," said Ben. "Do you care, Devo?"

"Like I give a fuck," said Devoid.

"I meant a boss," Gene said. What had Blair said the supervisor's name was supposed to be? Dupry? He realized that they hadn't even seen the guy.

Ben snorted at this suggestion. "For the last time, Wheeler, the bosses definitely don't give a shit. We had a great night. The machines ran smooth as silk. As long as we don't start killing each other, they could care less."

"But what happens tomorrow," Gene said. "Is somebody else going to teach me?"

"Oh, no," said Ben. "Tomorrow you're on your own. Day after tomorrow we'll probably have you training somebody new. You never heard of that: See one, do one, teach one?"

"You're kidding."

"Yeah, I'm kidding. You do only get a babysitter today, though. Tomorrow we'll all help you out, like we did today after Blondie split."

"So, I'll be working with you guys again?"

"Yes and no," said Ben.

"Yes and no?"

"Well, Devo and I will be here, but Hood actually works on Number Four, so he'll be back over there tomorrow." He nodded toward the machine on the other side of the corridor.

"So, who's going to take his place?"

"Devo's going to slide down to that position."

"Then who's going to run the winder?" Gene asked, but the grimace on Ben's face told him the answer before he spoke.

"Hawkins," Gene said, beating him to the punch.

Passing Time

"You got it, kiddo," Ben said. "You, me, Devo, and Blondie. Just one big, happy family."

When it was time to go, Gene joined the line that threaded its way back through the paper canyons. With every step, the temperature dropped a little more, the sounds faded into the background. He felt someone fall in step beside him. It was Hood. He had taken off the headband and hair net, and his thick, black hair was wild around his face and halfway down his back. Gene nodded to him and he smiled. "It's so quiet out here compared to back by the machines," Gene said. Hood smirked and tapped a finger on the side of Gene's head. Gene realized the he still had earplugs in. He popped them out. "That was dumb," he said.

"Don't sweat it, man," Hood said. "You don't really remember me, do you?"

"Of course, I do. We didn't hang out with the same crowd, but we were in the same school."

"We always figured your kind didn't even know our kind existed."

"We knew."

He nodded. "So, what happened to college, man?"

"I fucked it up."

"Still, you didn't have to come back here. Don't you think you're too good for this place?"

"Even if I did, I know a few professors who probably think I'm right where I belong."

Hood chewed on that. "You got teachers telling you that you suck."

"Yeah."

"My man," he said, sticking out his hand.

Gene took it, and Hood twisted their hands into a Black-Power-Harley-Davidson-Brotherhood shake. "Who would have thought we'd ever see this day?"

As they reached the door and walked down the ramp toward the bridge, a cool breeze blew in their faces. "So what did you think about your first night in this fucking loony bin?" Hood asked.

Gene shrugged. "It's okay. I just wish Hawkins wasn't such an asshole."

"Don't sweat it," he said. "It won't last long. He just wants to see what you're made of."

"What I'm made of?"

"Sure, he doesn't want to waste his time on you if you're a loser. I think he figured out you were okay when you told him off."

They clattered back across the bridge. Hood waved toward the south end of the lot when they reached the other side. "My truck's parked over there. Where are you?"

"I'm walking, man."

"You want a lift?"

"No, I need some air."

"Suit yourself. I'll see you tomorrow, man."

"Aren't we working on different machines?"

"I'm working on Number four. Right next door. I'll still be around."

"Thanks," Gene said.

"No problem," Hood said. "Remember what I said about Hawk, man. You've got to listen to what he says, not how he says it. He knows this shit better than anybody. He'll teach you everything you really need to know."

Gene smiled. What he needed to know. Hawkins had said that when he'd asked him about smelling formaldehyde in the pulper, that he didn't "need to know." Maybe that was the problem. It wasn't that he looked like a kid. Hawkins thought they were working for the CIA, and Gene just didn't have the proper clearance, yet.

Chapter Three

When Gene got to work the next afternoon, light glared from the bare metallic cylinders at the front of Number Five in a wide, Cheshire cat grin. There were thick slabs of paper all over the floor, covered by a single, long sheet twisting back and forth between the winder and the machine, as if the cat had been playing with a giant roll of toilet paper. He realized he was about to find out what "all hell breaking loose" was really like.

Halfway up the aisle between the machines, Ben appeared, his T-shirt soaked, his hair spiked out in all directions. He waved toward the other end, and then darted back out of sight. Devoid stood back, peering intently into the machine. He played with the torn collar of his ragged T-shirt. Gene couldn't see his fingers from this distance, but the image of them flashed in his mind: bits and pieces of what they were supposed to be. He figured he'd better head down to them, though he didn't have a clue what he was supposed to do.

He walked between the machines, and the heat closed in behind him. The cylinders loomed up on either side. He counted them as he walked: four, eight, twelve, sixteen. Sweat stung his eyes. He tasted salt at the corners of his mouth. He watched the thick mist rise into the silver hood that encased the top. He wondered how so much heat could be escaping and it still be so hot.

When he reached Devoid, Ben jumped out from between the rolls and ran right into him. "Jesus, Wheeler," he yelled, "What the hell are you doing here? Get down to the wet end where you belong." He pointed toward the far end of the machine. Gene backed out of his way. Ben jumped back into the space between the rolls, a narrow corridor just like the pulper. Hawkins stood just inside. His face was flushed. He looked so different, nervous and unsure. Gene liked it.

Here, the sheet was only two feet wide, cascading from the cylinders on one side into a wide gap in the floor. Hawkins swiped at it, but it kept slipping through his hands. Ben elbowed him aside, tore the sheet in one movement, and threw it across the gap into the pulleys on the other side. The pulleys dragged it in, wrapping it around the first roll and the next one and the next. Further along, it ran smooth and flat against each roll, weaving in and out, touching every one as it flowed toward the front of the machine.

"Yes," Ben punched the air with his fist, a wide grin on his face. Hawkins stood behind him, wiping the sweat out of his eyes. Then he saw Gene. "What the hell are you waiting for?" he bellowed. "Get to your post!"

Ben winked at Gene. "Better move it, kid."

He walked away, still smiling. Nice to see that there were parts of this job that gave Hawkins trouble, too.

At the back of the machine, he took a breath of the thick, moist air. It was a relief after the way the dry air tore at his lungs.

Two guys argued by a control panel. Gene wondered where they'd been yesterday. One wore bib overalls and rubber boots. His hair was pure white, his skin bright red, his nose laced with smashed blue veins. The other had hair as black as Ben's. That's where the similarity ended, though. His face was soft and pale. His clothes were different, too. Not just from Ben's, but from everyone's. He wore a neon-green tank top and pink jeans. He was dressed like a clown as the machines raged around him.

The old guy pointed at the gauges and waved his hands. The clown twirled the ends of a pink bandana around his neck. Suddenly, the old guy threw his hands up and stalked off. The clown studied the panel, and Gene thought he was finally paying attention to what the old guy had been telling him, but when he smoothed down his hair, Gene realized he wasn't looking at the gauges, but at his reflection in the bright metal.

He felt an arm on his shoulder. It was Hood. He flashed his "no-worries" grin. Of course, he was working on the other machine tonight. He didn't have to worry what was going on with them.

"So listen," Hood said. "Hawk split yesterday without telling you what your job was down here, didn't he? Follow me."

Passing Time

They walked past the short stacks of cylinders to the conveyer belt. Ben had called it the screen. This was where the fibers in the pulp mixture meshed. Gene remembered how Ben had locked his fingers together.

Hood stopped at the end of the screen, where a thick, white waterfall tumbled into a huge vat. "First thing you got to do is keep your eye on this," he pointed toward the mixture as its level rose toward the top of the vat. "When it gets full, you've got to pull that lever to drain it." A guy in a green uniform stood by the lever. His hair was slicked back, a hairstyle from the fifties, but when Gene studied his face, he realized that he was their age. Another mechanical arts alumnus like Hood, though Gene didn't recognize this guy.

"That's Riendeau," Hood explained. "He's doing your job on the day shift. Watch him."

Riendeau's gaze jerked back and forth between the rising level in the vat and the rest of the crew, who were now spaced out along the length of the machine. The mixture touched the lip of the vat, and he leaned over and tugged the lever up, letting it drain, exposing silver walls. Gene wondered if this thing was like the pulper and he'd get a glimpse of the infamous blades churning at the bottom, but even as he thought this, Riendeau slammed the lever back down again, and the foam began to creep back toward the top.

Hood walked over to Riendeau. "You my relief?" Riendeau asked. Hood shook his head, and then jerked his arm in Gene's direction. "Yesterday was Wheeler's first day. They didn't have a break all night long. I'm going to walk him through it. How's it going?"

"It's been a fucking nightmare," Riendeau raked his hair back out of his eyes. "They changed the order at noon. We still haven't had a decent roll. And you know these guys are fucked with The Flamer back here." He nodded toward the guy in the wild clothes.

"He'll be all right once he stops playing and listens to Old Man Grenier," Hood said.

"How come I didn't see those two guys yesterday?" Gene asked.

"They're the top men on each crew, the machine tenders," Hood said. "Their work is down here. Even if you came down here, they lay low unless there's a break. Fucking machine tenders live in their own little world."

"Fucking Flamer," Riendeau said. "He is one worthless asshole. He spends more time on his fucking wardrobe than he does on learning his fucking job."

"Don't get us wrong, Geno," Hood said. "We wouldn't really care about him being queer, but he is one sorry machine tender. If Number Five didn't practically run herself, you guys would be seriously fucked."

"Damn." Riendeau pushed his hair back out of his eyes. It fell back down as soon as he pulled his fingers away. "I need a butt so fucking bad."

"So, get out of here," Hood said.

"You sure, man? I can stay for a while. You don't need this shit."

"It's okay. I'll just walk Geno through the first time. He picks things up fast."

Riendeau smirked. "That's not what I hear."

He walked away, and Hood shook his head. "Don't mind him. He's a fucking retard." He glanced at the vat, and then peered down toward the front. Ben emerged and pointed away from the machine, his posture as stiff as a hunting dog's. Hood grabbed the end of a long wire just above the lever and began to back up slowly.

Gene realized that the wire was attached to a hose. The nozzle of the hose sliced across the waterfall, dividing it into two streams. The larger one tumbled down into the vat, but the other part somehow ran on into the rest of the machine, up the belts and through the wringers and on into the stacks of cylinders. As Hood pulled out on the wire, the nozzle moved out across the sheet at a diagonal, and the part that fell into the vat got smaller, while the part running on the cylinders got wider. When he reached the other end, there was paper running all the way across the machine again.

Hood waited for a few minutes, still staring intently toward the other end. Finally, he nodded. "Let's go," he said.

They walked back down and stopped at the place where Ben and Hawkins had been when Gene came in. "After the sheet breaks," Hood said, "we've got to rethread it through three different sections of the machine. It's impossible to pass it when it's full size."

"Because there's so much water in it," Gene said.

Hood frowned. "I thought you said Hawk didn't show you this part of the job," he said.

"He didn't. Ben showed me around. I asked him how the machine worked."

"But he didn't show you your job down here?" Hood asked.

"It didn't come up," Gene said.

Hood shrugged.

"I guess that makes sense," he said. "You're right. There's too much water in the sheet at first, so you pass different sizes. That's why you work the hose. You watch Ben to see what size he needs. Back at the start, the sheet is really wet and he can only pass a couple inches. Between the presses and the dryers," he pointed first at the wringers and then at the stacked cylinders, "he needs a foot. Right here, he needs a couple. Even then it's a bitch. It takes one coordinated motherfucker to get it past this point." Gene thought of Hawkins being shoved aside by Ben and couldn't help but smile. "When Ben points out and away from the machine," Hood continued, "that means it's time to go all the way out. You've got to pull slow and steady because if you jerk the hose, the sheet might snag, maybe even break again." He stuck a finger in Gene's face. "Your co-workers will not be happy with you if it does."

They walked to the front of the machine. Ben moved back and forth, cursing. The sheet ran onto the roll, again. Hawkins and Devoid sat on one of the spare metal cores that the sheet wrapped itself around. Hood sat down beside them and motioned for Gene to sit down, too.

"Once you got the sheet back on again," he leaned in close to Gene's ear, "your troubles aren't over. That messy shit is no good for the winder." He pointed toward several red rings on the side of the roll. "Each one of those is from a break in the sheet. You'll have to make splices. You're going to have to start and stop. Sometimes the paper will break in the winder, and when the big machine does settle down, it'll run faster than the winder, and you'll never get caught up."

The heat blew off the dryer rolls, and the vibrations rumbled up through the floor. An image flashed in Gene's mind of sitting in the middle of a railroad track as an engine bore down on him.

A whistle sounded. "Jesus," Hawkins said as he jumped to his feet. Suddenly, the flow of paper stopped. One second it stretched out across the machine, then paper gave way to metal, and the roll flapped a long tail. The Cheshire cat was back.

"You're on your own this time," Hood said, but he motioned for Gene to wait a minute as the others disappeared into the corridor. "Remember, you got any questions, you ask Hawk. Don't let his bullshit get to you."

"Thanks, man," Gene said and headed to the back.

Things went smoothly. Ben passed the sheet through the different parts of the machine, making the signals to show how far he wanted Gene to pull out on the hose. He moved easily down the machine, and Gene only had to drain the vat a couple times before Ben was at the front, waving for him to take the hose all the way out. He pulled steadily, and the sheet grew to its full width, blanketing the surface of the cylinders. He hoped that he wouldn't be seeing them again for quite a while.

When he got back in front, Ben was slicking his hair down. Hawkins stood beside him. Devoid and Hood were in the smoking area. Hawkins waved for him to come over. "You've got to get this mess cleaned up," he said.

Gene bent over and grabbed at some loose sheets on the floor, wadding them up in his arms, wrestling a wad as big as himself toward the pulper. The edges of the wad fanned out and away from him like wings. He'd almost reached the front of the machine, when someone grabbed his shoulder. It was Ben. He pointed up. One of the wings of paper was a foot away from the cylinders.

"Jesus, Wheeler," Ben said. "If that end gets dragged in, all hell's going to break loose again. I think we got things straightened out, so don't fuck 'em up, okay."

"Sorry," Gene said and pulled in his wings. He bulled his way into the pulper space but kept an eye on the sheet above his head. He stuffed the paper down between the pipes. It floated for an instant on the surface before it was dragged into the whirlpool.

When they got their first roll, Hawkins waited for Gene by the winder. He had changed his T-shirt, back to crisp white again.

Hawkins watched Gene when he turned on the winder. He watched him when he rolled up the samples and carried them to Ben. He got down on his knees and watched Gene when he crawled under the winder. He didn't go back to the control panel until Gene was out and around to the back.

Hawkins ran the winder much more slowly than Devoid had the night before. Gene realized this was not a twenty-minute roll. When they reached the first red mark, Hawkins shut the winder down. They cut away several inches of messy paper around the broken part and spliced together the good ends with a long roll of transparent tape. They started up again. Gene had taken care of the loose stuff, so now he dragged slabs to the pulper, handling them carefully, so he wouldn't get cut by the edges. They hadn't even finished the roll when Ben turned up another, picked it up with the winch, and set it on the floor.

Gene emerged from the pulper in time to see the sheet explode in the winder. The surface of what was still in the stand in the back shredded like so much tissue paper, filling the air with a storm of confetti, some tiny scraps, some a foot-square, drifting down, covering the floor.

Hawkins walked back to the roll, took a sample, and held it up to the light. He waved it at Ben and drew his hand across his throat. Ben frowned, but leaned on the horn on the front of the machine. It was soon answered by one on the other end. The Flamer raised his arms toward the ceiling in exasperation.

Hawkins brought the scrap of paper to his face as if to smell it, then grabbed his nose and grimaced. The Flamer rubbed his fingers together, the universal gesture for money. Hawkins made as if he were signing his name to something and buried his finger in his chest. The Flamer folded his arms across his chest and stamped his foot, but then he exhaled, his whole body a sigh, and drew his hand across his throat. Ben shrugged and turned away.

Hawkins pulled the roll out of its rack and set in on the floor. Hood came over and sat down beside Gene.

"What was all that about?" Gene asked.

Hood laughed. "They wanted Hawkins to run the rest of that roll, but he told them it was garbage."

"What did it mean when Hawkins was holding his nose?"

"There's too much water in the paper. When that happens, we say it's curdled, like milk."

"So why did The Flamer do this?" He rubbed his fingers together in the money gesture.

"That's one of his favorites. 'Water is cheap.' He's always trying to get as much water into the mix as he can, sometimes he just goes too far."

"And that screws up the paper?"

"Oh yeah."

"But I thought The Flamer is the top guy on the machine, why doesn't Hawkins have to do what he says?"

One long strand of hair had slipped out from under Hood's hairnet. He twirled it around one finger as he thought about his answer.

"I suppose he'd have to if The Flamer stood his ground. Thing is, Hawk is the top guy on the winder, and his name goes on the rolls that we ship out. He just refuses to put his name on shitty paper. The Flamer usually backs down. Especially when he knows Hawk is right."

"Doesn't Hawkins ever get tired of being right?"

Hood grinned. "Hell no. He's made a career out of it." He tucked the strand of hair back into place.

Gene shook his head. "So, let me see if I got this straight. Supry is the foreman here, but we never see him. The Flamer is the head man on Number Five, but Hawkins really runs the show."

"You could say that."

"And Hawkins doesn't get in trouble for messing with The Flamer?"

"For what, making him better than he has to be?"

Hood pulled a book from his lunchbox. Gene looked back toward the others, standing by the front of the machine. So, that was how it worked around here. If Gene was going to make it, he was going to have to play ball with Hawkins.

They had two more breaks in Number Five. With the splices and the extra broke, Gene spent most of his time running back and forth to the pulper. He worked alone. Even Hood just sat at the table with his nose buried in his book.

Passing Time

When they had good rolls, Hawkins ran them slowly. They ended up with rolls backed up all the way to Number Five like planes in a holding pattern.

At nine-thirty, Gene finally got caught up. He sighed and stretched out on the picnic bench. He dozed off and awoke with a start as his body slid over the edge of the bench. He sat up and looked toward the front of the machine, where every member of his crew tore at the roll that Hawkins had refused to run. They went at it like a pack of demented dwarves, whistling, joking, slashing it with their box cutters as slab after slab of paper slid down to the floor. Gene realized this one roll would make as much work for him as everything else he'd done that night. Their smiles got wider as the pile grew.

He walked over and stood beside them, arms folded over his chest. He felt the blood creeping up his neck.

"Got a problem, Wheeler?" Hawkins had stopped, and the others were watching.

"No problem."

"I don't know," said Ben. "That's a hell of an ugly color your face is turning."

Gene shrugged.

"Come on, Wheeler," Hawkins said. "We don't want you stroking out on us. Tell us what's on your mind."

"Do you have to make a party out of fucking me over?"

"Fucking you over?" said Hawkins. "Where'd you get that idea?"

Gene pointed toward the slabs of paper. "You're laughing because I'm the one that has to clean up this mess."

Hawkins shook his head. "Actually, Wheeler, you are the furthest thing from our minds. We're laughing because stripping a roll can be a bitch, but when you get it right, it's a blast. Hey, I know it's not brain surgery, but we like it." He turned back to the roll and dug into the edge. They went at it just as quickly, but none of them smiled.

Finally, they backed away, leaving a pile of paper that was almost four feet thick, three across, and twelve feet long. Gene knew he'd have trouble moving it if he were driving a forklift.

"You know, Wheeler," Hawkins said. "Everything isn't about you." He turned and walked away. Devoid shook his head sadly.

Ben shrugged and winked, but he walked away, as well.

Gene leaned over and grabbed the first thick slab and dragged it to the pulper. He couldn't believe no one was helping him. He didn't expect much from Hawkins, but Ben had always been pretty decent, and Hood had helped him out a lot in the last two days.

Hood stayed at the table, reading and listening to music. Hawkins was right beside him. Ben came over and saw Gene looking at Hood. "The Hood's not going to help you out," Ben said. "Teaching is one thing, but hauling broke is a different story. Besides, if he helps you out when things are going bad for us, then you'll feel obligated to help him out when he has a bad night. Before you know it, we'd all be working every night."

"We don't want that, do we?" Gene said.

Ben shrugged and went back over to the smoking area. When Gene came out of the pulper, Ben and Devoid chatted and laughed up a storm the way they always did. It was as if he were invisible.

As he got closer to the bottom of the pile, the slabs got wider. It was harder and harder to jam them between the guardrails on the pulper, and finally, one got stuck. He kicked it but it wouldn't budge. He jammed his foot down on it. He stamped once, twice, three times, then grabbed the railing with both hands and climbed on top of the slab, throwing all his weight down on it. It broke free as his hands slipped on the damp metal of the guardrail. He jerked back, twisting his spine in a way it was never meant to go, landing flat on the edge of the pulper. He hugged the bottom rail, his face out over the edge of the pit. Beneath him, the slab swirled in the grip of a whirlpool. It disappeared as a white bubble formed on the surface and popped, the harsh exhale almost a sigh. Maybe next time, it said.

He rolled onto his back and closed his eyes, gasping for breath. He felt someone standing over him and knew it had to be Hawkins, that goddamn smug grin on his face. His eyes shot open.

It was Ben.

"Jesus, Wheeler, are you okay? What the hell happened?"

Gene shook his head as he scrambled to his feet.

"Just relax, kid. Take a few deep breaths. That's it."

When Gene finally got his breath back, he told him what had happened.

"Didn't I tell you to be careful?"

"The slabs are so wide that they jammed up in the mouth of the pulper. What else could I do?"

"Wheeler, Wheeler, Wheeler," he draped an arm over Gene's shoulder. "Nobody expected you to ride the fucking thing down into the mix, that's for sure." He picked up a tool that leaned against the machine. It had a sharp point jutting from the top of a three-foot, wooden handle. About three-quarters of the way up, a metal tine curved out, sickle-shaped. "Try this thing, next time. Lumberjacks call it a cant dog. They use it to wrestle logs. Get the sharp point into the slab, and then use the sickle part to lift up and jam it down. For now, though, have a seat and catch your breath. We're just getting used to you, for Christ's sake. We don't want to have to break in another guy so soon."

Gene tried to catch his breath, but sitting right beside the roll, he could see how quickly Number Five was catching up to him. He sighed, leaned the cant dog by the entrance to the pulper, and went back for the next slab. He bent down and a sharp pain tore down his back and into his legs. He jerked back up, then took a deep breath and squatted down to grab the paper.

He used the cant dog and got the first slab in without trouble, but the second one jammed. He dug into it, but couldn't get the sickle under it. He stood up and slammed the sharp point into the edge of the paper. It didn't budge. He jabbed at it again and again, harder and harder. "You goddamn, fucking piece of shit," he railed. Just then, the slab came loose, and the cant dog slipped through his hands, both plunging straight down into the mixture. They disappeared, never even coming back to the surface. He expected to hear the grinding of metal on metal as the tool jammed the blades. He expected a warning siren, whistles, bells. Nothing.

He glanced up at the sheet passing overhead. If the blades had ground up the tool, he expected to see streaks of brown splinters, flecks of steel appear, fouling the sheet. Finally, the horn blasted. Caught. He was almost relieved. He stumbled out of the pulper, looked around, waited for the hammer to come down on him. Ben raised his eyebrows and turned up the roll.

He spent the next half-hour waiting for disaster, but it never came. The machine just kept rolling on. Obviously, Hawkins had been lying when he'd said that Gene would fuck up the entire run by falling in the pulper. If he fell in, he'd simply vanish without a trace.

"Hey, Wheeler," Ben said at the end of the shift, "did you walk to work or drive."

"I walked."

"Let me give you a ride home."

"Okay."

In the parking lot, he led Gene to his pick-up truck.

"Hey, Ben," Devoid called over the roof of a beat-up Ford station wagon, "ain't we going to The Bone?"

"I'll be over in a few minutes. I'm going to run the kid home."

"Bring him along."

"What say, Wheeler? Want to have a beer with us?"

"Maybe some other time. I'm really beat."

Ben started the truck, and they headed up the hill. Gene's back ached, and his palms were full of splinters, souvenirs from the cant dog.

"So," Gene said, "I'll bet everyone had a good laugh when you told them about me."

Ben's face flushed. "Jesus, Wheeler, what kind of guy do you think I am? I didn't tell them anything. It isn't bad enough you almost killed yourself, you think I want you to die of embarrassment, too?"

Gene couldn't believe how relieved he felt. He didn't think he cared this much about what the guys thought, but he did.

"Thanks, Ben. Thanks a lot."

"Don't worry about it."

"No, I mean it. All I need is the rest of the guys thinking I'm a fuck-up."

Ben reached out and roughed up his hair. "Just remember that I've always got your back, kiddo."

They pulled up in front of Gene's house. "Anyway," Ben said, "now that I showed you about the cant dog, you won't have to be climbing on top of the slabs of broke in the pulper."

Gene studied his face for a minute. Could he tell him? Why not? He'd already proven that he was a friend.

Passing Time

"You're not going to believe this," Gene said.

By the time he'd finished telling Ben how he'd thrown the cant dog in the pulper, how he'd spent the next half-hour waiting for it to get caught up somewhere in the system and screw up the entire run, they were both laughing hard enough to cry.

"You're right," Ben said. "I can't believe it. I just can't fucking believe it."

When they'd both calmed down, Gene opened the door and climbed out, suppressing one last giggle.

"Well, Wheeler, I figure there's only one way for you to look at all this. You've already done two of the stupidest things I've ever seen anyone do on this job. Things can't get any worse."

"You could be right, Ben."

"I'm always right."

"I thought that was Hawkins."

He frowned. "Leave Blondie out of this. We're having a good time here. Don't blow it."

"Sorry. Thanks again."

"Don't mention it. See you tomorrow."

Chapter Four

Ben drove away, and Gene walked down the driveway. The house was dark. That was one advantage to working evenings. His parents were both on the day shift, and they hadn't seen each other since he'd started work. It was as if he were living alone. He walked around to the back door. His room was in the basement, and he had his own entrance. There was a note tacked to the door in his mother's handwriting.

"Staci called. She'll be up late studying. Call anytime."

He unlocked the door, kicked off his shoes, and lay down on the bed. He glanced at the clock. It was after one, but the note had said to call anytime. He dialed her number. The phone was on its eighth ring before it was picked up. "Hello." The voice was too small. It sounded like a little girl.

"Could I speak to Staci?"

The little girl chuckled. "This is Staci," she sounded more like herself with every syllable. "That's great. Gone two days, and you've already forgotten me."

"You sound different on the phone."

"You'd better get used to it. We're going to be doing a lot of this in the next few months."

"Don't remind me."

"I'll be doing a lot of that, too." Okay, now he knew it was her. At five feet tall and barely one hundred pounds, Staci gave no quarter. Her image flashed in his mind: her long hair, in a wild perm, framing her face like a fierce, dirty blonde halo.

When he'd told her he was leaving school for a while, he'd expected her to be angry, but at first, she was only stunned. She was taking classes at an accelerated pace, careening toward her future, bristling most days because it was taking too damn long, and he was getting out of school.

Once she'd recovered from her shock, they had a hell of a fight.

"Did I wake you? The note my mother left said you'd be up for a while."

"I thought I was going to be," she paused, and her silence became the tail end of yawn, as if she'd tried to cut it off and failed. "I pulled an all-nighter yesterday to finish up Shakespeare. I finally crashed. I've still got one more paper to do, but that's a purely research thing. It'll write itself. I'll knock it out tomorrow."

"I'm glad you called," he said.

"I thought you might need a little cheering up," she said. "Either that or we could fight some more about your sabbatical." Again the chuckle. It was so deep that it was hard to believe it came from someone so tiny.

"Let's try the cheering up, okay?"

"Okay. I can't believe you're already working. I figured you'd have a few days to think about all this, but here you are already on the job. They don't fool around in this company of yours, do they?"

"They tricked me. I figured it would take a while to process paperwork, so I went down as soon as I got back, but they put me right to work."

"So what's it like?"

"It's okay. The work is pretty easy, but the guy who's training me is a real jerk. I already had a huge fight with him."

"You're just not used to working with regular folks."

"Speak for yourself. I started working with my dad when I was fourteen. The guys there were all pretty regular. Besides, I'm doing okay with everybody else."

"Sorry," she said. "Bad guess."

"No problem."

They fell silent. He would have been happy for another yawn to fill the void, but it didn't come.

He wasn't used to uneasy silences between them. They'd clicked from the first day they'd met. Not that it made any sense. She was an English major, he was slumming in a liberal arts course, but it had never seemed to matter. He wondered if there were more of these silences in their future.

"I called for another reason," she said.

"What's that?"

"My folks have a house on the coast of Maine, and I was thinking I'd run up there Saturday. I realized that might not be too far from you."

"Where is it?"

"Old Orchard Beach."

"You're kidding, that's only a couple of hours from here."

"I figured it would be the perfect chance for you to see me in a bikini."

Gene rolled onto his back, reaching out to turn off the bedside lamp. The room went dark, except for a sliver of light that came from the bathroom, its door slightly ajar.

He pictured her in the bikini. She had the body for it. In his mind, green triangles of cloth hugged her hips and stretched tight across her breasts.

They made plans for the weekend. She figured she'd be in Maine by noon on Saturday. He told her that he'd plan on getting there at two or three, in case she was late. "I don't want to be sitting around with your parents waiting for you." Even though they'd been going together since the first semester, and her dad taught at their school, he'd never met her folks.

She chuckled, the sound deep and rich on the phone. "Who said my folks are going to be there?"

Chapter Five

Friday afternoon Gene stopped in the middle of the footbridge on his way into the mill and stared down at the white water as it tore through the river channel a hundred feet below. He'd been upset when they put him to work so fast, but now he was happy to have the first two days behind him. He was ready for the weekend.

Two rough arms wrapped around him and pulled him back from the railing, lifting him off the ground.

"Don't do it, Wheeler!" a voice rasped in his ear. "We all feel this way sometimes, but it isn't worth throwing yourself in the river." The arms got tighter and then were gone. Gene stumbled into the railing.

It was Ben. Devoid, of course, was right behind him. "Jesus, Wheeler, we have one bad night and you're contemplating suicide already," Ben said.

"How the hell will we go on," Devoid said, "knowing that your blood is on our hands?"

It was the longest sentence Gene had heard Devoid utter. It didn't sound like him at all. He wondered if Ben had a hand up the back of Devoid's shirt working his mouth for him. Gene laughed aloud.

"That's the spirit, Wheeler." Ben threw one arm over his shoulder and the other over Devoid's. "Whatever the she-bitch has in store for us today, we'll just laugh in her face."

"Fucking A," Devoid said.

When they got inside, things were running well. "That's the funny thing about the she-bitches," Ben said, "they might drive us crazy sometimes, but they know when to let up. Just like a woman."

"Maybe your fucking woman," Devoid said, glaring at Ben. "Leave mine out of this."

Ben just smiled. He tapped Devoid on each shoulder with the backtender's stick. "Calm down, Devo," he said. "You know I don't mean anything. I'm just shooting the shit. I forget that your wife is a fucking princess, and you're her knight in shining armor."

"You'd better believe it," Devoid said without a trace of irony in his voice, clueless, it seemed, to Ben's sarcasm.

On the first roll of the night, Gene walked over to the control panel to start the winder, turned quickly, and ran into Hawkins. "Take the winder down a notch," he said. "It's spinning a bit fast."

"Whatever you say."

They were back to square one. Hawkins shadowed him everywhere, even crawled under the winder with him. Obviously, he'd been distracted the day before by the shitty paper they'd been running. Today, Gene was back in boot camp.

When the sheet was through the winder, Gene hauled the broke to the pulper. At least Hawkins let him fly solo on that. When they pushed the rolls into the hall, Hawkins followed him and waited until he'd marked them before he went upstairs, as if lettering was more high tech than dragging slabs of pulp.

When Gene went back in and sat down at the table, the rest of the crew had already scattered. Ben and Devoid were in the smoking area. He knew Ben would call him over in a few minutes, but it was nice to be at the table by himself.

Or was he? He could hear something. Heavy breathing? Not exactly. Snoring? That was it.

He looked around, but there was no one else in sight. Then he realized that the noise was coming from the bench on the other side of the table.

He stood up and looked over. An old man slept on the opposite bench, snoring with his mouth wide open. Actually, Gene was glad he was snoring, otherwise, he would have thought the man was dead.

His skin was pale, his face like a bare skull. He'd curled up in a fetal position, and although Gene would have expected him to be tossing and turning, trying to get comfortable, he lay perfectly still, the only movement was the stirring of his lips as his breath whistled in and out.

"So you've met Saucier?"

Passing Time

Gene turned to Ben and Devoid. "We haven't actually been introduced."

Ben smiled. "They haven't been introduced. God, I love this kid, Devo." He poked Gene on the arm with his stick. Gene wondered if he took the thing home and slept with it.

"Allow me, Wheeler," Ben said. "La Sauce this is Wheeler, Wheeler, La Sauce." He jabbed his stick into the old man's chest. The old man frowned, swiped at it, and rolled over onto his back. Gene didn't know how he managed without falling off the narrow bench.

"La Sauce?"

"His name is really Saucier, but most of us call him La Sauce."

"Why?"

He nodded toward the old man. "Take a whiff."

Gene leaned over. The smell of alcohol and rotten teeth washed over him. "God," he said as jerked back from the stench. "He's drunk."

"He's always drunk," Ben said. "The way we figure, if he ever came to work sober, we'd have to retrain him."

"And nobody cares that he's drunk and asleep on the job?"

"Like I said, Wheeler, he was drunk when he trained for the job, so he probably couldn't do it sober. As far as sleeping is concerned, as long as he wakes up when the horn sounds, nobody gives a shit."

"Why doesn't he sleep at home?"

"He doesn't have one. Oh, he rents a room, but he's never there. He goes straight to The Bone after he gets off work and closes the place, then he opens The Moose Club for breakfast every day."

"I didn't know they served breakfast at The Moose." The Moose was the local men's club.

"Sure," said Ben. "They got a full breakfast menu: eggs, toast, bacon, a shot, and a beer."

The horn sounded on Number Four, the machine just across the aisle from Number Five. The old man's eyes slid open sluggishly. He struggled into a sitting position, scratching at his thick stubble. The tips of his fingers were yellow with nicotine. He stood up, cleared his throat, and spit something at Gene's feet that was the same sickly yellow as his fingertips, then headed off toward his machine. Ben smiled at Gene. "You know, Wheeler. I think the old guy really likes you."

An hour later, Gene was introduced to more members of Number Four's crew. He'd seen some of the guys who worked on it in passing, but the only one he really knew was Hood. It seemed like most of the time they were running off in opposite directions.

Not today, though. He realized that for the first time, both of the machines were running in synch.

The new guys were quite a pair. One of them was huge, maybe six-foot-five and at least three hundred pounds. His complexion was bright red. He had a fringe of white hair around the edge of his skull. He reminded Gene of those guys in the movies who play the senators in ancient Rome. All he needed was a toga.

The other guy was incredibly skinny with dark skin and a white sailor's cap perched on top of his head.

They each carried a lunch box, but the boxes were as different as the men carrying them. The big guy's was the standard model, battered, black-metal, but the little guy was carrying a huge wicker basket with an embroidered cloth draped over the top. The big guy also had a backtender's stick like Ben's, but he had tucked his into his belt. It seemed almost an afterthought for him, not an integral part of his personality. "Mind if we sit down?" he asked.

"Be my guest."

The big guy held out his hand. When he opened his mouth, the illusion of the Roman senator was complete. "Sorry we haven't had the pleasure, yet. It's like that sometimes when the machines are out of synch. We're in the same room but we might as well be a hundred miles apart. Better make the most of this chance to socialize while we can, before the ladies go wild on us again. I'm Phil Judson."

He took Gene's hand. It was twice as big as Gene's. He applied pressure gently, but it felt as if he could easily crush it if he wanted to. Gene was relieved when he let go.

Judson turned to the little guy. Gene had never seen anyone so skinny. His white sailor's cap sat on top of his head like a crown. "This is Bill Duschene," Judson said. "We just call him Dub. Don't let that name confuse you, though. While a Dub is usually another name for a fuck-up, this boy is actually a fine worker. He got the name when he was young because he looks and acts so goddamn goofy, and it just stuck."

Dub flashed a huge grin and jabbed his hand out, took Gene's, and sawed it up and down. His face flew through a dozen expressions of pleasure that at first Gene thought were facial ticks. "You're the tough guy who told Hawkins where to get off," he said.

"Your reputation precedes you," Judson said as he placed one of those huge hands on Dub's shoulder. It made Gene think of a man and his dog.

Dub set a huge white plate out on the table and tucked a red-checkered placemat under it, then arranged a fork, knife, and spoon before he pulled a full rack of barbecued ribs, dripping with sauce, from the basket.

"The boy is a bit of a culinary genius," Judson explained. "Or at least his mother is. I see it's those famous ribs tonight, Dub."

Dub's head bobbed up and down like a toy with a spring for a neck. "These are made with Ma's special sauce." He winked at Gene. "Ketchup and molasses and cloves and a dash of mustard and a couple other things I can't let you in on because she'd kick my ass." He reached back in and pulled out two plastic tubs. One was baked beans, the other coleslaw. "Ma likes to use purple cabbage in her coleslaw for a dash of color." He surveyed the table and seemed satisfied. He pulled out a napkin and tied it around his neck like a bib.

"What's for dessert tonight, son?" Judson asked.

"Strawberry shortcake."

"Fresh berries and whipping cream?"

"But of course," Dub faked a lousy Parisian accent. Gene half expected him to pull a bottle of cream and a whisk from the basket.

Hood came back around the corner and eyed Dub and his spread. He shook his head, leaned over, and whispered in Gene's ear. "I swear this sorry little shit lives to eat. He must spend every fucking cent he makes at the grocery store. You should see the piece of shit car he drives. I wouldn't be caught dead in it."

"What do you drive?"

Hood brightened. "A Chevy pick-up. I modified it for off-road. It's a fucking gas. We've got a lot of pretty country around here, and I've seen most of it. I put a camper on the back, too." He nudged Gene in the ribs. "Comes in handy when my folks and my girl's folks are both home at the same time."

"It must have set you back a lot."

"Oh yeah. I'll be putting a fucking huge hunk of my check toward it for the next four years, but it's worth every penny."

They stayed in synch with Number Four all night, and Hood was right about Dub. Every time there was a break in the action, he came over to the picnic table and dipped into his magic basket. Gene began to wonder which was more bottomless, the basket or Dub's stomach. He realized that eating was Dub's favorite trick to pass the time.

First, there was a chicken salad sandwich on homemade wheat bread. The ingredients of the chicken-salad were a secret, of course.

"Jesus Christ," Hood muttered. "It's chicken salad. Chicken, mayo, a couple of hunks of celery. What's the big deal?"

Dub shook his head sadly.

Chicken salad gave way to blueberry muffins. Muffins to bagels with scallion cream cheese. Bagels became brownies. It was hard to tell where supper stopped and snacking began. Dub finally pulled out a sausage-on-a-stick that was as big as a baseball bat.

"Jesus," Ben nudged Devoid. "Will you get a load of that."

"Would you like a bite of my sausage, Ben?" Dub said.

"No thanks, Dubster," Ben said, "you're not my type." He leaned against Devoid, laughing at his own joke.

"But you're not my type either, Ben," Dub's dead-serious answer was a better joke than Ben's.

"I guess he told you," Gene said.

Ben sprang forward, grabbing Gene in a headlock, riffling the rough stubble on the top of his head. "Wheeler, Wheeler, Wheeler," he said. "What am I going to do with you?"

Later, Gene sat at the table with most of the guys. Hood sat on the winder reading his paperback. Saucier lay beside him, sound asleep. Devoid played solitaire. Judson kibitzed over his shoulder.

Passing Time

Devoid didn't seem to like it, though; he fingered the ragged collar of this T-shirt.

Dub cracked opened a thermos. Gene smelled coffee and a trace of vanilla.

"French vanilla," Dub said. He winked, collapsing half his face in the process. "Ma grinds her own beans." He poured the coffee into a thick, pink ceramic mug that looked like someone's first try on a potter's wheel at summer camp. Its surface was rough, and the lip of the cup was too thick. Dub took a sip and leaned back, patting his stomach.

Ben came in with three copies of the town's weekly paper. "Hot off the presses, gentleman," he said. He pulled the front section from one and threw the rest down on the table. Judson and Hawkins grabbed a front page. Devoid scooped up another. "Jesus," Hawkins said. "Can you believe this?" he asked Judson, holding up the headline: Negotiations stalled. Union reps declare impasse.

Judson raked his fingers through his hair, making the white fringe stand up straight.

"Bunch of fucking bullshit," Devoid said.

"What does it mean, Mr. Judson?" Gene asked, but Judson didn't look at him. His hand shot back up into his hair.

"The union and The Company are negotiating a new contract," Hawkins said. "As you can see, things aren't going well."

"Those cocksuckers take everything we've got and don't want to give us shit," Devoid said. He waved his hands, giving all of them a good view of his mangled fingers, a visual aid of how much he had given to The Company. "We fought long and hard for everything we got," he said. "We ain't giving nothing back."

Devoid glared at Hawkins, who simply looked away. Ben laid his stick on the table and began to roll it back and forth along the surface.

Judson cleared his throat, and the others turned toward him. He ran his fingers through his hair again, but this time, he flattened it down, undoing the damage he had done just a few seconds before.

"I know that concessions has always been a dirty word," he said. "But The Company is in trouble. Maybe it is time to give a little back."

"Bullshit," Devoid said. "If it was up to guys like you, we'd have been taking it up the ass from The Company for the last twenty years."

Judson pulled his stick from his belt, but Gene didn't think he was going to roll it on the table. From the look on his face, he planned to beat Devoid within an inch of his life. Devoid seemed to have the same thought. All the color drained from his face as he leaned back from the table.

"Don't talk to me about the union, you little shit," Judson said. "I was shop steward when you were jerking off in your bedroom and your daddy was putting a roof over your head."

Devoid stared down at the table. Ben rolled his stick back and forth until Judson finished, and then looked him straight in the eye.

"Everybody knows what you did back then, Jud, but that's ancient history. The question is, what are you willing to do now? Whose side are you on?" Ben picked the stick up and lined Judson up with it as if it were a gun.

The words hung between them, but then the horn blasted on the other end of Number Five. They all turned. The Flamer waved frantically as the sheet disappeared from the machine.

The others groaned, but Gene was glad for a timeout.

He walked with Ben and Devoid down to the wet end. "I can't believe that sorry bastard," Devoid said. "Where would we be without the union? Struggling along at minimum wage, trying to make ends meet. Putting off going to the doctor because we can't afford insurance. Fucking scabs."

Gene nodded, but he couldn't help but wonder. Ben had said that Judson was living in the past, but wasn't that what Devoid was doing? Gene thought those struggles were over, material for the history books. He'd never expected to find them here. But the blood in Judson's face and the anger in all their voices made it clear that they were very much alive.

Chapter Six

During the next break in the machines, the two groups kept their distance. Gene stayed with the "union guys" in the smoking area, while the "scabs" sat around the picnic table. Ben surprised him when he broke the ice. Then again, it did make sense. If the guy believed in brotherhood so much, he had to be the one to reach out first.

Ben watched the guys around the table for a long time. He juggled his stick, flipping it a foot or so above his hand and catching it on the other end. He finally nodded as if he'd come to a decision. "I'll be right back." He went out into the hall. Gene glanced at Devoid. He shrugged.

Ben was only gone a few minutes, and then he came back through the door. "Let's go, men," he said.

"Go? Where the fuck are we going?" Devoid asked.

"To make peace with our brothers."

"Peace. I ain't making peace with fucking scabs."

"Yes, you will," Ben said. He walked away without looking back. Devoid scowled, but he went. Gene took up the rear.

"Hey, Jud," Ben said, walking up beside him.

"What now, Ben?" Judson asked without looking up. "You want to talk more bullshit about the union?"

Hawkins and Hood looked up from their books and magazines. Dub put down the turkey leg he was gnawing on and leaned so far forward that he almost fell off the bench.

Ben shook his head. "Look, I know we all got a little carried away before. I don't blame you guys. I blame it on the fucking papers. They're blowing the whole thing out of proportion just to make headlines, you know?"

Judson shook his head. Hawkins rolled his eyes.

"All I'm saying is that we need to chill out, you know?" Ben laid his stick on the table, pulled out a deck of cards, and dropped a brown lunch bag down beside the stick. The corners of the bag broke and a stream of quarters spilled out across the table. "Let's forget this union bullshit and play some poker."

It was if they'd all been waiting for this cue but had forgotten it when the union talk began. La Sauce came out of nowhere with a purple Crown-Royal whiskey sack filled with change. Dub reached into his basket and pulled out a can of mixed nuts, but when he cracked open the cover, it, too, was full of silver. Gene felt a hand on his shoulder. It was Hood.

"Slide over. You're in my lucky spot." Gene slid down the bench, and Hood pulled six rolls of quarters from his pocket, fresh from the bank. He gave Gene a sheepish grin. "I didn't do so hot last week," he said.

Gene thought Hood should be looking for a new spot.

"You guys do this a lot?"

"Every payday." Ben poured a pile of coins out onto the table. "I'm going to put my kids through college on the money I win from these suckers."

Ben held the cards out for Gene to cut. He drew the ace of spades.

"Look out," Ben said. "My boy's hot today. Want to join us, Wheeler?"

"I don't have any change."

"I can stake you," he said.

He shuffled quickly, and then drew his hands apart, the cards like an accordion between them.

"Slick," Gene said. Ben smiled.

"Almost as slick as his fucking hair," Hood whispered in Gene's ear.

Ben's smile disappeared. "I guess The Hood wants to play partners with Wheeler," Ben said. "He must think we're playing pitch or some such pansy ass game."

"Come on, come on, man," Devoid said. "Don't let the little cocksucker get to you. Just take his fucking money the way you do every week."

"I like that idea," Ben said as he handed the deck to Gene, but Hawkins reached across the table and took it away.

"Actually, Wheeler," he said, "before we let you in the game, do you play real poker, or are you one of those guys who likes gimmicks?"

"Gimmicks?"

"Gimmicks. You know, smoke, mirrors, wild cards."

"I can go either way," Gene said.

"Now, now," Ben said, "he didn't ask you about your sex life, he asked you about poker."

"I don't play very often," Gene said. "I don't really have an opinion."

"Don't have an opinion?" Hawkins said. "How can you not have an opinion?"

"Oh, Jesus," Devoid said. "Here we go again."

Judson cleared his throat. Everyone looked in his direction. It was if he had puffed up to twice his size. "There are some things that a man has to have an opinion about, son. Wild cards or straight poker is just one of them.

"Christians love Jesus, and the Jews killed him. The Yankees stole Babe Ruth from the Red Sox, which makes them crooks to some and geniuses to others. Republicans steal from the poor to line their cronies' pockets, while the Democrats try to funnel the money the other way."

"The Company assholes try to fuck us over, and our union brothers stop them," Ben said.

Judson glared at Ben. "I thought we were chilling out, Ben."

"You're right, Jud," Ben said. "My apologies."

"But it's just a game," Gene said.

"Actually, choices like this tell us a lot about a man," Judson said.

"Deal the cards," Saucier said. "Quit diddling around with the kid and let's get this motherfucking game going. Who the . . . fuck . . . cares . . . what he thinks . . . about . . . goddamn wild cards?" Gene thought the pauses were for emphasis, but then he realized Saucier was out of breath. He threw his hand over his mouth and hacked a half dozen times. He brought up a huge yellow gob and leaned back to spit it out on the floor.

"What's your hurry, old man?" Ben said, "Didn't I take enough of your money last time?"

"For Christ's sake, Ben," Dub whined. "Deal the cards. We haven't got all night." He glanced at the machines. He shuddered. It started at the top of his head and made his white sailor's cap dance, and then ran down the whole length of his body. "You know as soon as she realizes we're playing cards, she's going to start messing with us."

There it was again. He was talking as if the machine were alive. Gene thought it was the goofy part of him coming out again, but the others just nodded. Ben shuffled the cards and eyed Number Five.

"Who plays which way?" Gene asked. "Who likes wild cards?" Ben, Devoid, Hood, and Saucier raised their hands. "Straight poker?" Hawkins, Judson, Dub. That made sense. Ben and Devoid always seemed ready for a good time. Hood and Saucier were always in some sort of altered state.

Hawkins and Judson, on the other hand, seemed dead serious about most things. Why not cards? The only one who seemed out of character was Dub. He was so goofy most of the time, Gene figured he'd want to play with every wild card in the deck.

They cut the cards for the deal, and Hawkins got a king of hearts. He took the deck from Ben and shuffled smoothly.

"We'll start with a little seven-card stud. Dollar ante, twenty-five cents for every card. Two-dollar limit on raises. And, of course," he glanced at Ben, "no wild cards."

"Of course," Ben rolled his eyes.

Hawkins won the first hand with a full house, beating Devoid, who had a flush. "Of all the shitty luck," Devoid muttered. "A fucking full-house natural."

"It isn't luck." Hawkins raked in the pot. "I keep telling you that. It's skill. A skill you don't have because you keep playing with wild cards. They're like a crutch," he said as he handed Devoid the deck.

Devoid just grinned. "Baseball," he said. Hawkins moaned.

"Baseball?" Gene said.

"Same setup as seven-card stud," Devoid explained. "Except threes and nines are wild. A four gives you an extra card."

Gene frowned. "I don't get it."

"A free pass, like a walk, four balls," Judson said as he rolled his eyes toward the ceiling.

Judson stayed disgusted, even when he won the hand. He had five of a kind: two threes to go with three eights, natural. He beat Hood, who worked two wild cards of his own into the middle of a straight flush. "I hate winning this way," Judson said as he pulled in the pile of silver, and from the sad look on his face, Gene believed him.

Dub dealt next. He chose five-card draw with no wild cards, jacks to open. He dealt the cards deliberately and leaned back, stroking his chin. He grinned expectantly, but it only took one trip around the table to discover that no one had the necessary pair of jacks.

"That's just pitiful," Ben growled. "Let's hear it for real poker." He glared at Hawkins, who shrugged his shoulders. "I never said playing natural was perfect, Ben. Just better."

They left the pot in the middle of the table.

Hood chose seven-card stud on his deal, spicing it up with one-eyed jacks wild. He had dealt each of them three cards when the horn sounded.

"Jesus holy fucking Christ!" Devoid growled. They turned toward Number Five. Her sheet was gone, the cylinders flashing harsh metal.

"Fucking crazy she-bitches." Saucier hocked up another yellow glob and aimed it in Number Five's direction.

"You'd think a man could play a few hands of cards without her getting her skirt up her crotch," Ben said. He picked up his stick and waved it in her direction. "One of these days, bitch, I'll show you who's boss."

"She already knows," Hawkins said.

When Gene got down to the wet end, The Flamer stood with his hands on his hips, resplendent in an orange tank top with a yellow bandana and jeans. He watched the overflow from the screen. "What happened?" Gene asked. "What went wrong?"

"Nothing went wrong," The Flamer said. "Everyone thinks that I must have screwed up. I didn't. Everything's perfect. I can't find a thing wrong with the pressures or the tensions or the mix."

"Then why did we lose the sheet?"

"Because you and your buddies had to play cards, that's why."

He stomped away.

They got the sheet back easily, but when they got back to the table, Number Four had turned up, so Dub, Saucier, and Hood were at their winder.

Gene went over to the smoking area with Ben and Devoid.

"Can you believe this jealous bitch?" Ben nodded toward Number Five. "She does this every time we try to play. We were in synch with Number Four before she pulled this little trick."

"That's the idea," Devoid said.

At eight o'clock, Gene folded early in the hand. He'd been winning early on, but his cards had taken a turn for the worse, so he decided to take a break.

Hawkins stood at the front of Number Five, covering for Judson. He walked along the length of the roll, thumping the surface with Judson's stick as he went.

"Why do you do that?" Gene asked. He regretted the words as soon as they were out, knowing he'd probably get the "need to know" speech again, but Hawkins just kept tapping his way along the roll.

"It's important to keep tension on the sheet consistent all the way across," he explained. "If you don't, you get soft spots and the rolls run together in the winder. When you do this you can hear them."

"Really?"

"Really," he said and went back across. This time Gene heard the dull thumps that he made with every whack.

"They all sounded the same to me."

"That means everything's okay. When it starts to sound like you're playing a xylophone, that's when you've got trouble."

Gene nodded. There was a lot a guy had to know here, if he wanted to do right by this job.

"You give up on the game?" Hawkins asked.

"My last few hands have been pretty sorry," Gene said. "I think I'll sit out a few."

Hawkins glanced at his watch. "You don't have a few hands, Wheeler," he said. "The next one will probably be the last."

"But it's eight o'clock. We've still got three hours to go."

"We have to change the order at eight-thirty. Once we do that,

Passing Time

we'll be lucky if we have time to take a piss, let alone play cards."

"I don't get it." They'd changed the order a couple times in the last few days. It usually meant a break in the sheet and some extra broke, but it wasn't usually a big deal as long as The Flamer listened to Old Man Grenier.

"Play the last hand," Hawkins said. "Enjoy it while you can."

Back at the table, the others echoed his words. "Time for one more hand before we head off to our doom," Ben said.

"I signed on to make paper," Devoid said. "Nobody told me I'd have to mess with fucking cardboard."

"What's so bad about this order?" Gene asked.

Judson shook his head sadly. "You'll find out soon enough, son." Judson took the deck from Ben and riffled the cards in those huge hands. "At least it's my deal," he said. "The last hand will be an honest one. Seven card stud. Two dollars to ante, fifty cents a card, unlimited raises."

Gene dug into his pocket and pulled out a handful of change. He threw two dollars in the pot, as Judson dealt each of them three cards, two face down and one showing. Gene checked his hole cards, a jack and a seven, both hearts.

"So," Judson said, "what have we here? Wheeler with a queen of hearts, Saucier with a six, Dub with a nine of diamonds. I've got the ten of spades, and Ben is the boss with the king of that same suit."

Hood had already gone broke and sat on the winder, watching. Devoid had done the same and stood behind Ben.

Ben threw fifty cents into the pot. The rest followed suit. "Anybody raise?" Judson asked. They all shook their heads. "Everybody's cool," he observed. "Biding their time."

Judson dealt Gene a ten of hearts, Saucier another six. Ben got a five of diamonds. Dub grinned when his card was an eight of clubs. Judson gave himself a three of the same suit.

"Well, well," Judson said. "My little buddy is working on a straight. Saucier takes the lead with his puny little sixes, but let's keep our eye on Wheeler, working on a flush."

Everyone stayed in and Judson dealt the next round. No heart for Gene, no six for Saucier. Nothing good for Ben or Judson. Dub got a five of clubs.

"What garbage," Ben said, sliding his cards toward Judson. "Thanks for nothing, Jud."

"Don't take everything personally, Ben," Judson said. He folded his own hand without a comment.

"Two pair showing," he said. "Potential straights and flushes. Quite a variety, but the old man's sixes still bet."

Saucier threw fifty cents into the pot. Gene called and raised a dollar. "Ah, yes," Judson said. "The plot thickens. Does Wheeler have hearts in the hole? Does Dub have his straight? It will cost you a cool buck-fifty to find out."

Dub slid his money into the pot. Saucier threw his cards down in disgust.

"Jesus fucking Christ all to hell," he said. He took off toward the smoking area, muttering under his breath.

"And then there were two," Judson said. "One more up on top," he said, tossing the cards out. Gene drew the six of spades. "No help there," Judson said without emotion. Dub grinned when he got the nine of spades, although it was no help for his straight.

"Well, well," Judson said. "You don't suppose Dub's got nines down there, do you?"

Dub threw in a dollar. Gene stared at his hole cards for several minutes. Dub didn't have anything showing on top. The only reason he'd be willing to bet was if he did have nines in the hole. At least one. Maybe he had the nine of clubs in the hole and needed the nine of hearts to fill them out. If that was the case, Gene had just as much chance of drawing it as he did. Then again, maybe he didn't have a thing, and he was bluffing, trying to buy the pot. Now there was a thought. Underneath that goofy exterior, maybe Dub was just a stone-cold card shark. Gene threw two dollars into the pot. "Call and raise," he said.

"See you and raise you two," Dub countered.

"Call and raise you two more," Gene said, throwing in the coins.

Dub picked up his hole cards and rubbed them together nervously.

"Well, well," Judson said. "We've got a battle royal on the last hand."

Dub reached for the coins in front of him as he rubbed his hole cards together. The horn blasted and both hands jerked in the air, scattering coins, sending his cards straight up into the air. He swiped at them, tried to pull them back in, but he flapped his arms so wildly that he only stirred up the air in front of him, and the cards landed face-up in the middle of the table: two nines, clubs and hearts. He had his four of a kind and the nine Gene needed to beat them. Dub clawed at the cards, dragging them back in, as he struggled to get to his feet. Gene threw his hand down.

"Hey," Dub said. "We're not finished. I'm going to call and raise. You've gotta pay to see my cards."

"What the hell for?" Gene said. "You just showed them to me."

"But—"

The horn sounded again. One short burst that was clipped off almost before it began. Dub wheeled around. Hawkins, still covering for Judson, stood with his hand resting lightly on the lever that sounded the horn on Number Four, glaring at Dub. His expression said, 'Don't make me sound this thing again.'

Dub glanced back once at the pile of quarters in the middle of the table, then turned so quickly that his legs got tangled in the bench, and he tumbled over onto the floor, losing his sailor's hat. It rolled across the floor like a loose hubcap, disappearing under the winder. He scrambled to his feet and ran to Hawkins.

Ben watched him go. "So tell me, Wheeler," he said. "How high were you going to go?"

Gene shrugged. "As high as it took. How often do you get a chance for a straight flush natural? It was worth a shot."

"Can you believe Dub?" Ben said, shaking his head. "That is one bizarre little motherfucker, I'll tell you that."

"That's true," Gene said. "Actually, it's kind of a relief. I don't think I could stand it if Dub was a card shark. A guy's got to have a few things he can depend on."

Chapter Seven

When they switched over to a new order, Gene saw right away what they'd been complaining about. The dark brown stock flowed off the end of the screen like mud. When Ben passed the sheet, it looked like soggy cardboard. "God, I hate this shit," he said as he moved off down the machine.

It took them an hour to get it to stay on the reel. The first roll had so many breaks in it that they just dropped it on the floor. When they got a good roll, it was harder to pull samples, harder to thread it into the winder. It seemed as if Hawkins barely got started before he began to slow back down. Gene looked for snags or breaks, but there weren't any. When it stopped, Gene stood back, not sure what was up. The rolls were only about a foot in diameter. Normally, they were at least thirty-six inches. "What are you waiting for?" Hawkins yelled. "We have to pull those rolls."

"But they're too small."

"Not for this order."

They rolled them out, pulled the shaft, and sent them into the hall. Gene went to the winder to get the numbers from the order sheet. "We get five sets of these for every roll that comes off Number Five," Hawkins explained. "This is as close to an assembly line as it gets around here."

"At least we'll be going home in an hour," Gene said, looking up at the clock.

"Maybe," Hawkins said.

"What do you mean, maybe?"

"I mean that if any of the guys on the night crew checked the orders for today, then right about now they're calling in sick, and if it's one of our mates who's doing it, then we're fucked, because nobody is going to volunteer to work sixteen on this order."

Passing Time

Mates? Sixteen?

Before Gene had a chance to ask, a guy who he had never seen before came around the corner. He was about six feet tall with short, white hair and glasses. He wore a white shirt with a blue bow tie and blue suspenders. He stared down at a piece of paper in his hand as he walked. He almost ran into Hawkins, looking up at the last minute. "Hello, boys," he said.

"Hey, Dale," Hawkins said. "Who's the lucky man tonight?"

"Wheeler," he read from the paper. "Who the hell is Wheeler?"

"I am," Gene said. "Who the h—" Hawkins jabbed him in the ribs.

"You want to work sixteen tonight?" Blue Bow Tie asked.

"Sixteen?"

"A double shift. Your mate called in sick."

"My mate?"

"You know," he said. He eyed Gene as if someone had just dropped him on his head. "The guy who's supposed to relieve you at eleven."

"Like you relieved Riendeau at three o'clock," Hawkins offered.

"Oh sure, I forgot about that," Gene said. "Do I have to stay?"

"Not if somebody else is willing to work. I'll ask around and get back to you." He looked back down at his paper. "Your man isn't going to make it either, Hawk. Did you want the shift?"

"You know I don't want any part of it," Hawkins said.

"Me, either," Gene said.

The guy didn't seem upset with Hawkins, but he glared at Gene. "I told you I'll check around, but I wouldn't be making any plans if I were you."

Ben, Devoid, and Hood walked up.

"You want to work a double, Ben?" Blue Bow Tie asked.

"No, sir."

"Hood?"

"Nope."

"Devoid?"

"You know I don't do weekends."

"Come on, Devo," Ben said. "You know you could use the money."

"I don't do weekends," he said. "You know that. My girl is

waiting for me."

"Jesus, Devo," Ben said. "Could you be more pussy whipped? You're married. When you're dating, you worry about weekend nights. Once you tie the knot, you do what you damn well please, and your wife is waiting in the bed when you get home. That's the way it works."

"Not for me," Devoid said.

"Don't know why I even bother with you jokers," Blue Bow Tie said and headed toward Number Four.

"Who was that?" Gene asked.

"That's Dale Supry," Ben explained. "Remember? He's the foreman."

"Where's he been all week?"

"He stays up in his office most of the time. He does the schedule, takes care of call-ins, that kind of stuff."

"He looks goofy. I'll bet he's worked in an office his whole life."

"Actually, he was a hell of a paper-maker before they kicked him upstairs," Hawkins said. "He worked here in the room for twenty years."

"And he's still got all his fingers," Hood said. He grinned at Devoid and flicked him a sharp salute.

"Fuck you, too, faggot," Devoid said as he flipped him the finger of his good hand.

"What was he saying, though?" Gene asked. "If no one else wants to work, I have to stay and work all night?"

Ben shrugged. "You can't leave until you get relieved. If nobody else wants to work nights, then your next relief will be here at seven a.m."

"Great."

"Damn," Hawkins said. "I knew this would happen. Billings, my relief, always checks the orders, and he's pretty tight with your relief. The two of them are probably having a beer right now, laughing at us."

Supry was only gone a few minutes. "I've got good news and bad news."

"What's the good news?" Hawkins asked.

"Saucier is going to work for you, Hawk."

Gene knew what the bad news must be. Nobody wanted to work

for him.

After Supry left, Hawkins smiled at Gene. "Tough luck, kid," he said. He pointed toward the table. "You ought to sit down, while you've got the chance. It's going to be a long night."

Gene sat. It was bad enough he had to stay all night, but there was no way he'd be able to visit Staci at the beach if he worked all night.

At eleven-thirty, Riendeau came in and stood beside Hawkins. They talked for a few minutes and Hawkins waved for Gene to come over.

"What the hell are you doing here?" Gene asked Riendeau, knowing that he usually worked days.

"I volunteered," he said.

"Are you nuts?"

"Don't knock it," Hawkins said. "This is a big break for you. Officially, Riendeau's here to relieve Devoid. Saucier's the one who volunteered to work for me, but I'll bet he lets Riendeau run the winder most of the night. That's probably why the old coot agreed to work. It's all yours, man," he stood back and let Riendeau take his place at the controls. "I'll see you Monday, Wheeler," Hawkins said. "Have a good weekend."

"Yeah, right," Gene said.

Riendeau headed for the smoking area as soon as they finished the roll. "Come on," he said. Gene had a hard time keeping up with him as he sprinted across the room.

"So it looks like you guys had a rough time getting started?" Riendeau said as he threw himself down on the bench and lit the cigarette that had been dangling from his lips since he'd arrived. He leaned forward, and his hair fell into his eyes. He raked it impatiently aside.

"It's been pretty crazy."

"It usually is on this frigging order. Once we get a little bit ahead, we'll strip down that roll over there." He nodded toward the first one they'd turned out, the one that was pure junk. "I'll help you drag it to the pulper."

"Do you think we'll ever get ahead?"

"Oh, sure. The machine tender on this shift is much better than The Flamer. The backtender can run rings around Ben, too." He smiled. "Of course, I can't hold a candle to Hawk. Not yet, anyway."

"Don't you usually work my job?"

"Sure, but I'm not going to stay at the bottom forever. I work the winder every frigging chance I get. Shit, I'll get more experience tonight than I would in a normal week." He stubbed out his cigarette eagerly as the machine accelerated. "See what I mean?"

After they had threaded the sheet, Gene watched Riendeau at work, intent on the gauges and the rolls in the winder. He reminded Gene of the kids at school who could do calculus and of Staci when she talked about the stuff that she read. Riendeau wanted to move up in the world, and for tonight, he seemed happy to have jumped a couple rungs on the ladder.

Instead of going through the motions several times an hour, they had to do them every five minutes. Stop the winder, cut the sheet, pull the rolls and the shaft, push the rolls out, mark them, start again.

At first, things were pretty rough, but as Number Five settled down, every repetition went more smoothly. Gene would have never volunteered to work with Riendeau and Saucier, but they made a good team. Riendeau was good at the winder, and Saucier was better as a fourth hand than in his regular slot.

Gene wondered what Hawkins would say if he could see them. Maybe they were even living up to his high standards.

Between rolls, Gene sat in the smoking area with them and even smoked a few cigarettes.

"I'm glad we got this chance to work together, kid," Saucier said. "Really glad. We've never had a chance to talk before. You seem like a good egg. Not like the rest of these assholes around here."

"Thanks," Gene said.

"There's too much in this place," Saucier muttered. "Too many fucking assholes, and then there's the machines." He shuddered again and pulled a cigarette from his pocket. He lit a match, but his hands shook so violently he couldn't get the cigarette lit. He threw the match away and crushed the cigarette in the ashtray by the bench.

"Crazy fucking she-bitches," he said. He swirled his arms over his head in wild circles as if he were trying to fend off a mass of insects. Gene realized that he was imitating the endless swirl of the machines, the cylinders, the ropes and pulleys, the blades of the winder. Crazy fucking she-bitches.

"They say that you get used to it," Saucier said. "Can you believe that? Used to it. And most of them do. They get careless. They take the bitches for granted, and that's when it happens. A piece of a finger, two or three joints. Shit, old Savage lost his whole fucking arm," he said, referring to the old guy who swabbed the toilets in the locker room. He grabbed Gene's arm. "Not me. They ain't getting me. Not La Sauce. Not you, either, I'll bet. You're a smart boy." He waved his fingers in Gene's face. "I'm keeping these. Yes, sir, I sure as hell am."

All Gene could do was nod.

Between each roll, Saucier disappeared. Every time he came back, the smell of liquor was stronger on his breath, and his mood got better.

"So kid," he said after one of his trips, "tell me about the sweetest girl you ever fucked." Gene just stared at him. Saucier didn't seem insulted, though. Instead, he grinned even wider. "Oh, I get it, you're a gentleman. No names." He pressed a finger to his lips. "Let's just talk in general. I've heard that nowadays, all the girls fuck. Even the good girls. In my day, there were nice girls and there were whores. The only ones who put out were the whores, and you were taking your life in your hands every time you stuck your dick in them. Crabs. VD. Damn. Some nights I'd soak my dick in alcohol as soon as I got home. Nothing worse than the crabs."

"Don't I know it," said Riendeau. He aged thirty years before Gene's eyes, becoming another Saucier, complete with rotten teeth and lungs and yellow fingertips. Gene found it hard to believe that either of them had ever had sex.

They had a break in the machine at six a.m. Gene worked the hose by the screen, watching for signals from Shelton, the backtender on this shift. He was an older version of Ben with slick, black hair and sideburns, though there was a touch of gray in his hair, and his paunch was out of hand, hanging out over his tight jeans. He emerged from between the rolls and waved for Gene to go all the way out, then turned and headed for the front. Saucier waited at his post halfway down the machine. Gene had reached the end of the hose when he noticed a long scrap of paper sticking out of the side of the machine down by Saucier. It bobbed up and down, stuck on the end of one of the rolls, caught between the metal and the rope. Saucier reached up to pluck it out before it fouled the sheet. He grabbed it and the long, brown scrap became a tongue, wrapping itself around his wrist and pulling him in. His feet were jerked off the ground. His free hand tore at the air.

No one else had noticed. The machine tender was in back. Riendeau and Shelton were out of sight. Gene jerked on the hose and snapped the sheet.

"What in fucking holy goddamn shit do you think you're doing?" the machine tender screamed as he ran toward Gene, waving both fists. Riendeau and Shelton appeared at the other end, arms raised, mouths wide, but then they saw Saucier, dangling from the side of the machine, and sprinted toward him.

Gene turned away. He retched, but nothing came up. He stood with his hands on his knees, staring at the floor. He could still see Saucier's frail carcass hanging like a toy from the side of the machine. Somehow, he knew that he would always see it.

He forced himself back up and looked down the corridor. The men clustered in the center of the aisle. Either they had pried Saucier loose, or Number Five had pulled him in.

When he finally got up the nerve to go down, they parted and let him through. Saucier lay on the ground, shivering. Shelton's bare belly hung out over his pants. He had taken off his shirt to wrap Saucier's arm. An ugly red line appeared just above Saucier's elbow and disappeared into the bandage. There was a trail of blood leading back to the machine.

"Fucking Christly she-bitches," Saucier muttered. "They got me. They fucking got me." He opened his eyes, and Gene smiled at him, but he seemed to look right through him. Tears welled up in Gene's eyes. Fortunately, they mixed with his sweat, and the others didn't notice. He pulled up the bottom of his T-shirt and wiped it all away.

After the paramedics carted Saucier away, they all just stood around. Riendeau came over. "Did you see his arm?" he said. "The pulley tore him raw right to the bone. You could see everything."

"Is he going to be all right?"

"If he is, it's thanks to you. Another few seconds, and he'd have been in up to his shoulder."

Gene smiled in spite of himself. He knew Riendeau was right.

"Oh, Jesus," Riendeau looked over Gene's shoulder. "Just what we need. Fucking Lambert. Supry's evil twin."

Gene turned. A guy careened down the hall with his arms pumping and his chin stuck out, just waiting for a right hook. He wore a white shirt, suspenders, and a bow tie. Gene guessed that was the uniform for a supervisor, but otherwise, he seemed as different from Supry as possible.

"Okay, okay," he said. "That's enough excitement for tonight. Let's get back on line."

Nobody moved. "Show a little respect," Shelton said. "We just lost a man."

"He wasn't our man," Lambert said. "He's a rummy working our shift to make a few extra bucks. If the union hadn't shoved him down my throat, I never would have let him work on my time."

"You sound happy that he got messed up," Gene said. The words were out before he had a chance to think.

Lambert looked at Gene, puzzled. "Who the hell are you?"

"This is Wheeler. He works evenings," Shelton said. "Saucier *is* his man." The others all grumbled their approval.

"Jesus, kid," Lambert said. "I didn't mean nothing. Everyone knows Saucier's a rummy. You must know it better than me."

"He still did his work," Gene said. "He was always there when the horn sounded."

Lambert's hair fell in his eyes the way Riendeau's did, and he raked it away. "This is bullshit," he said. "There's nothing we can do for him, anyway. They'll stabilize him in town and ship him out to Mary Hitchcock. They do great work down there. Besides, that's a million-dollar wound. Lifetime permanent disability. From now on, he'll be splitting his time between The Moose Club and The Bone. He won't have to come here to catch up on his sleep."

Gene looked around the circle. Shelton met his stare and winked. "We aren't moving until we hear the old bastard is okay," he said.

Lambert's face got so red, Gene thought it would pop off his shoulders.

"We need to get back on line," Lambert said.

"We need to find out if the old man is all right."

"I—"

"We don't give a shit about you, Lambert. Take it up with the fucking union."

One by one, each man nodded.

"The rest of you still have to make a living," Lambert said. "Let's make some paper."

"We get paid by the hour. We're not moving until you call the hospital," Shelton said. He nodded toward the machine, toward the bloody trail that led back to it. "We've got to clean up this mess, anyway."

Lambert glared at him. His chest puffed up but just as quickly deflated, as if someone had stuck a pin in him. "I'll be back in twenty minutes," he said. "You men better be ready to work." He wheeled and stalked away. Shelton put his hand on Gene's shoulder. "You're all right, kid," he said. The others nodded.

Lambert pulled out a hose and started to wash things down between the machines. The others stood around, talking and waving their arms. Gene couldn't stand to listen. He headed back to the wet end.

Back at his "post," he stared into the machine as the sheet tumbled off the screen and down into the vat of the save-all. He could feel the machine's anger, her disappointment at getting only a piece of Saucier. He knew it made no sense, but he still felt it.

Lambert didn't come back for almost an hour with the news that Saucier had been stabilized at the local hospital and was on his way to the trauma center.

"Now can we make some paper?"

"Be my guest," Shelton said. "It's time for us to go home."

Amazingly enough, all their mates showed up. Gene's, of course, was Riendeau who was going to stay for his regular shift.

"This is crazy," Gene said. "They've got to find someone to work for you."

"You want to work twenty-four?" he asked.

"Hell no."

"Then get the hell out of here. I'll be all right. Remember, I volunteered for this shit." He stuck out his hand. "Some night," he said.

"I guess so."

"You're all right, Wheeler."

"Thanks. So are you."

Chapter Eight

It seemed like the phone had been ringing forever. Gene couldn't figure out why nobody answered it. He picked it up.

"Wheeler? This is Phil Blair."

Gene's eyes snapped open.

Last week, Phil Blair had been on the phone when his secretary ushered in Gene. He snatched Gene's application and waved at the chair across the desk from him.

"Jesus-H-Christ, Maurice," he yelled into the phone. Thick glasses sat in the middle of a fat, red face. Traces of blue lined his lips. "I told you I don't have anyone to give you today. No one. Are you fucking deaf?"

Whoever Maurice was, though, he didn't give in. Blair paused as a voice exploded from the phone. He rolled his eyes at Gene. "Maurice, what part of this don't you get? I sent every spare man I got out this morning. Hell, I'm going to have to send a goddamn rookie down to work on the fucking paper machines tonight. That's right, the machines. No, you can't have him. Well, fuck you, too, Maurice."

He slammed the phone down and chuckled. "So," Blair had said as he'd glanced at Gene's application, "what are you doing this evening, Mr. Wheeler?"

Now, Phil Blair was on the other end of the phone, two hours after Gene had gotten home from the worst night of his life.

"Wheeler," he repeated. "Are you there?"

"I'm here, Mr. Blair."

"I need you to work this afternoon."

"I can't, sir. I'm going out of town."

Blair laughed. "This is your first week, Wheeler. You're not supposed to have a fucking life. You're supposed to work when I need you."

Passing Time

"I'm sorry, sir. I even worked a double shift last night."

"You think I don't know that, Wheeler? I'm the goddamn employment director." He chuckled. How could a sound that was supposed to be joyful sound so evil?

"Let me tell you how this works, kid. If you don't want to work, unplug your phone, get your mother to lie for you, get out on the road before I call. Once you've picked up the phone, you have to work. The only excuse I'll take is that you've got a goddamn bullet in your brain."

Gene shook his head to try to clear it. People didn't talk this way. It had to be a bad dream.

"I didn't know about any of this, Mr. Blair," he said. "I'm really sorry."

"Sorry? What the fuck good does that do me?" His breath rasped in the phone. When he spoke again, there was a kindness in his voice. "Look, kid, I'm the one who's sorry. Nobody's answering their phones today. My options are extremely limited."

That made two of them. "Where did you want me to work?"

"Your usual spot on Number Five."

"What about the guy who's there now? Why can't you make him work?"

"He's already worked sixteen."

Of course, Riendeau. "Okay, Mr. Blair. I'll be there."

"Good boy. I'll make it up to you sometime."

"Thanks," Gene said. He could start by calling Staci.

After Blair hung up, Gene stared at the phone. He dreaded the call. He dozed off, then jerked awake. Ten minutes had passed. He pulled himself up on the edge of the bed and dialed her number.

"Gene," she said. "Calling to let me know you're on your way?"

"Not exactly." He lay back down and covered his eyes with his arm.

"You sound awful," she said. "Are you all right?"

"I'm okay, but I can't make it this weekend."

"Why not? Is something wrong?"

He pulled his arm away and struggled back up. He didn't want to worry her. "I'm okay. I really am. I'm just beat. I drew a double shift and worked all night. Then I dozed off when I got home, and the wild man who makes the schedule called me, and I didn't know that if I answer my phone when he needs someone to work then I can't say no, so I have to work this afternoon, too."

"Isn't that dangerous?" she asked. "You'll be half-asleep. Can't they make the guy who's there work like they made you last night?"

"The guy I have to relieve worked with me last night. He's already worked a double shift."

"That's crazy," she said. What he heard was, 'Let me talk to that guy who makes the schedule, I'll give him a piece of my mind.' He could picture her and Phil Blair going at it. He'd definitely want tickets to that.

"It's really okay, Stace. I'll sleep until I have to go back in, and I'll be fine. I'm just sorry I have to bail on you."

"Don't worry about that. Go back to sleep. Get as much rest as you can."

"I'm sorry."

"Don't apologize. I'm hanging up. Get some rest."

He lay back in the bed. When *would* he see her again? How could he sleep with that question hanging over his head?

He woke with a start at two o'clock. A twenty-minute shower and a pot of coffee got him to the door of the machine room. He didn't have a clue what would get him through the rest of the shift. Riendeau shook his head when he saw him. "I didn't think they could find anybody who was worse off than me," he said.

When Hawkins came in, he looked them up and down. He didn't seem to like what he saw. "Are you guys coming or going?" he asked.

"I'm going," said Riendeau.

"I'm gone," Gene said.

"No, really," Hawkins said.

"I'm on my way out the door," Riendeau said.

"And I just got back," Gene said.

"You worked that double, and now you're back?" Hawkins asked.

"That's right."

"Don't bitch at Wheeler," Riendeau said. "Me working twenty-four was your only other choice."

Hawkins headed over to check the orders, shaking his head. Gene nodded his thanks to Riendeau. They shook hands, and Riendeau staggered off toward home. Gene lay his head down on the picnic table.

He had already dozed off when Hawkins's voice jerked his head back up.

"It says here that we have to run this shit for another three hours. There should be less than an hour left. How the hell did you lose two hours?"

"We lost them when Number Five tried to swallow Saucier," Gene said as he lay his head back down.

"That's not funny."

"No," Gene said without raising his head, "it wasn't."

"You're serious?"

"Damn right." He sighed and turned his face to look up at him.

"Is he okay?"

"I don't really know. The last I heard, he was on his way to Mary Hitchcock."

Hawkins headed over to the smoking area. Gene had never seen him move so fast. Both crews milled around there, even The Flamer and Old Man Grenier. Ben and Hood stood with their backs to Gene. Judson's head towered above them all. Dub's white sailor hat bobbed in and out of view. Most of the guys from the day crew were there, too, as if they were too excited to go home. Suddenly, a dozen heads turned toward Gene, as if it had finally occurred to them that while they were swapping second-hand information, he was an actual eyewitness.

They stampeded the picnic table. The horn sounded at the other end, as the machine tenders demanded their relief. The Flamer and Old Man Grenier flipped a coin and The Flamer sashayed angrily toward the back of the machine when he lost.

"So tell us about it, Wheeler," Hawkins said.

"Tell me what they've heard from the hospital first."

"Oh, come on, Wheeler," Ben said. "La Sauce is history. That's a fucking million-dollar wound he's got. He only needs one elbow to bend, anyway."

Gene waited. If he could stand up to Lambert, a supervisor he didn't know, he could stand up to Ben.

"Supry just got a report from the hospital," Hawkins said. "Saucier's still in surgery. They have to restore circulation in his fingers and repair his tendons and nerves. Everything was torn to shreds. That takes a while."

"There," said Ben. "You got your update. Now tell us what happened."

"I'm sure you've already heard," Gene said. "He reached up to pull a scrap from the pulley and got dragged in. I was the only one who saw it happen."

"So you cut back the sheet?" said Old Man Grenier.

"I figured that was the fastest way to get everyone's attention."

He chuckled. "You got that right."

They asked a million questions, and he tried to answer them. When Ben turned up the roll, they sent Hood to do his work. Most of them seemed sorry that they'd missed the show. He wanted to tell them that they'd feel otherwise if they had seen what the machine had done to Saucier's arm. He felt like a kid who grows up on war stories and thinks the whole business is cool until he sees his buddies get their arms and legs blown off.

They acted as if he'd scored the winning touchdown or captured the enemy flag. Meanwhile, Saucier was knocked out on an O.R. table as they tried to piece his arm back together.

The excitement got him a brief respite from his work, but it was business as usual on the second roll. He just went through the motions, always in somebody's way. Hawkins followed him around the whole night, poking and prodding him through every step of the job, but it was different. He wasn't his usual, heavy-handed self, but almost gentle. Gene marveled at that miracle.

The party started all over again when the night shift came back in, but this time Gene sat it out because they each had their own version of the story. Arms flailed above the crush of bodies in the smoking area, imitation Sauciers being jerked around as if their bones were jelly.

Hawkins came over. Gene tried to work up the energy to head home.

"You know, Wheeler," he said as he gathered up his lunch bucket and folded up his newspaper, "about the only thing those jokers over there can agree on is that you're a hero."

Passing Time

"It could have been anybody."

"Not really," he said. "There's no telling what would have happened to Saucier if you hadn't acted as quickly as you did. "He stuck out his hand. Gene took it, and they shook.

"You did great," Hawkins said.

"Thanks."

Just over his shoulder, Gene saw Ben watching them, his eyes locked on their handshake. A huge sigh rippled through Ben's body, as if Gene was making a deal with the devil.

Ben came right over. "Hey, Wheeler," he said. "We're all going over to The Bone, and you've got to come."

"I'm dead, Ben. What I need to do is get some sleep."

"But you're the guest of honor, man," Ben said, grabbing his shoulder and shaking gently. "Everybody's going. Hell, it's even okay with me if Blondie comes along."

"I'll pass, Ben," Hawkins said. "But thanks for asking."

"Oh, come on," Ben said. "Be a team player for once."

"No. I'll give Wheeler a ride over, though, if he wants one."

Ben's eyes got big. "Better take him up on that one, kid. The rest of us mere mortals have never had a ride in Blondie's Magic Machine."

Magic Machine? Gene wondered what he was talking about, but he was too tired to ask. Too tired to say no to Ben. "Okay," he said. "I can't stay long, though."

"That's the spirit," Ben said and gave both of them a pat on the back.

Hawkins's Magic Machine was a Porsche, silver with a black vinyl roof. The sleek body clung to the ground. He bent down to put the key in the lock. "You sure you don't want me to just take you home?"

"I'd better not," Gene said. "Ben will be disappointed."

They climbed into the car. The engine ran so smoothly that Gene didn't realize Hawkins had started it until they were moving. They glided across the lot and onto Main Street. He glanced at the speedometer. They were up to fifty in an instant.

"Great car."

"There are some benefits to working here," Hawkins said. "You could get wheels, easily enough. Your folks might have to co-sign for you, but you're making good money."

"I might not be sticking around."

"That's right. Hood said you were college prep. How long did you go?"

"A year."

"Me, too."

"Really? Why did you quit?" Gene wondered if he had trouble with math, too. That would be too good to be true.

"I just didn't see much point to it. I figure you go to school to find something you like to do, and I got that here."

"Don't you get bored, sometimes?"

"Not really." He smiled. He was his old self, judgmental and superior. "You're at the bottom now, Wheeler. There's a lot to learn as you move up the ladder. I could teach you if you want."

"Really? Why would you do that? I thought you'd already pretty much decided I was a fuck up."

He laughed. "No, not really. I know I come on pretty strong sometimes, Wheeler, but you're all right. I suspected it when you stood up to me that first night, and I know it now, after what you did for Saucier."

"Thanks." Gene leaned back into the seat. The leather molded to his body, supporting every inch. His aches and pains faded away.

"Wheeler," Hawkins shook him awake. "We're here. Are you sure you just don't want me to take you home?"

"No. This might be cool. Maybe you should come, too."

"That's okay. I like to keep my home and work lives separate."

"Okay." Gene savored the seat for one more minute. "I hate to move. This is a great car." He pulled the latch on the door. He barely had the strength to push it open. Hawkins reached across his body and pushed it for him.

Gene struggled to get up. The seat didn't seem to want to let him go. He finally made it out and leaned back down. "Thanks again," he said.

Hawkins held out his hand. "You did good, kid."

The Bone was a well-known local dive, a place Gene had always heard about but, somehow, his eighteenth birthday had come and gone, and he'd never been inside. He decided that he hadn't missed much. It was a long, narrow tube, the whole place twenty feet wide, the walls painted black. On one side, the bar ran from end to end, while the other side was booths with black leather seats and black tables. The aisle that separated them was only three feet wide.

Just inside the door, a guy sat in the first booth, a full-length leg cast stretched out across the aisle, blocking the way. He glared at Gene when he tried to get past, but Ben came over and slapped him on the back of the head. "For Christ's sake, Jimmy," Ben said. "Let Wheeler by. He's the goddamn guest of honor."

This didn't seem to improve Jimmy's opinion of Gene, but he slid his leg down to the floor to let him past. He propped it back up as soon as he passed.

"How much longer are you going to be in that thing, Jimbo?" Ben asked.

"I'll be out of it on Monday," he said. "I'm already cleared to come back. Don't you know I'll be glad to be rid of this sorry piece of shit?" He reached over and dug at the space between his toes and the plaster with a straw. "Sometimes it itches so much it drives me nuts."

The place was packed. Ben shoved his way down the aisle, and Gene followed him. Devoid sat at the end of the bar guarding two empty stools.

"Sit," Ben said. Gene looked back down the bar. The only one missing was Hawkins. Dub and Judson sat in a booth, each nursing a beer. The Flamer and Old Man Grenier squabbled as if they were still back in the machine room. Supry played with his bow tie.

Hood sat in a booth by himself with his hair out, long and full, free of the hairnet and bandana. His was the only one with long hair in the place, though. Obviously, this was no place to meet women. The cigarette smoke was thick. The music was loud. The lights were turned down low. The white plaster of Jimmy's cast cut across the aisle like a florescent tube.

The bartender came over. "How's it going, boys?"

"Can't complain, Billy," Ben said.

"That's too bad," Billy said. "I always thought there was a lot of fun to be had in complaining."

"You could be right. I want you to meet Wheeler, a new guy in the machine room and the star of the night."

Billy turned and held out his hand. "Nice to meet you, Wheeler."

"Billy owns this place." Ben swept his hands around to take everything in. It didn't take long.

"Nice to meet you, sir," Gene said.

"Call me Billy. Everybody does."

The front door opened and a girl strode in. She didn't look much more than fifteen or sixteen, but when she paused, Gene didn't think for a moment that she was intimidated. She was striking a pose. She wore a black cowboy hat and had long, blonde hair. She wore a leather jacket over a white T-shirt and tight jeans. Hood whistled, and she slid into the booth beside him. They kissed. Hood's cheeks bulged as she slid her tongue into his mouth.

Billy whistled. He shook his head and pointed to the door. Hood gave him a smile and his middle finger. He saluted Gene and went out hand-in-hand with the girl.

"Hood's an idiot," Billy said. "One of these days that jail bait he's messing with will come back to haunt him."

"Forget about him," Ben said. He motioned for Billy to come closer and whispered something in his ear.

Billy let out a sharp whistle, and the bar fell silent. "Ben's buying. The first round is on him." Everybody cheered. Gene nodded to Ben, and he blushed. He stood and raised his glass. "Let's drink to Wheeler," he said.

"A good man," said Judson.

Everyone drank, but as soon as they put their glasses down, they settled into talk about past accidents.

"Remember that time those two guys were down working on the pulper blades and the bosses started up with them still down there?" Ben asked. He shivered. "How long ago was that, Old Man?"

Old Man Grenier looked down at his hands as if he had to count on his fingers, but since they were as badly mangled as Devoid's, they probably wouldn't help much. "At least twenty years," he said, finally.

"Were you there?" Ben asked

"No," he said. "I was off that day. Glad I missed it. I heard they got ground up into little pieces, like hamburger meat."

"Is that true, Dale?" Ben asked Supry.

Supry shivered. "It's a fact. Hope I never see anything like that again as long as I live."

"What about the day that Savage lost his arm?" Ben asked, mentioning the guy that Saucier had talked about just before he got hurt.

"I was there," said Old Man Grenier. "He got sucked into the rolls. Damn she-bitch tore his arm out of the socket. Fucking bosses were down within an hour trying to get us to start up again."

"That happened this morning," Gene said. "Some guy named Lambert tried to get us running as soon as they had Saucier in the ambulance."

"Word is you told him where to get off, Geno," Ben said. "Is that true?"

Gene grinned. "Not exactly."

"Now, now, don't be modest," Ben said. "Your stock is sky high with the boys on the eleven to seven. You saved the old man and stood up to Lambert."

"It wouldn't have done any good if their backtender hadn't told Lambert to fuck off," Gene said.

"Dave Shelton," Ben said. "A man who shares my job and my finer qualities." He raised his glass, earning a round of hoots and hollers from the guys.

"Savage's best friend worked machine tender the night he got hurt," Supry said. "He knocked one of the bosses out cold when the damn fool kept telling him to start up again. He never even got suspended. The union went to bat for him."

"That's what happened last night, too." Gene said. "Shelton told Lambert that we weren't budging until we got some kind of word on Saucier and to take it up with the union if he didn't like it."

"Let's hear it for the union," Ben said.

Everyone raised their glasses, but Gene noticed Judson and Dub didn't look happy when they did.

By the time they staggered out the door, the sky was pale gray. Most of the guys had left hours before, but Gene had stayed with Ben and Devoid. They waited after hours while Billy closed up. His first night in the place, and he was already a regular.

"Come one, Wheeler," Ben said. "I'll get you home."

"I'll be fine."

"Fine, my ass. The cops will find you in a ditch somewhere."

"They'll find all of us in one if you drive."

"I'm fine," Ben said. "I'm used to this. You'll get used to it, too."

Now there was something to look forward to.

They walked to Ben's truck. He opened the door and shoved Gene up. Devoid climbed in right behind him.

"All aboard," Ben said. "Ben's taxi is about the leave the station."

Gene leaned his head back on the seat. He dozed off. He heard some lady jawing at Ben. It was Devoid's "girl." Gene knew there was something about her that would make it worthwhile to open his eyes. Of course, he wanted to see what she looked like. What kind of woman marries the ugliest man in the world? He giggled and opened his eyes, but it was too late, they were already pulling away. All he saw was the back of a head and a pile of wild black curls.

Ben fiddled with the dials on the radio. Gene caught a whiff of smog from The Company's smokestacks and gagged. "Stop the truck, Ben." Ben slammed on the brakes, and Gene ran around to the back, where he emptied his stomach on the pavement. He felt Ben's hand on his shoulder. "I didn't know you were such a rookie," Ben said gently. "I guess we should have let you go home at closing time."

Ben gave him a rag from the back of the truck, and he wiped his face. Ben scuffed the hair on the top of his head. They made it home without another attack. "Thanks, Ben," he said as he slid unsteadily down to the sidewalk.

"Don't mention it, kid. You did great."

It was strange to hear the same words that Hawkins had used come out of Ben's mouth.

"You know," Ben said, "Blondie shook your hand tonight, but he'll turn on you in a minute if you screw up the slightest on Monday. He'll be right back on you."

"You're probably right, Ben. I don't worry about that anymore."

"That's my boy."

"Thanks for the ride."

Passing Time

Ben drove away, and Gene started down the driveway. He paused when he saw a car parked beside the house, a BMW with New Jersey plates. He walked to the back and saw a figure sitting on the steps, a young girl dressed in black, her face stark white in the moonlight, beneath a black beret, framed by a tangle of dark curls. Maybe Ben was right about his shaking hands with Hawkins. Maybe he'd sold his soul and this apparition had been sent to claim it.

"Hey," she said. He reached out one finger, twirled a strand of hair around it and brought it up to his face. He took a deep breath. The devil couldn't smell like this.

"Hey, Stace," he said.

"Where have you been? Did they make you work overtime again? I've been waiting for hours."

"What are you doing here?"

"After I hung up the phone this morning, I knew I couldn't wait another week to see you." She leaned into him. "I'll probably regret admitting that."

"I'm glad you came."

"Where are your folks? I thought they'd let me in when I got here, but nobody's home. I was starting to think I got the address wrong."

"They went to our summer cottage last night. They go every weekend."

"You mean we've got the house to ourselves?"

"Yes. Your folks aren't in Maine, mine aren't in New Hampshire." He giggled. "We're a couple of orphans."

She took his face in her hands. "You're drunk."

"Guilty."

"You were supposed to be at work."

"I was. We went out after. We were celebrating."

"Celebrating what?"

"It's a long story. I promise I'll tell you all about it in the morning." He closed his eyes.

She took his hand. "Where do we sleep?"

"Downstairs."

She led him down to his room. He turned on the lights and fell onto the bed, draping an arm over his eyes.

"So you worked twenty-four hours out of the last thirty-two," she said, "and then you went out and got drunk. Quite a life you've got going here." Her anger finally cut through the fog in his head.

"I'm sorry," he said. "I didn't know you were coming." He tried to hug her, but she pushed him away. He tumbled on to the bed.

"You smell like a homeless person," she said. She unlaced his boots. He grabbed the headboard as she jerked them off. She fiddled with his belt and the zipper on his pants. She tugged them down. They got tangled up around his ankles, but she worked them free. "Scoot over," she said. He slid to the edge of the bed and she pulled the covers back. He tried to get up. "I need a shower," he said.

"It'll wait until tomorrow." She rolled him over onto his stomach and pulled the covers up to his waist.

He struggled to roll back, but she already had him pinned, straddling him. She rolled up his T-shirt and began to knead the muscles in his back. She had strong hands, and she worked his muscles hard. He felt her thighs around him, her pelvic arch pressed into his back. Some distant part of his mind whispered how much he wanted her, but the rest of him was fast asleep before it got the message.

Chapter Nine

He woke up with a sliver of sunshine in his face and Staci pressed up against his back. He glanced at the clock. It was almost five p.m. He disengaged himself and sat up. A sharp pain tore at his skull. When he stood, the pain shot down his back.

He went into the bathroom, brushed his teeth, and took the shower that he desperately needed. Then he crawled back into bed and lay down face to face with her. She wore one of his T-shirts. He traced her spine through the worn fabric. She opened her eyes. "I know why I slept so late," he said. "What's your excuse?"

"Who says I've been asleep all this time? I slept a couple hours after you passed out and then got up and read all day. I finally got tired of waiting and decided to take a nap."

She studied him. He knew she wanted to see just how hung over he was. He forced a smile to his face, but even that hurt. He winced.

She rolled away from him and sat up on the side of the bed. "So, is staying out all night and getting drunk a requirement on your new job?"

He sat up and put his arms around her. She shrugged them off and went into the bathroom. Standing before the mirror, she pulled out her hairbrush and attacked her hair. She tore at the tangle of black curls, taking her anger out on it as she often did.

"I told you," he said. "It was a one-time thing. Something happened at work, and the guys wanted to celebrate. I went to be sociable."

"What can you have to celebrate in a place like that?"

"This old guy I work with got hurt Friday night. He got caught in the machine, and it tore up his arm pretty bad."

"And you and your buddies took that as an excuse to get drunk?"

Drunk? Buddies? Okay. She'd come all this way. He'd made her wait and been passed out all day, but enough was enough.

"We celebrated because it could have been a lot worse," he said. "I had to go because I probably saved his life. I was the only one to notice when he got pulled into the machine, and I did just the right thing to let everybody else know."

That got her attention. She laid the brush down on the sink and turned back to him. "That's incredible," she said. "Most people would have panicked. What did you do, sound the alarm?"

Gene thought of the red faces and the enraged voices when he broke the sheet. He smiled. "Something like that."

"Oh, Gene. I'm so proud of you." She took a step in his direction, but stopped. "Is there any way you can get hurt like that?"

"Not really. You have to get careless, have to take the machine for granted, and sh— . . . it still scares me shitless."

"So, you're not going to do anything crazy and get hurt like that old man did?"

"Of course not."

"Good. It's bad enough I lose you for a few months to that place, I want to at least get you back in one piece."

She turned back toward the mirror. He walked up behind her and rested his head on the top of hers. It was a good fit. He smelled her hair. She sighed and turned toward him.

They kissed and he slipped his hands under the T-shirt and the thin fabric of her underwear. He lifted her toward him. She was so light, it was as if she were floating on the palm of his hand.

The next time he awoke, no light came through the window. When he stirred, Staci climbed on top of him, and her hair fell down around his face.

"I'm starving," she said. "Are there any places around here that have good fried clams?"

Coming up from the cellar was often like coming out of a cave, but tonight the sun had already slipped behind the mountains, making the gray twilight easy to take.

They climbed into her car and drove toward downtown. They pulled into the parking lot of The Clam Barn. She got out and sat on the hood of the car while he got the food.

He slid up on the hood beside her with the tub of fried clams and two large drinks. She perched the cardboard tub between her legs, balanced her soda against it, and dug in.

She held a clam up to him. He took a bite and the stomach burst, burning the inside of his mouth. He grabbed his soda and doused the fire.

A truck pulled up next to them. Its sound system blasted the air, rippling the metal on the roof of its cab. Staci rolled her eyes at him. "Get a load of this bunch," she said.

Two girls in cut-off jeans and halter tops tumbled out of the passenger side. One of them had blonde hair, the other dark black hair that hung all the way down her back. The blonde glanced their way and gave Gene a huge grin, then poked her friend in the side. On the driver's side, Hood stood up in the doorway, looking over the roof of the cab. "Geno," he called.

Staci turned to Gene. "Geno?" she mouthed.

"He's one of the guys I work with," he explained.

"How you doing, my man?" He came over and threw one arm over Gene's shoulder. His breath rivaled Saucier's on his worst day. His eyes glittered.

"We're doing fine," Gene said.

Hood flashed Staci a huge smile. "And who's we?" The blonde materialized at his shoulder, as if she'd smelled the chemicals he was tossing toward Staci with his smile. Gene realized it was the girl from The Bone.

"I'm Jenna," she said. She wore a lot of make-up: thick, blue eye shadow, bright-red lipstick.

"Nice to meet you. This is Staci," Gene said.

"You're not local," Hood said to Staci. "I'd know you if you were."

"I'm up from Maine for the weekend," she said.

"Where in Maine?" He ignored Gene completely. Gene watched the hole Hood was digging himself into get deeper and deeper in Jenna's eyes.

"I know a lot of people in Rumford," Hood said.

"My folks have a place in Old Orchard."

"Old Orchard, huh? I used to hang there where I was a kid, but I haven't been there in a long time. Guess I need to check it out again. Give me your address, and I can look you up the next time I'm down there."

It was hard to say who was angrier: Staci or Jenna. Gene figured he'd better jump in before somebody took a poke at Hood.

"What are you guys up to tonight?"

Hood, totally focused on Staci, jumped at the sound of Gene's voice. He glanced at Gene, who expected him to show some kind of remorse, but he just winked.

"Nothing fancy tonight," Hood said. "Just our usual. We're getting in gear to party down. Headed up the mountain. You guys should hang with us. We're just stopping in here for some grub, but we've got all the other provisions we need in the truck, if you know what I mean."

"We can't," Gene said as he put an arm around Staci. She leaned back against him, getting into the act. "Staci's going back to Maine tomorrow, so we're just going to hang with each other tonight. You know how it is."

"Oh, yeah," Hood winked again. "Well, don't let us keep you. It was nice to meet you, Staci. Make sure Geno calls me the next time you're in town, and we can all get together and par-tay."

"We'll do that," Staci said. "Nice to meet you, Jenna." The young girl stared icily at her. Her friend stood behind her. At first, Gene thought she was trying to catch his eye, but every time he looked at her, she looked away.

"Catch you later, man," he said to Hood. "Bye, Jenna." She broke down long enough to smile at him. They all waved as they got into the take-out line. By the time they reached the window, Gene and Staci had finished eating. They climbed back into the car and drove away. Hood waved.

As soon as they pulled out of the lot, Staci's smile disappeared. "Cute kids," she said.

"Hood's all right."

"I have a hard time when I think of you spending your time with people like that," she said.

"People like that?"

"A drugged-out low-life and his slutty little girlfriends. They can't be more than sixteen. They should be throwing your pal in jail. If you're not careful, you could end up in the cell next to him."

He couldn't believe what he was hearing. He glanced in her direction. She glared back at him.

Passing Time

"Come on, Stace," he said. "I work with the guy. I don't hang out with him."

"I bet he's asked you to. I bet he wants to fix you up with that little tramp with the black hair. Didn't you see the way she was looking at you?"

He tried to pull her closer to him, but she jerked away.

"This is crazy," he said. "I've never met those girls."

"The blonde acted like she knew you."

He slammed on the brakes and pulled over to the side of the road. "So now I'm lying?" he said.

"Maybe," she said. "Who knows what you've picked up hanging around with people like that."

"People like that? Can you hear yourself? You act as if we're better than them."

"We are."

"Oh, Jesus. This is fucking bullshit."

"So now you even talk like them."

He threw the car into gear and pulled away.

"There is no us and them, Stace," he said. "Kids at school do drugs and screw around. What's the difference?"

"The kids at school will grow out of it. Your buddy Hood will probably be stoned and sleeping with high school girls when he's forty."

She had him there.

"He's just one guy. There are lots of other guys at work who are serious about what they do. Why should you care what Hood does in his free time? You're just freaking out on me."

She shook her head. "I'm freaking out on you? You're the one who ditched school so you could work in a factory and hang out with low-lifes. This isn't what I signed on for, Gene."

"I don't remember signing anything," he said.

"Maybe that's the problem."

Later, they raided the refrigerator and curled up on his bed with a half-gallon of ice cream.

"You know," she said. "I'm still angry."

"I know," he said. "I don't like the idea of being away from you either."

"And it's your idea. Imagine how I feel."

"I'm sorry."

"You should be."

They reached the bottom of the carton and scraped the last few spoonfuls from the corners of the box, getting closer to the kind of silence they usually shared. "We need more ice cream," she said. "We'd better make a grocery run." She rolled over onto her stomach and groped under the bed for her shoes.

"The stores are all closed."

"You're kidding. Doesn't this town have a 7-Eleven?"

"No. Everything shuts down at nine o'clock."

"Oh, great. The city that needs its sleep. And you want to live here for the next few months? I give up. I just don't get it."

She picked the carton back up and stared into it again, as if maybe there were a few morsels that she had missed, but she finally shook her head and tossed it into the trashcan.

"Actually, I'm glad this town is so dead. If I have to suffer, at least I know you'll be suffering, too."

She woke up Monday morning before six, shook him, planted a kiss on his lips before he had a chance to come fully awake, and was gone. As he lay back in bed, he wondered if he was dreaming. It couldn't be a good sign that he was always asking himself if his girlfriend was a ghost or a dream.

Chapter Ten

When he got to work that afternoon, both crews were gathered around the picnic table, even the machine tenders. Jimmy, the guy with the cast from The Bone, was sitting beside Ben and Devoid, without the cast, of course. Ben waved and pointed toward an empty seat on the bench beside him.

Supry stood at the winder, drumming his fingers on the panel.

"Let's get started," he said. He probably felt weird being out of his office.

"We're all ears, Dale," Ben said.

Supry stared down at a scrap of paper he held in his hand.

"Good day, men," he said. "You're probably wondering what this meeting is all about."

Gene looked around the table. Dub's face was screwed up in intense concentration. Hawkins and Judson hadn't even unfolded their magazines. Ben tapped his stick impatiently on the table.

"You're all aware of Saturday morning's accident," Supry said as he worked the scrap of paper in his hand. "Saucier is still in Mary Hitchcock. The doctors managed to save his hand, but he won't get back much of the function in it. Since his injury was job related, he will receive full disability, of course."

"I told you, Wheeler," Ben whispered in Gene's ear. "A fucking million-dollar wound."

Supry glared at him, but Ben just smiled.

"Accidents usually cause a great deal of confusion with our staffing," Supry said. "It just so happens, however, that even as Saucier is leaving us, another member of our crew, Jimmy Cooper is returning from his own medical leave. Because of this, Gene Wheeler, who would have been bumped out of the department by Jimmy's return, will be staying with us on a permanent basis."

Gene felt Ben's hand on his shoulder. "Welcome to the team,

Geno," he whispered.

Supry frowned at Ben, but pressed on, as if he'd decided the best thing to do with Ben was to ignore him. "I would like to take this chance to say that I'm glad that Mr. Wheeler will be staying with us. I can't say I know him very well. Before Friday night, he was just another body, someone Phil Blair stuck us with because he didn't have an experienced man. Friday, though, he really showed us what he was made of. Old Saucier may have been a pain in the ass, but who knows what would have happened if Mr. Wheeler hadn't acted as quickly as he did. We toasted him the other night, but I'd like to ask you one more time to show him how glad we are to have him on the team."

"Way to go, Geno!" Ben crowed.

"My man!" said Hood.

The others applauded. Gene glanced over at Hawkins and he nodded. High praise, indeed.

"All right, men. That's enough," Supry raised his hand. "I didn't come here just to commend Mr. Wheeler. The main reason is that I've decided to take this chance to make some changes with the crews that a few of you have been requesting for months. Frankly, I'm going to let you try them just to shut you all up." He glanced at Ben.

"As of today, the crew for Number Five will be Flamand, Ben, Devoid, Cooper, and Wheeler. Number Four will be manned by Grenier, Judson, Hawkins, Dub, and Hood." He looked around the table. "Any questions? Anybody have a problem with this?" Gene wasn't sure what to think. Hood's hand went up. Ben frowned.

"What is it Mr. Hood?" Supry asked.

"I was just wondering," Hood said. "Since I got more seniority than Wheeler, I could bump him, couldn't I, get his slot on Number Five?"

"Of course," Supry said.

"But he'd better not," Ben muttered.

"You got a problem, Ben?" Supry asked.

"No," Ben said. "Not yet, anyway," he whispered to Gene.

"So, Mr. Hood," Supry said. "Did you want to make that switch?"

"No, I'm cool. It's no big deal. I'm just thinking out loud, you know?"

Passing Time

"Fine. For now, we'll go with the crews as I've just called them, but since Hood brought it up, there is one thing you should all keep in mind. The only two people who are out of place by seniority are Hood and Wheeler. If Hood asks for a change, we'll do it. That's the rule under the union contract." He looked at his scrap of paper, even though by now it was shredded into little pieces. "That's it," he said. "Get to work, men." No one moved. Supry looked over his shoulder. Both machines were fifteen or twenty minutes away from turning up. He stuffed his paper back into his pants pockets. "When the ladies need you, of course," he said.

After he had gone, Ben stood. He waved for them to follow. They found their usual bench in the smoking section. Jimmy and Devoid sat down on either side of Ben.

"So, Ben," Gene said. "I guess this was all pretty much your idea."

"Of course," he said. "I just thought that it would be nice for us to be able to do our jobs without having to deal with Blondie's bullshit all the time. Don't get me wrong, just because we're all friends here, doesn't mean I'm going to let you slack off. When the horn sounds, you'll still have to be there, and if you're not, there'll be hell to pay. We just don't have to listen to Blondie bitch because we don't meet his goddamn expectations."

"Amen," Devoid said.

"Fucking A," Jimmy said.

Ben held out his cigarettes to Jimmy and Devoid and offered the pack to Gene. He shook his head. "You can't refuse, Wheeler," Ben said. "This is a celebration of our being a team."

"Well, I guess if you put it that way," Gene said. He took one.

"Actually, I'd rather crack open a bottle of champagne." Ben lit a match and held it out for all of them. "But that will have to wait until we get to The Bone."

Devoid snickered. "As if Billy has champagne."

Ben took a long pull off his cigarette and held it up like a small sword. "All for one, and one for all," he said. Devoid and Jimmy touched the tips of their cigarettes to his. Gene did the same.

"To the A-Team," Ben said.

"Right on," Devoid said. Gene glanced over at Hawkins and

Judson who talked quietly at the table. Dub sat beside them, hanging on their every word. The horn sounded, and Old Man Grenier waved wildly to them. Judson raised his stick in a calm salute and turned back to Hawkins. Ben had referred to his group as the A-Team, but Gene had to wonder. How could they be the A-Team when all the best workers were on Number Four?

They ran their next roll and were back in the smoking area before Gene knew it. "So, tell us about your weekend, Wheeler," Ben said and patted the bench beside him.

"Not that much to tell," Gene said, sitting beside him. "A friend of mine from school came up."

"A friend, huh?" Ben winked at Devoid. "A lady friend, maybe."

"Wheeler got some," Devoid said.

"Well, it's not like he's the only one, Devo," Ben said. "We know you've been fucking the little lady's brains out all weekend."

Gene tried not to show his doubt on that one. It was still hard to imagine someone as ugly as Devoid having a wife, let alone spending the weekend having wild sex.

"Damn straight," Devoid said. "Don't act like you weren't doing the same, Ben."

Ben waved this away with a flip of his hand. "It isn't the same once you've been married as long as I have. For one thing, the frigging kids are always in the way. You can maybe get a little taste after dark as long as you're quiet, but lord knows the old lady won't even make a peep. It takes the fun out of it, you know?"

"No," Devoid said, "I don't."

"You son of a bitch," Ben said, but he couldn't hide a grin. "I envy you young studs. You have all the fun."

"Oh, Jesus, here we go again." Devoid rolled his eyes at Gene.

"Come on, Ben," Jimmy said. "You're not that old."

"I'm forty, kid," Ben said. "My best days are behind me." He buried his head in his hands. "You don't know what it's like. You young bucks are tasting sweet pussy night and day, but it's just a distant memory to me."

"Come on, Ben," Jimmy whined. "Don't be like this."

"There's only one thing that keeps me going," Ben's fingers finally parted. "You guys can tell me about your fucking weekends. And I do mean fucking."

"You want to live vociferously?" Devoid asked.

Ben smiled. "Close enough. You go first, Geno."

"I don't know, Ben," Gene said. "That's personal."

"Personal?" Ben said. "We're all friends here. We got no secrets." His smile faded. "Or do we?"

"I just don't like to talk about my girl that way."

"That way? Jesus, Wheeler. What other way is there? Even Devo talks about fucking his wife, and he's the most pussy-whipped man on the face of the planet. You know Jimmy would be shooting his face off every day if he ever actually got any."

"That's right," Jimmy said and turned bright red when he realized what he'd just admitted. Ben slapped him on the shoulder to show him everything was all right.

Ben looked at Gene. He waited. Gene thought of Staci wearing only his T-shirt. The way she'd rested so lightly on his palm. It was a good memory, but it was his. It wasn't meant to be a scene in a porno movie.

"Okay, okay," Ben said. "You got issues. We'll let Devo show you how easy it is. And remember, this man thinks his woman is God's gift to this green Earth."

"Damn right," Devoid said.

"What's the little woman's favorite position, Devo?" Ben asked, holding out his backtender's stick like a microphone.

"Doggie style."

"Pussy or ass?"

Devoid closed his eyes and then he smiled. "She likes it in the pussy, but the ass is a whole other thing. She just loses it. Sometimes I'm afraid she's going to break my dick off inside her."

"See, Geno," Ben said. "That wasn't so hard. Now, you try."

"No," Gene said.

"Okay," Ben laid his stick on the table before him and began to roll it back and forth. "Let's start slow. Your girlfriend came to visit."

"That's right."

"Where did she drive up from?"

"Old Orchard Beach."

"She lives there?"

"Her folks have a summer place."

"A place at the beach," Ben said. "Maybe that's the problem, men. Geno's girl is a rich bitch. He doesn't want to talk about her to lowlifes like us."

"Jesus, Ben," Gene said.

"No, no," Ben said. "I'm just trying to figure this out." He flipped the stick back and forth more quickly. "If that's just the summer house, where's she live full time."

"In New Jersey."

"New Jersey. That's a long way, off, my man. How did you meet her?"

Gene glanced at Devoid and Jimmy. "I met her in school," he said, finally.

"School?" Devoid said. "How'd she get in Jersey? Did her family move away or something?"

"I met her in college. The college is in New Jersey."

"College?" Devoid said. "You went to fucking college? How the hell did you end up here?"

"He went one year," Ben said. "He's taking some time off." He picked the stick up and tapped it in his other palm.

"Who the fuck takes time off from college?" Devoid asked. "You go to college, you graduate, you get a real job. It's probably a bullshit job, but you don't end up here."

"It doesn't matter why Geno's here, why he got out of school," Ben said. "The only reason we need to know is that it helps us understand why he won't talk about his girl. She's obviously too high class for us, a rich-bitch college chick. Either she's an uptight white girl and there's nothing to tell, or she's a raging whore in the bedroom who would die if anyone but her lover boy ever found out. Whatever the case, she's too fucking good for us to talk about. And I guess Wheeler must be too good for us, too."

"Fuck you, Ben," Gene said and walked away.

He went back over to the picnic table and sat down beside Hood, who turned off his tape player and stuck a scrap of paper in his book to mark his place. He ran his hand over his head as if to smooth down his hair, but of course got only red bandana and hair net. He grinned. "Force of habit. So, how you doing, man?"

"I'm okay."

"You don't look okay."

"Ben's busting my chops."

"I thought he was your good buddy now, the captain of your team."

"I thought so, too."

Across the table, Dub had already spread out his dinner. He smiled at them, but Hood ignored him. Dub shrugged, his head pinched between his shoulders like a turtle's bobbing out of its shell. He dug into his basket and pulled out a casserole in a flowery-colored ceramic dish. "Chick-en tet-tra-zeen-nee," he mouthed to Gene, and then winked at Hood and held a finger up to his lips as if they were keeping a secret. Gene smiled, and Dub dug in.

Hood nodded toward Ben, Devoid, and Jimmy. They were talking and laughing again. Devoid lit a cigarette and handed it to Ben. Jimmy lit one off Ben's.

"Will you look at those three," Hood said. "They always seem to be having one hell of a good time, don't they?"

"I guess."

"They hang out together outside of work, too," Hood said. "They probably spend more time with each other than they do with their women. Shit, I wouldn't be surprised if they were fucking each other."

"Get out of here," Gene said. "They're not like that. They're pissed off at me because I wouldn't talk about fucking my girl."

"They want details," Hood said.

"They want to live *vociferously*," Gene said.

Their laughter came together. Dub fought to hold back a grin. Gene thought Dub's head would split wide open.

"Fuckin' lame assholes," Hood said. Dub nodded sadly.

Things ran smoothly for most of the night, at least as far as the machines were concerned. Ben still wouldn't talk to Gene.

They didn't have any breaks in the machine. Gene saw his team only when they had a roll. It had to be the shortest honeymoon on record.

At eight o'clock, he watched Ben, Devoid, and Jimmy in the smoking area. With all the talk about sex, it made him wonder again what Devoid's wife looked like.

"Have you ever seen Devoid's wife?" he asked Hood.

Hood snickered. "I know where you're going with that, man. Devoid is so fucking ugly that you figure his wife must be a real dog. She's not bad looking at all, though. I'd take a taste of that."

"Ain't that the truth," Dub said. He smacked his lips and glanced at the drumstick he munched on as if it had lost its taste.

"Devoid was single when I started working here," Hood said. "Then he got engaged and everyone started riding him about the wedding coming up. The big day comes and goes and Devoid comes back from his honeymoon sporting the widest gold wedding band that you have ever seen. Obviously, the little woman wanted everyone to know that her man was off the market. Can you believe that shit? The fucking ugliest human being in the world, and she wants to brand him so no other broad would try to cut in."

"So what happened?" Gene asked.

"He hadn't worked an hour before the winder snagged the fucking thing and he was three fingers in before Hawkins could shut it down."

"That's how his hands got so messed up?"

"That's how." Dub nodded sadly. "It's his own fault, though. He shouldn't have rubbed that ring in Number Five's face."

"You're saying the machine was jealous?"

"I know it sounds crazy, man." Dub glanced over his shoulder as if he were afraid of being overheard. "But I've seen too much around here. You won't find me messing with these machines. You'd be smart to do the same."

"And I'll tell you something else you need to do if you want to get along around here," Hood said.

"What's that?"

"Talk about fucking your girl." He nudged Gene in the ribs as if he wanted his share of the juicy details.

"Oh, Jesus," Gene said.

"What's the big deal? Are you trying to tell me you never sat around with your boys at school and talked about getting laid?"

"Of course I have," Gene lied.

"So do it with the guys here," Hood said. "It's nothing. It's how we talk. It's not like your girl will know." He frowned. "Unless you tell her, that is. You can't be that fucking whipped, can you?"

Later that night, Judson came over to the table. He carried his backtender's stick in one hand and a huge bottle of pink antacid in the other. Gene thought he'd looked sick in Supry's meeting, but he'd stayed over by the front of the machine all night.

His skin had lost its usual fiery red glow. His hair lay flat on his head instead of dancing around the fringe of his bald spot in its usual, wild manner.

He sighed and dropped on the bench beside Hood. Dub did a double take, one right out of a cartoon. "Gosh, Big Buddy," he said, "you look like hell."

Judson grunted in reply.

"I don't know why you don't just hook yourself up to an IV," Hood said. He seemed to be enjoying Judson's pain. Dub glared at Hood, stood up, and hovered over his friend. He rummaged in his basket as if there was something inside that would make Judson feel better. Why not? Maybe his Ma was a witch doctor, too.

"Sit down, Dub," Judson said. "We all know the only thing you have in that basket is food, and the thought of eating turns my stomach. I'll be fine, son. I'll just have to ride this one out."

Dub sat, but he didn't seem happy. He fidgeted in his seat, glancing at the basket every few seconds. Gene realized he didn't want to eat because it might bother his friend.

Judson looked up and smiled. "Go ahead, son."

Dub sighed with relief and dug into the basket. He came up with two sandwiches and held one out to Gene.

"That's okay, Dub."

"Take it," he said. "I usually share with my big buddy, anyway."

"Okay," Gene said.

Dub gave him the sandwich and poured him cup of coffee, too.

The sandwich was good, chicken-salad. It had a different flavor. Gene was at a loss to name the secret ingredients. The coffee had a heavy taste, almost like espresso. Of course, with all the noise, Dub could have had a machine in the bottom of his basket, and they wouldn't have noticed if he fired it up. "Thanks, Dub," Gene said. "This is all great."

After he'd finished the sandwich, he sipped the coffee, cradling the mug in his hands.

Things ran smoothly most of the night. Gene decided the machines were happy with the new crews, too.

The horn blasted.

Gene wheeled around, expecting to see the sheet gone, the bare metal of the rolls mocking him, but they remained hidden beneath the white of the sheet.

He walked over to the roll and looked down the corridor toward the wet end of the machine. He expected to see The Flamer, but Old Man Grenier leaned on their horn, instead. Ben came up beside him, hit the horn, and stood with his hands high, his palms open. What the hell was going on? he asked without words. Old Man Grenier lifted one arm, held up an open palm, brought his fingers down, and then opened them again.

"What's he trying to say?" Gene asked.

"I don't know," Ben said. "I've never seen this sign before."

"Five," Gene said. "It's like he's holding up five fingers. What does that mean?"

"It doesn't mean a thing," Ben said. "I told you, he just made up a new sign." Old Man Grenier hit the horn twice and pointed at Ben, then pointed at Gene and snapped off five, short, shrill blasts, then waved his hand in a beckoning gesture. Gene felt someone walk up beside him. It was Hood. Old Man Grenier pointed at Hood, than at Gene and knocked out five more blasts.

Ben laughed. "Five," he said. "Two blasts for me, the number two guy on the crew and five for you and Hood, the low men on the totem pole. He wants to talk to you."

"Me? Why does he want to talk to me?"

"Or maybe Hood. Maybe he wants to welcome him to his new crew."

Gene looked over at Hood.

He shrugged. "What the fuck. Let's check it out."

At the other end, Old Man Grenier sat with his lunch box open and a sandwich broken in two on the table. Crumbs leaked out the corners of his lips. "You hungry, boys?" he asked.

"I'm okay," Gene said.

Hood shook his head. "I'm good."

"What's up?" Gene asked.

"I wanted to tell you again how good you did the other night,

Wheeler," he said. "I never saw somebody move so fast when there was trouble. Number Five would have fucked Saucier up a lot worse if you hadn't acted when you did."

"Thanks," Gene said.

He pointed at Hood. "And I wanted to talk to you, too."

"What did you want to talk to me for? I ain't got no fucking medals coming to me."

Old Man Grenier picked up half the sandwich and stuffed it in his mouth. He chewed thoughtfully. Hood rolled his eyes at Gene.

"I was wondering," Old Man Grenier said, finally, "if you were ready for the new day around here?"

"New day?" Hood asked. "What the fuck are you talking about, old man?"

"I wonder if you're ready to be a part of our new team."

"What the fuck?" Hood said. "I know what I have to know to do my job."

"That's my point," Old Man Grenier said. "You just want to get by. That might have been okay before, but it won't do now."

"Okay," Hood said, "I'll bite. Why won't it do?"

"Just look at the guys you're working with. You used to have The Flamer as your machine tender and Saucier fucking things up at the winder, but now you've got me and Hawk. We got a good group from top to bottom, though I guess the bottom part is up to you."

"You've got to be kidding me," Hood said.

"Not for a minute, boy. Things are going to be different if you work with us."

"I can fix that. Working with you, that is."

"Suit yourself."

Just then, the horn sounded back at the other end. Old Man Grenier frowned and looked at his watch. "What the hell?" he said. He got up and peered down that way. Ben leaned over the roll. This far away, Gene couldn't hear the acceleration of the turn-up, but Ben's arm dropped over the roll and Gene knew he'd cut the sheet and started a new roll. He wondered where Judson was, but then he remembered how sick he was. Maybe he was upstairs in the bathroom. Old Man Grenier shook his head. "Ben's early," he said. "The roll's light. He'll be within specs, all right, but I don't like it, it's sloppy." He seemed to be talking more to himself than to them. "You'd better go," he said finally. "They're starting without you."

They were pulling samples when Gene and Hood got back. Hawkins gave Hood a dirty look. "Start the winder," Dub muttered. Hood trotted toward the control panel, and Gene walked over to the smoking area. Hawkins waited for Hood, tapping the rolled-up samples impatiently against his palm. Ben stood just behind Hawkins.

Ben waved an arm. Gene ignored him at first, but then he realized that Ben was trying to get his attention. Had he forgotten he was pissed off at Gene? Maybe having Hawkins as their common enemy trumped all of that.

Ben made a terrible face, curled up his nose, and pinched his lips tightly together. He planted one fist on his hip, and the stick in his other hand became a rolling pin. He was the mother of all shrews. Gene smiled and headed over to him. "How come you turned up for them instead of Judson?" Gene asked.

"Jud's still up in the can," he said. "I'm covering for him while he's indisposed."

"That's great," Gene said and headed back over to the picnic table. Hood came over and sat down beside him after he'd lugged his broke to the pulper. Hawkins had the winder up to speed, and Dub stood beside him. Hawkins leaned over and whispered something in Dub's ear. Dub glanced over at Hood and nodded, his face grim, and took over the controls. Hawkins came over. Gene recognized the look in his eyes, the same, dull sheen that always appeared when he talked about other people's screw-ups. The way he'd looked at him that first day, as if he was channeling the machines.

"Look," Hawkins said. "I know you were down there talking to Old Man Grenier, but that's still no excuse for getting down here late. I know he likes to talk about making paper, but you've got to keep track of time. Actually, I blame him more than you. He should know better."

Hood just rolled his eyes, but Gene couldn't keep quiet. "Old Man Grenier was watching the time," he said. "He said Ben turned the roll up a few minutes early."

"Really?"

"Really," Hood said. "He said the roll's going to be light."

"We'll see," said Hawkins, turning back toward the winder.

"And don't be worrying about me spending time down at the other end picking Old Man Grenier's brain," Hood said. "It wasn't my idea in the first place, and it won't happen again."

Hawkins looked Hood up and down. "That's too bad." He turned quickly, dismissing Hood's attitude again with that speed.

"Jesus-H-Christ," Hood said, as he watched him walk again. "What the hell is it with these guys? They've all gone fucking nuts."

He was right. Ben and his gang seemed happy enough with the changes in the crew, but they were sure on edge on Number Four.

When they pushed the rolls into the hall, Gene went out with them. Hawkins pulled a tape measure from his pocket and checked them. "Goddamn," he said. "They are light."

"But they're okay, aren't they?"

He shrugged. "They're within company specs, but they aren't within mine. I need to talk to Ben."

"But he was just trying to help you guys out," Gene said. "Because Judson's sick."

"He shouldn't have done anything if he wasn't going to do it right."

He stalked over to Ben. Hawkins had his back to them, but he did the talking first. Ben listened, and then glanced in Gene's direction. Gene expected a sneer, but hurt flashed across Ben's face instead.

By the time he looked back at Hawkins, though, Ben's sneer was in full force. Hawkins held two fingers out, and Gene knew if they had a ruler, it would have showed exactly how light the roll had been. Ben stretched his arms apart before him as if he were showing a huge fish that had gotten away, one that got bigger with every telling. Finally, he brought his hands together and got down on his knees, begging for forgiveness. Hawkins walked away.

Ben came right over, and the hurt was back in his eyes. "I covered for Judson," he said. "I tried to cheer you up, reminded you what a pompous jerk Blondie is and you sicced him on me."

"I'm sorry, Ben. He was giving Hood so much shit. Then he said it was Old Man Grenier's fault that Hood was late."

"Oh, I see," Ben said. "You stood up for The Hood and Old Man Grenier, anyone but me."

"I didn't mean it like that."

"That's okay, Wheeler," he said. "I can see where I am on your list." He walked away, shaking his head.

"Jesus, Wheeler," Hood nodded toward Ben. "Do you have to work at pissing people off so much, or does it just come naturally?"

"I never had this problem before I came here," Gene said. "These people are crazy. They've always got their nose out of joint about something."

"They do take this shit pretty seriously," Hood said. "Hawkins is nuts about the work, but Ben always wants you to think about him and the team, first and foremost. With Hawk, nothing is personal. With Ben, everything is."

"Everything?"

"Everything. The only thing that Ben cares about is teamwork."

Judson came back through the door, still sipping from that economy-sized bottle of antacid. Hood filled him in on the excitement. "I should have known," Judson said. "You get spoiled working with a third hand like Saucier. Next time I'm under the weather, I'll stay home. No slacking off when you work with Hawkins." He took a long drink.

"Tell me about it," Hood said. "The more I think about it, the more I wish they'd put me on Number Four. The crew's a bunch of losers, but at least they're not fanatics. Sometimes I think I should use my seniority and switch over there."

"I wouldn't do that if I were you," Judson said. "Ben's had it in his head to change the crews for months. It's best not mess with his scheme. Besides, working with Hawk could be good for you. As they say in sports, he helps the rest of us raise the level of our games."

"Oh, great," Hood said. "He's the fucking Hondo Havlicek of the machine room."

Ben stayed away from Gene for the rest of the night. Even when they ran their rolls, he acted as if Gene wasn't there. At eleven,

Passing Time

Gene walked out behind him and the others. He caught up to Ben when the others had gone to their cars. "Hey, Ben," he called.

Ben paused but didn't turn around. "What is it, Wheeler?"

"I just wanted to say I'm sorry. You've been really good to me since I started here, and Hawkins is a real asshole. I didn't mean to rat you out about the roll being light. He surprised me, and I just blurted it out. You were trying to help out, and Hawk was a jerk about it. I know I screwed up, I'm sorry."

Ben spoke without turning around. "Blondie," he said.

"What?"

"I said call him Blondie. Hawk's too good a nickname for an asshole like that." He finally turned and grinned at Gene, reaching out to rough up his hair.

"Blondie it is," Gene said.

"Let's get a beer," he said.

Jimmy and Devoid seemed surprised to see Gene when they walked into The Bone.

"Why's *he* here?" Jimmy said.

"Because I want him here, Jimmy. You got a problem with that?" Ben said.

"No," he mumbled, staring down into his beer.

"Good. You want the usual, Wheeler?"

"Yeah."

At closing, Billy chased everyone else out. Gene was already well on his way to being as drunk as he'd been on Saturday night. Ben got up and stood behind them, draping his arms over their shoulders. "I thought the rest of them would never leave," he said.

Jimmy and Devoid settled back in their seats. Ben kept his arm around Gene's shoulder. "So, Geno. Maybe now you want to tell us about your college girl."

"Her name is Staci."

"Pussy or ass?"

Maybe it was the beer, or Hood's advice. After all, the guy had been living in this world his whole life. Talking to the guys wouldn't hurt Staci. She'd never even know. Somehow, it just didn't seem to matter anymore.

"Well?" Ben said.

"Up the ass," Gene said. "Definitely up the ass."

Chapter Eleven

Ben didn't carry a grudge. Once Gene started talking about Staci and apologized for taking Hawkins's side over the early turn-up, everything was back to normal. Ben seemed determined to make Gene a regular at The Bone, dragging him there every night after work. It left Gene sick and shaken by Friday afternoon.

When Gene got to work, he realized he'd grown accustomed to the sounds and vibrations of the machine room because his hangover made it seem like his first day all over again. Everything was too loud. The heat off the machines was like a furnace. His legs trembled with the vibrations that had become second nature. He could hardly wait for his first trip to the pulper. One good whiff of formaldehyde would be the coup de grâce for his swirling stomach.

Ben and Devoid came over as soon as he walked in. Neither of them looked the slightest bit uncomfortable. "Jesus, Wheeler," Ben said. "You are one sorry looking child."

"Fucking rookies," Devoid said.

"Don't worry, Geno," Ben said. "The first couple weeks is always the worst. By the end of the month, you'll be logging your Bone time every night, and you'll be past this shit. It's just like riding a horse. You get thrown, you've got to climb right back on. Show your body who's boss."

Gene shook his head. "I don't know, Ben. I've never felt this bad in my whole life. This isn't natural."

"Trust me, Wheeler. I know what I'm talking about. Have I ever steered you wrong?"

"No," Gene said, "but I need to take a night off, tonight. This is killing me, and I'm going out of town tomorrow."

"I suppose I can let you slide this one time," he said. "But I'll expect you back in the saddle come Monday, you hear?" He waved his stick in Gene's face like a teacher wielding a pointer at the blackboard.

"Okay," Gene said. He would have said anything to get him to stop talking. Ben's voice was one more noise banging against his skull.

"Fucking lame rookie," Devoid said, revising his earlier opinion. They headed off for the smoking area.

Hood sat beside him and slapped down a fresh paperback. Gene winced. Hood pulled out his tape player, but Gene knocked his hand away from the Play button. He'd moved too fast. His stomach roiled in protest.

"What the fuck?" Hood said, but then he looked at Gene. "Oh, man, I thought you'd hit rock bottom yesterday, but you look even worse today."

"My head is killing me," Gene said. "I can't take any music."

"How many nights have you gone to The Bone this week?" Hood asked.

"Every one."

"And how long did you stay last night?"

"I don't have a clue." He lay his head down on the table. It felt good at first, but then he felt the vibrations of the machine singing in the wood. He sat back up.

"I don't know why you waste your time hanging out with that sorry bunch of geezers," Hood said. "You saw my girl. Wouldn't you rather be hanging out with me and her friends? You know you'll never get any pussy hanging out at The Bone." He put the tape deck back into his lunch pail and pulled out his hairnet.

"You know I'm not really looking for that right now. I've got a girl."

"Is there a law that says you get to have only one?" Hood asked. "You could have the ideal set up: local and long-distance pussy."

He slipped his fingertips inside the hair net. He spread them out as wide as he could. He looked like he was playing Cat's Cradle.

"Billy didn't seem to think much of your girl being in the bar the other night," Gene said, trying to change the subject.

"Ah, he's fucking paranoid about his license. He's like an old woman. My mother has more balls than he does."

He pulled the net down over his hair. He tucked the loose ends up under and pulled the red bandana from his back pocket.

"But your girl is underage, isn't she?" Gene asked.

"Who cares?" Hood said. "I'll bet she could teach you a thing or two. Age is a fucking technicality."

"Be sure to mention that at your trial."

"You're a funny guy, Geno. You know, if you play your cards right, we'll both end up in jail. Jenna's best friend saw you the other day, and she's really got the hots for you. They want me to bring you up the mountain with us after work."

Gene thought of the girl they'd had with them at the Clam Shack, the one Staci had said was checking him out. Maybe Staci wasn't so paranoid after all.

"Not tonight. I'm going to see my girl tomorrow."

"Going to sample the long-distance pussy. That hot little piece you've been telling us about?"

"Don't remind me."

"That she's a hot little piece?" He seemed confused.

"That I let you talk me into telling the guys about her. Don't tell Ben, but I made half of it up."

"Really?"

"No, not really."

"You dog," Hood said. He slapped Gene on the back. Even that made his stomach jerk.

"You had me going there for a minute," he said. He swiped at Gene. Gene jerked away too fast, saw spots, and everything went black.

When he opened his eyes, Hood, Ben, and Devoid were looking down at him. "Jesus, Wheeler," Ben said. "You fucking passed out. Are you all right?"

"Yeah," he said. He sat up. No spots. Ben held out his hand and pulled him to his feet.

"I'm okay."

"Fucking lame-ass rookie," Devoid said. Gene wondered just how many levels of rookies there were and how far he could fall.

"You should go home," Ben said.

Dub came over, munching on a smoked turkey leg. "You know, Wheeler," he said, "my Ma has a great hangover remedy. I'll have her whip up a batch, and I'll bring it in for you tomorrow."

"I won't be here tomorrow."

"Why can't you just give him the recipe now?" Ben asked.

"Yeah," Devoid said. "He might not make it 'til Monday."

"You know I can't give out my Ma's recipes," Dub said. He looked over his shoulder as if he were a spy who'd just been asked to break his cover. "If Ma found out, she'd kick my ass."

"We wouldn't want that," Ben said.

"I'll be okay," Gene said. "I'll just go upstairs to the locker room for a minute."

"Take your time. We'll cover for you if Supry comes around."

"Thanks."

He walked up the stairs to the locker room. The spots crept back in at the edge of his vision. He closed his eyes and felt his way along the railing to the top. In the locker room, he clung to the window that opened out onto the roof. He stuck his face into the breeze. "I just need a little air," he said, trying to convince himself, but he finally walked into the stall, closed the door, and emptied his stomach.

"Fucking sorry lame-ass rookie," he said. To think that his college had been rated one of the top three drinking schools in the Mid-Atlantic States. Obviously, "Bone time" was a whole new ball game.

At five, Hawkins, Judson, Hood, and Gene sat around the table, reading. Gene's head had cleared. Dub rummaged around in his basket and pulled out a huge plastic bag of trail mix. Not the store-bought kind, of course. "Way too heavy on the raisins and peanuts," he explained. "I'm partial to cashews and dates." He sipped coffee from his ugly pink mug. Gene smelled hazelnut. His stomach didn't protest, and he decided me might live after all.

Ben came around the corner with his boys and tossed three copies of the local paper down on the table without commenting on the headlines. He had already pulled out a sports section for himself. The others grabbed at the rest. Hawkins and Judson each took a front page.

After Devoid scooped up a sports section, Jimmy shoved Dub aside and took the last one. Dub hit the floor. His hat fell off and rolled under the table. Judson looked up and frowned, but Dub held up a hand. He burrowed through the tangle of legs to get his hat.

"Hey," Ben yelled.

"Jesus-H-Christ!" said Devoid.

"Get the hell off of me, you fucking retard." Jimmy swiped at him with the paper. Judson grabbed his wrist. Jimmy pulled away, but Judson squeezed. The blood drained from Jimmy's face.

"Take it easy, Jud," Ben said.

Dub emerged from the other side, his hat back in place. He grinned. Judson let go of Jimmy. He glanced at the paper in Jimmy's hand and raised his eyebrows. Dub shook his head. He sat next to Ben, reading over his shoulder.

One of these days the uneasy truce between these guys was going to break, Gene thought. He hoped he wasn't in the middle when it did.

"I don't know why you guys waste your time reading that political crap," Ben said. "The real news is the preview of this year's flag football season."

"To each his own, Ben," Judson said. Hawkins didn't even look up. Gene reached over to take the remaining front section. He expected to see a lead story about city council business, but the headlines read: Union ponders strike vote. He glanced at Hawkins who shook his head and looked back down.

"What do they say about flag football?" Dub asked, leaning into Ben. "Do they talk about us?"

"Of course, they do," Ben said. "How could they leave out the defending champs?" He winked at Gene.

They were all on the same team, sponsored by The Bone. Ben was the quarterback and middle linebacker. Jimmy played line on both sides of the ball. Devoid was fullback and free-safety. Amazingly enough, Dub was a star wide receiver. "You should see the moves this little monkey's got," said Ben. "He gets the defenders going in three directions at once." Dub demonstrated without getting up from the bench, his neck and shoulders and arms all going in different directions, as if his bones were made of rubber.

"Yeah," said Devoid. "When the Dubster starts shucking and jiving like that, he leaves the other team grabbing at thin air. It's a beautiful thing."

Ben slapped Dub on the back. They both beamed.

"You should come to tryouts, Wheeler," Ben said. "They're a week from Saturday. We've got a couple slots open."

"But you'll probably ride the bench," Jimmy said.

"Oh, come on," Devoid said. "We had so many blowouts last year, everybody got to play."

"Maybe Wheeler doesn't like football," Jimmy sulked. "Maybe he doesn't like contact."

"Isn't that why you wear handkerchiefs on your hips in flag football?" Gene asked. "So there won't be too much contact?"

"Oooh," said Ben. "Score one for Wheeler. Just for the record, though, things can get pretty rough out there."

"Sounds good to me," Gene said. There had always been some kind of intramural league going on at school. During the fall, they spent more time playing football than going to class.

Ben looked at his watch. He folded up the newspaper and stuck it in his back pocket. "I need a cigarette before we turn up. Who's with me?"

"I'm in," said Jimmy.

"I could use a butt," said Devoid. He left his paper on the table. Dub scooped it up.

"You coming, Wheeler?"

"I think I'll finish this article about your team." Gene picked up the section that Jimmy had left.

"Suit yourself. We'll see you at the winder."

They were barely out of earshot when Hawkins slammed the paper down on the table. "I can't believe it," he said. "Those goddamn union reps have lost their minds. They've got to be bluffing."

"Maybe, maybe not," said Judson.

"What's going on?" Gene asked.

Hawkins shook his head. "This says the union walked away from the bargaining table last night. They've given The Company two weeks to come up with a new proposal or they're going to call for a strike vote."

"They threatened to call a vote?" Dub said. He tossed down the sports page and grabbed the newspaper from Hawkins's hands.

"That can't be right."

"We're going on strike?" Gene said.

"The committee can't actually initiate a strike," Hawkins said. "They have to put it to a vote of the membership, but a vote is usually just a rubber stamp."

"The committee never calls for a vote unless they recommend a walkout," Judson explained. "If they figured they could get a better deal done at the table, they'd have stayed there. I can't remember the membership ever going against the recommendations of the negotiating committee."

"But it can't just be business as usual, this time, Jud," Hawkins said. "We can't line up like sheep to the slaughter just because that's what the committee wants us to do. You saw the last draft of what The Company was offering. It's a good deal. There's nothing in there that I can't live with. I can't see how anyone in their right mind would vote to strike."

"Who said anything about a right mind?" Judson said.

"I don't know, big buddy," Dub said. He pulled off his hat and twisted it in his hands. "I heard they're talking layoffs. I don't think anyone should have to lose their job."

"They're going to make all the cutbacks with early retirements and generous severance packages," Judson said. "Hell, I might retire myself. It's the most reasonable plan I've ever seen in this type of situation."

"And what type of situation is that?" Gene asked.

"The Company is losing money hand over fist." As if to prove his point, he flipped to the business section. He ran his fingers down the page until he found the stock market listing for The Company. "Down three more points," he said. "They've lost a quarter of their value in the last year. They're bleeding money."

"But maybe that's all bookkeeping," Gene said. "And who can figure out the stock market anyway? It's like voodoo or something."

"Actually, Wheeler," Hawkins said, "I understand the market just fine."

Of course he did. He probably had a portfolio that would make a Rockefeller proud. He could probably afford to retire. He only worked because he loved making paper.

Passing Time

"I don't believe the numbers are a smokescreen," he said. "The payroll in this company is bloated beyond belief. Who's it going to hurt if we cut back? In the long run, The Company gets stronger. That's good for all of us. It's almost as if the union doesn't want The Company to make money. Heaven knows we get our share."

"You know you shouldn't say that kind of shit," Dub said. He shuddered. He looked toward the doorway as if he was afraid Ben and the guys might come back in and overhear. "Even if you think it, you can't say the words."

"Oh, that's right," Hawkins said. "I forget that it's the workers against fat cats. Us versus them."

"Come on, Hawk," Judson said. "You're getting ahead of yourself. It's another couple of weeks before they ask for a vote. Maybe cooler heads will prevail by then."

Hawkins rolled the paper tightly in his hands. "I just got a bad feeling this time, Jud. There are too many idiots in this place who seem willing to shoot themselves in the foot just to spite The Company. One of these days they're going to take us all down with them."

"We'll cross that bridge when we come to it," Judson said. "If they do call for the strike vote, that'll be the time to fight. I just can't see stirring everybody up for no reason."

"I suppose you're right," Hawkins said.

"You know he is," Dub said, nodding forcefully. He winked at Gene.

Everyone picked up their sections of the paper, and things were quiet again. Gene picked up the paper but only pretended to read. He wondered how all this would affect him. He'd wanted to get out of school and figured working here was a good way to pass the time. He couldn't help but appreciate the irony. For a hundred years, the men of Cumberland had crossed the river to make their living, grumbling about it all the while, telling their sons to make a better life for themselves and not to end up like them. He had tried college and come here as a backup plan, and now they were going to take that away, too.

But what if it came to a vote? Should he vote for a new contract just to keep the place going for the months he needed it? Should he vote with Ben and his guys for the sake of brotherhood? Should he vote with Hawkins and Judson just because they made the most sense? This seemed to be a choice between the head and the heart. Whose side *was* he on?

When Ben came back after his cigarette break, he had a sly grin on his face. He looked like he was ready to stir things up, and Gene feared another union fight.

"Sometimes you guys act as if we're working in a frigging library," he said.

Sure, Gene thought. A library with machines as loud as freight trains in the reading rooms.

"Not that I have anything against reading," he said. "Just your choice of materials."

He pulled a smudged sheet of newsprint from his back pocket and opened it luxuriously. The entire front page was a picture of a woman with her legs spread wide open and her fingers buried in her vagina. Her head was thrown back so far that it was invisible. "Faces," Ben said. "Who needs them? Give me two legs and a bush, anytime."

"I've never seen that one." Dub's tongue darted across his lips. Gene had never seen anything like it, period. The pin-ups in the dorm rooms were nuns in Sunday school compared to this. At least they had faces.

Dub leaned over Ben's shoulder and reached out to touch the page. Ben slapped his hand away. "'I like to watch,'" Ben read aloud. "'Italian stallion does my wife, and I can't get enough.'" He turned the paper sideways to ogle the centerfold, pointing out some of the finer points to Devoid. Hood walked away, but Dub stayed just behind Ben, oblivious, it seemed, to the sounds of Judson turning the roll: the acceleration, the blast of air, the crack of the sheet beneath the stick, even the sound of the horn. Gene glanced over toward the front of Number Four. The other members of the crew were there, but Dub just stared at the newsprint in Ben's hands.

"'Black cocks are the best,'" Ben read. "Of course, I'm just reading," he added. "I have no personal opinion on the subject."

"You been holding out on us, Ben," Dub said. "Did we get a new shipment?"

"No," Ben grinned. "I've just been saving this one for a rainy day. I'd say things are pretty moist, wouldn't you?" He ran his fingers lovingly across the page.

"I got it after you guys," Dub licked his lips again.

"Got anything to trade for it?" Ben asked.

"If that's the only one left," Dub said. "What the hell can I trade?"

Ben nodded toward Dub's picnic basket.

"Maybe you've got something in there that would be worth a peek."

"What would Ma Duschene think about that?" Devoid asked. "I'll bet she'd kick his ass."

The horn sounded again. Dub turned. Judson glared at him. The white fringe of his hair looked like the hairs on the back of an angry animal. Hawkins and Hood had the roll racked up in the back spools and were taking samples without Dub. Dub ran over to the roll, trying to push past Hood, who was in his spot, but Judson pointed underneath the winder with his stick.

"That ain't my fucking job," Dub pushed his sailor's hat back off his forehead at a defiant angle.

"It is, now," Judson said, reaching out with the stick and pushing Dub's hat back down over his eyes. Dub jerked the hat back up but slunk under the winder.

Ben and Devoid took their seats at the table, still studying their prize. Jimmy hovered over their shoulders. Ben glanced over at the winder and shook his head. "Frigging Dub," he said.

"What's the big deal?" Gene said. "He was just a few minutes late. You distracted him with that magazine."

"What did we tell you that very first day, Geno?" Ben asked.

"That the machine is our real boss, and she decides when we work."

"Go to the head of the class, Geno," Ben said. "The she-bitch decided, Judson sounded the horn, and Dub was nowhere to be found." He shrugged. "When you've only got one rule, it's important that you follow it."

They rode Dub for the rest of the night. After his first protest, he never said another word.

At ten-thirty, Gene sat at the table with Hood. Hood tucked his book into his back pocket and turned off his tape player. "I'm going out to the loading dock to get some air, you want to come?" he asked.

"Are you sure it's okay?" Gene asked.

"You got twenty minutes until you turn up," he said. "I got twenty-five."

"What if there's a break in the sheet?"

"We're not going that far. We'll be able to hear the horn. You know that fucking thing could wake the dead."

They walked back down the corridor toward the guard shack, but turned before they reached the end of the warehouse, moving down a side passage to a door leading to the outside. Gene smelled propane as he stepped into the doorway, but Hood grabbed his arm. "Incoming," Hood yelled, as a forklift whipped around the corner. Hood stuck his head around the corner. "Now it's clear," he said and dragged Gene onto a loading dock that overlooked the railroad yards. Boxcars lined the edge with their doors opened. The same brightly colored safety signs were on every pillar, but there was one Gene had never seen before: NO HUMPING.

He followed Hood to the edge of the dock, a spot that opened out onto the rest of the yard. Hood sat on the edge and dangled his legs over like a child on a playground swing. There was a cool breeze blowing here, a nice change from the hot wind of the machines.

"I understand most of the signs," Gene said, "but what the hell is 'no humping' about?"

Hood laughed. "That's for the fork-lift drivers. Some of the machines turn out bales of pulp. When they load the boxcars, they have to be careful not to jam them together, or 'hump' them. They have a hard time keeping those signs around, though. Most of us have one at home."

"I can imagine," Gene said. He jumped as another forklift burst through the door behind them, slid across the dock, and disappeared into a boxcar, rocking it as it slammed into its far wall.

"Humping," Hood said. Gene laughed.

He looked out over the yard. The wind felt good in his face, but he couldn't ignore the smell, the usual sulfur base from the mill with a high note of diesel fuel and motor oil. The moonlight reflected off pools of the stuff standing between the tracks.

"What's the story on that magazine Ben had?" Gene asked. "I don't think I've ever seen anything like it."

"Tabloid pornography," Hood said. "Pretty raunchy stuff. It makes *Penthouse* and *Playboy* look like fucking kids' books. You can't even buy them around these parts."

"So how did Ben get it?"

"The Company brings in old newsprint for recycling by the boxcar." He waved toward a low building on the other side of the yard. "Ben scouts out every load as soon as he gets wind of it. We haven't had a shipment for a while. He must have saved that one from the last batch." He rolled his eyes. "Wait until they get the next big shipment. It's a regular party around this place when those come in."

"He sure got Dub riled up, didn't he?"

He made a gun with his finger and pointed it at one of the pools of oil. "Like shooting fish in a barrel." He pulled the trigger. "The goofy little bastard didn't know whether he was coming or going."

"So how much longer are you guys going to ride him?" Gene asked.

"Just tonight."

"I still don't get it," Gene said.

"What's there to get?" Hood said. "The horn sounded, and he didn't answer. We had to teach him a lesson."

"But it was only a couple minutes. Everybody fucks off sometime. Shit, we usually fuck off half the night."

"Fucking off *is* human nature," Hood said, "but there's nothing human about when we have to work and why, the machine decides. Dub forgot, and we can't have that."

"And what if somebody doesn't want to answer to a machine?" Gene asked.

This time he pointed the gun in Gene's direction. His lips formed a single word, "Pow," and then blew smoke away. "Then they need to get the hell out of here, my man. I know you got stuck down here by accident, but the rest of us are here by choice. We've all worked at a lot of other jobs in this fucked up company. There are some real assholes out there, always trying to get out of work and sticking it on the next guy. We don't play that way.

"We all chose to be here. Dub chose, too. You'll have to do the same thing, eventually."

Gene wondered how all this fit in with the new alignment of the crews. Hood didn't seem to be too happy since he'd been teamed up with Old Man Grenier and Hawkins. Maybe he was rethinking his own choice.

"Not that we're fanatics, or anything," Hood said. He reached into his pocket and pulled out a cigarette. He lit it, and the sweet smell of pot blocked out the rest of the smells on the dock. He held his breath and passed the joint to Gene, his fingers pinching the end. Gene looked back toward the door. "Are you crazy? What if somebody sees us?"

Hood shrugged, coughed, and finally spoke, his voice a high smoker's whine. "Nobody gives a fuck about shit like this as long as we do our job. You want a hit or not?"

Gene saw rolling cylinders, drums, pulleys, and gears.

"Aren't you afraid you'll stick your hand in the wrong place if you're high?"

"Who said anything about getting high? It's just a couple hits. Not like we'll get really stoned." Hood held it out to him again. Gene took it. He inhaled and held his breath, felt the smoke ease up into his head. He giggled.

"What?" Hood said, a big grin on his face.

"We're sitting out here smoking a joint, discussing how Dub wasn't doing his job. It's weird."

"That's the fucking beauty of only having one rule."

They passed the joint between them. Hood was right. This was good. Just enough of a buzz to take the edge off. Not enough to get messed up. He held it out to Gene again. He shook his head. Better not push it.

Hood smoked the joint down to the nub, held it until Gene could smell the skin on his fingertips burning. Finally, Hood stubbed it out on his boot and stuck it in his pocket.

"So, tell me, Geno," he said. "What do you do for fun when you're not in this fucking dump, besides hanging out at The Bone?"

"Not a hell of a lot," Gene said. "Everybody I used to hang with in this town is gone."

"I've already told you if you're looking for someone to party with, just let me know."

"Thanks," Gene said.

Hood looked at his watch. He stood up. "Come on, we'd better get back."

They walked back into the room just as Judson turned up. Dub got up from the table and went to start the winder. As Hood walked away from Gene, a movement at the table caught his eye. Ben lifted the lid of Dub's basket. Gene thought Ben was helping himself to a snack, but he slipped the porno rag in, instead. Ben looked over. He set the lid back down, held one finger up to his lips, and winked.

Chapter Twelve

Saturday morning the phone started ringing at seven o'clock. Gene ignored it the first time, and when it rang again at seven-thirty, he pictured Phil Blair pounding on his door and dragging him off to work, so he decided to hit the road.

Between his early start and good luck with traffic, he made it to school much earlier than he'd told Staci to expect him. It was a beautiful day, so he waited on the steps of her dorm. She'd told him she was going to be at the library all afternoon, and he knew she'd come back this way.

He decided she must be the only person in the library. The rest of the student body sprawled out on the campus green before him. They were on blankets and lawn chairs, sunbathing with their books open. They tossed Frisbees and softballs back and forth. Musical styles: rock and classical and even country battled for supremacy, with none getting the upper hand.

He stretched out on the warm concrete and enjoyed the sun, the music, the scenery, grateful he didn't have any summer studies.

It was almost an hour before he saw her coming across the green. She wasn't alone.

She laughed and talked with a guy he'd seen around campus but didn't really know. He was tall and skinny, dressed in green army fatigues and a T-shirt with the sleeves hacked off. Amid this sea of shorts, halter tops, and tank tops, he had the anti-establishment thing going big-time.

He had silver wire-rim glasses, hair down past his shoulders, and a scruffy beard that only seemed to be growing under his chin, Amish style.

Staci didn't see Gene. They seemed to be having a hell of a time, one step removed from holding hands or walking arm in arm. They kept their distance, but their hands darted back and forth.

Passing Time

Just before she reached Gene, she threw her head back and laughed, reached out, and touched the guy's arm.

Then she saw Gene. The guy looked over, too. It was hard to tell which of them was most confused.

Gene stood up, and she ran to him. She threw her arms around him. "You're early," she whispered in his ear.

"Apparently."

She blushed. Just what he needed, a physical confirmation of guilt. She interlaced her fingers with his and turned back to her new friend. "Daniel, this is Gene. You remember him, right?"

"Of course," Daniel said as he stuck out his hand.

"Daniel's in a couple of my classes this session."

"Chaucer and Henry James," he said.

"Fun stuff," Gene said.

"We like it," they answered at the same time.

"I studied James with Doc Marble last semester," Gene said. He was the head of the English Department, and the difficulty of his classes was legendary.

"He's pretty rough," Daniel said. He pulled off his glasses and wiped them clean on the tail of his shirt. "He doesn't hang around for the summer sessions, though. We got Mr. Clemons. We call it James-Lite. So, you're down for the weekend?"

"Yes," Gene said. "I have to head back early Monday."

"It was good to see you."

"Thanks. You, too." Gene figured that was that, but Daniel turned back toward Staci.

"So what do you want to do about the assignment for Tuesday, Stace?"

"I'll dive into it after Gene heads back on Monday."

"Okay," he said. "I'll call you. We can figure out something to dazzle Old Man Clemons with."

She smiled. "We like to freak him out with our brilliance," she explained.

"That must be fun," Gene said.

"It is," they said. Again with the chorus.

He watched Staci as she watched Daniel walk away. He didn't like the look in her eyes. He pulled his hand away from hers.

"You know," he said, "I don't think I like the thought of you hanging around with people like that."

"What are you talking about?"

"You freaked out when you saw Hood and the girls back home. You acted crazy about people I don't even hang out with, and here you are already auditioning my replacement."

She blushed. Again with the guilt.

"Your replacement?" she said. "What are you talking about?"

"I'm not blind. I saw the way you two looked at each other."

"Don't be ridiculous," she said. "We're just friends. He's in my classes. There aren't that many people around in the summer who are serious about being here." She nodded toward the party on the green, as if to prove her point. "We talk about the stuff we read, that's all."

"You dazzle Mr. Clemons together. You're a team."

"About books, that's all. For God's sake, Gene. This is what I do." She reached for his hand, but he jerked away. "Have you gone nuts? Even when you were here, I had other friends."

"But I'm not here."

"Whose fault is that? Do you expect me to shrivel up and die while you get your head straight in your factory job?"

"No," Gene said. "I just hoped we'd stay together through this thing."

"We will. Daniel is just a friend." She reached for his hand, and he let her take it this time. "He's not even my type. He's kind of goofy, you know. God, he's a regular Ichabod Crane."

He did have the scarecrow thing going. Gene decided that's what he was trying to hide with the hippie-radical look.

"We just have some fun," she said. "How can you even think that way?"

"You should know how. You were jealous of Hood's slutty girlfriends."

She laughed. "Okay, you've got a point. This sabbatical of yours is making us both nuts. Hey, I've got a good idea. Why don't you just come back to school, and we can get our lives back."

"I will. Just give me a little time."

She dragged him up the stairs toward her room, stepping over a broken bottle on the second landing. A poster on the door announced that dollar tequila shots would be available at 8:30 in the lounge. Gene remembered those parties. Maybe Daniel was the only guy on campus who actually cared about Henry James.

Three hours in Staci's room provided a temporary fix to their problems. When he suggested they go out to dinner and a movie, she chuckled. It was a sound that always made him feel that things would be all right.

"You do everything backward," she said. "You haven't even graduated, and you're taking a sabbatical. You're supposed to take a woman to dinner and a show and then drag her back to her room."

After dinner, they walked the deserted pathways of the campus and settled down by the fountain in the middle of the academic quad. A six-foot wide circle of jets shot a ring of water straight up in the middle of the pool, splashing down around the spotlight that shone at the center. A breeze came across the green and brought the mist to them.

The sound of the tequila party was a dull roar beyond the walls of the courtyard, but it was quiet here.

The Campus Security van pulled up next to Gene's car. Its door popped open, and a man limped out and started toward them. Gene knew the limp, and as the man came closer, he recognized the face and the smooth, balding head. Doc had been on night patrol for twenty years. He studied them with an angry scowl, though he mostly kept his eyes on Gene. When he finally focused on Staci, he smiled and the tension seemed to go out of him.

"Good evening, Miss Thomas," he said. "I didn't know it was you. Thought it might be townies. Have to run them kids off two or three times a week."

"Sorry if we worried you, Doc," she said.

"No worry," he sat down on the rim of the fountain and lit a cigarette. He glanced over at Gene. "Hey," he said. "I know you, too. You used to have hair, though."

"I'm taking some time off from school, Doc. I had to cut it to get a job."

"It looks sharp. Don't see much of that around here, these days. Better watch it, though," he said, running his hand over his smooth, white skull. "You don't want to end up like me."

Doc finished his cigarette and limped back to the van. Gene put his arms around Staci, rested his chin on the top of her head, and inhaled. They listened to the soft sound of the water splashing from the metal ring to the surface.

"There's something else I don't get about all this," Staci said.

"What?"

"Aren't you bored working in that place? It can't be much of a challenge."

"Actually," he said, "I've had my hands full so far. I still have a lot to learn about the job."

"I know it might seem cool now, but what happens when the novelty wears off?"

"I'll worry about that when the time comes, Stace."

"And I'm just supposed to wait for that to happen?" He could feel her body stiffen in his arms.

"It's only for a few months. Besides, once you get into your fall schedule, you probably won't even notice I'm gone."

"That's not funny. I work hard, but I have feelings, too. Somebody has to in this relationship." She tried to stand, but he pulled her back down.

"I'm sorry."

"Is it so bad that I want you to be here for me? You know I love to tell you everything."

"We'll talk on the phone."

"It's not the same."

"It isn't going to be that long."

This time when she pulled away, he let her go. She walked to the edge of the circle of light that blossomed from the fountain. When she turned back, he couldn't see her face in the darkness. "I just don't understand," she said.

"I don't expect you to." He stared at the water. "Everything comes easy for you. You don't know what it feels like to fuck up the way I did."

"Easy? I work my ass off."

"And I worked my ass off and still flunked calculus. That's the part you don't know anything about. I know the next few months are going to be rough, but I don't want to make any big decisions while I feel like this."

"Like what?"

"Like shit," he said. "I'm all turned around, that's all."

She came into the light and stood beside him. She took his hand.

"I know you're messed up. I want to help you, but I can't help you when we're so far apart. Why do you have to take this crazy job? What is it, some kind of penance or something?"

Penance? Why did it have to be something besides what it was? Why couldn't it just be a job?

"I've told you why I'm working there. It's something to do while I figure out what I'm going to do next. I'll be back before you know it."

"I think you're running away."

"Think what you want. It's not your life."

"Oh, yes, it is."

He awoke in the middle of the night, Staci pressed against his back. He lay still for a few minutes, listening to the sound of her breathing and the party outside her dorm room.

He gently pulled away from her. She mumbled a sleepy protest and rolled over onto her back, one arm over her eyes.

He walked to the window and sat on the ledge. He thought about what Staci had said, that he was running away. Was that really it? His life had been on cruise control until this. Now he'd hit a wall and didn't know what to do. Was The Company a place to figure things out or a place to hide?

He thought of the other thing she'd said. He'd told her it wasn't her decision, that it wasn't her life.

"Oh, yes, it is," she'd said.

It made him happy. It also scared him to death.

When he woke up the next morning, Staci sat in the chair by the bed, her hair pulled back and her reading glasses on. She scribbled in the margins of the book in her lap.

"Hey," she said.

"Hey. What's on the schedule for today?"

"Not a thing. I'm all yours. I did want to run by the bookstore this afternoon, though."

He glanced around the room. Every available inch of wall-space was lined with books. There was a pile in the corner that he took for this session's assignments. "Don't you think you've got enough books, already?"

"We're buying for you."

"Me?"

She nodded toward the pile. "I figure you should buy a copy of every book I have to read this fall. From what you tell me, you have plenty of time to read when you're at work. We'll talk about them on the phone or when you visit."

"That might be fun." And it wouldn't hurt to remind her that Daniel wasn't the only one who could wow people about Henry James.

"It'll be like we're taking classes together again. It'll keep you sharp."

And if he could beat Daniel at his own game, it might keep the guy from becoming her type.

He got up at four a.m. on Monday. He figured that would give him time to beat the traffic and take a quick nap before he went to work. Staci walked him to the car. As they stepped outside, he was grateful that the first gray light was already creeping over the horizon, but he couldn't help but think how hard this was going to be in the winter when four a.m. was still pitch black.

"I'll see you Saturday afternoon," she said.

"Okay."

"Do you think that crazy old guy who makes out your schedule will want you to work?"

"I'm supposed to be okay as long as I don't answer the phone."

"So, I guess you'd better not answer it."

"I won't."

He climbed into the car and started it up. She leaned in the window and wrapped her hands around his head, locking her fingers together as if she'd never let go.

"I'll see you Saturday," he said.

"Okay." She kept her fingers together for another second and finally slid them apart. She stood back, and he pulled away. He watched her figure in the rearview mirror. He remembered the night he'd come home from The Bone and found her waiting on his doorstep, a dark angel.

She didn't look like an angel now, just a sad young woman who missed her boyfriend. Why was he doing this to her? Was it really worth it, just to get away from school for a while? That was the problem when you tried to step back from life. Life didn't stop; it just kept on going all around you.

Chapter Thirteen

Gene got to work and relieved his mate, but he could tell it would be fifteen or twenty minutes before they turned up the roll, so he went upstairs to use the bathroom. When he got back, Riendeau was just inside the door, pacing back and forth. Gene hadn't seen him since the night Saucier had gotten hurt. He remembered how well they'd worked together. They'd even made Saucier part of their team.

"Hey, man," Gene said. He held his hand out.

"Wheeler," Riendeau said, but he ignored the hand. He raked his hair out of his eyes. It flopped right back down. He pulled a cigarette from behind his ear and jammed it between his lips, but then remembered he couldn't he smoke it here, so he pulled it back out and shoved it behind his ear again.

"What's wrong?" Gene asked.

"Fucking Hood is late. He hasn't called to say whether he's coming or not. The little cocksucker is going to stick me with his goddamn shift."

"I thought you liked working overtime."

"I do when it's my fucking choice. It's the goddamn principle of the thing, you know?"

It was hard to keep up with all the principles in this place, Gene thought.

"Damn that sorry little motherfucker," Riendeau muttered as he grabbed the cigarette again. This time he lit it, took a long drag, and exhaled a huge cloud, even though they were still in a non-smoking area. The cloud drifted over to Hawkins as he read a magazine at the table. He coughed and looked up, but he seemed to know this wasn't the time to mess with Riendeau.

"He didn't even call," Riendeau said. "So he needs another day to recover from his weekend, what do I care? At least if he called,

I'd have a choice whether I was going to stay or not, but this way, I'm fucked. What the hell is wrong with him? You think for one minute he'd remember that I'm stuck until he gets his sorry ass here."

"I don't think Hood's thinking too much about any of us, these days," Hawkins said, just as Hood sauntered through the door.

"My man," he said to Gene, ignoring Hawkins and Riendeau. He didn't seem to know he was late. If he did, it was obvious he didn't care.

"Jesus Fucking H-Christ," Riendeau ground out his cigarette beneath his boot and charged Hood. He stopped six inches away from him. "Don't you even know what time it is, you sorry little son of a bitch?"

"Hey, man, back off," Hood said, though he was the one to back away. "So I'm a couple minutes late, sue me."

"Sue you?" Riendeau swiped his hair out of his face with one hand. He buried one finger of the other into Hood's chest. "Sue you, my ass. You're fucking late, and if it ever happens again, I'll kick your sorry ass from here to goddamn China. If I didn't have things to do tonight, I'd have Supry send your ass home, because as far as the contract is concerned, this is my fucking shift."

"Hey," said Hood. "That's fine with me. Take the fucking shift. Take the fucking job for all I care." He turned to go, but Riendeau grabbed his arm. Hood jerked it away and got in Riendeau's face. "Don't touch me you retarded motherfucker!"

"I'll touch you anytime I want. You're the one who's retarded here, not me. I told you this was my shift if I wanted it, but I don't. You're staying here, and I'm going home. I got things to do."

"Don't make me laugh," Hood said. "All you're going to do is go home, lock yourself in the bathroom, and jerk off."

Gene got between them. Riendeau glared over his shoulder at Hood for a few seconds, but then he grinned.

"Not bad," he said. "Too bad the only thing that still works on you is your fucking mouth. Be on time tomorrow, fuck-up."

"If I feel like it," Hood said, but Riendeau was already out the door.

After Riendeau was out of sight, Hood threw himself down on the bench. "What an asshole!"

"You were late." Hawkins folded up his magazine as he stood up. "You didn't call. That makes you the asshole." He walked away. Gene looked over toward Number Four to see if they were ready to turn up, but there was still plenty of time. Hawkins just didn't like the company around the table.

"Maybe you'd better split, too, man," Hood said. "You don't want to be caught hanging out with a fuck-up like me."

"You left the guy hanging," Gene said as he sat down beside Hood. "He was already pissed off about that, then you gave him attitude."

Hood shrugged. "Yeah, yeah, I know. I just figured I could stonewall Riendeau, he's such a retard."

"About some things, maybe," Gene said. "Not the job."

"A retard's a retard," Hood said. He flashed a silly grin. "Jenna's folks weren't home when I dropped her off this afternoon. I went in, and one thing led to another. You know how it is, man."

"Sure," Gene said, "but you should have called, man."

"I know." He looked into Gene's eyes for the first time. They were the same bright red that they'd been the time they'd run into him at The Clam Barn.

"Jesus, man," Gene said. "Are you already high?"

"A little," Hood said. "Ask me again after my first break."

"Bad idea," Gene said. "You should be more careful. Things are different now that you work with Hawkins."

"Yeah, yeah. Tell me something I don't already know. I'm so tired of this shit."

"You've got to be cool, man. A joint at ten o'clock is one thing, but you can't be smoking all night long."

"I've built up a tolerance, that's all. I need to smoke more to get a buzz. I can still do my job."

"I don't know," Gene said. "You need to be careful."

He glanced over to front of Number Four, where Judson, Hawkins, and Dub stood by the roll. Judson had given Dub his backtender's stick. Dub used it to measure the roll, to see how long it would be before they had to turn up. He held the stick out at arm's length as if it might bite him. Judson turned away from Dub. He talked to Hawkins, but Gene saw that Judson was watching Dub the whole time out of the corner of his eye. A smile played at the corner of his lips.

"Don't you get fucking paranoid on me, too, man," Hood said. He pulled the thin black net from his pocket and gathered the long strands of his hair in one hand. He stuffed them into the net and smoothed everything out. Next came the red bandana. Gene realized that it didn't really do much about holding his hair in place. He probably just wanted to hide the hair net as much as he could.

"I mean it, man," Hood said. "It's bad enough I have to work with these up-tight motherfuckers, don't you get all serious on me, too."

"I just don't want you to screw yourself, that's all."

"I know. You got my back, right?"

"I'll try." Gene looked back toward Number Four. Judson patted Dub on the back. Dub beamed. Even Hawkins smiled. Was there anywhere for Hood in this scene? It didn't seem likely. Hood had helped him out when he'd started, and Gene would watch his back as much as he could, but he wasn't sure how much good it would do.

The horn sounded. Hood jumped. "I'll start the winder for you," Gene said. "Get over with your crew."

"Thanks, man."

Standing at the controls, Gene watched them. They pulled the samples, and Hawkins handed them to Hood, but when Hood turned to look for Judson, he was halfway across the room, and Hawkins was already turning the roll and tearing the sheet. Hood stuffed the samples into his pocket and dived under the winder.

He was a step behind them the whole time. Hawkins, of course, did little to hide his anger. Even Dub rolled his eyes the whole time. Hood seemed oblivious to it all, just fumbled through, helped Dub tear the sheet, crumpled it into a ball, and headed for the pulper. When he got to the back of the machine, he swung the wad onto his hip and reached down to get the slab that they'd taken off the top.

Gene went over to help him, but Hood waved him off. "I'll just kill two birds with one stone. We don't mess around on the A-Team, you know."

When he came out of the pulper, Judson stood with his hand

outstretched. "You got my samples," he said. Hood reached into his back pocket, but his hand came away empty. "Oh, Jesus," he muttered and ducked back in.

"Well?" Judson said, still waiting when Hood came out. "I guess I dropped them, man," Hood said. "Let me look around."

Gene helped him look, but they couldn't find them anywhere. Hawkins watched them the whole time. Dub slid up beside Gene. "Did you guys lose something?"

"The samples," Gene said. "Don't tell Hawkins, yet."

"Don't worry," Dub said, "I'll let somebody else do the honors on that one."

They returned to Judson empty-handed. "I don't know what happened, man," Hood said.

"I'd say you got them mixed up with the rest of the broke and dumped them in the pulper," Judson said. "I really need them, you know."

"Can't we just tear some off the top of the rolls when they're done?"

"That's sloppy," Judson said.

"Can't we just blow them off this one time?" Hood whined.

"I don't think so."

"But we already started the roll. What the hell are we going to do?"

"We could stop the roll, take our samples, make a splice."

"Jesus Christ, Judson," Hood said, as the color drained from his face. "Hawkins will have a fit. That's a hell of a lot of work for nothing."

"That's why we do it at the start of the roll."

"Can't you give me a break, man? Please?"

"I don't know, son," Judson said. "You've been around too long to make rookie mistakes like this. If I let it go, you'll probably just pull more of the same shit. We might as well deal with it now."

"Look, man, it won't happen again."

"Supry will have my ass if he notices."

"Supry doesn't notice shit."

"He notices more than you think."

Gene looked toward the winder. Hawkins raised an eyebrow. Gene shrugged.

Passing Time

"Come on, man," Hood said. "Don't do this to me."

Judson shrugged. "I'll let it go this time, but I'm telling you, son, you need to get your act together, and I mean yesterday. You're playing with the big boys now."

"Sure, sure. Thanks a lot, man." Hood said as he threw his arms around Judson. "You won't be sorry, man." He winked at Gene over Judson's shoulder.

Hood disappeared as soon as they finished their roll. Gene followed him out to the dock. He was just lighting up when Gene got there.

"Hey," he said, but Gene held out his hand.

"Give it to me, and anything else you're holding."

"What the fuck, man?"

"You screwed up, and they're watching you. If you screw up again, you sure as hell can't be high."

"Screw up? When did I become such a screw-up? I've worked here for two years. Nobody had any trouble with me before."

"That was before they changed the crews. Before they invented the A-Team."

Gene still had his hand out in front of Hood. "Give," he said. Hood pulled three more joints out of his pocket. "Did you want to search me?" He threw his hands into the air. Gene stuffed the joints into his pocket. "I'll give these back to you after we get off tonight."

"Thanks for nothing," Hood said.

They walked back to the room without exchanging a word. Gene had to wonder if he was wasting his time. He wanted to help Hood, but he couldn't do this by himself. If Hood didn't get his act together, Hawkins was going to eat him alive.

Hawkins and Judson were still by the front of the machine. They saw Gene and Hood and turned their backs.

"I guess they're afraid we can read lips," Hood said.

When they turned up the next roll, Judson came over with them and stood in the spot where Hawkins usually pulled his samples. Dub took his regular spot, but Hawkins stood back. Hood looked at them and frowned but got between Dub and Judson.

After they pulled the samples, Hood rolled them up and handed them to Judson. Judson stuck them in his pocket and turned the roll. He tore the sheet and slid it over to Dub. He was doing Hawkins's job. When Hood slid under the winder, Hawkins went with him.

"What the fuck?" Hood said. Gene heard the murmur of Hawkins's voice, but he couldn't get the words. It wasn't too hard to figure out, though. They thought Hood needed a refresher course, and who better to give it than Hawkins?

As he watched Hawkins shadow Hood around the winder, he felt a jolt in his stomach, a sense of déjà vu, his first day all over again. He saw the look in Hawkins's eyes, the cold reserve. Hood's eyes were full of anger and frustration. He remembered how it felt. He felt sorry for Hood. Still, he couldn't help but be happy that it wasn't him, this time.

At eight, Ben came over to the table with Jimmy. He'd left Devoid watching the roll. "Come on, Geno," he said. "Jimmy and I are going on a little expedition. You want to come?"

"What kind of expedition?"

"You'll see."

They followed the path to the loading dock, but when they got outside, Ben slid down into the railroad yard. He pointed toward a line of boxcars on the far side of the yard. "The building on the other side of those is wastepaper recycling. My sources tell me that there's a new shipment of porn in one of the cars. Your mission, if you choose to accept it, is to help us scope it out."

Gene sat on the edge of the dock.

"Will we be able to hear the horn all the way over there?"

"Of course, we will, Geno," he said. "We wouldn't be out here if we couldn't hear."

"But how will we know if it's for us or Number Four?"

"Because they sound as different as night and day," Jimmy said.

"Like women when you fuck them," Ben said. "You know that no two of them make the same sounds."

"Maybe he doesn't know," Jimmy said. "Maybe he's only fucked one girl in his whole life."

"At least I've fucked one," Gene said.

Jimmy lunged at him.

"Okay." Ben blocked Jimmy with an outstretched hand. "That's enough of that. We're wasting time. You girls can settle this later." He put his free hand on Gene's knee. "Listen, Geno, this isn't a big deal. We do it all the time. The horns do have different tones. We'll know if Number Five is howling for us, trust me. I hear her calling for me in my sleep, sometimes."

The man did have a way with words.

"So, are you coming or not, Geno?"

Gene jumped down.

"That's my boy," Ben said. They moved off into darkness. Gene struggled to catch up. He smashed his boots against a railroad tie and crashed to his knees. He scrambled back to his feet. Ben and Jimmy didn't struggle at all. Obviously, this was familiar ground to them.

By the time Gene got to the boxcars, Jimmy was nowhere in sight. Ben's legs hung out the door but then they disappeared, as well. Gene pulled himself in and caught the smell of moldy newsprint. The car was filled with ragged bales. They scampered up and down the piles, scanning the top page of every bundle. "Bingo," Jimmy crowed, and Ben wheeled, leaped several piles, and landed by his side. He shoved him out of the way. "Hey," Jimmy said, but Ben whipped a pair of wire-cutters from his back pocket and snapped the binding on the bundle. He pulled the first few sheets away from the top and sat down on the nearest bundle, his eyes intent on the pages. Jimmy moved in and grabbed one of his own. "These people ain't even human," he muttered.

Ben had broken the bundle into three piles. He handed one to Gene. He glanced at the one on top. A tall, dark-haired woman was bound at the wrists and ankles, her naked body spread-eagle against a wall. She was pinned by a set of stocks from Puritan times, but the holes enclosed her breasts, as well. The caption read: BEWITCHED, BOTHERED AND BEWILDERED.

Gene felt Ben's hand on his arm. "We got what we came for, Geno. We'll have plenty of time to read when we get back."

"First we had to drag him here, and now we've got to drag him back," Jimmy said. "Fucking rookies."

When they got back to the room, all the guys crowded around, but Ben glanced at the roll on Number Five and pushed them aside. "Time for that later," he said. "We have work to do."

"Maybe you guys are ready to turn up, Ben," Dub pointed toward their roll, "but we still got a few minutes. Let us have a crack at them."

"Now, now, Dubster," Ben said. "You know the rules. Besides, you remember what happened the last time you saw one of these beauties. I wouldn't want you to get another demotion."

"Aw, Jesus, Ben," he said. "I learned my lesson."

"Maybe, but I feel responsible for that last mess. I'm going to protect you from yourself this time." He waved for Jimmy and Gene to follow and led them over to the front of the machine, where he stacked the rags right beside the roll. He winked at Gene. "Let them drool for a few minutes."

Ben let Devoid turn-up when the time came while he stood guard over the pile. The sheet got too much slack, surging up almost six feet high behind the roll. Devoid cursed and slapped at the sheet with the stick, the sweat pouring down his forehead, but Ben never moved. Devoid finally got it under control and got the new roll started.

"Not bad," Ben said finally. Gene expected him to rag Devoid on his rookie-like performance, but he just smiled. "Everybody has to learn, has to practice. We have to help Devo out while he does. That's what teamwork is all about, covering for each other, right Geno?"

"That's right, Ben," Gene said. What was a little extra work among teammates?

When they finished their roll, Ben finally brought out the pile of porno rags, and Gene learned the rules of this new game, one played as seriously as poker. Ben always got first pick. He skimmed through the pile, picking out the titles and photos that caught his eye.

He showed them one picture, all black lace and pubic hair. The woman was laid out flat, licking her lips, touching herself. "What I like about these is they're not all artsy-fartsy like *Playboy* or *Penthouse*, with the pictures all shiny and the defects brushed away."

"You never get good beaver shots in those," Devoid agreed.

"And those girls are goddamn fashion models," said Jimmy. "They'd never give guys like us the time of day."

Passing Time

"But this lady is for real." Ben licked his lips and passed his fingers lovingly over the rough newsprint.

He took his time. Gene guessed he wanted another chance to make the guys drool.

"Okay," he said finally. "Next pick goes to the gentlemen who made the trip with me."

Jimmy dived in first and grabbed a thick wad without looking at the pictures.

"Easy, boy," Ben said, but Jimmy shrugged him off and strode away, protecting the magazines like an animal guarding his part of the kill.

"Geno," Ben said.

As Gene sifted through the pile, he couldn't believe what he saw. He thought he'd seen pornography before, but this was different. The photos were low quality and the stories were incredible. There were combinations of people he had never thought possible. There was lots of bondage, lots of guns and knives. Some of it turned his stomach, but he knew enough not to let it show. It would be like not telling them about sex with Staci. He'd have to hear all that, "Geno thinks he's too good for us" crap again. Better just to be quiet.

After Gene picked, they went by seniority. He wondered if that was in the union contract. Hawkins surprised him when he took a turn. Gene expected him to turn up his nose the way he did at most of their antics. Ben smiled and slapped Hawkins on the back.

After everyone had taken a stack, Ben surveyed the room. "Okay, gentlemen," he said, "let's read us some por-no-gra-phy."

For the next few hours, every minute between running the rolls became a reading orgy. Guys ran back and forth across the room, waving pictures and stories in each other's faces. Gene remembered Jimmy's comment in the boxcar, and he had to agree. The people that he met in these pages weren't even human.

Of course, Number Five had her say about all this. Gene was sitting beside Ben on an empty reel when the horn blasted down on The Flamer's end. "Oh, shit," Ben muttered. He stuffed the magazine into his pocket as he jumped to his feet. They ran into the aisle.

The Flamer stood down at the other end. When he saw them, he made a fist and pointed across the machine. Gene expected the sheet to disappear. Instead, a huge tear appeared on the far side of the sheet, flashing a glimpse of the metal drums for just an instant, and then everything went back to normal. Ben stared at The Flamer for a moment, but when he only shrugged, Ben crossed over to the other side of the sheet and dropped a red, cardboard square into the space between the roll and the metal drum. It jutted from the side of the roll like a warning flag. They waited. The sheet held. The Flamer hit the horn again, and they sprinted back into the aisle. The Flamer blew a kiss. Ben gave him the finger and pulled the porn from his back pocket.

"What was that all about?" Gene asked.

"There's about a million filters and screens to keep lumps and debris out of the mixture, but sometimes stuff gets through. When it does, it gets caught up in the presses and makes holes, bad spots, and tears. We're lucky that it just tore a piece out of the side. Usually a divot that size will rip the whole sheet." He smiled. "We dodged a bullet that time." He glared at Number Five. "Is that all you got, old girl?"

Phase two of reading por-no-gra-phy began when each of the guys had finished with the ones he had originally claimed and began to look around to see which others he could trade for. The trades were never straight up. They bargained the things like baseball cards, and certain ones had greater value. Three *Screws* were worth one *Rampage*. Two *Ruts* were worth one *Screw*. Don't bother trying to trade for a *Swank*.

And the guys had their personal favorites, ones they would no more trade than they would have cashed in a Joe Pepitone on a vintage Mickey Mantle even up.

Hawkins and Judson passed on Phase Two. After they'd read theirs, they gave them to Dub. This gave him a lot of bargaining power, and from what Gene could see, he needed all the leverage he could get. The other guys ran him in circles until he was drooling like Pavlov's dog. He needed three times as many as the others just to break even.

In the final phase, Ben read his favorites aloud. He had quite a voice, really, better than most guys Gene had heard do poetry readings back at school. Ben had a sense for it. He climbed up on the table to read. He even had gestures for his favorite words, like the signals he exchanged with the machine tenders down the length of the machine. As they say, however, sometimes the best performances are the simplest.

"She's begging for it," he said, holding up the first picture he had found. "They always do." He climbed up onto the table. "Don't," he cried.

"Stop," Devoid chimed in.

"Don't."

"Stop."

"Don't."

"Stop."

"Don't stop!"

Gene thought back to the first day, when Ben had told him about the importance of finding ways to pass time. He wondered if this was what the old timers had in mine when they'd coined the phrase.

Gene walked out with Hood that night. He thought Hood would still be pissed at him, but since he was holding the guy's dope, he knew they'd at least get to the car, and maybe they could talk.

When they got to Hood's truck, he jumped up on the hood. Gene handed him his dope. He lit one and passed it back.

"You sure, man?" Gene asked.

"Yeah. I was pissed at you before, but the truth is, you saved my ass. I don't know what would have happened if I'd fucked up again tonight while Hawk was shadowing me. Shit, who am I kidding, I know exactly what would have happened. He'd have had me and Supry in the Nurse's office, and I'd have been pissing in a cup so fucking fast my head would have been spinning."

Gene climbed up beside him.

"You did say you needed me to watch your back."

"I never said you should steal my fucking dope. I almost went nuts tonight, man."

"I guess you're going to have to get used to it. Hawkins is definitely watching you." Gene leaned on the hood.

"I thought I was past this shit, man. Back when I started, he figured out what I was up to out on the dock and he shadowed me for a while. He saw it didn't really affect my work, and he left me alone after that."

"I guess you'll just have to show him again, quit screwing up for a while."

"Screwing up? I still can't figure out how I got to be a screw-up. I know my job, man. It's not me, it's these goddamn new crews. When Supry first did it, I figured it wouldn't be any big deal, that I was getting the lesser of two evils. I mean, Ben's a real asshole. I never wanted to be one of his boys, you know. The other guys, Hawk and them, they just want to work, and I've always done okay, so I figured it would be fine."

"But it's not fine."

"No, Hawk and the others have gone crazy."

"Supry said you could switch if you wanted," Gene said. "It's in the contract."

"I wouldn't do that to you, man," he said. "Besides, Ben would throw a fucking fit if we messed up his gang."

"So what are you going to do?"

"I'll let it ride, man. I'll wait until the novelty wears off for Hawk, until he stops trying to run the perfect fucking roll. Even he has to chill sometimes."

"You think?"

He took a long drag and held it. He giggled and smoke billowed from his mouth. Gene almost expected it to come out of his ears, too.

"Not really," he said. "Either way, I'm fucked. I'd never take you down with me, though." He stuck out a hand. Gene took it and they whipped their hands around, locking wrists.

Gene had to admit he felt relieved. The last thing he wanted was to be back with Hawkins now that he had gotten even crazier. He felt bad for Hood, but if he switched over to Ben's crew, Ben would be pissed off.

Just then, The Flamer came out and stood by the shack, leaning against a telephone pole at the center of a circle of light. He had changed from his work clothes into a one-piece black-leather jumpsuit. It had a zipper down the front, and he had it open halfway down his chest. He wore several gold chains and, as a final touch, white cowboy boots. "Jesus," Gene said. "Get a load of that outfit. Guess he must be going cruising."

"He's waiting for his ride," Hood said, just as a black Lincoln Continental pulled up. The Flamer walked over to the driver's side and opened the door, and in the overhead light, Gene saw a woman behind the wheel in profile. She was stunning, her features elegant, her red hair piled on top of her head. She wore a white blouse with a high collar and a single gold chain. She slid over toward the passenger side, but it couldn't have been more than a couple of inches. The Flamer still managed to slide in beside her.

"Who the hell is that?" Gene asked.

"His wife."

"His wife. I thought you said he was queer."

Hood passed the joint. "Sometimes queers get married, Wheeler. Everything isn't always black and white, you know."

"But that woman is gorgeous."

"She is sharp for an old broad," Hood said.

"So what's she doing with him?"

"Who knows? Maybe she's lesbo and they're covering for each other. Maybe they like to wear each other's clothes. The Flamer was born to wear those high, silk collars. She might love the crazy motherfucker." As if on cue, the Flamer turned toward her, and their silhouettes merged in a long kiss.

Hood took a long drag from the joint and passed it along. He exhaled a luxurious cloud. His voice was high and shaky.

"Black and white, my man," he said. "It ain't all black and white."

Chapter Fourteen

Gene's phone rang early on Tuesday morning, and hoping it was Staci, he picked it up, but the chuckle that he heard wasn't Staci's.

"Mr. Wheeler," Phil Blair said. "Returned from whatever frigging corner of the globe that you've been hiding out in. A place, I'm sure, where there is no running water, no electricity, and sure as hell no telephones. I called you eleven times on Saturday, son."

"I left early, sir."

"Just as I advised you. I knew you were a quick study."

"Thank you, sir."

"Don't mention it." He took a deep, harsh breath. Gene could see his blue skin, feel the cool flesh of his fingers. How was this guy still walking around?

"Sorry, kid," Blair said, "but it's time for a new lesson. You need to stop by my office before work this afternoon. We need to talk. Be here at one."

"Yes, sir," Gene said, but as usual, Blair had already hung up.

Gene waited in Blair's outer office for half an hour, listening to the dull roar of his phone conversations on the other side of the door. His secretary wore the same suit that she'd had on the day Gene had put in his application. Her earrings were huge yellow sunflowers. He stared at them for a while, but she caught him, and he looked away.

The door burst open, and Blair came through, coughing and wheezing and waving his arms. "Get Larry Sanschagrin on the phone, Phyllis," he said. "That sorry little cocksucker has pulled this shit on me one too many times."

"Yes, sir," she said, not missing a beat at his language.

Blair finally noticed Gene.

Passing Time

"Wheeler. Come on in."

Gene followed him into the office. Blair sat down and folded his hands together. He seemed ready to speak, but then he paused. "Phyllis," he barked.

"Line one," she said.

He grabbed the phone. "Larry, Phyllis told me that you called twenty minutes ago to say that you want to keep those two guys I gave you from the labor pool for three more days. I told you when I gave them to you that I needed them back by tomorrow. I already got them scheduled in the Lime Kiln." He paused, listened. "I don't care if the job is going slower than you expected, Larry, I need them back." He paused again. The voice on the other end was shrill, angry. Blair cut him off. "Larry," he said. "You're not listening. My job is to give you the manpower you need. Your job is to get the goddamn work done on time. You said you needed two men for three days and that's what I gave you. I don't give a flying fuck why the job isn't done. I need those two in the Lime Kiln tomorrow, and if they're not on the job at six a.m., the next time I send a laborer to your fucking department will be after you've retired." He slammed the phone down and turned toward Gene. If Larry Sanschagrin was lunch, then Gene figured he was going to be dessert.

"So, Wheeler. What do you think about that call?"

"I'm glad I'm not Larry Sanschagrin, Mr. Blair."

"Good answer," he said. "Good answer." He stood up and paced back and forth behind his desk. "You remember what I told you the first day you were in here?"

"That I could start work that afternoon."

"That's right, and why was that?"

"Well, you said you needed a body."

"That's right." He threw himself back into his chair. "You see, Wheeler, I don't think you realize just how lucky you were, the timing and all. I needed somebody down on the machines, and I didn't have anyone to send. Zero." He formed a circle with his thumb and middle finger.

"I don't usually start people on the machines," he said. "I got a few other spots that I send new guys to, spots that help a guy figure out if he really wants to work for us. You missed out on those. You started out on the machines, instead, a damn good job, but that was only supposed to be for a few days. After that, Jimmy Cooper was due back from his broken leg and that would have bumped you out of the machine room and back into the labor pool. If Saucier hadn't stuck his hand into Number Five, that's where you'd be."

"What is the labor pool, Mr. Blair?"

"When you're in pool, you report to me every day, and I send you wherever I need an extra hand. Basically, you never know where you're going to work or who you're going to be working with from one day to the next. How does that sound?"

"Pretty lousy, sir."

"Damn right it is. It stinks." He chuckled.

"When Saucier got hurt, that opened things back up for you. You stayed on the machines when most guys don't get a steady assignment like that for almost a year."

Blair picked up the phone, but instead of dialing, he waved it at Gene.

"Do you think it's just a coincidence I talked to that asshole Sanschagrin while you were in the office?"

"I guess not, sir."

"I wanted you to see what you're missing."

"Am I going to the labor pool, Mr. Blair?"

"That depends on you, son. If you want to stay on the machines, you need to start working Saturdays. Labor pool guys get called on Saturday morning, so they can ignore me. Regular guys get their schedule in advance, and that includes Saturdays. If you can't work them, I'll have to give that slot on the machines to someone else."

Work every Saturday? When would he see Staci? She was already pissed off at him. If this happened, she'd kill him.

"When do I have to decide?"

"This Saturday is already decided. You're on the machines this week, and you're scheduled to work Saturday, unless you want out of the machine room right now."

"No, sir," he said. "I'll work this Saturday, but I'd like to think about doing it full time."

"That's fine," Blair said. "You can have the week. Let me know by Friday what it's going to be." He stood up and held out his hand. Gene took it and was amazed at how warm his grip was. Obviously, jerking people around got his blood going.

"Actually," Blair said, and Gene wondered if he'd read his mind, or maybe just his face. "I like you kid, but rules are rules, and I wanted you to know how lucky you've been. You got one of the best jobs in The Company. You don't get your schedule screwed up because assholes like Larry Sanschagrin piss me off. But you have to do this one thing for me, this Saturday thing. Is that so much to ask?"

"I'll have to think about it, sir."

"Sure, sure," he said. "Call me Friday. Talk it over with your co-workers, see what they have to say."

He opened the door and led Gene out, his arm resting gently on Gene's shoulder. Phyllis looked up and smiled. She mouthed, "Line one." Blair patted Gene on the back and retreated. He picked up the phone. "This is Phil," he said, but Gene thought of something. "Mr. Blair?" he asked, even though he could hear a voice on the other end of the phone line. Phyllis shushed him, but Blair said, "Hold on, Vashaw," and clamped his hand over the receiver.

"Will I have to work Sundays, sometimes, too?"

"Hell, no," Blair said. "The Company pays double-time for Sunday. Guys kill to work Sundays. Help me out with Saturdays, and we'll be golden."

"Okay," Gene said. "Thanks."

At ten-thirty that night, he sat on the winder. Everyone else gathered around the table. Ben pulled out a deck of cards. "No time to get a decent poker game going," he said. "But we could play a little Blackjack." He looked over at Gene. "What do you say, Geno, up for a few hands?"

"I don't think so, Ben."

"What's wrong, kid? You seem down tonight. Did that little girl in Jersey hurt your feelings this weekend?"

"I had a chat with Phil Blair today."

"No wonder you're bummed out." Ben held his hand up to his ear as if he were talking on the phone. "This is Phil," he roared, mimicking Blair's voice perfectly.

"What did he say?" Hawkins looked up from his magazine.

"He told me how lucky I was to be working down here, and that if I didn't want to get dumped into the labor pool, I was going to have to start working every Saturday."

"Uh-oh, nookie alert," Ben said. "The old guy is really trying to cramp Wheeler's style."

"He's right about one thing," Hawkins said, ignoring Ben. "You are lucky. I don't think I've ever seen anyone else who ended up down here on their first day in The Company."

"Amen," said Judson.

Gene looked around and realized that he had everyone's attention. Even Hood had turned down his tape player.

"Blair said most guys get bounced around for months before they get a steady position," Gene said. "He hinted that some of the other jobs are pretty nasty. Is that true, or is that more of his bullshit?"

"Oh, it's true all right," Hawkins said.

"Absolutely," said Judson.

"No doubt about it," Dub piped in.

They tripped over each other with horror stories about the other departments.

"The wood room," Ben said. "Now there's a frigging hole if I ever saw one. That's where everything starts, where they grind the logs into the chips that make the pulp mixture. I swear the fucking machines are all a hundred years old. So are the guys that work there. They walk slow, and their eyes are squinty, and none of them have teeth. Imagine a department where the whole crew looks like Saucier.

"When you get assigned there from the labor pool, they give you a shovel and a wheel-barrel and tell you to clean up, as if there was any point in that. There you are poking around under this maze of rickety old conveyer belts, trying to shovel sawdust while the stuff is raining down around you every minute. God, you cough the shit up for a week after you've worked there."

"Still," Dub said, "it ain't as bad as the lime kiln." He shuddered.

"Why would they have a lime kiln in a paper mill?" Gene asked.

"Lime is a key ingredient they use to break down the wood

chips," Hawkins explained. "They use so much and it's so expensive that it only makes sense to cook it up themselves."

"But it isn't just the lime they cook in that place, it's the workers, too," Dub said. "The kiln is this giant tube that's about three thousand degrees, and the lime dust that's floating around the place burns your skin so you have to wear coveralls, gloves, goggles, a face-mask, and that makes you sweat like a pig."

He clawed at his skin as if he were coated in sweat and lime.

"Blair usually sends everybody to the lime kiln for their first month," Hawkins said. "It's an initiation."

"You definitely lucked out when you missed that place," Dub said.

"I hated that lime kiln bad as anyone," Devoid said, "but at least it doesn't stink like the Kraft mill." He pinched his nose between his fingers. "I'd come home every night, and my girl would make me take my clothes off on the porch. She saved them in a plastic bag and took them to the Laundromat. Said she didn't want them in her house. I think if we could have afforded it, she'd have just thrown them away. And to think there's guys that work there their whole lives."

"Maybe their wives aren't as delicate as yours," Jimmy said.

"Hands off my girl," Devoid said.

"That's not what she told me yesterday."

"You little cocksucker." Devoid lunged at Jimmy, who leaned back just out of reach.

"You're not kidding when you brag about what a hot little piece she is," Jimmy said.

Devoid dove across the table and rode him to the floor. "Jesus!" Ben yelled as Jimmy's head hit the concrete.

Ben grabbed Devoid, but he couldn't hold him back. Devoid snapped Jimmy's head back up, ready to drive it down again. Judson grabbed Ben with one hand and Devoid with the other. He tossed Ben aside, picked up Devoid, and pinned him face down on the picnic table. "Take it easy, son," Judson said as he leaned down on him.

Ben scrambled back to his feet and leaned down close to Devoid's ear. "He's an idiot," he said. "Let it slide. You know she'd never give him the time of day."

"I'm going to kill him."

"I think you already did," Judson said,

Jimmy didn't move. Dub and Hawkins leaned over him. Devoid turned his head toward them. "Serves him right," he said. Hawkins pinched Jimmy's ear. Jimmy groaned and swiped at him, then covered his eyes with his arm. "Open your eyes or I'll pinch you again," Hawkins said.

"Fuck off."

Hawkins pinched him again. Jimmy pulled his arm away. Hawkins flashed a light in his eyes.

"Hey," Jimmy said. He covered his face again.

"He'll live," Hawkins said. "He'll have a hell of a goose-egg on the back of his skull, but he'll live."

"Too bad," Devoid said.

"If we let you up, will you behave yourself?"

"I suppose."

"You'll have to do better than that," Judson said.

"I'm okay," Devoid said.

Ben got off. He nodded at Judson, who did the same. Devoid lay for a moment with his face pressed against the table, and then he sprang to his feet. Judson stood poised to tackle him if he went after Jimmy, but he turned and stormed out the door.

Ben went to Jimmy, who was still lying on the floor, and offered him his hand. Jimmy took it, and Ben jerked him to his feet. "You okay, kid?" he asked, still holding his hand.

"Yeah."

"You sure?"

"I'm sure." He flashed a grin. He seemed pretty pleased with himself.

"Good," Ben said. He slapped Jimmy's face.

"Jesus, Ben! What the hell was that for?" Tears came to his eyes.

"What the hell you talking like that to Devo for? You know he's crazy as hell when it comes to his girl. I should have let him kill you."

"I was only joking."

Ben slapped him again. "Don't joke about that man's wife. Joke about mine or Judson's. Joke about Dub's mother, for Christ's

146

sake, anyone but Devo's wife."

"But you're always kidding him about her. Saying that he's pussy-whipped."

"That's talking about *him*. I never talk about his woman."

They headed off to the smoking area. Judson went over to check on his roll. No one said a word. What was there to say? Gene glanced over at Hawkins, who just shook his head. Dub shook like a small dog. Hood moved his finger in a circle by the side of his head.

"I can't believe Ben just slapped Jimmy's face like that," Gene said. "Why would Jimmy let him do that?"

"Jimmy's just a big kid," Hood said. "Actually, he's more like a giant puppy. You can't reason with someone like that. You have to smack him every now and then to get his attention."

"And you don't have a problem with that?"

"Why would I care? If it keeps Jimmy in line and out of our hair, I'm all for it."

"I don't know," Gene said. "It just seems wrong to me. Guys are supposed to keep their hands to themselves."

He thought of Hawkins grabbing him on the first night.

A grin flirted with the ends of Hawkins lips. "That's true most of the time," he said. "Not for Ben and Jimmy, though. Jimmy can't look up to someone that he's not afraid of."

"I don't get it."

"You don't have to."

"The one who's really scary is Judson," Hood said. "Did you see the way he pulled Devoid and Ben off of Jimmy?" He lifted his paperback over his head and slapped it down on the concrete. Dub jumped when the book hit the floor, but then he perked up. He beamed with pride for his friend.

Gene thought of how Dub looked up to Judson. Would it still be the same if Judson slapped him around? There were different ways to look up to someone. He was glad that Jimmy's wasn't his.

"Old Jud is one man I wouldn't piss off in a million years," Hood said.

"You know," Gene said, "before all that started, you guys were telling me how crazy things are in the rest of The Company."

"There's different kinds of crazy, Wheeler," Hawkins said. "You run into assholes wherever you go. What we just witnessed was personal bullshit. Out there," he said, waving his arm to include the world beyond the machine room, "the bullshit is part of the job. It's institutionalized.

"Once you walk outside the door of the machine room," he said, "the work barely matters, it's knowing how to play the game, how to manipulate the contract so you can get paid for doing nothing. I could be wrong, but you don't strike me as that type of guy."

Gene shook his head. Since when did Hawkins have such a high opinion of him? "So why is it different here?"

Hawkins smiled. "The machines protect us," he said. "You know the ladies play by their own rules."

"Okay. I'd hate to have to deal with bullshit every day, but the only time I get to see my girl is on the weekends. She's pissed off with me already for leaving school."

"I keep telling you, Wheeler," Hood said, "there are plenty of girls right in this town. Shit, I can find you one that you can see every night, not just on weekends."

"So you think I should do the Saturday thing just so I can stay here?" Gene asked.

"Damn right," Hood said.

Hawkins shrugged. "We all have to decide what's important to us."

They walked out together that night. Nobody said anything more about the job. When they got to their cars, everybody split up. Hawkins climbed into the cockpit of his Porsche and rolled down the window. "I'll see you gentlemen tomorrow," he called, and as he pulled away, Gene wondered if he had a girl and what she was like if he did. An Aryan goddess, no doubt.

"Earth to Wheeler," Hood said, snapping his fingers in Gene's face.

"Sorry," he said. "Does Hawkins have a girlfriend?"

"He probably does. But he sure as hell isn't going to bring her around any of us."

"You got a point."

"I got another point, too, you know. If your girl dumps you, I can fix it so you still get laid on a regular basis."

"Great," Gene said. "We can be cellmates when they throw us in jail for screwing minors."

"Just let me know," Hood said, ignoring the jailbait comment. Maybe those laws really were out of date, and Gene was the only one who still worried about them.

Hood turned on the headlights and the dual spotlights on the top of the cab and revved up his engine. "Just remember, Geno," he said. "A lot of things are optional in life, but a job you can live with and regular sex aren't two of them."

As he watched Hood drive away, Gene thought that if he worked Saturdays and Staci blew him off, then Hood could fix him up with Jenna's friend. "It's nice to have options," he said. Even if he was only half-serious, it felt good to say the words. It had been a while.

When he got home, he stared at the phone for a long time. He knew he should call Staci and talk about this. As if he didn't know which way she'd vote. Or maybe it didn't matter to her. Maybe part of her had already moved on. He could give up his spot in the machine room, throw himself into the mess of the labor pool, and that wouldn't be enough for her. Maybe he needed to decide for himself and let her figure out what that decision meant to her.

Ben dragged him to The Bone every night after work for the rest of the week. He put on a full-court press, telling Gene how crazy it would be to give up his slot in the machine room for a woman. Hood was after him on a different front, reminding him how he could hook him up with Jenna's friend. Local nookie. If he said those two words one more time, Gene swore that he'd take a poke at him.

Thursday morning, Ben dropped him off at six, steadying him with an arm over his shoulder as he puked behind the rose bushes on the front lawn. "Damn, this is the life," Ben said.

He was awakened at two by a loud knocking on his door. He lurched up and toppled over the chair by the bed. "All right," he yelled. "I'm coming."

He stumbled to the door. "Who is it? What do you want?" He threw the door open.

Hood was standing there with a fat joint jutting from between his lips and a six-pack under each arm.

"What the hell are you doing here?"

"Well, my man, I figured this was a big night. Tomorrow you're going to give that old fart Phil Blair your answer, and I figured I couldn't let you do that before I showed you just what's at stake."

"What's at stake?"

"You keep thinking what you'll lose if you piss off your girl. Fuck that shit. I want you to see what you could be doing instead." He put one of the six-packs down by his feet and passed Gene the joint.

He waved it away. "We have to be at work in an hour."

"No, we don't. We called in sick."

"We did?"

"Yes, we did," Hood said. "And let me tell you, it turns out I wasn't lying about you. You are fucking green. Damn, you look like hell." He shoved past Gene and turned on the light.

Gene followed him back in, turned out the light, and crumpled back down on the bed as he threw his arm across his eyes. "How could you call in sick for me, anyway? I thought we had to do that personally."

"I do a great imitation of you." Hood sat ramrod straight, and his face got stiff and stern. So that was how he saw Gene. It probably wasn't that far off.

"Besides," he said, "how the hell would Supry know the difference, anyway? He's probably heard your voice twice in his entire life."

"Thanks," Gene said. "I guess I could use a night off. I need to clear my head."

"That's right, my man. We have to get you straightened out. I'm glad the girls are meeting us up the mountain."

"Girls?"

"I'd hate to have anyone else see you like this. We gotta get you some coffee, some food, something. I'm worried about you, man, you're in a rut, hanging out in that sorry dive all the time with those losers. You need a change, and I'm the man who's going to give it to you. I'm talking drugs and booze and girls, all enjoyed in some of the prettiest country on God's green earth. That little chickie of yours will be sorry she ever left you to your own devices."

"What are you talking about?"

Passing Time

"We're going to party tonight, Geno. Everybody who's anybody in this town is going to be up on top of Mt. Page tonight, and we are going to make that scene."

"I think I'm going to die," Gene said.

A half-hour later, they sat in Hood's truck in the parking lot of The Clam Barn. Gene had a thermos of coffee in his lap and sipped from its mouth. He knew Dub would have frowned on this breech of etiquette, not to mention the fact that this was store-bought instant crystals, not freshly ground Colombian Mocha Java. Gene smiled. If Dub's mother found out, she'd probably kick his ass.

He'd gotten to the point where he could sip without gagging. But when Hood came back with a huge tub of fried clams, the smell of hot grease set him off again. "Sorry, man," Hood said. "Why don't we sit in the back?"

He let down the tailgate, and they sat on the edge. Of course, out here they had to contend with the smell from the mill. The wind was driving the clouds right to them. Gene took a tentative breath. Nothing. It was a start.

"Should we really be sitting out in the open like this? What if someone from The Company sees us here?"

"Yeah, right," Hood said. "The Truant Officer trolls the parking lot here every night to find bad boys who are playing hooky. Jesus, Geno, we're not in grade school anymore. We don't even need a note from a doctor until we've been out for three days."

"Let me guess. It's in the union contract."

"You got it."

Hood ate his clams. By the bottom of the tub, Gene even managed a few. Hood finally put it on the ground, stomped it flat with his boot, and tossed it in the trash barrel.

"You ready, man?" he asked. "Time to ride. We got mountains to climb, kegs to tap, joints to roll." He smirked. "Girls to roll, too."

They headed out of town and came at Mt. Page from the logging roads in the forest behind it. This was a part of life in Cumberland that Gene had never known when he was in school. He'd always heard about parties "up the mountain" but had never been to one. They were for Hood's crowd, not the college-prep kids he hung out with. He was moving up in the world. Or down, depending on who you asked. He knew which way Staci would vote.

As they bounced along, the road changed: first, it was asphalt, then gravel, then mud ruts. They careened on as the branches of the trees slapped against the windshield, clawing at Gene's arm until he pulled it into his lap in self-defense.

"Yee-ha!" Hood yelled.

Gene realized his stomach was taking the rough and tumble of the road without a tremor. Hood must have sensed this, too, and kicked the cooler on the floor by Gene's feet, cracking open the lid. "I think you're finally ready, my man," he said. "It's about goddamn time."

Gene opened a beer and took a long drink; the beer slid cold and rich down his throat. He sighed, relaxing for the first time all day, now that his body had stopped reading him the riot act. The guys who hung out at The Bone never looked rough the morning after. Gene was still worthless until the late afternoon. Maybe someday he'd be able to recover as quickly as them.

The party was in a clearing at the top of the mountain, a meadow just behind a wide cliff that formed the forehead of the Elephant, the smooth rock face that was visible from the valley. A bonfire raged in the middle of the clearing. A ring of logs ran all around it, reminding Gene of the campfire ceremonies that had always been a part of his Boy Scout weekends. A ring of trucks, most of them like Hood's, with campers mounted on the back, stood just back from the logs, their tailgates hanging down, sagging under a load of coolers, boom boxes, and drunken kids. They had barely come to a halt when a girl broke away from one group and came running over, dragging another by the arm. It was Jenna and her friend from The Clam Barn. Jenna had on her black cowboy hat. She wore tight jeans and a red tank top. The friend had on a white bikini top, jeans, and a Red Sox hat. Gene remembered the time he'd seen her before, how she'd always turned away whenever he looked at her, but now she returned his gaze boldly. He hadn't noticed before how pale she was, her cheeks red from too much sun, the skin peeling off her nose.

"You remember Jenna?" Hood asked as he slung an arm over her shoulder, his hand resting easily on her breast.

Passing Time

"Of course."

"This is my friend, Lisa," she said. The other girl nodded, still not looking away. Gene was the first one to look down.

Lisa and Gene were paired off from the start. Hood and Jenna did most of the talking. All he had to do was open Lisa a beer when she needed one and pass the joints along to her when they came around. Dusk came, and they took a turn scrounging up some firewood. Lisa had slipped into a red-checkered flannel shirt as it cooled off, but it hung open in the front, and the white bikini flashed in the light from the campfire as they dragged their prize, a thick, half-rotten stump, back into the ring.

At first, the party was all loud music and illegal substances. One of the guys had a huge tape player that he'd hooked up to a spare car battery, so the rest didn't have to worry about running down the ones in their cars. He blasted them with heavy-metal tunes as they smoked and drank and talked. But as the party settled down, as the bonfire burned down to a dull red, he started playing softer songs, make-out music, and kids disappeared into the bushes or into the backs of the trucks. Some of them just went at it by the fire.

Gene felt relaxed. Lisa leaned into him, and her face was an inch from his. He kissed her, saw the white of her top, and slid his hand into the cup. She moaned and buried her tongue in his mouth. They kissed for a long time. He squeezed her breast gently and pinched the nipple. She squealed and pulled back, a huge grin on her face. Her teeth flashed in the firelight, the thick double row of her braces glaring out at him like a neon warning sign. Why did she have to be so young?

He closed his eyes and pulled his hand slowly away, stroking her hair. He took her hand and led her away from the fire.

They followed the path until they reached the high point of the mountain. Gene sat down on a wide, granite ledge, looking out over town. She nestled into his arms.

Just below, he could see the lights of the city, the glare of the mill yards. She turned back to him and they kissed, but he knew she felt the difference. She settled back into Gene's arms.

"Don't you like me?" she asked softly.

"I like you a lot. I've got a girlfriend, that's all."

"Hood didn't tell me that."

"He wants me to forget."

"You did for a while."

"Yeah."

"So where is she?"

"She's in New Jersey. I met her in college down there."

"You went to college?"

"One year. I had some trouble, so I figured I'd work for a while."

"Doesn't she come to visit you?"

"We see each other every weekend, but I may have to work every Saturday, so we'll have to go longer between visits."

"I can see why you're stuck. You have to punch a time clock, but what's her problem? I always heard college kids pretty much make their own hours, that they can blow off classes whenever they want."

"Some can, but she's pretty serious about school."

"I'd do it," she said, turning back to him, taking his chin in her hands and staring him full in the face. "If I had to blow off school to be with you, I'd do it in a minute. She doesn't deserve you."

"I wish it was that simple."

"It should be."

They sat for a few minutes. Headlights moved up and down the streets. He thought of what Staci had called this town, "the city that needs its sleep." He felt Lisa's warm body against him.

Lisa shivered. "Do you want to go back to the fire?" he asked. She shook her head, even as she got to her feet. "You stay here," she said, pushing down on his shoulder as he tried to get up with her. "I'll be right back."

She returned with a six-pack, a joint, and two sleeping bags. She smiled when he seemed puzzled by the bags. "Hood didn't tell you we were spending the night?"

Gene shook his head.

"He's such a jerk."

As they sipped the beer, she unzipped the bags and then zipped them back together. "I don't know if that's such a good idea," he said.

"Don't trust yourself with me, huh?"

"That's right."

Passing Time

"Don't worry. We can keep our clothes on, but you don't want to hear the abuse you're going to get if somebody stumbles on us in separate bags. They'll hound you all the way back to New Jersey. Besides," she said, "it's cold." She crawled in and pulled the bag over her head. He wanted to finish his beer.

She pulled the covers away from her face and tossed something to him. "If you change your mind," she said, as she burrowed back down in. It was another six-pack—a six-pack of condoms.

He awoke just before dawn with Lisa snuggled against his chest. He desperately needed a drink of water. He gently disengaged himself and crawled out.

He made his way back to the deserted fire. He figured everyone was in the campers or sacked out in the bushes. By some standards, it was a pretty tame orgy. Everyone was paired off. At least he thought they were. He decided not to test his theory by looking in Hood's camper.

There were several coolers by the fire, and he rummaged through them until he found soda and several gallon jugs filled with water. Either someone in their midst was a teetotaler, or someone had planned ahead. He tore the cap off the water and gulped down several long swallows, taking the bite off his thirst. He took out two sodas and sat down on the cooler, finishing one in a couple of swigs. God, he'd never get used to being this thirsty. He sipped the other as he headed back.

Lisa was still snoring, so he slipped past her and walked to the edge of the cliffs. He dangled his legs over the edge. The sun was just coming up across the valley. It was nice to see it as he was waking up, not staggering home.

He wondered what to do about working Saturdays. He'd put Lisa off by telling her he had a girlfriend, but was that even true anymore? Things had always been good between him and Staci, but maybe he had to be the person she wanted him to be for it to work out. For him, working in The Company was just a temporary thing, but maybe his being here told Staci something about him that she couldn't ignore. Maybe Daniel was a better fit. Would she even be satisfied if he got out of the machine room and into the labor pool? Maybe in a month she'd start complaining about weekend visits. This didn't have anything to do with her. Maybe he was kidding himself to think it did.

Lisa stirred in the sleeping bag behind him. He finished the soda and crushed the can with the heel of his boot.

He crawled back into the bag, and Lisa nestled up against him, her sure hands sliding down the front of his jeans. He opened his eyes, and she stared at him, one hand undoing his zipper, the other sliding in, caressing him. She closed her eyes and kissed him. He slid his hands under the flannel shirt and undid the halter. They slipped off each other's clothing, one piece at a time. When they were naked, she cracked open one of the condoms and slipped it into place. This time, he didn't stop, even when she smiled.

The party broke up at noon. The four of them tumbled down the backside of the mountain jammed in the cab of Hood's truck. He wasn't sure what Lisa would expect after their night together, but as they pulled up to his house and she slid out of his lap, she gave him a quick kiss on the cheek. "Later," she said in a tone that didn't ask for anything. It didn't make any promises, either. He didn't know whether to be relieved or disappointed.

He called Phil Blair when he got home. When he told him he wanted to stay in the machine room, he seemed happy. Gene half expected him to be disappointed, thinking of all the chances he was losing to jerk him around, but when Blair chuckled, it was a joyful sound. It was as if he and Staci had switched places.

"You made the right choice, kid," Blair said.

Gene figured that was that, but when he got to work, everyone was waiting for him, even Old Man Grenier. Just as he came through the door, the horn sounded, and the guy who Old Man Grenier was supposed to be relieving raised both hands in exasperation. Old Man Grenier waved him off. The guy leaned on the horn, but he gave him the finger and turned his back to him.

"So what's it going to be, Wheeler?" Ben said, appointing himself the spokesman for the group, as usual. "Don't keep us in suspense."

"About the job?" Gene asked.

Passing Time

"What else?"

"I'm staying."

"High five," Ben said, holding his hand up for Gene to slap. Gene gave it a good, hard smack, realizing for the first time how happy he was with the choice.

Their high five set off a chain reaction, from Ben to Dub to Old Man Grenier and on to The Flamer. The Flamer slapped hands with Hood and wouldn't let go. Hood tried to jerk his hand away, then just started laughing and swiped at Hawkins's hand with his free one. Hawkins slapped palms with Judson, who got Jimmy's, turning him around with the force of the blow. That left Jimmy facing Devoid. Gene thought about their fight the day before, but that was obviously ancient history to them. They never missed a beat. Their high five was as enthusiastic as all the others.

One by one, they came over to slap Gene on the back and shake his hand. He realized that it was the first time they'd all been together about something. The closest they'd come to this before was when they went to The Bone the night after Saucier's accident; but even then, Hawkins had begged off. He realized that what they said was true. Whatever their reasons, working on the machines was their choice, and somehow, it made them happier to know that it was his, as well. Of course, none of them had ever had to choose between a woman and this job.

The horn sounded, and Old Man Grenier wheeled back toward the machine. "For Christ's sake, hold your horses, MacKensie—" he roared, but the words died in his throat. This wasn't MacKensie's impatience they were dealing with, but Number Five's. She'd snapped her sheet and needed their attention. Gene felt a hand on his shoulder. It was Hawkins. "We'd better move, kid," he said. "She's waiting."

Chapter Fifteen

When Gene first met Staci, if anyone had ever told him that a day would come when he would dread seeing her, he would have laughed in his face. He thought of her first visit this summer, the feel of his hand inside her as she danced on his palm. Then he remembered Lisa beside him in the sleeping bag. How had things changed so fast? He knew he couldn't tell Staci about Lisa, but if he didn't, would she still sense a change in him?

She sat in the chair beside the bed when he got home on Friday night. He had called to tell her that he had to work on Saturday, but hadn't said a word about it being permanent. It was her turn to travel, anyway, so she hadn't complained. She said she'd still come on Friday as she had plenty to keep her busy while he was at work.

The reading lamp was the only light in his bedroom. She was intent on her book and didn't hear him come in. He stood in the doorway.

She wore her reading glasses. The lamp sent slivers of light off the frames to the wall over the bed. Her hair was tied back in a tight bun. She looked every inch the college professor she would be in a few years. He felt the distance between them. He missed her already.

She looked up and smiled. She put down the book, took off the glasses, pulled the comb from her hair, and shook it out. It fanned out around her face. His girl again.

"Hey," she said.

She climbed out of the chair long enough to let him sit down, then climbed back into his lap. He stroked her hair. Its fragrance filled his nostrils. He ran his fingers through it, wrapping one long strand around his fingers.

"So, how was work?"

"It was fine."

"Did you have a special assignment or something? Is that why you had to work Saturday?"

"No, this is actually going to be a regular thing from now on."

She pulled away from him. He tried not to meet her eyes, but she got right in his line of vision.

"Why didn't you tell me when you called the other day?"

"I figured it would be better if I told you in person."

She climbed out of his lap and stood over him. "I thought you said you only had to work on Saturday if that crazy old guy caught you at home."

"It turns out that's for people who don't have a regular assignment. Since I do, I get it scheduled in advance."

"I see." She turned away.

He stood up and put his arms around her. She let him hold her, but her body was rigid and unyielding.

"Come on, Stace," he said. "I don't really have a choice in this."

He felt the tension drain from her body.

"It's probably for the best," she said. "I won't be able to travel so much when classes start back in the fall."

"I guess I already knew that," he said, but he thought of what Lisa had said, that while he had to punch a time clock, Staci could work around her schedule.

"We both have to do what's right for us," she said. "For some reason, you need to be here. I can't drag you kicking and screaming back to school, just because it's what I need, any more than you can keep me here to pack your lunch and send you off to work."

"You mean you don't want to play housewife to my factory worker?" he asked. As if that was what he wanted.

"Hardly." She chuckled. It was her chuckle, not Phil Blair's. "I just have too much to do the next few months. I'm ready to move on, Gene, and you want to get out of the game."

"I just can't see myself back in school right now," he said.

"And I can't see myself anywhere else."

"So, what do we do?"

"Let's go to bed," she said. "We can talk in the morning."

He awoke with pre-dawn gray leaking though the window. They

had three quilts piled on top of them. Staci was curled up against his chest. His hands were like ice. He slid them between his legs until the skin had lost its icy feel. Then he ran them over her body, up through her hair, across her chest, and brought them finally down between her legs.

She clamped her legs together and they lay for a long time without moving. He felt her skin against his hands. He pressed into her and she pushed back.

The motion inched across their bodies. Their tongues met in the dark. He should have realized that this was something different, but he didn't.

When they were done, Staci rolled away from him. She turned her back to him and curled up in a ball. He encased her with his body, resting his head on top of hers, taking the same position that he always did. He had drifted back to sleep when he felt her crying, sobbing quietly at first. The sobs grew louder, shaking her whole body. It was a sad parody of what they'd just been through.

"Hey," he whispered. He hugged her and tried to turn her face to his, but she just pulled more within herself. He could only lay there in the dark and hold her and wait for the sobbing to subside.

"You just don't get it," she said.

The alarm went off at nine. He tried to kill it, but Staci lay on his arm.

She opened her eyes.

"Good morning," she said. It was as if nothing had happened at dawn, as if it was all a dream. "You set the alarm on Saturday morning. Am I forgetting something?"

"You said you wanted to do something today. You've been complaining that we never get out of my bedroom when you visit. I figured we could take a hike today. You know Mt. Page, those cliffs behind the house."

"But don't you have to work this afternoon?"

"It won't take us long. Maybe an hour up and another one back down. We can eat lunch at the summit and still have plenty of time."

"I don't know." She burrowed back under the covers. Her voice was muffled when she spoke. "You're sure this whole thing was my idea?"

"Yeah.

"Oh, well," she said, throwing the covers back and swinging her legs over the side of the bed. "Nature calls."

At nine-thirty, they went into the backyard and climbed over the fence. Ten minutes later, they were at the base of the cliffs, the wide granite slabs looming over them. Staci eyed the rocks doubtfully, but most kids in town had climbed Mt. Page before their twelfth birthday. They'd also driven up the back roads by the time they were eighteen, but best not to mention that.

They kept the cliff face on their right as the trail cut up through the trees. It was like being in a time warp. Gene half-expected a mob of screaming twelve-year-olds to come out of the woods at any time. They worked their way up quickly. He stopped twice to let Staci catch her breath, but the second time, she blew right past him. He caught up with her at the base of a granite ledge. "What happened to the trail?" she said. He pointed toward a series of red arrows that were painted on the stone.

"I thought you said we stayed off the cliffs?"

"These aren't really cliffs." The ledge was steep, but it was still passable.

"If you say so," she said. They scrambled up the stone. Another ledge jutted up on their right, sheer and rough. It was covered with orange letters as tall as they were. CLASS OF 76 was the first line. EAT SHIT was the second.

"Is that one message or two?" she asked.

"I'm not sure."

Blueberry bushes pushed out of wide cracks in the granite. They pulled themselves up with the thickest stalks and collapsed in the middle of the patch. "Snack time," he said, scouring several handfuls of berries from the low bushes. Their tart flavor curled the edges of his lips. He washed them down with a swig from his water bottle and passed it to Staci.

Looking up, he studied the path. They were in a ravine that split the steepest ledges. They could follow it all the way to the summit.

"Ready?"

"Sure," Staci said.

They moved quickly. The ground was rough, but they made good time, and each time they stopped to catch their breath, they got a better view of the valley.

They stopped a hundred feet short of the summit. Both of them were breathing hard, their faces flushed and sweaty.

"I must be quite a sight," Staci gasped.

"You're beautiful," he said.

When her breath was even, he said, "This is the last push. Ready?"

"Sure, why not."

He took a deep breath and focused on the cliffs above them, scrambling up through the brush. He crested the rocks and threw himself down. He heard Staci thrashing up behind him. He struggled to his feet, still breathing hard.

"God," she said, "this is fantastic."

They had a perfect view of town. The Company was spread out across the river like one gigantic machine, while the neighborhoods stretched out below them: the Avenues, The Hilltop, The North End, and Little Norway. When he was in grammar school, the Irish nuns had always told them to watch out for Lutherans. He might have paid more attention to that one if he'd known Hawkins then.

"So," Staci said, and he realized that she wasn't looking at the town but at the mountains. She looked to the south, where the Presidential Range towered over the others, its ridges gray-blue, every one of them pushing up past the timberline. Across the valley were the smaller, wooded peaks of the Mahoosucs, his favorites.

"It's so beautiful." She spread her arms and spun, taking in the final two directions. "And you said you've climbed most of these."

"When I was in high school."

"Who did you go with?"

"My friend Steve. He was really into it. He had all these maps and guidebooks. I'd just show up every weekend once the snow thawed, and he'd have picked out a new mountain to climb."

"What's he doing these days?"

"He's at UConn."

"What's he studying?"

"Geological Engineering. He always did like rocks." Math, too, but Gene didn't mention that. He sat down on the rocks and shrugged off his knapsack. He unzipped it and pulled out lunch: ham sandwiches, apples and bananas, and sodas for each of them. Dub would have found this spread pitiful.

Staci stood looking out over the valley, though by now, her sights were on the town itself. The wind drove the clouds from the smokestacks toward them. She took a deep breath and frowned. "It smells so bad," she said.

"I barely notice. You get used to it."

"Now there's a scary thought. Isn't it illegal to pollute the air like that?"

"They actually clean up the worst of it before it hits the air."

"Why don't people complain about the smell more?"

"They figure the town would dry up and blow away if The Company left. They're probably right."

"It just seems like a waste." She came back over and nestled between his legs. "You're surrounded by all this beautiful country, but then that monstrosity is plunked right down in the middle of it."

"It does give us a unique perspective."

She laughed. "I guess that's one way to look at it." She grabbed an apple, a large, green Granny Smith, and took a huge bite out of it, then held it up for him over her shoulder. He took a bite and winced at the tart taste. She nodded toward The Company. "It's hard to get away from that place, isn't it?"

"Yeah."

"And you really want to stay here for a while, don't you?"

"I was thinking I might work until next fall," he said. "School was so crazy this year. It seems like I just got out. I don't think I'm ready to throw myself back into all that again."

"And if you work Saturdays, we won't even be able to get together on the weekends."

"You said the other night that might be for the best."

"I know." She pulled away from him and walked to the edge of the rocks. She flung the apple over the edge. He watched it plummet into the trees below.

"I've been kidding myself," she said, "Thinking that I can juggle things, running up here every weekend. Dr. Ellis, my advisor, and I have been mapping out my schedule for the last two years. You should see his face every time I tell him I'm headed up here for the weekend."

"It isn't any of his business."

"He and I have the same business."

"I didn't mean that kind of business," Gene said. "I meant your personal life."

"When you get to where I am," she said. "There isn't much difference between the two."

He walked up behind her and wrapped his arms around her. He expected her to pull away, but she didn't.

"I could do the driving," he said.

"To New Jersey and back in thirty-six hours every week?"

"It'd be worth it."

"That's what you say now, but who knows how you'll feel after you've made that run two or three times. Maybe you'll just want to stay up here and get drunk with your pals."

She pulled his hands from around her waist and walked to the edge of the ledge. The wind whipped her hair over her shoulders as if she were moving at high speeds, leaving him behind.

"So what are you saying? Do you want to break up?"

"I don't know. For God's sake, Gene, don't you get it? This is my future we're talking about. The next year is going to be one of the most important of my life. I need for you to be there for me. I figured we could ride out the next couple months, but I've been kidding myself."

He listened to her words. Me. My. Mine. What had happened to Us?

She came back without looking him in the eye and buried her head in his chest. "Why couldn't I fall for a nice, boring scholar? Somebody who'd be there to discuss our courses and the books we'd read. Someone I'd see at meals and late at night and go to movies and readings and plays."

"Damned if I know," he said and hated himself when Lisa's face popped into his mind. "We'd better start back down. There's a trail down the back of the mountain that's better for the descent."

They cut back through the trees, and soon they came across the clearing where he'd partied with Hood and Lisa and the others. In the center of the logs, there were still the remains of a campfire, a black circle of ash six feet wide. The sun played off crushed beer cans and shards of broken glass. There were fast food bags, bits of plastic, and torn condom wrappers.

"Jesus," Staci said. "What a mess." She glanced at the muddy road that led off into the trees.

"I thought you said that this was the mountain all the little kids climbed before they were twelve."

"It is," he said. "After that, they drive up here and party."

"Hood talked about coming up here that time we met him at The Clam Barn with his little friends."

"Yeah."

She turned toward him. She studied his face. Hers changed.

"You were at this party, weren't you?"

"Yeah."

She shook her head. "I thought you wanted to get out of school to clear your head. How can you do that if you're stoned out of your mind half the time?"

"I'm not getting stoned all the time. I went to one party."

"It doesn't matter," she said. "One party or a hundred. If you spend your time with losers like this, then I've really been kidding myself." She turned her back to the campfire ring. "Which way do we go to get back down?"

"Follow me."

When they got back to the house, she began to pack her things.

"What are you doing?"

"I'm going home. I don't belong here."

He touched her arm, but she shrugged him away.

"You can't be serious," he said.

"I'm always serious. I thought you were, too. I never would have started with you if I'd known you were going to piss your life away like this."

"I'm just taking some time off."

"I'm tired of hearing that. I don't have time for time off."

She threw her backpack over her shoulder and headed for the door. He cut her off.

"Get out of my way, Gene."

"I can't believe you're doing this."

"Believe it," she said. "Besides, in an hour, you won't even care that I'm gone. You can call Hood, smoke some good dope, have a few beers. He can bring his little girlfriend over. I'm sure he wouldn't mind sharing."

"You should hear yourself. You think you're so much better than them."

"I told you," she said. "I am. So are you. You used to know that. Now, get out of my way."

He stepped aside, and she walked to the car. She threw the backpack on the passenger seat and got behind the wheel.

"Is this it?" Gene said.

She didn't answer.

"Can I call you?"

"Don't bother. Why drag it out?"

She started the car and backed out of the driveway. He watched as she took the corner at the bottom of the hill and went out of sight.

He went back into the basement. In the corner by the bed, he saw the pile of books that she had bought for him, "their" reading for the semester. He crossed the room in two strides and took them out with one kick, sending them flying across the room, skittering across the carpet like stones on ice.

Chapter Sixteen

He felt strange walking to work that afternoon, as if for the first time he was officially out of school. As long as Staci had still been visiting him, as long as the best part of school was still coming to him, nothing had really changed. Today was really the first day of his sabbatical.

After they ran their first roll, Hood came over. "What's going on, Wheeler? You look like your goddamn dog died or something."

"It's nothing."

"Sure it is. You can tell me, bro."

"My girl freaked out on me this afternoon. She split. I think it's over."

"No shit, man. That's too bad. She was wicked cute."

"Tell me about it."

Hood glanced over at the machines. "I think we got about ten minutes before we turn up. You want to head out to the dock?"

"Why not?" Gene said. Maybe a couple hits would help his mood.

They walked out to their usual place on the dock. Hood sat on the edge, dangling his legs over the side. He pulled out a joint, lit it, and passed it to Gene without taking a puff.

"You're giving me first shot? Jesus, I'm not dead, man. I lost my girl, but I'll live."

"Suit yourself," Hood said.

Gene wasn't used to being out here so early. Somehow, darkness made it seem safer. He sat with his back against a post so he could have a clear view along the dock and back down the aisle toward the machine room. No sense taking chances. Supry had been known to come out of the office every now and then before supper.

Hood had no such worries. He exhaled, grinned, and passed it to Gene.

"So what the hell happened?"

Gene inhaled and felt it wash up into his head. He exhaled, coughed. "You know how it is, man. She's in school. She wanted me to be in school, too. I figured she'd stand by me until I sorted things out, but she couldn't wait." He smiled at the high-pitched whine in his voice. He felt better already. He passed the joint back to Hood.

"I told you that long-distance shit was no good, Geno," he said. "It ain't natural. People got needs." He frowned. "It's usually the guy who cracks, first, though." He nudged Gene in the ribs. "You did tell us she was pretty hot in the sack. Guess she was one of those princess-slut types."

"Don't go there," Gene said. Why did he ever talk about Staci with these assholes? He held out his hand as soon as Hood exhaled.

"Did she find out about what happened with Lisa? Is that what finished things off?"

"You think I'm crazy?"

"Well, you are the sincere type. I figured you maybe had the need to come clean."

Gene shrugged. Had he been the sincere type before he started working here? Was that behind him now? He took another hit. He giggled. He was past his limit. And it wasn't even suppertime.

"It never came to that," Gene said. "It was about where our lives are heading. She knows exactly where she's going, and I'm up in the air. She couldn't deal with it."

Gene glanced at his watch. "You think we should head back?"

"We got time. Seriously, man. I know you're bummed out and shit about this, but it's probably for the best. And it's not like you weren't having doubts of your own. If you weren't, you wouldn't have got it on with Lisa the other night."

He had a point. Gene hated to admit it, but he'd made his choice on Thursday night. Today was about Staci making hers.

"Am I right?"

"You're not too far off."

"So, you have to move on. You know we're going to party up the mountain tonight. I'll call Jenna and tell her to give Lisa the good news."

"Not tonight, man," Gene said. He wasn't ready to jump from

Staci to Lisa. He knew this might be for the best, but it still hurt like hell. Not that he could tell Hood that.

"It must be time to turn up." Gene got to his feet. Hood offered him another hit, but he shook his head.

"Come on, man," Hood said. "You know you want it. Take your mind off your little girl." He winked. "Get you thinking about the next one."

"It's time to go back in, man. I've had enough. If you ask me, so have you."

"Jesus. Here I am trying to help you out, and you're acting like my fucking mother. As if there weren't enough old ladies around here already. I told you, man, I need a couple extra hits every night because of the fucking bullshit."

"I'm not trying to be your mother," Gene said. "I'm trying to watch your back, remember?"

"I'm sorry, man." Hood stubbed out the joint and stuck the butt into his back pocket. "I'm trying to watch your back, too, you know. That's why we're out here. That's why I want you to party with us tonight."

"I just need some time, man. I'll be there for the next one."

"Count on it."

When they walked back into the room, Hawkins stared at Hood. Hood fiddled with the lid of his lunch box and dug out his tape deck. Hawkins never took his eyes off him. Hood looked up and their eyes locked. Hood looked away first. He slammed the lid back down and went over to sit on the winder.

"You know, Wheeler," Hawkins said. "You better watch yourself around Hood. You carry yourself pretty well around here, but then again, he used to, too. He's slipping, and I don't want him to take you down with him."

"Why don't you ease up on the guy?" Gene asked. "He's only slipping because you're riding him so hard."

"I just want him to do his job."

"No, you want him to do his job the way you think it should be done."

Hawkins smiled. "That's what I do with everybody. I did it with you."

"And I didn't like it any better than Hood does."

Hawkins nodded. "There's one big difference, Wheeler."

"What's that?"

"You told me where to get off, and then you learned everything you needed to know without me. Hood's all talk. He can't back it up."

"You're hopeless, man."

"Actually, Hood's the one who's getting hopeless."

Gene looked over at Hood, who sat on the winder with a silly stoner's grin on his face. You'd have to be blind not to see it. Gene looked back at Hawkins. Of course, he'd seen it, too.

"I just can't let it go," Hawkins said.

Hood's tape player had gone silent. He popped out the tape and brown cellophane swirled from it. "Jesus Christ," he said. Hood tore at the tangle and tossed it into the trash.

Hawkins frowned. "You know as well as I do that the only thing Hood cares about these days is getting high. He used to be able to balance things out, but I just don't see that anymore. He needs to get his shit together, if it isn't already too late."

"Because you say so?"

"I just don't want him dragging the rest of us down. We've got a good thing going."

There it was again. The Real A-Team: Old Man Grenier, Judson, Hawkins, and Dub. No slackers allowed. It seemed like all of them were in synch except for Hood. Gene remembered the night he'd worked with Saucier and Riendeau. It did feel good to mesh that way.

Hawkins smiled. "You do know what I'm talking about."

The horn sounded. Hood put up his stuff and went to the winder. Hawkins looked Gene in the eye. "Later, kid," he said. "I got a job to do." He walked over behind Hood. Hood tried to stare him down, but lost again. Gene watched until they slid under the winder, and then he had to walk away.

Gene was grateful when they had a change in the paper on Number Five. It was enough of a difference that they were down at the wet end for almost an hour. He stood beside Number Five, listening to Ben curse as he tried to pass the sheet through the first set of wringers. It crumbled in his hands. Still, it was better than watching Hawkins torture Hood.

Gene knew Hawkins was right, that Hood was slipping and needed to get his act in gear, but he hated what Hawkins was doing to get that done. It was hard not to feel bad for Hood.

The Flamer and Old Man Grenier squabbled about adjustments. Ben leaned over and whispered in Gene's ear. "I don't know why The Flamer always makes such a big show out of bucking Old Man Grenier. We all know he's going to do what that old fart says, eventually. Meanwhile, I have to keep trying to pass this shit even though I know it ain't going to happen."

"I guess it's just a matter of pride," Gene said.

"Actually," Ben said, "I think he just likes to put on a show."

"Maybe that's the same thing for him."

"You got a point."

"Have you ever seen his wife?" Gene asked.

"Sure," Ben said. "She usually picks him up on Friday night, and they go dancing at the VFW."

"How do you think they ended up together?" He wondered if Ben ever took his wife dancing.

"How does anybody ever end up together? Maybe he knocked her up and they had to get married. That was probably the last time they ever had sex, though."

Old Man Grenier threw his hands up in disgust and stormed away toward Number Four. The Flamer watched him go, and then fiddled with the dials.

"We're on," Ben said. "You know, it's like watching a play. That was Act One. In Act Two, now that the old man's gone, The Flamer can do exactly what the old man's been telling him to do for the last twenty minutes."

"That's good for us, isn't it?" Gene asked.

"You bet. That's one thing I'll say about The Flamer, he puts on a show, but when the chips are down, he'll always go with Old Man Grenier's advice. He knows which side his bread is buttered on."

By nine, they had everything back in line. No one on Gene's crew had eaten, so they all sat down together. As soon as he saw them, Dub dipped into his magic basket. He pulled out a giant plastic tub of coleslaw. Next came baked beans, thick, brown syrup streaming down the side of the white plastic. Finally, he pulled two smaller baskets from the mother ship, both lined with red-checkered napkins. One had biscuits, the other an entire fried chicken.

Gene felt disappointed. He'd seen all these dishes before. This was the first time Dub had ever repeated one of the daily specials.

Ben eyed the chicken. He nudged Devoid in the ribs with his stick. "The only recipe in the world more guarded than the Kentucky Colonel's," he said. Devoid grunted and cracked open his own lunch pail.

"You got that right," Dub said solemnly. "If I ever gave you this recipe, Ma wouldn't just kick my ass, she'd have to kill us both."

Judson and Hawkins came though the door carrying their lunch pails. It wasn't often that everyone ate together. Gene was so used to watching the show Dub put on every night, he'd never paid much attention to what the others brought.

Devoid's dinner came packaged in a plastic tray as neat as a store-bought TV dinner, but the meals were all homemade. They smelled as fine as anything that Dub's Ma fixed. Only the proportions were different.

What else would you expect from Devoid's girl? The care she took with each meal was as evident as the gold band she had made him wear, the same one that had cost him half his fingers.

Gene was surprised when Ben opened his, though. His box was a mirror image of Devoid's, as neatly and lovingly arranged. It made him wonder about Ben's wife. Ben never mentioned her. Was he holding out on them? Did he have a "girl" stashed away at home?

Judson's meal reminded Gene of what he'd been sent off with in high school. There were two sandwiches, one peanut butter and jelly, one baloney. He had cheese crackers in a baggy held with twist ties, a juice box, and a chocolate cookie, as if Mrs. Judson was a good mother and Judson was her only child.

Hawkins had actual TV dinners. Everything cooked to perfection and flash frozen at the factory, laid out in squares and rectangles, covered in foil. The only missus in his kitchen was Mrs. Swanson.

The only one missing was Hood. Gene wasn't surprised. He'd

Passing Time

been spending more and more time on his own.

Hood always talked about Dub spending his whole paycheck on his stomach. He said that he had better things to do with his money. The bottom half of his lunch pail was for his tape deck, of course. The upper portion was stuffed with cassettes, comic books, and cheap paperbacks.

Hood never did the math, though. He got his lunches straight from the vending machines. Two bucks for a sandwich, fifty cents each for a coke and a bag of chips. It cost a quarter for an apple, and this stuff might as well have been a Chinese dinner, because he was right back staring through the glass within an hour or two.

Gene walked out into the hall, and sure enough, Hood was at the vending machines.

He dug into his pockets, but came up empty. "Jesus-H-Christ," he said, then pulled a bill from his wallet and jammed it into the change machine between the glassed-in cases. The machine took singles but also five dollar bills. It scanned his money, paused, took the few extra seconds it needed to figure out that it was Abe Lincoln and not George Washington that it was reading, and then quarters cascaded down into the trough like the payoff from a slot machine in Vegas. A few coins jumped the metal lip and fell on the floor. Hood ran after them, trying to stomp them flat with his foot. He waved in disgust when they disappeared under the machine.

He turned back to the food machines. He fed them quarters as if they were slot machines, as well. This time, the payoff was the swish of cellophane, the thump of candy bars, the rumble of the cans down their chutes, each sound as sweet as the jingle of the coins when they rained down.

He banged on the machine. The payoffs weren't coming fast enough for him. Gene shook his head. Maybe Hawkins was right. Maybe Hood was too far gone to make it back. If Gene tried to watch his back, would Hood take him down with him?

Later that night, they had breaks in both machines at the same time. They were having a rough time getting the sheet through Number Four. Hood stood with his eyes glued on Judson as he moved through the passes. Gene glanced over. Stock bubbled over the edge of the vat he should have been keeping an eye on. Gene ran over and jerked the lever. Hood jumped back as he pushed past him, then giggled, just as Old Man Grenier charged toward them.

"What the hell is wrong with you, boy?" the old man bellowed. "You been working here for two years and a frigging rookie has to do your work for you?"

"Go fuck yourself," Hood said.

"I should fuck myself?" Old Man Grenier said. "That's big talk, considering you're the one who's fucking up. We can't afford to waste good stock by pouring it down the sewer."

"If the stock was any damn good," Hood sneered, "it would be running through the machine, and I wouldn't have to worry about it going down the drain. Why don't you do your own job, old man, before you start giving me shit about mine?"

The horn blasted at the other end. Judson stood with his arms raised high. When he saw that he finally had their attention, he pointed for Hood to take the sheet out.

"Do your job," Old Man Grenier growled, then turned away.

"Fucking asshole," Hood said and jerked out on the hose. He was the one who had taught Gene to do this slowly and carefully.

"Watch out, man," Gene yelled, "you're going to tear—" but before he could finish, the sheet snagged on the first press and tore all the way across. Hood dropped his head in his hand, and then pulled all the way back. "I don't need this fucking bullshit," he said as he watched Judson, Hawkins, and Dub trudge toward him, their faces red, their shoulders sagging.

Gene walked out with Hood at the end of the shift. They didn't say anything. When they reached his truck, Hood leaned against the side, hanging his head.

Hawkins, Judson, and Dub walked through the gate. They were always together now. All they needed was Old Man Grenier. Hood looked over at them but quickly looked away. Hawkins looked toward them and shook his head. Judson nodded. Dub saluted. They all split up and headed toward their cars.

"I don't know how much more of this I can take," Hood said.

"I'm sure the way they're riding you won't last forever," Gene said. "It'll be like that time Dub was late answering the horn and they made him do your job. Hawkins will follow you around for a while, and then things will get back to normal."

"I don't know, man," Hood said. "They're all so uptight now. You'd think we were doing brain surgery or something. We're making paper, for Christ's sake."

"You know they're all crazy about the job," Gene said. "You used to tell me everyone was here by choice, even you."

"I know I did. Lately, though, I'm starting to wonder." He finally stood up straight. Gene expected him to ask again about going up the mountain. "You need a ride home, man?"

"No. I'll walk. It's too nice to ride."

"Suit yourself."

Gene was surprised. Hood never gave up this easily when he wanted to party. Maybe this was really getting to him.

Hood got into the cab and started the truck. The lights glared on behind Gene. He got ready to wave as Hood peeled out on his way by, but Hood stopped beside him. He had a troubled look on his face. "You're all right, man," he said. Hood stuck his hand out the window. Gene took it, and they locked arms.

"I'll bet things will be better for you tomorrow," Gene said.

"Count on it," Hood said, but he didn't seem very happy about the prospect. He held Gene's hand a second too long. "Later," he said, finally letting go. He peeled out, tossing gravel in his wake. Gene waved, but Hood didn't look back.

Chapter Seventeen

When Gene got to work on Monday, Supry stood at the winder. Gene's crew sat at the picnic table. Ben glared at Supry and tapped his stick on the table. Devoid tore at the collar of his shirt. Jimmy winced every time Ben's stick hit the table. They were not a happy bunch.

The guys from the "real" A-Team were at their winder. Hawkins worked on the blades that cut the sheet, the slitters.

He pulled one off and handed it to Judson. Judson ran it over a sheet of paper, slashing it in two. Dub whistled, impressed. Gene wasn't sure if Dub was more impressed by the razor-sharp blade or the way his big buddy handled it.

Supry worked his scrap of paper in his hand. He crumpled it into a tight ball. The first time he'd talked to them as a group, Gene had thought the paper must be his notes, but he never looked at them. Now Gene figured he just had it to have something to do with his hands.

When he saw Gene, he nodded and tossed the wad into the trash.

"Mr. Wheeler. We've been waiting for you."

"Am I late?"

"No. I just wanted to talk to everyone before they scattered, and you know they get restless."

"So, what's up?" Gene glanced at Hood, who sat on the winder for Number Five. He looked down, but not before Gene saw his eyes. He'd seen the same look the night before. Guilt. Gene promised him that today would be better for him. What had Hood said? "Count on it."

It all clicked. Gene realized why he'd been so sure. Hood was selling him out—taking his slot on Number Five.

This was the guy who shook his hand in brotherhood and said

he would never do such a thing, who would never take Gene down just to get away from Hawkins.

"Have a seat, Mr. Wheeler," Supry said.

Ben frowned and shook his head. He slapped the stick on the bench next to him for Gene to sit beside him. Gene walked as close as he could to Hood. Hood wouldn't look at him.

"When we changed the crews," Supry said, "we knew that the only one who was out of line in seniority was Mr. Hood. At that time, he seemed okay with the situation but said he might want to make a change in the future. He's decided to make that change. Effective immediately, he will be working on Number Five with Flamand, Ben, Devoid, and Jimmy Cooper."

"Now wait a fucking minute." Ben glared at Hood with pure hate. "I know the little punk has seniority, but things have been working out just fine since we switched. Aren't we keeping everything in specs?"

"Yes," Supry said. "Both of your machines have been within specs. Number Four has exceeded them."

"You see," Ben said, "we're doing good work, and everyone but Hood is happy. So, now, we're going to mess everything up because somebody hurt Hood's feelings. Why would you want to fuck with a good thing, Dale?"

Supry sighed. "What I want isn't important, Ben." He looked so miserable that Gene knew he would have been more than happy to leave things the way they were. "What is important is the contract between the union and The Company. Hood has seniority, and this gives him the right to choose his position."

"Fuck the contract," Ben said. "You know we make our own rules down here. We do what works. Or at least we used to, back when we had balls."

Blood crept up Supry's neck and into his face. By the time it disappeared beneath his hairline, Gene figured he might pop the bow tie right off his shirt. Supry took a deep breath.

"I've worked in this room for thirty years, Ben," he said. "I'm not some asshole who wandered in off the street. Sometimes I don't like the contract any more than you do, but it's my job to enforce it. If Hood wants to change crews, then he can. I sure as hell don't have to clear it with you. Just because I don't rub it in your face all the time that I'm in charge around here, doesn't give you the right to forget it."

"Actually, Mr. Supry," Ben said, "I haven't forgotten who's in charge. Maybe you have, though. You're the first one who ever told me that the machines are the only ones we ever listen to. Now, you're saying we're no different than anybody else who works for The Company. We can't lift a finger without checking the goddamn contract. Won't you be surprised the next time we got broke piled to the goddamn ceiling, and I slap a grievance on anybody who tries to give The Hood a hand. If the little prick can't do his own job, then you'll have to call Phil Blair to send us someone from the labor pool."

Supry winced at the name. Ben knew how to push Supry's buttons, too.

Supry shook it off and glared at Ben. "I've had enough of your shit, Ben. I put up with it most of the time because you're a hell of a backtender, but one more word out of you, and you'll be working in the lime kiln so fast, it'll make your head spin."

Ben grinned. He seemed ready to talk, to have that last word, but he thought better of it. Maybe down deep, Supry's thirty years in the machine room did mean he was not someone to mess with. Maybe Ben knew that he had pushed him as far as he could.

Gene suspected that Supry couldn't do what he'd just said, that the contract, the union, probably made it impossible. He was stuck with Ben, just as much as Ben was stuck with Hood. One big, happy family. And he'd stayed in the machine room and lost Staci to avoid personal bullshit.

Ben and Supry stared at each other for a few more seconds, and Ben finally dropped his gaze.

"So," Supry said, "this will leave a crew on Number Four of Grenier, Judson, Hawkins, Dub, and Wheeler. Does anyone else have a problem with this?" He looked around the table, but there were no takers.

"Good." He turned and stalked out the door as if he couldn't get away fast enough. Even then, Hood beat him out. "You'd better run you little punk," Ben called after him.

"Calm down, Ben," Hawkins said. "The guy's got seniority. He's within his rights."

"Stay out of this, Blondie," Ben said. "You're just happy 'cause you'll have Wheeler under your thumb again."

Leave it to Ben to think of that. Gene wondered how true it was. Sure, Hawkins had been saying good things about him since he'd switched machines, but would he have to start all over again? Would Hawkins shadow him, shove him out of the way, brush his questions aside as if he were a twelve-year-old?

Hawkins stared at Ben, then his eyes shifted to Gene. "Don't listen to his crap, Wheeler," he said. "I've got no beef with you. All that is in the past." He nodded toward the winder on Number Four. "Are you coming?"

Ben moved between them. "Wheeler will be over when the fucking horn sounds and not a second before. He may have to work with you, but leave him alone between rolls."

"Maybe he'd rather speak for himself," Hawkins said.

"Go ahead, Geno," Ben said. "Tell this asshole where to get off."

"I'll be over in bit," Gene said.

"Suit yourself," Hawkins said.

"He damn sure will," Ben said. "Come on, Wheeler. I need a cigarette."

They walked over to the smoking area, and Ben threw himself down on the bench. "I can't believe this shit," he said. "Just when we get things set up our way, The Hood has to screw it up."

"He does have seniority," Jimmy said. "Wheeler's as low as you can get around here. Hell, he wouldn't even be here anymore if Saucier hadn't fucked himself up."

"We're stuck," said Devoid. "It's in the contract."

"We'll see," Ben said. "We have to take Hood. It doesn't mean he's going to want to stay with us. He might have a change of heart, you know?"

"What are you going to do, Ben?" Gene asked.

"I'm not exactly sure. Though I can say that your ex-pal Hood will find out real quick that he's not wanted around here. He thought Blondie was on his ass, but he ain't seen nothing yet."

He glared toward the picnic table where Hood sat with his tape deck and a detective novel. Judson and Hawkins were also there, the newspapers spread before them.

"This is what I'm talking about," Ben pointed toward them.

"What's wrong with this goddamn picture? We're all sitting here, while the bookworms are over there. Those three are made for each other." He dismissed them with a wave on his arm. "It just rubs me raw."

The horn sounded on Number Five. Gene walked over to the winder and started it up before he realized that Hood was standing beside him. "Hey, thanks, man," Hood said, "but we switched out, remember?"

"Oh, yeah," Gene said. He turned away. "Force of habit."

"Well, if you feel forced to haul my broke, too, go right ahead," Hood said.

Gene faced him, and Hood grinned. He obviously enjoyed the trick he'd pulled on Gene.

"I thought we were friends, man," Gene said, and as Hood's smile evaporated, he realized that Hood had been trying to stonewall the way he'd done Riendeau that time he'd been late. Maybe he wasn't enjoying fucking over Gene.

"I'm really sorry, man," Hood whined, "but I had to get away from Hawkins and the others. They were driving me nuts."

"And you couldn't find a way to save yourself without screwing me? You told me you wouldn't do that."

Hood raked his hands through his hair. At least he tried to. His fingers slid over the hairnet and the bandana. He didn't even notice.

"I would have had to transfer out of here or quit altogether," he said. "I can't afford to quit, and I don't want to work in another department. You know how I feel about that. It's just that those guys on Number Four have gone nuts since Supry put them together. They just wore me out."

"Like they won't do the same to me?"

"No, no," he said eagerly. "I think you'll get along okay with them. You're their type. You'll fit right in."

"You've got to be shitting me." Gene wondered who Hood was trying to convince.

"No, really. You're a serious dude. Deep down inside, you probably care about this shit. Me, I just want to come to work and do my job and read a little and listen to my tunes and smoke out on the loading dock. I think you can handle Hawk and the rest of them. We're both in the right place." He stuck out his hand.

Could he really believe that? Better yet, was he right? When had Gene become a serious dude? Maybe he had been one back at school, before calculus, that is, but since he'd gotten here he'd done his best to live the life Hood had just described for himself.

Sure, the machines were cool, and it might be fun to learn a little about them, but was he ready to get thrown head first into the fanaticism of the A-Team?

"What a crock of shit," Gene said. He left Hood with his hand hanging out in front of him. Gene didn't know what Ben had in store for Hood, but he planned to enjoy the show.

When the horn sounded, Gene started up the winder and went over with Hawkins and Dub to get the samples. Dub stuck out his hand. "Nice to have you aboard, Wheeler."

"Thanks."

"Although I don't know what kind of a team we're going to make, what with you and Hawk hating each others' guts," he said. He slapped himself on the forehead.

Hawkins smiled. "Come on, Dub. I don't hate Wheeler's guts. That's old news. Not that it matters, though. We don't have to be friends to work together. We just have to care about doing the job."

"But it helps if you're friends," Dub said.

"I'm not so sure," Judson's voice came from behind them. Gene turned in his direction. "Sometimes," he continued, "being friends is actually a problem. It complicates matters. Work, after all, is black and white, while relationships are the grayest of gray areas."

Gene thought of how Judson had straightened Dub out when he hadn't answered the horn. Gene guessed Judson didn't have that gray problem.

"So, being friends ain't so good?" asked Dub.

"Not always," Judson said.

"Being enemies is better?"

"Sometimes."

Dub nodded decisively. "Then working with Hawkins and Wheeler is about the best deal I can get."

Judson smiled. "As frightening as it seems, you might be on to something, son."

Dub beamed. Hawkins turned to Gene. His fingers went to his upper lip, and Gene thought he was smoothing his mustache. Then Gene realized he was trying to hide a smile.

"So, Wheeler," he said, "your job is pretty much the same here as it was on Number Five. Each winder and machine has its own little quirks, though, so it'll take a while for you to get used to that."

"I'm sure you'll fill me in," Gene said.

"Not me. I'm still learning, myself. This winder is Dub's baby. Follow his lead for a while." Dub's face split in a pained grin, as if he were worried about being in such a position of responsibility.

Judson tapped him on the shoulder with his backtender's stick, as if the stick was a sword and he was knighting him. "You heard the man," he said. "Show Wheeler the ropes."

Dub took a deep breath. "Follow me, Wheeler." He crawled under the winder, and Gene followed him.

After they had threaded the sheet, Dub took the controls, while Hawkins stood beside him. They gabbed back and forth. Toward the end of the run, Hawkins took over, and Dub tried to sit down, but Hawkins shook his head and motioned for him to stay beside him. Supry had said Number Four consistently exceeded the specs. This was a whole new ball game. Gene wasn't sure he wanted to play.

After they finished, Hawkins went over to the winder and started fiddling with the slitters again. Saucier had never done it, and Devoid never did it more than once or twice a week.

"What're you doing?" Gene asked.

"I'm checking to see if these are sharp enough. If they're not, I'll have to replace them."

"How come Devoid doesn't do it as often as you do?"

"Checking once or twice a week is enough to keep within specs."

"What happens if you just leave them like everybody else does?"

"If they aren't sharp enough," Hawkins said. "They don't really cut the paper, they tear it. You can't see the tears, because they're microscopic, but they show up as dust on the side of the rolls. We call it slitter dust. If quality control finds it, they drag the rolls over to refinishing and vacuum them. I keep the slitters razor sharp, and nobody has to do that."

"I guess that makes sense," Gene said. Hawkins smiled and moved on to the next blade. Gene looked toward the smoking area. Ben waved for him to come over.

"You'd probably better go," Hawkins said. "See you in twenty minutes."

"I'll be here."

By seven o'clock, the machines were out of synch. Ben and the others had just finished their rolls, while Gene's crew was five minutes away from turning up. Ben went up to the locker room and burst back in a few minutes later with a huge grin on his face. "I was just talking to Evans over in recycling," he said. "There's a new shipment of newsprint over there, and he says one of the boxcars has an especially promising vein of porn. We have to get over there before word spreads."

"Count me in," said Jimmy.

Ben looked at Gene.

"I can't leave," Gene said. "We're almost ready to turn up."

"Oh, Jesus," Ben said. "I forgot. That's okay. We'll wait."

"We're totally out of synch," Devoid said. "There won't ever be a time that you can take Wheeler with you."

"I know," Ben said, and then he brightened. "But we'll give you first crack at them after us when we get back, Wheeler."

"Those aren't the rules, Ben," Jimmy said.

"I'm the one who made the rules, Jimbo," Ben said. "I'll just change them." He smiled. "Yeah, maybe I'll change more than one of them. We'll catch you later, kid."

"I'm not going anywhere."

They came back just in time for their own turn-up, so they stashed the bundle in their pulper. Judson and Dub snuck over and tried to get a peek, but The Flamer appeared out of nowhere and shooed them away.

When it came time to divide up the magazines, Devoid, Ben, and Jimmy each took theirs, but when Judson stepped up to take his, Ben held up his hand. "There's been a little change in the rules."

"Oh," Judson said. "And what change is that?"

"Well," Ben said. "We figure that Geno would have been with us on our excursion if he was still on our crew. Of course, he was stuck back here, chained to Number Four through no fault of his own, so we want him to get the next shot."

An easy grin crossed Judson's face. "Why not," he said. "Change is good. After you, son." He twirled his stick over the magazines like a magic wand.

Gene stood up and leafed through the pile, the usual mixture of grainy, black-and-white photos and lurid headlines: HANDCUFFED TO THE BED AND PANTING, I WAS A SHAMELESS, COCK-HUNGRY SLUT. He grabbed a couple and moved away. He checked out the pictures and then turned back to the first article. He remembered how his friends in high school used to joke about reading *Playboy* for the articles. The truth is, the stories in these were so insane, they actually were the best part.

He heard the guys behind him, Judson and Hawkins and Dub all taking their turns with the usual hoots and catcalls, but suddenly, everything got quiet. Gene looked up.

Hood stood in front of the table, leaning over to grab a paper. Ben slapped his hand over Hood's, pinning it down.

"What the fuck?" Hood said, pulling his hand away.

"You know, Hood, this is my show, and I'm thinking I don't want you involved."

Hood laughed. "Are you shitting me, Ben?"

"No. I'm just wondering why I should let you read my magazines when you're fucking up my plans for the crews."

"They're not your magazines, Ben," Hood said.

"Technically, no, but me and Jimmy and Devo are the ones that found them and got them here, so that should count for something."

"So why don't we ask Jimmy and Devoid what they think?"

"Why don't we?"

Ben glanced at Jimmy, who was standing right beside him. Jimmy grinned and made a thumbs down sign. Devoid did the same.

"And what about Wheeler?" Hood asked. "He's the one who I switched with. Why don't you ask him if he gives a flying fuck? Maybe he's glad to get away from you but doesn't have the balls to say so."

Passing Time

Oh, Jesus, Gene thought. First, Hood had fucked him over, and now, he was trying to mess up things between Ben and Gene. Gene sure knew how to pick his friends.

"So, what do you say, Wheeler?" Ben said. "The Hood wants your opinion on this, too. I guess he's got a short memory, since it's been less than four hours since he royally fucked you over and stole your job. What do you say, should I let him have a turn?"

Gene remembered the first nights when Hood had helped him out, their nightly joint, the party on the mountain. Still, he'd sold Gene out in a heartbeat to get away from Hawkins.

"Earth to Wheeler," Ben said.

"Fuck him," Gene said. "Let him read the world news."

"That's the spirit," Ben said.

Hood stared at Gene in disbelief. Gene glared back. "Let's read us some por-no-gra-phy," he said.

They moved over to the smoking area and began their usual routine of reading and comparing stories. Ben was in rare form, almost giddy. Gene glanced over to the winder for Number Four, where everyone was reading quietly, as if the incident with Hood had taken some of the fun out of things. Hood, himself, was sitting beside them, grimly reading his spy novel. Dub looked over, and when he saw that Ben wasn't looking, he slid one of his magazines over to Hood. Hood shook his head, then spit, the huge, wet glob landing right in the middle of the page.

The horn sounded. Gene looked up and saw a break in the sheet. "Shit," he said as he folded up the paper so he could stick it in his pocket, but Ben held out his hand. "I'll hold on to that for you, kid," he said. "We wouldn't want it to fall into the wrong hands."

Later, Gene sat with Dub at the picnic table. Dub offered him some macaroni and cheese.

"Did it come from a box?" Gene couldn't help asking.

"Of course not." Dub explained the elaborate process his Ma used, complete with hand graters and double boilers and one particular wooden spoon that had been in the family for years. If his Ma had heard Gene suggest that it came from a box, she probably would have whipped him with that spoon.

As Dub explained, they turned up on Number Five. After they racked the roll and took the samples, Ben crawled under the winder with Hood. Gene realized that he was going to shadow Hood just the way Hawkins had done the last few days on Number Four.

Ben played the part of Hawkins perfectly. He even had the facial expressions down. Ben followed Hood to the back when they tore off the sheet and trailed him all the way to the pulper, where Hood finally wheeled around and got right up in his face. "What the fuck is your problem, Ben?"

Ben smiled innocently. "No problem. Just doing my job."

"Your job. Since when is watching me part of your job?"

"It's always been," Ben said. "The Flamer is the top man on the crew, but he's down at the other end. Everything down here is my responsibility, even you." He waved his arms in a sweeping gesture that took in everything around them.

"And how is it that you never worried about this before?"

"I was lax in my duties," Ben said. "But I've seen the light." He nodded toward the slab of broke that Hood had dropped when he'd turned to confront Ben. "We really shouldn't be gabbing, you know. You've got work to do. We can discuss it some more if you get caught up."

"You mean when I get caught up, asshole."

"Whatever."

Hood dove into the opening for the pulper, and Ben came back toward the table. He winked at Gene, and his hand flashed out just as he went by the table. Gene thought he had grabbed his lunch pail, but it was still there. Then he saw that Hood's was gone.

Judson turned up, and they went over with the others to get samples. Looking back toward the table, he saw Ben jawing with Devoid. Hood's lunchbox was back.

The next time the machines were in synch, Gene went back to the table with Dub. Hood turned his back on them. He took out his tape deck and punched the Play button. Nothing happened. "Damn," he muttered. "It's dead. This goddamn thing eats batteries. I just put in new ones." He opened the battery compartment. It was empty.

"Jesus," said Dub. "You weren't kidding. It really does eat batteries." Hood threw it back into his lunch pail in disgust.

Passing Time

"Fucking Ben," he said.

Gene tried to hold back a grin but couldn't.

Hood caught him. "You're loving this aren't you, Wheeler?"

"You're the one who had to get away from Hawkins and his team."

"So you think I deserve this bullshit?"

"You said it."

Hood shook his head. "Do you really think I'm going to give up my spot because Ben doesn't like me, Wheeler? No fucking way. I got seniority, and I'll work where I damn well please. Goddamn Ben. Goddamn pretty-boy, candy-ass motherfucker. You'd think a grown man would have better things to do with his time than this junior-high bullshit. I ain't going anywhere, Wheeler. I'll do my job and mind my own business. We'll meet the specs, and Supry will keep us together. Ben's going to have to do a lot better than this if he wants to get rid of me."

Gene smiled. Somehow, he knew that Ben was just warming up.

Ben shadowed Hood constantly the next day, calling him on even the tiniest mistakes he made. "Pretty soon, he'll be giving me a grade on my penmanship when I mark the rolls," Hood muttered as he threw himself back down at the table.

Dub grinned. "He'll probably set up a blackboard and have you write the alphabet five hundred times."

"There really is no excuse for those sloppy a's you've been turning out," said Judson.

"We can barely tell the difference between your d's and your b's," added Hawkins.

Hood smiled and flipped open his lunch box. "Hey," he said, his smile fading. "What happened to my book?" They heard a loud whistle and looked over by the front of Number Five. Ben stood at the end of the pulper space, waving something over the opening. "Oh, for Christ's sake," Hood said, and Gene realized that Ben had Hood's book. When Ben saw they were all watching, he took a step back and tossed it into the pulper with a pretty, fade-away jump shot. He turned and took a bow. Jimmy and Devoid gave him a standing ovation. Hood shook his head. "Good thing it only cost me a buck-fifty," he said. "I'll just have to buy another one tomorrow."

"Better buy two," Hawkins suggested.

Hood held out until Friday. Ben followed him everywhere, but Hood had become a perfect worker. He'd left Number Four to get away from the fanatics there, but Ben was turning out to be even tougher. Hood never let his tape deck out of his sight but brought extra batteries, anyway. When Ben stole one of his books and dumped it in the pulper again, drop-kicking it this time, Hood didn't even blink, just went upstairs to the locker room and returned a few minutes later with another copy of the same book, saluting Ben with a flourish.

At seven o'clock, when everyone pulled out their quarters for poker, Hood slipped into the seat beside Gene. Gene gave him a dirty look, but he just glared back. There was the same uneasy silence there had been when Hood had stepped up to get his share of the porn tabloids. Gene glanced around the table, and everyone stared at Hood.

"Now what?" Hood said.

"Well," Ben said. "We've been talking."

We? Gene thought. He glanced over at Devoid and Jimmy, and they nodded as if on cue.

"We've decided that we don't want you in the game."

"Why the hell not? I've been playing with you guys since you started."

"We just don't feel the same about you since you fucked up the crews."

"Poker was never about which fucking crew a guy was on," Hood said.

"And it still isn't. Hawkins, Dub, and Wheeler are all welcome to stay in the game. This is about you being a back-stabbing punk."

Hood stood up. "This is just more of the same bullshit, Ben, but it isn't going to work. You couldn't pay me to play with you assholes, now." He looked at Gene, who couldn't meet his eyes.

"Why don't you play a hand to settle this?" Hawkins said.

"It's already settled," Ben said. "Hood's out."

"Maybe not," Hood said.

Hawkins came over and took the deck out of Ben's hands. "One hand," he said. "If Hood wins, he stays. If you win, he goes."

Passing Time

"I like it," Hood said.

"Sure, why not?" Ben said. "I could beat you in my sleep, you sorry little punk."

Hawkins held out the cards, and Ben tried to take them. Hawkins pulled them away. "Cut for the deal," he said.

Ben frowned. "What's the game going to be?"

"If you get the deal, you can call anything you want."

Ben cut the cards and got a jack of hearts. He smiled. Hood got the king of spades.

"What's the game?" Ben said. "It better be real poker. Something like seven-card stud. A man's game."

Hood got a wicked grin on his face. "Seven-card stud is for pussies," he said. "I call Indian poker."

"Oh, Jesus Christ," Ben said.

What the hell is Indian poker? Gene wondered.

Hood dealt each of them two cards face down. He looked up at Ben and nodded. Without looking at their cards, they lifted them up and plastered them to the middle of their foreheads with the faces showing, the bright colors like painted feathers. Hood had a pair of threes. Ben had the king of hearts and a four of clubs. Each focused on the other's cards for just a second and then their glances locked. They gazed into each other's eyes, searching, it seemed for a clue. Ben flicked his tongue over his lower lip. Hood broke into a huge grin and slammed a roll of quarters down on the table. "Ten bucks is the bet, motherfucker. Are you in?"

Ben slapped his cards down and began to count out ten dollars in quarters. "This shit ain't even poker. I should have known you couldn't play me man-to-man."

Hood laughed and got to his feet. "Don't worry," he said, "I'm still out. I just wanted to see you squirm." He glared down at Ben. "Cards and porn are one thing. Changing machines is another. See you at the winder, motherfucker." He gave him the finger with a grand flourish.

As Hood walked away, Dub shook his head.

"You got a problem with any of this, Dubster?" Ben asked.

"You better believe it," Dub said. "You should have told me you were going to dump Hood. I would have brought more money. He's the only guy here I could beat."

Chapter Eighteen

For several days, Gene stared at the books Staci had bought him before he finally picked one up.

She was registered for Great Works of Fantasy: Tolkien and C.S. Lewis. Since she wasn't around to tell him which to cover first, he chose *The Lord of the Rings* trilogy. The first book was slow going, but he forced himself to finish it. He wasn't sure why he bothered. Wasn't one of the advantages of being out of school not having to do things you didn't want to? Maybe he wanted to prove something to Staci.

The second book, *The Two Towers*, was a different story. He started it one night after work, a rare night off from The Bone, and read until dawn. He slept a couple hours and dived back in after lunch. At two-thirty, he stuffed it into his lunch pail and took it to work. He figured it would be a perfect way to pass the time.

He lucked out. The machines were running out of synch, so Ben and his gang were always working when he had a break. Every time they got back to the table, he had to run his rolls. Every time he had a break, he dived back into the book. He got annoyed every time he had to put it down.

At eight-thirty, the horn sounded, and he slammed the book down.

"Must be pretty interesting," Hawkins said.

"It's great," Gene said. "I can't wait to see what happens next."

Hawkins folded up his newspaper and shook his head. "What happens next," he said, "is that Number Four will pick up on this vibe you've got going with your book, and all hell is going to break loose."

"Oh, come on." Gene glanced toward the machine. Judson upped the speed and hit the air hose. The sheet inched up only a few inches before he cracked it with his stick. "Don't start with that 'the machines are jealous' crap again."

"It isn't crap. You'll see."

When the sheet snapped a half-hour later, Hawkins waited for him by the winder.

"I told you so," he said.

At the back of the machine, he took his post, and Judson took his at the end of the screen. He flicked his wrist, and the narrow strip of pulp flopped onto the first felt. He watched it for a moment, and then he held his fingers six inches apart. Gene eased the hose out.

They got the sheet easily through the presses and the first set of rolls. Gene watched them when they got down to the middle of the machine, but just as Judson ducked into the space between the rolls, Hawkins grabbed his arm and jerked him back. Saucier's accident flashed in Gene's mind: his body dangling from the side of the machine, jerked around like a rag doll.

Had Judson gotten careless and almost stuck his hand in the wrong place? They jawed back and forth. At first, Gene thought that Hawkins must be chewing him out for being so careless, but then Judson threw his head back and laughed.

Dub ducked in close to them, glanced Gene's way, and his face cracked into his full-face smile.

They stood in the aisle, waving their arms. Judson pointed toward Gene. Hawkins nodded and slapped Dub on the back. He broke away from them and headed Gene's way. When Dub got to Gene, he winked and smiled.

"You and I are switching places," he said. "I'll watch your stuff, you go down with them."

"Why?" Gene asked. "What's going on?"

"They'll tell you when you get there," he said. "Go on." He winked, his full-body variety.

Gene started toward them. What the hell was going on? Why did they want him to switch spots with Dub? They never usually messed with things like that. They stuck to the positions as if they were ranks in the army.

When Gene reached them, they each put an arm on his shoulder and drew him into a huddle. "Hawk tells me you caused this mess," Judson said. "You pissed off Number Four."

"Oh, come on," Gene said. "You can't be serious, Mr. Judson."

"Haven't you learned anything these last few months?"

"You made her jealous," Hawkins said. He patted one of the metal columns that supported the dryer rolls. "If you don't make amends, Wheeler, we'll be messed up for the rest of the night."

Gene didn't like the sound of this. They probably believed the machine was like a volcano and wanted to dump him into the pulper to appease her. At the very least, he could see his book taking the plunge.

"How the hell am I supposed to appease a machine?" Gene asked.

"She needs a little individual attention," said Judson.

"A little stroking." Hawkins broke the huddle and caressed a rough vein of metal on the column.

"What are you talking about?"

Judson wiped his forehead. He turned the gesture into a wild flourish. "We thought maybe you'd like to pass the sheet."

They'd thought wrong. This was a part of the job that even Hawkins had trouble with. That would certainly take all of Gene's personal attention.

"Come on," Judson said. "Show her you really care."

"Even if it is only for a couple seconds," Hawkins added.

"Quality time," Judson said.

Gene didn't seem to have any choice in the matter, so he slid between the rolls, then turned back to face Hawkins and Judson. The sheet tumbled off the roll about a foot across, flowing into the secondary pulper. Gene flexed his fingers just as Judson always did. Judson smiled and nodded. Gene grabbed the sheet, but couldn't even snap it. He only managed to divert its flow down to the floor, where his feet disappeared in a cascade of white. He stomped at it, trying to break it, but it was already out of control. He couldn't have screwed up any worse.

Judson nudged him aside, snapped the sheet as it came off the roll, and redirected it harmlessly down into the pulper. Gene kicked and pushed the pile of paper from his screw-up over the edge. He turned back to Judson only when the space was clean. Judson winked at him and motioned toward the sheet again.

On Gene's second attempt, he managed to break the sheet, but when he clutched it in his hand, it filled his palm like an explosion of ribbon candy, and then engulfed his chest and face, blinding him as he flailed out from under it and into the aisle.

Judson edged past him, smoothing the sheet back on the roll, guiding it back down into the pulper. The space filled up, but he pushed the loose paper out of sight.

"You're doing great," he said. He held his hand out before him with his thumb at a right angle to the rest of his fingers. He brought them together like the blades of a pair of scissors.

"You see?" he asked.

"Yeah, I think I do." Gene took a deep breath and slid back into place.

He drove his hand into the side of the sheet, clipped the edge with the web-space between his thumb and second finger and cracked it. He clutched the torn end with his fingertips, not blocking the flow with his hand but sending it on into the pulleys in one motion. It caught around the first roll and weaved through the next and the next, and he knew that it had worked, even before he glanced out at Judson, who pointed for Dub to go all the way out. It seemed like only a few seconds before the sheet spread out across the machine, a wide, flat roof above Gene's head. He leapt back out into the open, both hands clenched, waving at the sky.

"That was truly amazing, son," Judson said. "It was months before I made a pass that fluid." He held his hands high for Gene to slap. Gene unclenched his fists and slapped his open palms.

"I've never had one that good," Hawkins said.

"I got lucky," Gene said.

"Bullshit," Judson said. He took Gene's hands and studied them as if he wanted to tell his fortune. "You've got a great touch, kid," he said. "You've got a real future in this business."

They wouldn't let him get back to his book for the rest of the night. Even though they seemed sure that Number Four had been soothed by his touch, they didn't want to tempt fate. Besides, they were still buzzing about the way he'd passed the sheet.

Old Man Grenier came down from his end, and they gave him a play-by-play. Judson played Gene's part while Dub portrayed the sheet. He tumbled down to the floor at Judson's feet, circled around him, contorting himself into a jagged pile. Judson stomped him down and shoved him into the pulper. Finally, Dub flew past him, slithered up and down, in and out, around and around like the sheet in the dryers when Gene's pass had been successful.

Gene turned around, and Ben stood in the doorway. Ben didn't realize Gene had seen him, and his face was dark and ugly.

Gene tried seeing things through Ben's eyes: Judson waving his arms and pointing at Gene, Hawkins nodding, talking, touching his shoulder, Old Man Grenier roughing up his hair. Dub finally calmed down, collapsed at the table, and admired Gene, his eyes focused on him like a loyal golden retriever.

Ben saw that Gene was looking at him, and his face became his own again. He smiled. "So what's the party all about?"

"We let Wheeler pass the sheet," said Judson. "You wouldn't believe the hands on this boy."

"Smooth?"

"Smooth as silk," Dub said and sprawled, totally limp, on the surface of the table.

"It was a thing of beauty," Judson said. "I couldn't have done better myself."

Ben's eyebrows shot up. "Well, that is saying something." He glanced over at Gene. "Everybody knows that Jud's hands, in his opinion, at least, are the best ones in the house."

"No brag," Judson said. "Just fact."

"Well, kid," Ben said. "You really are moving up in the world. I hope you don't forget your friends when you get to the top."

"No chance of that, Ben," Gene said.

"Good. Then you can hang out with us for a few minutes."

"Actually," Judson said and glanced over at the roll. "We'll be turning up in a couple minutes."

"You're sure it's only a couple minutes?" Ben asked.

"A minute and a half, actually."

"Don't you want to measure?"

Judson shrugged.

"I don't have to," he said. "I've got eyes."

"And his eyes are just as good as his hands," Dub crowed. Judson tapped Dub's shoulder with his backtender's stick.

"Jesus," Ben said. "This mutual admiration society is a beautiful thing." He winked at Gene. "Maybe if you're really lucky, Wheeler, Jud will let you turn up."

"Now, that's a thought." Judson handed his stick to Gene. "Knock yourself out, kid."

"No way." Gene shoved the stick back toward him, but Judson held his hands up over his head and wouldn't take it.

"I can't—" Gene blurted out. "I won't—" He waved the stick toward Hawkins, but he shot his hands into the air. Dub did the same.

"I don't even know where to start," Gene said.

Judson's hand came over Gene's shoulder and took the stick back, rescuing him.

"I was just teasing, son," Judson said. "But your day will come. You're a natural." Dub and Hawkins grinned.

"Jud sure had you going," Hawkins said. Dub poked a finger into Gene's ribs and winked. Gene sighed with relief, knowing that his grin had to be at least as big as theirs. He turned to Ben, but he wasn't smiling. His face was grim again.

"What's wrong, Ben?" Gene asked.

"What could be wrong?" he said. "You and your boys are having a hell of a time. Everything's beautiful."

Judson sounded the horn on Number Four.

"You'd better go," Ben said. "Your crew is waiting for you."

Gene went to the winder and started it up. He pulled samples with the guys, and then slid under the winder and stared up at the spinning rolls, waiting for Hawkins to pass the sheet.

Why did Ben freak out every time the guys on the A-Team treated him right? Why couldn't he just be happy for him?

Hawkins passed the sheet, and Gene slid it up between the rolls. Dub's fingers snaked down and grabbed it. Gene rolled out and headed to the back. They broke the sheet off, and Hawkins started the roll. Gene went to the pulper.

He stood for a minute over the pit, watched the mixture churning ripples of white pulp. What the hell was Ben's problem, anyway?

The sheet broke, and he headed to the back of the machine. At least no one tried to blame the break on him this time. "What else do you want from me?" Gene mumbled to the machine as he moved through the stacks and took his position by the save-all.

"So," Old Man Grenier barked into his ear. "You did okay on your first pass. I hope you're happy working with us. I think we're going to have some fun."

"I'm not really sure," Gene said, glancing at the save-all, and then at Judson. "I got along pretty well with the guys on the other crew."

"That bunch of jerk-offs?"

"They're good guys," Gene said.

"What's that got to do with it?"

Judson followed the sheet through the first presses and waited by the dryer rolls. Gene liked watching him pass the sheet. His movements were so quick, so fluid.

"Save-all," Old Man Grenier said. Gene glanced down, and it was right on the edge. He yanked up on the handle and looked back toward Judson, who'd already passed the sheet along and needed him to go out to a two-foot width. He gently pulled the hose out.

"It's too bad about Hood," Old Man Grenier said. "I always thought he had potential, once you got past the hair and the music. I guess he's the one who couldn't get past it. Some kids just never grow up."

Gene shrugged. It seemed as if everyone had an opinion on this mess.

"It's funny, too, when you think about it," Old Man Grenier said, "how the union gets things backward. Take Hood. He's been here much longer than you, he's got experience and that's a valuable thing. We should be able to use that experience to get things running more smoothly. In the contract, though, experience becomes seniority, and that's something that Hood can use to get an easier job. The contract should be making him do the right thing, what's right for the job not for him, but it gives him a way out, instead." He shook his head. "How they've been able to make money in this place all these years is beyond me."

"Isn't that what The Company is saying now?" Gene said. "That they're not making money? Isn't that why there's a problem with the new contract?"

"That's what I hear."

Passing Time

"Do you believe them?"

He nodded. "But that's just between you and me and the old girl," he said, rapping his knuckles on the side of Number Four.

They got the sheet back through without incident. It seemed only a matter of minutes before Judson signaled him to go all the way out. They hadn't had any trouble in the middle this time. He told himself that Judson had probably passed the sheet for Hawkins.

He waited for a few minutes when he'd reached the end to make sure he wouldn't have to pull back. "I think we're safe," Old Man Grenier said.

"Thanks," Gene said. "See you later."

He held half a finger up to his lips. "Remember what I said about my opinion on the contract."

"Mum's the word."

At the front of the machine, things seemed to be running smoothly, and Dub had already hauled the broke to the pulper.

"Thanks, Dub," Gene said. "But you don't have to do that."

"Welcome to the real A-Team," Dub said.

Chapter Nineteen

Ben wanted everyone to go to The Bone after work. Gene wasn't in the mood, but he wasn't sure he could get out of it.

Ben had said he didn't want Gene on Number Four because he'd be stuck under Hawkins's thumb, but that was old news. Working with Hawkins and the other guys wasn't bad at all. Actually, it was fun. Sure, they were intense about the job, but that just made it more interesting.

Gene hated to admit it, but maybe Hood had been right after all. Maybe they were both in the right place. Not that he was going to tell Hood that. He couldn't tell Ben, either.

"You know, Ben," Gene said as they packed up to go home, "I think I'll just go home. I feel like hell."

"I don't know how many times I have to tell you, Geno," Ben said, "you just haven't built up a proper immunity to alcohol. You drink with us, but you don't drink enough. You need to drink yourself silly each and every night."

"Think quantity and quantity," Devoid said.

"Goddamn rookie," Jimmy mumbled.

"We'll make a man out of you, yet, kiddo," Ben said.

Gene walked out by himself at the end of the shift, hoping to get a little air before he dived back into Bone time.

Hood's truck idled by the guard shack. Gene thought he wanted to talk, but then Lisa got out on the passenger side, and Hood pulled away. "Hey," she said.

"Hey."

"There's a party up the mountain," she said. "I wanted you to come with us, but Hood's acting weird. What's up with him, anyway?"

"It's a long story," Gene said.

Passing Time

"He said I'm wasting my time asking you to come," she said. "That you'd be in trouble with your boys if you didn't go out drinking with them."

Gene shrugged. "They might not be too happy if I wimp out on them. Here they come."

Ben, Devoid, and Jimmy came through the gate. She took Gene's hand and squeezed it. "Let me handle this," she said.

"Hey, boys," she called to them.

Jimmy and Devoid grinned when they saw her. Ben didn't seem too happy.

"Can you believe this? I came down here to surprise Geno, and he tells me that he can't go out with me because he already promised to go out drinking with you guys."

"That's true," Ben said.

"Fucking stupid," Devoid said, "but true."

"I'll go out with you if he doesn't," Jimmy said.

Ben glared at him and shook his head. "I have never seen such a sorry, pussy-whipped bunch in my whole life. Pardon my French, little girl," he said.

"No problem," she said.

Ben held his frown for a minute but finally broke into a big grin. He grabbed Gene in a headlock.

"Get out of here," he said.

"We'll see you tomorrow, kid," Devoid said. "Have fun."

"Thanks so much," Lisa said and gave Ben a big hug. He actually blushed. Devoid winked at Gene.

"Where's my hug?" Jimmy said.

"Calm down, Stud," Ben said.

"Maybe some other time, Jimbo," she said.

"Where's your car?" she asked, after they'd pulled away.

"I don't have it," Gene said. "I always walk to work."

She laughed. "Hood knows that, doesn't he?"

"Oh, yeah."

"He's such a weasel," she said.

"You won't get an argument from me."

"You can walk me home. It's been a while since I did that with a boy."

"Okay."

As they walked across the parking lot, she slipped her arm into his. She wore a green men's shirt over a white T-shirt and cut-off jeans, her dark hair pulled back in a ponytail. She wasn't wearing any make-up, and she looked so young. Gene wondered what Jenna looked like without her custom paint job.

"Sorry you're missing out on the party," he said.

"I go to lots of those parties. Sometimes, they get old."

"That's how I feel about going to The Bone sometimes."

"They seem like a nice bunch of guys, though."

"They're okay. That's one of the good things about the job. It was rough, at first, but I get along with most everybody now."

"Except for Hood."

"Yeah, we got some shit going on."

"You want to talk about it?"

"Hood had trouble with the crew he was on, so he bumped me out of my slot. He had the right, he's been there longer than me, but everybody else was pretty happy with the way things were set up. My guys are giving him a hard time now."

"Typical," she said. "He fucked you over but acts like you messed with him. Serves him right if your friends are down on him."

"Sometimes, it sounds as if you don't like Hood much."

"What's to like? I put up with him because he's Jenna's man, but I don't have to like him."

"You know what's funny?"

"What?"

"I like working with my new crew. They're serious about the job, and they're starting to teach me. Hood told me that when he made the move. He said he didn't really think he was fucking me over. Still, it's hard for me not to think he sold me out."

"Let him sweat awhile," she said. "He might really believe you're better off where you are now, but he would have done it even if he didn't believe it. He's a weasel, and he always looks out for himself. You just got lucky if it worked out right for you."

The street took a wide, sweeping corner as it veered up the hill. Lisa took his hand and grabbed the fence that ran along the inside edge of the sidewalk. She pulled herself up the steep incline, dragging him along when he lagged behind. She sat on the top bar of the fence when they reached the top of the hill.

"So, what's going on with you and that girl from college?" She leaned forward, and her eyes fell behind the curtain of her hair.

"Not much," he said. "We had a fight last weekend, and I haven't talked to her since."

"Really? What happened?"

"She got tired of going out with a factory worker. School's her whole life, and she can't figure out what I'm doing here."

"That makes sense."

He reached out and brushed her hair out of her face so he could see her eyes.

"Weren't you the one who said you'd blow school off every chance you got so you could spend time with me?"

"That's just me," she said. "If she's serious about school, she had to take a stand. Why did you get out of school, anyway?"

He let her hair fall back into her face. She pushed it back, and he looked down at the sidewalk. "It just got weird for me. I bombed out in math. I didn't want to hang around and take courses I didn't really care about."

"You never told her you might stay here for a while?"

"We talked about it," I said. "She's just so into school, I guess she figured this life would get old real fast. She didn't think I'd like it here."

"But you do?" She took his hand and spread his fingers wide, then laced hers between them. "Aren't you itching to go back?"

"Not really. Things are going okay. I like the work. I like the guys. I get to learn from my new crew, and I still get to hang out with my old one. After the mess I was in last year, why should I go back right away?"

"Sounds good to me."

"That's the problem. I'm happy here, and she's happy in school. Doesn't do much for us as a couple."

She squeezed his hand. She leaned into him, took his head in her hands, and turned his face to hers.

"Her loss. My gain." They kissed.

They climbed down from the fence and walked the rest of the way to her house in silence, still hand in hand.

She led him down the walk to the front steps. She sat down and pulled him down beside her. "Maybe she's just trying to get you to come back sooner. Maybe she's tightening the screws." She squeezed his arm. "I know I would."

"Make up your mind," he said. "One minute you'd ditch school for me, the next you'd be busting my balls."

"I'm just teasing. I'm not much of a ball-buster." She leaned into him, and he could feel her breath on his neck. He turned to her, and they kissed again, their tongues twisting around each other. He brushed his hand across the front of her shirt. She sighed, pulled his hand away, and stood, leading him around into the darkness along the side of the house. He pressed her up against the wall and kissed her again, sliding his hand down the front of her jeans.

They pulled apart, both gasping for breath. "Why don't I walk you home," she said.

He couldn't hide the confusion on his face.

"We can get your car," she said.

Chapter Twenty

Hawkins was the first person Gene saw on Friday afternoon. He sat at the picnic table reading the orders. Gene sat down beside him and leaned back against the wall. It had been quite a week. Monday night with Lisa had been great. He'd been to The Bone with the guys every night since. He hated to admit it, but Ben's immunity theory seemed to be working. He'd been up until almost four and didn't feel half-bad.

He leaned over and read the order over Hawkins's shoulder. Talk about leading a double life. Stay up all night, and then come back to work ready to go. Work hard. Play hard. Now there was a concept.

Today, they would ship rolls to Blodget Business Forms in Hilldale, Illinois. "Do we have to make any changes in the paper tonight?" Gene asked.

"No," Hawkins said. "Blodget is one of our biggest customers. Sometimes, they keep us going for a whole week on just one grade of paper. Piece of cake, really."

"I wonder what they do with the paper that we send to them," Gene said.

"Well, if they're making business forms, they're cutting the paper down to size, punching holes, stuff like that. Their machines must be like the winder, only with a lot of blades and punches and special attachments."

He laid the order back on the table. Gene thought he would get out a magazine or newspaper, but he turned back to him.

"There used to be a division like that in The Company. It was called the Cutting Room. They phased it out in the late fifties. The real money is in bulk production."

"There must be a lot of money in this," Gene said, "if we can support everybody else on the payroll."

"The guys who work down here have always carried The Company," Hawkins said. "It makes you feel good, doesn't it?"

Gene had to admit he was right.

"What makes you feel good, Wheeler?" Ben said. He'd walked up behind them, Devoid and Jimmy on either side. He pulled a copy of the weekly paper from the top of the pile in the middle of the table. "Tell us what it is, and we'll be sure to do it more often."

"Just more talk about the job," Gene said.

Ben shook his head. "I'm starting to worry about you, kid." He peeled off the front page and tossed it to Hawkins. "Big news on page one, Blondie. I'm sure Jud will want to be alerted."

Hawkins glanced down, then got up and headed over to the front of Number Four, where Judson sounded the roll.

"What's the big news?" Gene said.

"Just union bullshit," Ben said. He winked. "Nothing new, really. I just wanted to get rid of Blondie." He sat down beside Gene and flipped to the sports page.

"So, are you coming to tryouts tomorrow, Wheeler?"

"I guess so," Gene said. "I hadn't realized it, but I miss playing sports the way I did in school."

"Is that the only thing you miss?"

"I miss my girl," he said.

"But that little chickie Hood fixed you up with must be helping ease that pain," Ben said.

Jimmy frowned.

"You know that Jimmy wishes he was getting some of that," Devoid said. He seemed to be enjoying Jimmy's pain.

"What about the rest of school?" Ben asked. "The classes and the teachers and all that shit?"

"I can live without it."

"Not much higher learning going on around here."

"There's enough," Gene said. "I'm learning a little about the machines. That's fun."

Ben frowned. "Better watch out, Geno. We don't want you getting all smug and serious about this. It's bad enough we gotta put up with Blondie and his disciples. We don't want you going over to that side."

"Don't worry about that, Ben. I know who my friends are."

Passing Time

And he knew who his crewmembers were. He wondered if he'd ever be able to get Ben to understand that he wanted both.

"Need a ride home, Wheeler?" Ben said when they got out of work.

"Home?" Gene said. "Aren't we going to The Bone?"

"We're in training. We go straight home to bed on Fridays from now until the playoffs. And remember, Devo," he said as he leaned out the window, "we are going home to sleep, not to bed down our wives, but to sleep. We will need our legs in the morning."

"Jesus, Ben," Devoid said. "It's only tryouts."

"You'd better watch out, boy," Ben said. "Do you want to lose your spot to some young stud who kept his dick in his pants tonight? Wheeler, for example."

"Maybe Wheeler's getting laid tonight, too," Devoid said.

Gene shook his head. "Tomorrow."

Devoid chuckled. "The boy grows on you."

Gene got up early on Saturday to get ready for tryouts. He made coffee. He checked the mail. He did a double take at a small purple envelope addressed with Staci's sure handwriting. He took a deep breath and opened it.

She might just as well have written it on a post card: "Greetings from Academia. Wish you were here."

She was keeping busy. The books she read were fascinating, and her classes were so alive. Her advisor treated her more like a colleague than a student. They had lunch together every day. He frowned. He had worried about her dating Daniel. Maybe he should have thought about Doc Ellis, instead. Gene had heard the guy wasn't above sleeping with his best students, and Staci was the best.

He sipped his coffee and read a bit more between the lines.

"This is where I am," she seemed to say. "So, where the hell are you?"

Tryouts were at the field just across from The Company. When the wind blew the wrong way, a thick cloud from the smokestacks hung over everything, making them taste every breath they took. Ben didn't seem to mind. "Don't you just love it?" he asked, inhaling deeply.

This was serious business. Billy coached, and all the returning players had T-shirts and heavy, hooded sweatshirts, with the bar's logo on the back and its name in thick red letters on the dark-blue fabric. "If you make the team, you get a T-shirt," Dub explained. "But you don't get the sweatshirt until your second year. We can't give them to just anybody, you know."

Billy ran them for twenty minutes before they started football drills. Gene saw a couple guys throw up before the running ended. He couldn't believe that Ben, Devoid, and Jimmy had so much stamina. They weren't even breathing heavy when Billy blew the whistle.

Ben told Gene he had a good chance to make the team as a back-up cornerback. What made Dub such a great receiver made him useless on defense, so Billy always carried extra cover guys. When Ben told Gene he might also see time on special teams—kick-offs and punts—he knew these guys weren't fooling around. It bothered him that if he went back to school next year, he wouldn't qualify for a sweatshirt. Maybe Ben would get him one.

After tryouts, they went to The Bone for lunch. Gene didn't know Billy served lunch, but then again, he hadn't been up in time for lunch in a long time. "We'll have a few beers this afternoon," Ben said, "but the real celebration is tonight, after work. By then, Billy will have posted the rosters."

"I can't come back tonight, Ben," Gene said. "I already made plans."

"Listen, Geno, from now on the weekends are all about football."

"I didn't know that when I made my plans."

"Which is why we'll let it pass this time. Starting next week, though, you have to get with the program. It's all part of being on the team, right guys?"

"Right," said Jimmy.

Devoid leaned over and whispered in Gene's ear. "Enjoy tonight, kid. It's hard to work and play flag football and still have time to get a piece of ass every now and then when you're single. I don't think I could handle it, anymore."

"Hey, hey," Ben said. "No whispering. We're a team here, aren't we?"

Billy brought out a scrapbook that had all of the teams from the last ten years. Jimmy and Dub had only been playing for a couple years, but Devoid and Ben were in all the pictures. "See what a handsome, young devil I was," Ben said.

Gene shrugged. Ben was still handsome, of course. Was it possible he didn't know it? Gene wasn't going to tell him. Ben pulled the book away and made the rounds of the bar, asking everyone else the same question. Every one of them followed Gene's lead and ignored him. Ben kept getting louder and louder until Devoid couldn't stand it anymore and burst out laughing. Soon, everyone in the bar was having a good laugh on Ben, and for once, he seemed more than happy to oblige. Gene sat back in the corner and sipped his beer. He remembered the first time he'd come here, how everyone drank so seriously. He glanced at the black paint on the windows just over his shoulder. It was dark in the bar, even though they'd left a crisp, fall sun outside.

What would he write if he were sending a post card to Staci about his life?

Greetings from Great Northeastern Paper.
Wish you were here.

He looked around. The weekend stretched before him: lunch and a few beers with the guys, work, a date with Lisa. Tomorrow would be football practice and more beers. On Monday, he'd be back at work, shooting the shit with these guys, working with Hawkins and Dub, Judson, and Old Man Grenier, learning more about the job. Maybe Judson would even let him turn up.

He'd leave out the part about Lisa and the party, of course, but the rest might go like this:

Dear Staci,

Things are going well. I'm working with a new crew. You remember Hawkins, the guy I fought with the first few days. Turns out, he's just crazy about this job. All the guys on my team are. That might sound like a problem, but it's okay. They want to teach me what they know. I think it might be fun.

There's another group of guys from work. They're the ones I hang with after hours. They aren't crazy about their work, but they know everything there is to know about loyalty and having fun.

Ron Roy

I don't know what the future holds, Staci. I just know that this life is how I'm passing time. Maybe it'll make me a better person when I get back in the game.

Chapter Twenty-One

Work was a bitch on Monday. Gene couldn't remember when they'd had it so bad. They switched grades in the paper at five-thirty, and even though there didn't seem to be much of a difference in the color and weight, they couldn't keep a sheet in the machine. They had half a dozen false starts, and Gene knew they'd have to trash most of the first roll when they got it off.

On the wet end, Judson tried to pass the sheet for what seemed like the hundredth time. When he finally got it, he stormed toward the middle without signaling to Gene and almost ran over Ben.

"Jesus Christ, Ben," Judson bellowed, waving his stick. "Don't I have enough to worry about without you looking over my shoulder?"

Ben jumped aside and threw his hands in the air as if the stick were a loaded gun. "Come on, Jud," he said. "You know I'd never second-guess you. I just thought my boy Geno might be thirsty."

He held up a can of soda. Beads of moisture formed on the metal and dripped down the side.

Judson dismissed Ben with a flick of the stick and walked away. Ben held the soda out to Gene. "I figured you could use this."

"Thanks a lot." Gene took the can and held it against his cheek for a few seconds, then took a long drink.

"Don't think I've ever seen Old Man Grenier have this much trouble with such a routine change," Ben said. "Maybe the old fart is losing his touch."

"There must be something wrong with the stock before it gets to us," Gene said.

He drained the can with his second swallow and crushed it under his heel.

Ben shrugged. "The old man isn't perfect," he said. "He just thinks he is. Of course, that seems to be a common ailment with the guys on your crew. I don't know how you stand them sometimes."

"It's not so bad. They just want to do things right, that's all."

Ben scooped up the can, wheeled around, and tossed it into the trash with a smooth fade-away jumper.

"There's right and there's right, kiddo," he said. "Be careful. Before you know it, you'll be walking around with your nose as high in the air as Blondie's. You won't be able to associate with the likes of me."

"Come on, Ben," Gene said. "I work with these guys. I hang with you and Jimmy and Devo. You're making it into something it's not, like I have to make a choice."

Ben threw up his hands. "I'm not asking you to make a choice, Geno. I just figure the fanatics around here might force the issue. I just want you to remember who your friends are."

The horn sounded at the other end of the machine, and Judson waved to take the sheet all the way out. Ben mimicked his motion perfectly, saluted, and headed back to the other end.

As he walked away, Gene thought about what he'd said, that it was Gene's new crew, the fanatics, who wanted him to choose. The same little voice that said they were the best workers reminded him that they didn't give a shit what he did after work. Hell, they didn't even care what he did between rolls. Ben was the only one who seemed to care. Why did he have to make everything personal? Why couldn't he just let it be?

When they finally got the paper to stay on the reel, Gene watched, with mixed feelings, as the roll grew steadily. He knew that unless it stayed on, things would never settle down. Still, there was so much junk on the bottom, they'd probably strip it and throw it in the pulper. Every minute it stayed on was going to be more work for him.

Old Man Grenier and Judson had that same debate. "For Christ's sake, Old Man," Judson said, "turn up the goddamn roll. The kid's going to be hauling broke for the next month at the rate she's going."

"That's how long he'll be hauling it if I don't get this shit straightened out," Old Man Grenier said. He glanced over at the roll and seemed to gauge the size. "Right now, it's only about a half-hour's work." Easy for him to say, Gene thought.

It was another ten minutes before he finally gave Judson the okay to turn up. They set the roll on the floor. No winder for this baby. Hawkins pulled samples, but Judson and Old Man Grenier stayed right at the front, studying the new roll.

"I think we got her licked, boy," Old Man Grenier said, suddenly near Gene's ear. "Mark my words. You're better off the way I handled it. I'm going to go back down and double-check everything, but I think it's smooth sailing now."

Judson walked across the length of the roll, thumping it with his stick. Gene could hear the soft rhythmic thumps, as steady as a beating heart.

"I think he's right," Judson said and pulled a huge handkerchief from his pocket. He wiped his forehead. "And not a moment too soon."

Gene felt a hand on his shoulder. It was Hawkins. "Let's go sit down while we can," he said. "We'll get to that later." He nodded toward the garbage roll.

Hawkins surprised Gene by walking right by the table and out to the loading dock. It was already dark.

"What the hell time is it?" Gene asked.

Hawkins laughed and showed him his watch. It was almost nine. That was the longest it had ever taken them to change an order.

Hawkins sat down on the edge of the concrete platform. He seemed out of place out here. Hood pulling out a joint, sure. Ben scooting off the edge, then hightailing it across the railroad tracks in search of porn, of course. Somehow, Hawkins belonged back at the picnic table with his nose in a magazine.

"Maybe we shouldn't get so comfortable," Gene said as he slid down beside Hawkins. "The way things have been going, I don't think we should trust the sheet."

"It'll be okay," Hawkins said.

"You heard Old Man Grenier and my big buddy," said Dub, who came through the doorway behind them. He sat down beside them and dangled his legs off the edge of the dock.

Hawkins slapped Dub on the back and turned toward Gene.

"I know you heard what Jud and Old Man Grenier said, Wheeler, but you also heard the machine."

"What do you mean?"

"Don't deny it," Hawkins said. "I saw your face when Judson sounded the roll. The thumps were even all the way across. You knew right then we'd be all right."

"Yeah," Gene said. "I guess I did." He smiled. Maybe Ben was right. Maybe he was turning into a fanatic.

A breeze came up and blew in their faces. Gene shivered as the cold air hit the sweat all over his body.

"We're in the wrong end of this business," Hawkins said as he turned his face into the wind. "We should have been lumberjacks."

At ten-thirty, Supry came through the door with the grimmest look on his face that Gene had ever seen. He wondered if the entire night crew had called in sick. Maybe they'd all been killed in a multi-car pile-up. Supry walked over to Number Four, blasted the whistle, and waited as The Flamer and Old Man Grenier scrambled into view. He waved for them to come on down, then motioned for everyone else to come to the table.

"I just got word from the union," Supry said as he worried the piece of paper in his hand. He fiddled with his bow tie. Gene expected him to start snapping his suspenders any minute.

"Negotiations have just broken off," Supry said. "The Committee has called a strike vote and is recommending that you walk."

As Gene looked around the table, he saw a dozen different emotions flit across the faces. Hawkins looked angry, but most of the others seemed anxious. Judson ran his fingers through his hair. Dub's tongue darted over the tight line of his lips.

Gene glanced over at Devoid, who looked as if he was in pain. Gene figured the hardest part for Devoid would be explaining all this to his girl, maybe suffering through a string of lonely Friday nights if she didn't like the way he voted. Hood's face was white. He never saved a penny, just lived from week to week. How long before the bank took back his truck? How long before his dealer cut him off?

Ben's face showed exhilaration. He obviously relished the fight to come.

Passing Time

"This is so much bullshit," Hawkins said.

Ben wheeled toward him.

"What the hell is that supposed to mean, Blondie?"

"Just what I said. They can't be serious. They can't expect us to walk out over the things they're down to."

He slammed his newspaper down on the table. Ben picked it up, rolled it into a tight wand, and pointed it in Hawkins's face.

"One of the concessions The Company wants is layoffs, Blondie. We're talking about people's jobs here."

"Layoffs?" Hawkins said, not backing down. "They're offering early retirement and generous severance packages. And the jobs they're talking about are jobs the union created years ago to pad the payroll. They're the reason The Company is losing money. I've got nothing in common with people like that. I don't owe them a thing."

"You pompous son of a bitch," Ben said. "Who the hell are you to talk like that about your union brothers?" Ben jabbed the newspaper in Hawkins's face, barely an inch away. If he was excited about a fight with The Company, then Hawkins would make a good warm-up bout.

"My union brothers?" Hawkins held out his hand for the newspaper. Ben slapped his hand away. Hawkins shrugged and shook his head. "Give me a break, Ben. The guys in maintenance have been riding on our backs their whole frigging lives, and they wouldn't get off their sorry butts to piss on us if we were on fire."

"Well," Dub said, "they might if they're not on break."

Every head in the room turned toward him. Ben glared. Dub blushed and looked at the floor.

"Gentlemen, gentlemen." Supry took advantage of Dub's interruption. He pulled out a handkerchief and rubbed his forehead. "We just have a difference of opinion here, that's all," he said. "We have to air those differences, get them out in the open. Once the decision is made, that's when we have to form a united front. For now, we have to state our opinions, and more importantly, we have to listen to everyone else's. That's how brothers treat each other."

Supry glared at Ben.

"Dale's right," Judson said. He stood away from the table,

towering over all of them.

"So, let's hear it." Ben set the newspaper back down in the middle of the table. Hawkins scooped it up and smoothed it out in front of him.

"I think the union is asking for too much this time, both from The Company and from us," Judson said. Hawkins nodded. Dub did the same but used his whole body. Jimmy and Devoid sat as still as dead men. Gene thought if he flicked his fingers at them, they would have gone over backwards and tumbled to the floor. Hood didn't look any better.

"You and the union want me to risk my job, so others can sponge off The Company until the day they die, or until The Company goes under, whichever comes first," Judson said.

"The Company isn't going under," Ben said. "That's just a smokescreen, for Christ's sake. Divide and conquer, that's their plan. They'd be dancing up in the boardroom right now, if they could hear you. This is just what they want. They want to turn us against our own kind."

As he spoke, he pulled out his stick and rolled it on the table in front of him. Gene expected him to start waving it in Judson's face, like he'd done with the newspaper and Hawkins, but he didn't. Of course, Judson had his own stick. He could fight back.

"Listen to yourself, Ben," Judson said. "You're spouting bullshit you learned at your grandfather's knee. It isn't the worker versus the bosses, anymore, it's the people who work versus the people who don't, and just because a guy uses his brain instead of his back, that doesn't mean he's our enemy."

This was good stuff. There was nothing backward about Judson's thinking. Ben was the one living in the past.

"Think, man," Judson said. "Divide and conquer? That's what the union's been doing for the last ten years. They drive a wedge between us and management, and we're the ones who lose."

"Gentlemen," Supry said. He plucked at his suspenders as if they were the strings on a bass. "I think it would help if we stuck to the facts."

"The facts?" Ben said. He seemed puzzled.

"What's being offered in the contract," Supry said. He gave his suspenders a rest and laid his piece of paper on the table. He glanced at his notes and realized for the first time that he had crumpled the paper up beyond recognition. He smoothed it out on the table.

"In terms of basic issues," he read, "The Company has been very fair. There is an across-the-board raise of ten percent—"

"For anybody who actually gets to keep their job," Ben said.

"All right, Ben," Supry said, as blood crept up the back of his neck. "You had your chance. For now, just listen."

"Yeah," Dub said. "How can we vote if we don't know what the vote's about?"

"It's about concessions, Dubster." Ben bristled at having to state the obvious. "And what concessions are about is giving up that first inch and finding out before you know it that you've given up a mile."

"Well," Supry said, "so much for listening to the facts or an exchange of ideas." He crumbled up his scrap of paper and tossed it on the floor. "The vote is the day after tomorrow at the union hall. The polls open at seven a.m. We should have the results by midnight. I don't want to hear another word about it until then. Is that understood?" He looked at each man and held their eyes until they nodded. He turned and headed for the door.

"Brothers, my ass." Supry threw the words back at them as he walked away.

Ben was in rare form when they got to The Bone. He stood guard in the booth by the door. Everyone who came though the door got sucked in, and Ben wouldn't let them leave until they stated their position. There were more people in the place than Gene had ever seen before.

Things seemed to be running pretty much fifty-fifty. With each vote, Ben got more sullen. Gene didn't get it. "It sounds to me like it's got a pretty good chance."

Ben shook his head. "You need a two-thirds majority to call a strike. I don't think it's going to happen."

Later, Gene went to the bathroom and stopped by the bar to get another round. "What do you think about all this, Billy?" he asked.

"Good for business."

"I can see that. What do you think about the strike vote?"

Billy looked down at the bar and swiped at a stain on the surface.

"Never ask the owner of a small business how they feel about unions and strikes," he said. "People always ask me what's the best thing about owning my own business, and I tell them it's being my own boss. When they ask me what the worst thing is, I tell them it's being my own boss."

Gene nodded. "I guess this must all sound pretty crazy to you."

"Damn right it does. I wear a dozen hats in this place just to get things done, and here's a bunch of grown men telling the whole world how unfair it is for them to have to do an honest day's work. Don't get me wrong, I'll take a man's money however he came by it. I just think it's funny sometimes."

Ben dropped Gene off at four a.m. He had rallied a little toward the end of the night. With just the regulars in the bar, there was no one to argue against his point of view.

"I think we might pull it off, Geno. It's going to be close, but I think we might just get it done."

Ben idled his truck as Gene climbed down from the cab.

"Do you think it'll be a long strike, Ben?"

"Hell, no." He gunned the engine. "The Company doesn't have the stomach for it. They don't have the cash reserves."

"You mean they really might be in trouble?"

Ben shrugged. "I guess we'll find out, won't we?"

Ben drove away, and Gene was more confused than ever. If The Company might really be in trouble, what the hell were they doing? He shook his head. He'd taken this job because he wanted to get away from his problems at school, but every time he turned around, this job was throwing more problems at him, telling him he had to make hard choices. Wasn't it enough that he had lost Staci? Now, he was supposed to throw the job away, as well.

Either way, he was screwed. If The Company went under, then he'd have no job, but even if it survived, and the strike dragged on for months, he'd be out of school and out of a job.

Still, this place wasn't really his life, his livelihood. He didn't have bills to pay, a family to support. He had to wonder what a strike would do to the rest of the guys. He had to wonder why Ben didn't worry about that.

Passing Time

Maybe Ben really did believe that standing by all his principles was the most important thing, even if it ruined the very brothers he professed to be standing by.

Chapter Twenty-Two

The union hall was packed, the crowd polarized. Strikers and anti-strikers lined up against the opposite walls of the room. The undecideds milled around uneasily in the middle. Gene stuck with Ben and his gang but made eye contact with Hawkins across the room. He glanced at Ben, then back to Gene and shrugged his shoulders. Gene figured he understood.

When Gene got into the booth, he stared at the board for a long time. He thought about Ben and his call for brotherhood. He remembered how much Ben had helped him those first few days on the job. Where would Gene be without Ben? Most likely, he'd be sitting at home with his tail between his legs. Of course, that's what Ben wanted them all to do now, sit at home. He heard Ben's voice in his head: 'But we sure as hell won't be doing it with our tails between our legs.'

He thought about what Ben had said the night before. He didn't think The Company had the stomach for a strike, that they didn't have the reserves. Didn't that contradict everything he said? Didn't that mean that The Company was really in a fix?

And what about the union? Sure, they'd been about fairness when they'd started out, but things had swung too far. Maybe they were out of whack. The contract should protect the men, but it shouldn't let them play games with their work. Maybe this vote wasn't really about concessions but about getting things back in synch, in balance. Gene thought of all the times he'd heard people talk about what they needed from their jobs, but he couldn't remember ever hearing anyone talk about what their jobs needed from them.

He punched NO STRIKE and pulled the lever.

"Well, I'm glad that's over," Ben said, as they climbed into his truck and headed to work.

Passing Time

Gene knew his next question should be how Ben thought the vote would go, but he was afraid that would lead to how he'd voted. He didn't have to worry.

"Nothing like a strike vote to get everybody crazy," Ben said, "but now, we get back to business."

"Business?"

"Sure, the day-to-day stuff."

"Like what?"

He reached out and ruffled Gene's hair.

"Like getting you back on the crew with us, where you belong."

They parked in the employee lot and crossed the footbridge. The day crew streamed past them on their way to the union hall. Ben shook a hundred hands, smacked his fists against a hundred more, but Gene knew these were union guys. There was no debate now, just confirmation that they were still on the same team.

They stopped in the middle of the bridge. The water slashed between the granite walls. The mist swirled around them. Ben leaned on the pipes and stared into the distance. "Don't get me wrong, Geno," he said. "I'll be mad as hell if the scabs win this one and start us on the slow, downhill slide of concessions, but I know I've done everything I could. Time to move on. I've got a few tricks up my sleeve when it comes to ridding myself of The Hood, and it's time for me to play those cards."

Gene knew he should tell Ben to let it go. He was happy where he was, but Ben looked so happy now, talking about getting him back with the crew. Besides, what harm would it do to let this thing play out? Nothing Ben had done so far had really bothered Hood. Let him get this crap out of his system. In the end, they'd all be better off. Gene would be where he wanted to be while Ben thought he wanted to be with him.

At ten o'clock, Gene sat in the smoking area with Ben and the guys.

Hood sat on the winder, reading. He glanced up at the clock, closed the book, and slid out the door. Gene knew he was on his way to the loading dock. He still smoked his nightly joint, although Gene was no longer invited. Hood seemed to be back to that one hit, though, because even when he disappeared early in the evening, he came back with clear eyes. Maybe his problem really had been trying to measure up to Hawkins and the A-Team.

He'd been gone only a few minutes, when Ben turned to Devoid. "Have you seen Supry tonight?"

Devoid looked puzzled. "No."

Of course he hadn't; they never saw the guy. What was Ben up to? Gene wondered if he wanted news about the election, but the polls were open until ten so that the night crew would have one last chance to vote.

"You know," Ben said. "I miss old Dale. We don't see enough of him. He's always up in the office. He needs to get down here more often, mingle with the guys, take a more hands-on approach."

Gene didn't know what this was about, but with Ben, there was always a reason for everything.

"Yeah," Ben said, "I think we should find the guy, roust him out of that stuffy old office. Get him some air."

Ben stood up, and Jimmy and Devoid followed. Gene glanced over at Number Four, wondering if he had time to follow, but the machine was only a few minutes away from turning up. Ben knew that and gave Gene a sad smile. After they left, Gene tried to figure out what Ben was up to. Then it hit him. Ben wanted Supry to get some air.

He took one look at the machine and sprinted out the door and to the loading dock.

Hood dangled his legs over the edge of the dock, taking a long drag on a huge joint.

"Hood!" Gene yelled.

Hood looked up and smiled, then seemed to remember that they were on the outs. He frowned and turned away.

"You have to get back inside," Gene said.

"I didn't hear the horn."

"It isn't the horn."

"Then what is it? We're long past the point where you can get on me about smoking."

He turned his back on Gene and took another long drag on the joint. He held it in and then let out a thick cloud. "Besides, since I got away from Hawkins, I'm hardly smoking at all. A few hits here and there. Shit. Listen to me. Why am I explaining myself to you?"

"Ben just went up to Supry's office."

"So what? Those two assholes deserve each other." Hood turned back toward Gene, inhaled, and blew it out in his face.

"I think he's bringing him out here. I think he wants him to catch you."

"Jesus-H-Christ." Hood ground the joint out on the cement and flicked it out onto the tracks even though there was still half of it left.

"Come on, man," Gene said.

"I'm coming, I'm coming." Hood scrambled to his feet. They headed back in, but Gene heard Ben's laughter around the corner. He froze. He wanted to warn Hood, but he didn't want Ben to know he had. He grabbed Hood's arm. Hood stopped, puzzled, but when he saw Gene's face, he understood. He ducked into a boxcar and dragged Gene in after him.

They heard footsteps and Ben's voice.

"Didn't I tell you this would be fun, Dale? You need to get out of that office more. Smell that air. Odd, I think I smell something unusual. Do you smell it?"

"I don't smell shit," Supry said. "Just propane from the forklifts and diesel from the locomotives and the goddamn crap from the smokestacks. I don't know why I let you drag me out here, Ben."

"But don't you smell anything else? What about you, Jimmy?"

"If I didn't know any better, I'd swear I smelled pot," Jimmy said.

"Pot?" Supry said. "You mean dope? How the hell do you know what it smells like?"

"I was at a party once," Jimmy said. Gene could hear the confusion in his voice. He pictured the look on Jimmy's face as he looked to Ben for help. Hood snickered beside him.

"And I know you left that party as soon as you smelled that vile shit," Ben said.

"Oh, sure," Jimmy said, the smile back in his voice.

"Good boy," Supry said. "If I ever catch anybody with that stuff, they're history."

"Yes, sir."

They waited until Ben led Supry out to Hood's usual spot and then returned. Supry grumbled about what a waste of time this had been. Ben said the same, though Gene knew it was for a different reason.

When their voices had faded, Hood held out his hand. Gene took it and beat Hood to the punch, twisting it into Hood's patented handshake.

"I owe you, man," Hood said. "After all the shit that's gone down lately, I'm surprised you bothered. When you let Ben bust my chops about the porn and the poker game, I was sure you were never going to forgive me for taking your slot."

"You pissed me off," Gene said. "Hell, I'm still pissed off. I just don't want you to have to get fired for me to get my slot back."

"Amen," Hood said. "Still, I don't want you joining me on Ben's shit list, so we'd best not be seen walking back in together."

"That's for sure," Gene said, but now that Hood was safe, he remembered there had only been five minutes before turn-up when he left. He sprinted toward the room.

"That's right, man," Hood's voice faded behind him. "You go on ahead."

He ran into the room, and the sheet was already in the winder. Hawkins glared at Gene as he adjusted the controls and brought it up to speed. Dub wagged his finger as he came back from the pulper.

"This had better be good," Hawkins said. "Either somebody died, or you stopped that from happening."

"Or maybe you brought somebody back to life," Dub said. He took off his sailor's hat and crushed it in his hands.

"You're close," Gene said. He told them about Ben taking Supry out to the loading dock while Hood was smoking.

Hawkins shook his head.

"I knew Ben was ticked off, but I never thought he'd go that far. Supry would have fired Hood if he caught him in the act."

"Hood's just lucky you don't hold a grudge for stealing your slot," Dub said.

"Jesus," Gene said. "I wouldn't want to get it back that way."

Hawkins smiled. "You're off the hook, Wheeler," he said. "We'll forget about you being MIA when we turned up. You're a regular lifesaver. First, you saved Saucier's skinny neck, and now, you saved Hood's job. You're all right, kid."

"Thanks."

Gene turned around and saw Ben staring. What gives, Wheeler? his eyes seemed to say, and Gene had no answer for him. Fortunately, Number Five turned up just then and got him off the hook, though he knew it was only a temporary reprieve.

On the next roll, Ben leaned against their winder, chatting with Devoid when it was time to pull the shaft from their rolls. Jimmy grabbed the end and nodded for Hood to take it out. Hood backed away without looking, slamming into Ben, who had ducked down on all fours right in his path. Hood fell hard on his back, and the shaft went flying, careening around like it had that first day when Gene had misjudged its weight. Ben rolled out of its path and sprung to his feet with a big grin on his face.

"Pancake," Jimmy crowed, as if this were a flag football game and they'd just blocked Hood flat on his back.

"Jesus," Hood moaned. He covered his eyes with his arm. Ben hovered over him. "You really need to look where you're going, son." Hood pulled his arm away and glared at Ben. Ben held out his hand, but Hood slapped it away.

"Get away from me, you fucking lunatic."

"Now, now, Hood. Temper, temper. You should have checked behind you."

"You should have stayed the fuck out of my way."

"That's what I've been trying to tell you to do, punk. Stay out of mine."

Hawkins brushed past Ben, helping Hood up. He turned back to Ben.

"Up to now, your bullshit has just been annoying, Ben," he said. "Actually, it's been pitiful, but somebody could have been hurt here."

"Not me," Ben said. Devoid and Jimmy stood behind him, one at each shoulder.

"You're fucking with the man's job, Ben," Hawkins said.

"And he's fucking with my team."

"It's not the same," Hawkins said. "Let it be, Ben."

"Make me, Blondie."

"I don't have to," Hawkins said. He pointed toward the offices upstairs. "You stick to your penny-ante bullshit, Ben—the tape deck, the books—and it's no skin off my nose, but if you try another stunt like this, you'll be answering to Supry."

"I'm shaking in my boots." Ben faked a shudder. "As if he gives a shit about anything except our meeting specs and filling our orders."

Hawkins shrugged. "You know how he feels about accidents. The big boys are still riding him about Saucier. Imagine if Hood threw out his back because of your horseshit. It won't be good."

"It's my word against Hood's."

"Actually, it's my word, too."

"And mine," Dub piped in.

"And mine," said Judson. Ben looked at the three of them and glanced back at Jimmy and Devoid standing just behind him. He nodded to Gene, sure that he'd balance everything out, four against four, a stalemate.

Gene shook his head. "You've gone too far, Ben."

Ben's face crumpled.

"So have you, Big Wheel," Ben said. "So have you."

He turned to go, then wheeled back around.

"You tipped The Hood off, didn't you?"

"What are you talking about?"

"When I brought Supry out to the loading dock, you warned Hood. That's why Blondie forgave you for being late on that roll. I knew it had to be something big, and it was. He's always wanted to put a knife in my back, and you did it for him."

"Come on, Ben. You were trying to get Hood fired. This shit has got to stop."

"Oh, don't worry, I'll stop." He dismissed Gene with a wave of his hand. "The only reason I did any of this was for you. You should have told me you were happy where you are. Then I'd have stopped making a fool out of myself a long time ago. Come on, guys, let's go."

He stormed toward the smoking area. Jimmy and Devoid slunk off behind him.

They almost collided with Supry. "Jesus Christ, Ben," Supry muttered. "Watch where you're going."

Ben tried to push past him. Supry looked confused.

Passing Time

"I've got the results of the vote," he said.

Ben stopped. They all did.

"Forty-five percent against," Supry said. "No strike."

"Yes!" Hawkins said. He exchanged a high five with Judson. Dub ran toward the back of the machine to tell Old Man Grenier. Gene felt like running, too, but he tried to hide it.

"Fuck," Ben said. Devoid kicked the table. Jimmy pouted like a confused two-year-old. Gene felt someone's eyes on him and turned. Ben stared at him. Gene blushed.

"Strike three," Ben said.

"What's that supposed to mean?"

"It means you voted with them. It's written all over your face. We went to the hall together. I drove you there, for Christ's sake. You weren't even man enough to tell me the truth."

"Jesus, Ben," Gene said. "I had do what I thought was right."

"What's right? How the hell do you know what's right, Big Wheel?" This time the new nickname registered with Gene.

"You're just passing through," Ben said. "You voted the way you did because that's what they think." He dismissed Judson, Hawkins, and Dub with the same wave he'd just used on Gene. It must be nice to have everything be so simple.

"Now look, Ben," Supry said as he worked the crumpled scrap of paper with the election results in his hand. "Everybody had to vote their conscience. We talked about this. Each man made his choice, and now we have to move on."

Ben walked away without looking back. Supry seemed relieved and walked away. Jimmy gave Gene a big grin and flashed his middle finger. Devoid shook his head and shrugged.

"Good riddance," Hood said. He winced and arched his back. "I can't believe that fucking asshole pancaked me."

"Maybe we should say something to Supry, son," Judson moved toward the door as if to call him back. "You shouldn't fool around about your back. Tomorrow, you might not be able to walk."

"I'm okay," Hood said. He put both hands on his hips and this time eased from side to side without showing any sign of pain. "I just had the wind knocked out of me, that's all."

"I don't know. You went down really hard," Dub said. He threw himself toward the ground, his arms flailing so wildly that he

225

seemed to levitate a few inches off the concrete instead of landing, then bounced back to his feet.

"I'm telling you," Hood said. "I'm okay. Ben is such an asshole."

"I don't think we've seen the half of it," Judson said. He glanced over toward the front of the machine. He turned back, satisfied that they had time before the turn up. He sat back down at the table. "Now that he lost that union vote, I think Ben will be a hell of a lot worse."

"Who cares?" Hawkins said. He sat down and pulled out his magazine. "So what if Ben acts like a miserable asshole? We're used to that by now."

"What the hell set him off, anyway?" Gene asked. "I know he's upset about the vote, but he was crazy even before that."

"I think I know," Hawkins said. He folded the magazine back up.

"You saw the look on his face when we talked about how well you passed the sheet the other day. We were having a hell of a time, and it tore him up. I guess he figured he needed to get you back on his crew before he lost you."

Lost him? What was that supposed to mean? Why did Ben care if he worked well with the guys from Number Four? He still practically lived at The Bone with Ben and his gang.

"I think you got something there, Hawkins," Hood said. He sat down on the winder, then seemed to think better of it and stood back up. "Remember a long time ago, Geno, when I told you that Ben didn't care about the work, that his thing was the fucking teams?"

"I remember."

"So, you're getting too close to these assholes over here." He nudged Gene in the ribs. "I told you that you belonged with these foolish motherfuckers, but you wouldn't listen."

"I suppose Ben wanted you back on his crew before you drifted further away," Judson said.

"I just figured I could work with you guys and hang with Ben and the others after work."

"That doesn't seem to be an option," said Judson. "Voting against the strike is the last straw for Ben. You're talking about something he really believes in, that union brotherhood crap. In his eyes, you really did knife him in the back. Maybe he could forgive the other stuff, but not that."

Gene tried, anyway, walking over to The Bone after work, even though the others left without him.

When he walked in the front door, the place got very quiet, and every eye seemed to be on him. Ben was the first one to turn away. "Say, Billy," he said, "what was the name of the last guy we cut Saturday, the short guy with the blond hair? We're going to need to get him back for coverage and special teams."

"Ben," Gene said.

"He looked pretty good," Ben said. He acted as if Gene weren't there. "It goes to show you that you shouldn't play favorites. I mean we never should have picked Wheeler. That other kid really did outplay him."

"Bullshit," Gene said.

Ben swung around on the stool and leaned his elbows back on the bar. "I didn't know you were there, Big Wheel," he said. "When did you come in?"

Gene nodded toward the booth by the door. "Can we talk?"

"Anything you have to say you can say in front of Jimmy and Devo. You should know that by now."

"I'm not sure what's going on here. I thought we were friends."

"So did I, but I know now that I was only fooling myself."

"Can't we talk about this?" Gene asked. He nodded toward the booth again.

Ben leaned back and draped his arms over Jimmy and Devoid's shoulders. "What's there to talk about?"

"Friends work things out."

Ben leaned back toward him. "It takes two to make a friendship, kid. I finally realized that when it comes to you and me, I'm in this by myself."

"How do you figure that?"

"How do I figure that?" He glanced at Jimmy and smiled. He winked at Devoid.

"Okay, Wheeler," he said, "I'll tell you a little story. Once upon a time, there was a sorry little fuck-up who had flunked out of college." Devoid and Jimmy looked puzzled. It had been a while since anyone had talked about Gene being in school. "With no place else to go," Ben continued, "he got a job in the factory in his hometown, but when he got to the job, he found himself working with a self-righteous prick who made his life hell. Of course, it didn't help that the little fuck-up wasn't just a school fuck-up, but a factory fuck-up, too. On only his second day, he almost got himself killed—"

"You never told us Wheeler almost killed himself," Jimmy crowed.

"You never told us he flunked out of college, either," Devoid said. "You said he was just taking some time off."

Ben just held up his hand. "Later," he said, and Gene imagined them sitting here after hours laughing over his bouts with calculus, the pulper, and the cant dog.

"But just when the little fuck-up was about to give up hope, a guy on the job came along and offered him a helping hand, told him not to take the asshole who was busting his chops seriously, showed him how to avoid killing himself, showed him ways to do his job without risking his neck. But most importantly, he never let on to anyone else just how much of a fuck-up the little fuck-up was."

He turned back toward the bar and sipped his beer, then set it down between his legs, balancing it on the edge of his stool.

"Should I go on, Big Wheel?"

"Why not?" Gene pulled out his wallet, waved a five-dollar bill at Billy. "Can I get a beer, first? I'm still allowed to do that, aren't I, Ben?"

Billy plunked the beer down in front of him but waved his money away.

"Don't worry about it, kid," he said.

"Consider it one for the road," Ben said.

Gene took a long sip. "So, where were we, Ben?"

"We were talking about a little fuck-up," Ben said. He spread his hands out before him, and suddenly Gene saw him standing on the picnic table at work, reciting his favorite porn stories. He was really getting into this, but Gene cared enough about him to let him have this shot. He owed Ben. Maybe this was what Ben needed, to get it all out, to vent the poison. Gene sipped his beer and sat down on the edge of one of the tables in a booth, so they were eye to eye.

"Thanks to the help of his new friend," Ben said, "the little fuck-up survived his first few weeks on the job. He settled in. His new friend took him under his wing even outside of work, shared his favorite hangout with him, got him home when he was too drunk to drive, held his head while he puked his guts out.

"At work, they hung out and played cards and read porn. Imagine that. One day, the little fuck-up is ripping his guts out because he bombed out in school, the next day, he's got a good job and good friends, and he's having the time of his life."

"I still want to know how Wheeler almost killed himself," Jimmy sulked.

"All in good time, Jimmy," Ben said. "All in good time. Am I leaving anything out, Big Wheel?"

"Say what you have to say, Ben."

Ben rubbed the bridge of his nose with one finger, as if he had a headache and was trying to rub it away. Gene watched the joy seep out of Ben's performance, but then he rallied.

"And then a funny thing happened to the little fuck-up. He got to working with a whole new group of guys, all of them serious and tough and definitely not in the least bit fuck-ups. They were perfect. And he learned his job, and he became perfect, too, and he forgot about the people who cared about him when he was just a little fuck-up."

"Jesus, Ben," Gene said, but Ben held up his hand.

"To tell you the truth, though, Big Wheel, I can live with all that. After all, you're just a kid. You're all caught up in yourself and the job and being perfect like Blondie and his gang.

"What really frosts me is the strike vote. You come in off the street and you've been working with us no time and who knows if you'll even be working here a year from now, and you vote for something that's going to affect the rest of us long after you're gone."

"A hell of a long time," Devoid said.

"Forty fucking years," Jimmy said.

"You didn't seem to mind when you thought I was voting your way, Ben."

"That's because my way is right," he said. "It's a vote for people." He nodded toward Jimmy and Devoid. They nodded back as if their heads were on a string. Gene remembered the first time he'd thought of Devoid as a ventriloquist dummy with Ben's hand up his back.

"People, Big Wheel," Ben said. "People have to watch out for each other, just like I watched out for you those first few days." Ben jabbed a finger in his chest. "I watched out for you."

"I know you did."

"That's just talk. I didn't just talk. I *did* things for you. You were supposed to *do* things for me."

"Like vote for the strike?"

"That's right."

"Even if I didn't believe in it?"

The hard wood of the table cut into Gene's legs. Perched on the edge, his muscles ached. His right leg began to shake. He held it down with his hand. He didn't want Ben to see.

"Jesus, Wheeler," Ben said. He didn't seem to realize that he had used Gene's real name. "You don't know anything about the union and The Company. You should have trusted me."

"A lot of people voted the way I did."

"And they'll regret it. The concessions have started, and who knows where they'll end."

Gene thought of the conversation on the bridge that afternoon. Ben had said that he was ready to move on, that he would let things fall where they may when it came to the strike. What had happened to that idea?

"I had to do what I thought was right," Gene said. He couldn't hold his leg still. Sweat itched on the back of his neck. He slid off.

"Bullshit, Big Wheel. You voted for what Blondie and Judson thought was right. You chose them over us, plain and simple."

Ben drained his beer and put it back on the bar. He raised an eyebrow to Billy, who brought him another.

"And the sad thing is that those guys don't really care about you at all. They care about the work, about the machines, about their goddamn rules. Shit, they aren't even human. Blondie's such a machine, I'll bet the only way he can get off is by jerking off in the back seat of his beloved Porsche. Don't come crawling back to me when you figure out what that bunch is really like."

"Don't worry, Ben, I won't." Gene said. He finished his beer. He knew better than to raise an eyebrow for another. Those days were gone. He leaned past Ben and handed the glass to Billy. He felt Ben's breath on his neck. He looked into Ben's eyes as he pulled away. "Just remember, Ben. You're the one who really made this choice."

Ben shook his head.

"I'm just honest enough to say what's what, Big Wheel."

That was it. Gene had given it his best shot. Obviously, Ben had a bottomless supply of venom. It was Gene's turn.

"What's what? I'll tell you what's what, Ben. You don't know what it means to be a friend. You don't want friends, you want flunkies like these two clowns." He pointed at Jimmy and Devoid. "They couldn't even take a leak without you holding their dicks. If that's your idea of being friends, then you can kiss my ass."

"Why, you little prick." Jimmy toppled his stool as he lunged toward Gene. Ben jumped between them.

"Don't waste your time, Jimmy," he said. "He isn't worth it. He thinks he's a man now. Hell, he's even learned the lingo, but none of it's real. Of course he's going to piss on what we have."

Jimmy glared at Gene over Ben's shoulder.

"Get out of my bar, Big Wheel," Ben said.

"I thought this place belonged to Billy."

"One more thing you don't have a clue about."

He walked away. He listened for footsteps, but Ben kept Jimmy in check. Talk about being a lap dog.

Gene got through the door and turned to trace the letters on the glass: The Bone. He knew he'd miss the place.

As he walked toward his car, the street was still alive with cars and people. Usually when they got out, everything was deserted.

He asked himself if Ben was right about the vote. Had he really voted the way he had because of Hawkins and Judson? Was he just following them instead of Ben?

He shook his head. Not this time, Ben. He had made up his own mind. Maybe the vote was like the work, black and white. Wouldn't it be great if everything could be that way?

Chapter Twenty-Three

Gene couldn't sleep when he got home. No surprise there. It was only one o'clock, and he hadn't gotten home from The Bone before five a.m. in weeks.

He missed it. He missed Ben. He might put on a tough face and pretend to blow Ben off, but the truth was, Ben had been a good friend. Gene depended on him.

He got up and turned on the television, flipped through news and sports and weather. He passed over a Tracy/Hepburn movie twice before he settled there. Something about the pair made him uneasy. What did everyone say about them, Tracy and Hepburn: the perfect team. On screen and off.

That's where all the trouble had started at work. Teams. Ben's guys and Hawkins's team. Hood stealing his spot, and Ben trying to get it back for him. He and Ben had been close, and now Ben hated him. Hawkins and he had hated each other, and now they were teammates. Hood and Gene were close and not close and now had made some kind of peace.

He sat up in bed and swung his legs over the edge. He didn't need Spencer's wise grin and Kate's cackle to remind him of what he'd lost.

He found his sweatpants and running shoes and climbed the steps into the backyard. The sky was clear, the huge globe of the moon rose behind the cliffs of Mt. Page. They seemed to glow with their own light as they towered over him.

He headed up the driveway, turned down the hill, and let gravity take him, just on the edge of falling, his feet slapping the concrete.

Halfway down the hill, he veered off to a side street that sloped more gradually and got himself back in control. His initial burst gone, his breath came hard. He hadn't run at all since school, and

Passing Time

he couldn't believe how out of shape he was.

He ran past the high school and its playing fields and turned onto a narrow path that led to a metal footbridge. It rang his footsteps back to him. Below him, the stream slashed across slabs of silver granite. Like crossing the bridge to get to work. What did he have to do to get away from that place?

He ran right down Main Street, deserted now. He passed a police cruiser parked in an alley with two heads back against the headrests. They didn't stir as he went past.

At the corner of Main Street and Washington Avenue, he took a right and headed back, coming toward Mt. Page from a different angle, climbing the far side of the street that rose to the highest point in town, and then dropped back to his house.

An A-frame chalet stood at the top of the street. He labored up, fixing his eyes on the spotlight that illuminated its front yard. When he reached the summit, he pulled up and leaned over with his head between his legs, grabbing for air. When he could finally breathe normally, he looked out over the city.

As his breathing became even and his heart stopped pounding in his ears, he became aware of the familiar sounds of The Company. It spit steam from dozens of stacks and vents. Trucks slid back and forth across the yards, their gears whining and grinding. Railroad cars linked and unlinked, slamming into each other like bumper cars. It was a giant, restless animal, worrying its nest all through the night.

When he was a kid, he had often walked up to this spot just to look at the factory. Sometimes, he brought a sketchpad and tried to draw its machines purely from his imagination. His mother called them his engineering sketches because they never had any people in them.

He should have stuck a few people in. That might have better prepared him for the last few months. There sure as hell were people in the picture now.

When he got back home, the run had only served to wire him up even more. The last two television stations had signed off. He stared at the test pattern for a while and listened to the tone, but, finally, he flipped it off.

He picked up the third book of Tolkien's trilogy, *The Return of the King*. Book Two had been so good, he had put off reading this one. It could only be a let down. He glanced at the clock: three a.m. He flipped to the first page. At least he didn't have to worry about upsetting Number Four.

He fell asleep at dawn and woke at one o'clock with the book lying open across his chest. He got up to shower and shave, and when he packed his lunch, he stashed the book in his lunch pail. He didn't know what to expect from Ben, but he knew his days of playing cards, reading porn, and shooting the shit in the smoking area were over. He was going to need something new to help him pass the time.

When he walked into the room, Ben sat in the smoking area with Jimmy and Devoid. Gene stood in the doorway and waited for Ben to look over. When he did, he seemed to look right through Gene, as if he weren't there. Ben snuffed out his cigarette and turned back to Jimmy. So that was how it was going to be: the silent treatment. Gene could live with that.

He looked around for the rest of the guys. He didn't see Hawkins, but Judson and Dub were on the backside of the winder, checking out what seemed to be a gigantic armchair. As he got closer, Gene realized it was some discarded rolls, arranged into a back, a seat, and two armrests—the bulky, off-white shape looked like an ice sculpture. He expected to see trickles of melting water on the concrete at its base.

Judson glanced at Gene when he walked up beside him. "How's it going, kid?"

"Okay. What's this supposed to be?"

"I think it's supposed to be a chair."

"I guess they had a miserable run this morning," Dub said. "Some poor bastard flipped out."

"Not exactly crazy," Judson said. "This little bit of creativity certainly beats stripping the rolls down and taking them to the pulper."

"You've got a point," Dub said. He stood on his tiptoes and patted the seat. "I think it's cool," he said, planting a hand on each arm and launching himself up. It was quite a leap, almost five feet off the ground, but he managed easily, flipping around, landing squarely in the middle. Football player and budding gymnast.

Passing Time

He closed his eyes and leaned back. "This is the life," he said with a sigh.

"It can't be comfortable," Gene said. "It has to be hard as a rock."

"Actually," Judson said, "those rolls are Duralon. They have a really high rag content. It isn't exactly goose down, but it should be all right."

"Rags? I didn't know they put rags in the paper," Gene said.

"Always have. Rags make really nice paper, actually. The A-rabs used them almost exclusively. If the demand for paper hadn't increased so much, a lot of people might still be using them. Now, we just throw a few bales of rags in every batch for texture. This stuff just has a higher concentration."

"Where'd you learn that? That stuff about the Arabs?"

"They offer a little course on Pulp and Paper Technology up at the tech school," Judson said. "I took it a couple years ago."

Dub grinned and jabbed a finger at Judson.

"Old Man Grenier thought that was the biggest joke," he said. "Learning about paper-making from a book. Remember, Big Buddy, he rode you like crazy that whole year."

"He did seem to enjoy teasing me about the course almost as much as I enjoyed taking it," Judson said. He glanced over at the roll on Number Four. "Guess I'd better sound that thing before it gets too much bigger. Want to give me a hand, Dub?"

"Sure thing."

Dub scampered down, and they headed over to the front of the machine. Gene decided to try the chair. He stuffed the book in his back pocket.

He gauged the height and jumped. He couldn't make it on the first try, so he grabbed another roll to use as a step stool, and finally made it up.

The paper really did have a lot of give to it. It was somewhere between paper and fabric, the sandy-colored surface rough to the touch. As an added benefit, the rolls absorbed the rumblings and grumblings of the machines. He got the book out of his pocket. Dub was right. This was the life.

He'd only been reading for a few minutes, when the chair shuddered and he had to grab the arms to keep from falling. He looked down, and Ben snickered up at him from the base. Jimmy and Devoid were right behind him.

"Jesus, Big Wheel," Ben said. "I knew you were getting pretty full of yourself these days, but I didn't think you'd build yourself a throne."

"I didn't build anything, Ben," Gene said. "These were here when I came in."

"But you sure do look at home up there." He glanced at Jimmy and jerked his head toward the chair. Jimmy threw himself at the base as if it were a tackling dummy. The rolls split apart like kindling, and Gene crashed to the floor as the arms of the chair came down on his head.

He lay on the floor, dazed, sore, and hearing nothing but their crazed laughter. Then he heard Judson's voice.

"What's going on here?"

"Nothing," Ben said. "Wheeler went high and mighty on us, so we took him down a peg."

The rolls on top of Gene were lifted away.

"You okay, kid?" Judson asked.

"I think so."

"He'll be fine," Ben said. "We were just having a little fun."

Judson studied Gene's face until he seemed satisfied that he was okay. He turned toward Ben. "I'm getting tired of this kind of fun, Ben. I think it's run its course. Let it be."

"Who's going to make me, old man?"

Judson smiled and held out his hand as if he wanted to shake. Ben studied him warily, but finally took it. Jud wrapped his fingers around Ben's, enclosing Ben's hand in both of his.

"We're all adults here, Ben," he said. "We need to end this. If I wanted to spend my days embroiled in petty squabbling, I'd just stay home and listen to my wife."

"Look, Jud," Ben said. "I don't know what we're shaking on. I ain't agreeing to nothing, so let go."

He tried to pull his hand away, but Judson held on. Ben grimaced. Gene looked back at the locked hands and realized that Judson was squeezing, increasing the pressure slowly but steadily. It was Ben's turn to squirm.

"Jesus Christ, you crazy motherfucker! Cut it out!"

"Are you going to leave Wheeler alone?"

"Hell, no," Ben said. "Goddamnit!" He dropped to one knee, tugging, trying to tear his hand away.

"I really think you should consider leaving the kid alone," Judson said.

"Fuck you, asshole," Ben said, but his other leg gave out and he was on his knees.

Jimmy moved toward them, but Judson's glare stopped him cold.

"You're breaking his hand, Jud," Devoid said.

"And you're breaking my heart," Judson said. He stared Devoid down. The tips of Ben's fingers were the same dark blue as Phil Blair's had been the day he'd hired Gene. Gene thought he'd never see another hand with so little blood in it.

"It's okay, Mr. Judson," Gene said as he grabbed his shoulder. "You don't have to—"

Judson shrugged Gene's hand away.

"I'll leave the kid alone," Ben whispered. By now, all the blood had gone out of his face, and he was gasping for air. Judson released his hand. Ben pressed it to his chest, cradling it against his body. He let his forehead fall to the picnic bench as he took long, deep breaths, trying to slow them down. Judson nodded and walked away.

"Jesus. Ben," Gene said. "I didn't want—"

"Get the fuck away from me, Wheeler," Ben said unsteadily.

Devoid ran to his side. Ben shook his head.

"Maybe you should see the nurse," Jimmy said.

"Yeah, right," Ben said. "Won't that be a hell of an interesting incident report."

"Jesus, Ben," Gene tried again. "I never wanted Judson to—"

"I told you to get the fuck away from me, Wheeler. Your bodyguards are waiting for you."

Gene looked over toward Number Four. Hawkins and Dub stood beside Judson. They did look ready to charge at the first wrong move from Ben and his gang.

Gene turned back to Ben.

"Get the fuck out of here, Wheeler," he said. "You're sure as hell not worth me losing a body part over."

Ben avoided everyone the rest of the night, sticking close to the front of the machine. Once, Gene looked over and caught him flexing his hand. Ben tried to shield the motion with his body, but Gene could see.

When Ben's crew ran a roll, he stood back. He went to the smoking area only when they were busy with a roll. Devoid tried to talk to him a half-dozen times, but he just shook his head and walked away.

At eleven-fifteen, Ben got relieved and went out the door alone. Devoid and Jimmy didn't see him go and looked all over when it was their turn to go.

"He split," Hood said when they came over to the table.

"Split?" Devoid said. Gene had never seen him so puzzled.

"You know," Hood said, "flew the coop, cashed in his chips, hit the road."

"I know what 'split' means," Devoid said. He and Jimmy eyed each other uneasily and went out the door together.

"Ben sure seemed in a hurry," Hood said.

"I think he just wanted to get home and lick his wounds," Hawkins said. "This wasn't exactly the best day for him."

"I hope he'll be okay tomorrow," Gene said.

"Don't worry about Ben," Hawkins said. "He'll bounce back."

"I hope so."

"After all the shit he put you through, you still forgive that asshole?" Hood rolled his eyes at Gene as if he had never known a bigger sucker.

"Why does that surprise you?" Judson said. "Wheeler forgave you when you stole his spot on Number Five."

"All right, all right," Hood said. He stuck his tape player in his lunch pail, getting ready to go home. "Don't rub it in."

Dub had been sitting quietly through this whole conversation. He got a grim look on his face.

"I was just thinking," he said. "Maybe Ben high-tailed it out of here so fast because he's got a gun in his glove compartment, and he's waiting right now in the parking lot to blow us all away."

"Where do you come up with this stuff?" Judson said as he pushed Dub's sailor's cap down over his eyes, the gesture of a father with his favorite child. "No problem, son. We'll just let you go first. Throw him one of those head-fakes you use in football, and he'll hit nothing but air."

Dub dodged an imaginary bullet and slashed into Hood with a body block. They tumbled to the ground. Gene went over to help them up, and even Hood grinned. "Bring him on," Dub crowed. "I'll pulverize him."

Ben didn't ambush them in the parking lot, and he did seem better the next day. He just made acting as if Gene were invisible into a permanent trick.

At ten o'clock, Gene headed out toward the loading dock with Hood, but halfway there, Hood took a different turn. They ended up at a window on the other side of the building, looking out over the river.

"What's up?" Gene asked.

"You'll see." Hood nodded toward a door several stories beneath them. It opened out onto a steep embankment that ran from the foot of the factory's basement to the ledges that lined the river. Ben and Jimmy emerged from the doorway and picked their way down a narrow path covered in loose stones. It was only a few seconds before they were both sliding, each sending an avalanche of gray stones before them.

"Jesus, Jimmy," Ben yelled as he was pelted with a steady stream, but he didn't really sound angry. He reached down into a crack in the rocks and came back out with a fishing rod. Gene looked at Hood, who smiled and shook his head, his expression saying that nothing he saw in this place surprised him anymore.

Ben and Jimmy hopped along the ledge until it jutted out over the rapids, just above the spray of the white water. They climbed down into a small, sheltered pocket, hopping along a string of stones. Ben finally stopped to cast his line into the pool. His rod bowed almost instantly and he jerked back on it. He played the line back and forth across the pool and wrestled a large fish up onto the rocks. Jimmy tried to grab it as it thrashed around on the rocks, but he slipped on the wet surface. He tumbled into the waist deep pool. "Jesus-H-Christ!" he bellowed.

Ben grabbed his hand and pulled him out, then gave him the rod and moved across the rocks. The white water misted up behind him, forming a soft halo in the light. He got the fish and held it up. Gene expected him to slap the fish's brains out on the rocks, but he slid the hook out of its mouth and gently dropped it back into the water. He pointed at his watch and waved for Jimmy to make another cast.

Jimmy tossed the line into the water, his movements stiff and awkward. Ben waited patiently for about five minutes as Jimmy jerked the line into the water and back out again, over and over, without a strike. Ben finally touched his arm and pointed to his watch again. Jimmy gave the rod up reluctantly, and Ben skipped across the rocks and dropped it back into its hiding place. He smiled and nodded toward the path. They skidded back across the rocks.

When they reached the path, Ben looked up and caught them watching. His smile disappeared. His face became sullen and angry. Jimmy looked up, but Ben shoved him toward the trail. They scrambled back up the path, spraying another avalanche behind them. Neither of them looked up again.

They waited until the others were out of sight. Gene thought of the look on Ben's face when he saw him. He shivered

"That's something new," Gene said. "The fishing, I mean."

"Poker and porn seem to have lost their thrill for them, so I guess they found another outlet," Hood said, as he climbed up on the ledge of the window and lit a joint.

"It's too bad," Gene said. "We used to have a lot of fun."

Hood shook his head. "You had it made, Geno. If you had played your cards right, you could be the one down there fishing with Ben. We sure as hell fucked things up, didn't we?"

Chapter Twenty-Four

The Bone Crushers went undefeated and played for the title of their flag football league on the third Sunday of November. Every Monday for the last few months, Ben had brought the paper in so he and the guys could relive their best moments. Dub reenacted all his catches, tossing his body around the machine room as if his bones were made of rubber. No wonder no one could guard "Our crazy little motherfucker," as Ben loved to call him.

Gene never joined in these conversations, but even sitting on the winder or up on his reconstructed throne, he caught most of it. He decided to go to the championship game.

A hill overlooked the playing field. It was far enough away that he figured he'd go unnoticed but would still be close enough to catch all the action. Not much different than the situation at work, really. He settled down on the grass just in time for the opening kick-off.

He marveled at the weather. The night before, he'd skipped the weekly party on Mt. Page and sat out on the roof and watched snow falling at the top of the mountain. They had escaped it in the valley, but as he'd looked up, the line between snowfall and clear ground had been as sharp as the edge of a glacier, and he knew it wouldn't be long before winter slipped the rest of the way down.

Today, that seemed like a dream. The sun had chased the snow back up onto the ridges. It was a perfect day for football.

It was touch-and-go for the Bone Crushers most of the game. Though they had dominated the league all year, their opponents, City Hardware, hung tough until Dub caught his third touchdown pass to push the lead to ten with just a few minutes left. Dub spiked the ball and leapt high in the air as the others mobbed him.

It made Gene long for the good times they'd had in the machine room before the crews had split: playing poker, reading pornography. For the first time all afternoon, he wished he hadn't come.

At work, Ben still acted as if Gene were invisible. Blackjack had replaced poker as the card game of choice for Ben and his boys. They spent endless hours at the table playing hand after hand. No one else was invited.

Fishing had replaced pornography as their secondary way to pass the time. Sometimes Gene would watch them from the window high above the river, always careful to stay back out of sight, so they wouldn't see him if they looked up.

They all still worked side-by-side but acted as if the others didn't exist. Hood hung out with Gene, but that was the only communication between the crews.

Gene found his own ways to get through each shift. Mostly he read, plowing through books at a rate that surprised Hawkins, the only one who kept track. He studied the cover every day when Gene came in to see if it was new. He'd roll his eyes and smile if it was.

Gene's back-up diversion was learning about the machines. This also served another purpose. It appeased Number Four. She forgave him for his books.

Hawkins taught him all the tricks at the winder. Old Man Grenier took him under his wing. He called him down to the wet end every day, droning on about the way things worked, dragging Gene after him as he made his rounds. Gene couldn't always give him his undivided attention as they scampered over catwalks high above the machine or dangled down into the vats of pulp. He was too busy trying not to get himself killed. Still, he learned a lot.

As time passed, these lessons made Gene realize that he missed school. Not just Staci and his friends, but the classes and the work. He wasn't ready to go back just yet, but he knew that he would be before too long. He might try engineering again. He might become an English major or study business, but for the first time in months, he knew that school was where his future lay.

One afternoon, he heard a loud whistle, not machine but human, and looked up from his book. Hawkins waved for him to come over to the winder. Hawkins had already pulled Dub away from a plate of ribs and given him the controls.

Passing Time

Hawkins walked over to the back of the machine and rested his hands on the surface of the paper as it surged toward the blades of the winder. He motioned for Gene to come over and do the same.

Gene walked over but instead of doing as Hawkins asked, he leaned toward him.

"You know you don't really have to do this."

"Why not?"

"I don't know how long I'm going to work here," he said. "I may never get higher than the job I'm in. I don't want you to spend a lot of time teaching me stuff and end up feeling like you wasted your time."

Hawkins took Gene's hand and held it just above the surface of the roll as it surged toward the blades along the top.

"I never thought you'd stay here forever, Wheeler," he said. "Some guys like to learn just for the hell of it. I thought you were that kind of guy."

Gene let his fingertips fall to the surface. The paper rippled beneath his fingers as if it were alive. He smiled.

"I'm not wasting my time," Hawkins said as he studied Gene's face. "The more you learn, the more use you'll be to me while you're here. And if you do get back to school and some asshole professor starts giving you a hard time, you won't have to take his shit because you'll know you made it in the real world and there's probably no chance in hell that he could do the same."

"I never thought of it that way," Gene said. "What am I feeling for?"

"The tension," Hawkins said. "Too much drag and the sheet will snap. Not enough and the rolls will run together."

Tension. Gene looked over at Ben and his gang at the table. Ben slapped a card down on Jimmy's Blackjack hand.

"Busted," Ben yelled.

Tension. Now there was something Gene knew a thing or two about.

"I thought it was you." The voice behind him pulled him from his thoughts.

It was Lisa. "Didn't you see me? I've been down there on the sidelines waving to you for the last twenty minutes."

She had on tight jeans and a bright green sweater. Her hair was combed out. He was used to seeing her in a ponytail.

"Sorry," he said. "I guess my mind was elsewhere."

He patted the grass beside him.

"Don't mind if I do." She passed her arm though his. "What happened to you last night?"

"I'm sorry. I just didn't feel like partying. I should have waited after work and told you myself."

"That's okay. It's not like we're anything official."

That was one of the great things about Lisa. She never pushed. He spread his fingers and slid them between hers. She leaned into him.

"I was surprised to see you up here," she said. "I thought you told me you're on the outs with these guys."

"Except for Dub."

"You mean that goofy little guy who plays wide receiver?" She jerked her neck back and forth like a turtle's jutting out of its shell.

He laughed. "That's the one."

"Weren't you on the team?"

"I made the team, but I never actually played."

"So they dumped you? Aren't you pissed off at them?"

He shrugged. "Mostly they're pissed off at me."

"Hood's right," she said. She squeezed his hand. "You're too easy."

She poked at him with her free hand. He caught it and pulled her down into his lap, pressing her face into his jeans. Anything to stop the questions, to avoid explaining what had happened between Ben and him.

She struggled to get free. He held her down. Her lips nuzzled his jeans and his penis responded to the playful pressure. He grabbed her shoulders and pulled her back up.

"You're crazy, girl," he said.

"It worked, didn't it?" She grabbed his shoulders and held him at arm's length. "So what happened with you and the head Bone Crusher dude?"

"It's hard to explain. Things got mixed up, working and hanging out, crew members and friends. I thought I had the best of both worlds, but I missed something."

"Things were going too good?"

"I guess."

She let him go and slid back down into his lap. He wished they were somewhere private, not sitting on this hillside where anyone could see them if they looked up. Not that she would have cared. For the hundredth time, he wished that he could be as free as she was. And that's when he asked himself what she was doing at the game.

"Lisa?"

"Yes."

"I know I'm here because I work with these guys, but why are you?"

"Promise you won't be mad?" He remembered all the times Staci had surprised him with questions and his body had given him away. Lisa's held no secrets.

"I won't know if I'm mad until you tell me."

"I ran into Jimmy last night when we came to pick you up. He asked me to come."

His body stiffened up on cue. She pulled away and studied his face.

"You are mad."

He tried to shrug it off.

"We have a good time together," he said. "Like you said, though, it isn't anything official." Unfortunately, that worked both ways.

"We could be official, you know. I just figure you're still carrying a torch for your college girl."

How could she know? He'd slipped so easily from Staci's bed to Lisa's sleeping bag up on the mountain.

He always thought of her as a kid, but she didn't look like a kid today. She was wearing a lot more make-up than usual. Give her a cowboy hat, and she was a dark-haired Jenna.

"Jimmy told me you went to school together," Gene said.

"Yeah. He's sweet. Not much for brains, but sweet."

Gene shook his head. "He never seemed very sweet to me."

"Maybe you're not his type."

"Jesus, I hope not."

On the field, the celebration had moved to the parking lot, where Ben cracked open the tailgate of his station wagon and pulled out a cooler full of beer. This, of course, was only to tide them over until they got to the real celebration at The Bone.

Jimmy was the first one in. He came out with a beer in each hand. Ben cuffed him and he dropped one back into the ice. Ben grabbed him in a headlock. Jimmy struggled, but Gene could hear their laughter floating toward them on the wind, intermingled with the sounds of the mill.

Lisa watched their antics, too. He wanted her to laugh at them, not with them, but she seemed to accept them with the same easy grace that she accepted Gene.

She turned back to him, smiling. "They seem to be having a pretty good time."

"They always do."

She squeezed his hand. "I guess you miss that, huh?"

"A little."

"It was that whole business with Hood that messed things up with you and them, wasn't it?"

"It was more than that."

He looked out over the field. On the side opposite his ex-pals, the guys from City Hardware were also gathered around their cars. They sucked down beer as easily as the Bone Crushers, but did so sullenly. Their coach yelled, his tone harsh. He waved angrily at the guy who had been trying to guard Dub.

Gene looked back toward Ben. He wondered how Ben would be acting if the shoe were on the other foot.

Both scenes played out under the sharp November sun. Maybe tomorrow it would disappear, not to be seen again until the early days of spring. Ben seemed to want to bask in it forever. It probably couldn't disappear fast enough for the guys from City Hardware.

On the edge of the crowd, Jimmy looked around. Gene guessed that he finally realized that Lisa had disappeared. Suddenly, he didn't want him to find her.

"You look great," he said.

"Thanks." She blushed.

"You never got this dressed up to party with me."

"You really are jealous, aren't you?"

"I know I don't have the right to be."

"That's okay. I like it." She drew her hair back and held it behind her head in her usual ponytail. "I didn't really do this for Jimmy, though. We're supposed to go to The Bone after the game, and I'm trying to fool the old geezer who runs the place. You know I'm not legal."

"You'd better watch it. Billy is usually pretty strict about those things." At least he could hope he'd be that way today.

"Jimmy says he gets so excited about this football stuff he closes down the place and has a private party for his boys and their wives and dates. You probably wouldn't recognize the place."

That might be true. It was hard to imagine The Bone full of women.

"The place is pretty much a dive, isn't it?" she asked.

"It grows on you."

"So, what's this going to be like today? I suppose the guys will get drunk and brag about what great jocks they are while the women sit around and watch them flex their muscles."

"That sounds about right." Gene pictured Ben dancing on a table in a booth. Now that was a sight she'd never forget.

"Ugh," she said.

"Doesn't sound like much of a date," Gene said. Maybe he should have taken her to a movie every now and then instead of always meeting her up the mountain.

"Who said anything about it being a date?" She poked him in the ribs again. "You know something? You're cute when you're jealous. I'm glad you are, though. It makes you human. Most of the time, I don't know what to make of you, Geno. You party with us every weekend, but the rest of the time, I never see you. Nobody does. I know you don't hang out with the geezers at The Bone anymore. What do you do with yourself the rest of the time, anyway?"

She ran her fingers through his hair. It was growing, not up to Hood's standards yet, but pretty unruly. He took her hand, let it fall to his lap.

"I read a lot," he said. "I used to run cross-country in high school, so I started running again. I lift weights at the club twice a week."

He smiled. He realized that he had just described a life that Staci might have tolerated while he was on sabbatical. She probably wouldn't have minded the way he spent his days now. Why had he waited until they'd broken up before he'd started living this way?

She squeezed his arm, ran a hand across his chest.

"Well," she said. "You are getting pretty buff. I don't get it, though. You're turning into a monk or something."

"I went crazy for a while when I first got out of school," he said. "I was messed up because I'd bombed out. This is actually more my style."

"You know," she said, "there's another party tonight. We can make up for last night."

"What about Jimmy?"

"I'm sure he plans on spending the night at The Bone. I'll go over for a couple hours, and then I'll just split. He probably won't even know I'm gone. We could pick you up."

"That sounds good," he said. He wanted her with him, not Jimmy. "Give me a call when you're ready."

"Count on it."

She stood and looked down at the people clustered around Ben's car.

"I have to go."

"Okay."

Gene watched her walk down the hill, but he turned away just before she reached the car. Part of that was not wanting to see her with Jimmy, but mostly, he didn't want to watch her at what should have been his party.

When he got home, Staci's car was in the driveway. He remembered the first time she'd come, the night after Saucier had been hurt. He'd come home from the celebration at The Bone that night to find her on his doorstep. Drunk and exhausted and high on his hero status, he had wondered if seeing her was just a dream. Tonight was no different.

He went down the stairs into the basement and left the sun behind him, stumbling in the shadows. He cracked the door open into the dark room. He waited in the doorway as his eyes adjusted.

She had pulled the shade on the one, tiny window, blocking out the sun. He felt the sun bristling against the window, but not a trace slipped through. He tiptoed to the window and pulled the shades apart a fraction of an inch. One narrow slit of light cut into the total darkness.

She slept in his bed with the covers pulled up to her chin, her hair spread out across the pillow like another comforter.

He sat down on the edge of the bed and began to stroke her hair. Her eyes opened. "Hey," she said.

"Hey."

"You always knew I'd show up back on your doorstep one of these days, didn't you?"

He pulled his hand away. "Not really."

"At least I came. That's more than you can say."

He touched her hair again. He didn't want to, but he did. His fingers were gentle. His voice wasn't. "You told me not to come."

"I didn't come all this way to fight," she said, lifting the covers. She was wearing one of his T-shirts. He slid his hand underneath and found the warm, wet spot between her thighs, stroking gently.

"Six weeks," she murmured.

The phone rang at six-fifteen. The shades were closed. The only light came from the cracked open door of the bathroom. He sat on the edge of the bed and stared at the white line on the floor.

"Aren't you going to get that?" Staci asked as she traced the length of his spine with her fingertips.

"I'd better not," he said. It must be Lisa. "It might be The Company, and if I answer, I'll have to go to work."

"Doesn't it bug you," she said. "Not being able to answer? It might be something important."

"You get used to it."

"I don't think I could," she lunged across his body and jerked the phone off the hook.

"No!"

"Hello," she said as she lay across his lap and squirmed over onto her back. She reached up and grabbed his hair, tugging his face down to hers.

"Oh, hello," she said. All the playfulness went out of her. She let go of his hair and rolled off him.

"Sure I remember," she said.

She remembered? How could she remember? She'd never really met Lisa.

"Sure. He's right here." She handed the phone to him over her shoulder. She didn't even look at him. "It's your buddy, Hood."

Gene finally exhaled. Sure, she was pissed off, but at least it wasn't Lisa.

She rolled off the bed and slipped into the bathroom. She slammed the door behind her, and he was in the dark again. He flipped on the light by the bedside.

"My man," Hood said.

"Hey, bud."

"How's it hanging, Geno? No, wait, let me guess, hard and high?"

"Not at the moment. What you calling for, man?" Gene asked. That was for Staci in the bathroom.

"You know why, you dog," he said. "Lisa called Jenna from The Bone. We're supposed to rescue her about nine, then swing by and pick you up. I suppose that is out of the question."

"You know it is."

The bathroom door burst open. Staci emerged and flopped down on the bed beside him.

"Don't be so hasty, my man," Hood said. Gene heard the wheels of possibility spinning in Hood's head.

"Maybe you could still get together with Lisa, and I could entertain that cute little college girl of yours."

"Yeah, right," Gene said. "You'd be a dead man in the morning. That's if you survived the night."

Staci raised her eyebrows at the word dead. Maybe he already was.

She pulled her jeans off the floor. She stepped into them and jerked them on. When she pulled up the T-shirt, Gene could see that she had panties on. She zipped the jeans and buttoned them. There was a finality to it all that frightened him.

"Chicks used to be more flexible," Hood droned in his ear. "Back when I was in high school, my buddies and I would trade off all the time." He sighed.

"Look, Hood, I've really got to—"

"You're leaving me with two options, man. I can leave Lisa at

Passing Time

The Bone with that sorry bunch, which is a hell of a thing to do to her, or we could show up, tell her you wimped out on us, and she should bring Jimmy Dwyer along with us to the party, which will annoy the shit out of Ben, so it might be worth putting up with that dim-wit for the rest of the night. Yeah, I like it. That's what it's going to be."

"Thanks, man," Gene said. "Maybe another time."

"I'll hold you to it," he said. "Anyway, I probably don't need to say this, man, but lay low tonight. This is a small town. Don't know who you'll run into if you're out and about."

"I think I can manage that," Gene said.

"I'm sure you can. I'll catch you later."

Staci was back in the bathroom. He got up and opened the door. She tore at her hair with a brush.

He should have kept his distance. He should have let the hair take the brunt of it for him. He touched her shoulder.

She wheeled around and smacked his hand away with the brush.

"Hey!" He jerked the brush away from her. She slammed her arm into his chest, a straight-arm any Bone Crusher would have been proud of.

He backed away. "Jesus Christ, Stace. What the hell is wrong with you?"

His legs caught on the edge of the bed, and he lost his balance. She lunged at him, and they hit the floor. She planted her knees in his chest and whaled away at him with both hands. He covered up, shielding his face with his arm. "Have you lost your fucking mind?"

She rolled away and sat on the floor beside him, sobbing.

He inched away from her and propped himself up against the bed. He gauged the distance to the door. He rubbed his chest. How could someone so small pack so much power?

"I'm such an idiot," she said. Her hair hung down over her face. He couldn't see her eyes. "I told myself not to come. I know things aren't right, but I figured we could pretend for a few days. We'd be together, and I could forget about school, and you could forget about your crazy job and friends. It could be like it was last year."

Her voice was harsh, almost strangled. She jerked out a

handkerchief and blew her nose. When she spoke again, she sounded more like herself. She looked up, shoved her hair aside, and there was a trace of a smile on her face. It wasn't a happy one.

"So, what happens?" she asked. "We're alone for a couple hours, and then your low-life, druggie pal is on the line trying to drag you away again. Don't let me stop you, *Gee-no*." She twisted her face into a bad imitation of Hood's. "Places to go. Losers to see."

"I'm not going anywhere," he said. "If you had listened you'd know that. Why would I go with Hood when you're here?"

She shook her head. "Who are we trying to kid? Nothing has changed."

"Actually," he said, "it has." He told her about his new routine. No more nights at The Bone. Only Saturday nights on the mountain. He left out the part about Lisa, of course. At work, he was learning about the job. The rest of the time he was running, working out, and reading the books that she had given him. He told her that he could even see himself back in school again. Maybe even as an English major.

As he spoke, the tension slipped out of her body. She held her hand out to him. He shook his head and lifted his shirt. There was an ugly purple bruise in the middle of his chest.

She blushed. "I'm sorry. I guess I went a little nuts."

"A little?"

She crawled toward him. The crack of light on the carpet was two feet away from him. That seemed like a safe boundary.

"That's close enough," he said.

She stopped, pulled her legs into a lotus position. She took a deep breath. That was rich. From wild animal to Zen master in minutes.

"You read the books for me?" She seemed pleased.

"For you? How could it have been for you? I thought I'd never see you again."

She pulled back as if he'd slapped her. "I never said that."

"You stopped calling. You only wrote one letter and that was to rub my nose in how different our lives were."

"I didn't mean it that way." She shifted her weight. Her legs knifed out in front of her.

"That's how it felt to me."

"Maybe that's because you were unhappy with your life." She jabbed a finger in his face. He batted it away. She reared back but seemed to think better of it.

He shook his head. "I'm not unhappy," he said. "Maybe that's the problem. You want me to be miserable because I'm not in school, because that's how'd you'd be. Maybe that's why you came. You wanted to see if I was ready to run back."

"I came because I missed you."

"You missed me? I thought you already found my replacement." After all, he'd found one for her. Someone who didn't judge him every minute of his waking life. Part of him wanted to scream the words, but he held his tongue. He didn't want to hurt her. He didn't need to. And maybe he wanted her back more than he'd ever imagined. Maybe he missed her, too.

"Your replacement?" she said. "What's that supposed to mean?"

"You know what I mean. You know who. That guy Daniel you were so chummy with when I visited you at school."

"I told you he's just a friend. How many times do we have to talk about him?"

"Maybe we should talk about Dr. Ellis instead."

"Dr. Ellis?" Her pale skin went red. Guilt? Anger?

"He's my advisor. He'd never—"

"I've heard he has. Lots of times. With every promising student he's ever had." At least the ones who looked as good as she did.

She shook her head. "This is insane. You're the one who ran away from us, not me."

There it was again. He'd run away. From school. From her. But had he really? Maybe, at first. Not anymore.

She reached for his hand again, and he let her take it.

"I didn't come here to fight," she said. "I missed you. That's all. Why can't we just leave it at that?"

He didn't want to hurt her, but he didn't want to get hurt either. He could see them doing this over and over again. A series of visits that were little more than strafing runs. She'd show up, they'd screw then fight, and she'd run away. He might have put up with that once, but not now.

"Because you can't breeze in here and act like nothing's changed," he said. "I've changed. I'm not the guy you knew in school, the one who ran home when he messed up. I'm not the guy you ran out on six weeks ago. I'm someone else. I'm not exactly sure who that is, but I'm not going to apologize for him anymore. Either accept things the way they are, Stace, or let it go."

He stepped over her on his way to the bathroom. Better not to watch her run away this time. He leaned on the sink and looked down. Anything was better than staring at himself in the mirror. He felt her hands around his waist.

"I couldn't stand to see you piss your life away. That's why I ran away. You came back here, and it seemed like all you wanted to do was drink and party. I saw that mess up on the mountainside, the beer cans and the trash. I thought I'd lost you."

"You should have trusted me."

"You didn't even trust yourself."

She had him there. He turned back to her. She buried her face in his chest. He winced when she touched the bruise, but he didn't pull away.

They made love. As soon as they were finished, Staci was hungry. Some people have to have a cigarette; Staci always looked for something greasy.

"We should get some fried clams from that little place downtown."

Just what he needed. What would happen if they ran into Hood and the girls stocking up before they headed up the mountain? Lisa was easygoing, but he didn't think even she would let that go.

"They're closed for the season," he said.

"I hate the off season. My favorite place in Old Orchard has been boarded up since Labor Day. Otherwise, I love this time of year down there. It's not as crowded. Too cold to swim, of course, but you can walk forever."

"I've never been to the beach this late in the season," he said.

"So, we'll go."

"Are you crazy?"

She jerked on her jeans, no panties this time, and hopped on one leg as she pulled on her shoes. She stumbled, held out her hand, and he supported her.

"This is crazy," he said. "You drove all day to get here, now you want to get back into the car and drive three more hours. The least we can do is take both cars, then you can head back from Maine tomorrow."

"No, I want to ride with you. Besides, I'm staying until Tuesday." She pointed at her monstrous backpack lying on the chair beside the bed.

"Tuesday? I didn't know you had time off from school."

"It's Thanksgiving break, remember?"

"But the break doesn't start until Wednesday. You can't afford to miss that many classes."

She reached down with her free hand, grabbed the backpack, and swung it up into his chest. He lost his balance and they toppled onto the bed.

"As you can see," she said. "I brought school with me."

"What's gotten into you? You don't do stuff like this."

"I never had a boyfriend who lived eight hours away before," she said. "I didn't think I could handle it, but now I'm ready to try."

It was dark when they got to the beach. The lane where Staci's folks had their house was lined with cottages on both sides, the buildings jammed together in the darkness. Several had smaller cottages in their backyards. Why waste good rental space on grass?

There were lights in only a handful of the buildings.

The front door of Staci's folks' house faced out onto the water, opening onto a stone patio with several Adirondack chairs looking out at the ocean.

Staci dumped her backpack next to one of the chairs and motioned for Gene to take the one beside her. They pulled the chairs together, but that still left a foot of wood between them, six inches for each arm. He cursed the designer of the chair.

The wind blew hard in their faces. She pulled up the hood of her sweatshirt. He buried his hands in his sleeves.

The tide crept up the beach. Gene could see by the line, where the hard packed sand turned to white powder and beach grass, that high tide would be only fifty feet in front of the cottage.

The beach was deserted. Cold and darkness would do that. If they had been in season, Gene knew there would be legions of kids playing along the sand or in the water, swimming.

"So," he said. "I'm still your boyfriend?"

"Yes."

"When did you decide that?"

"When I missed you too much."

"You couldn't find anyone to take my place."

"I didn't want to try."

"What about being apart? What about my not being there for you?"

"It won't be that long. Besides, it sounds like you're already on your way back."

"Maybe. It still might not be until fall."

"That's okay," she said. A breeze whipped over the patio, and she shivered.

"Want to go inside?"

"Not yet. I'll be right back." She got a blanket from the house and then crawled into his lap. He decided that maybe the guy who designed the chair had the right idea, after all. They arranged the blanket around them. They didn't speak, but it was a comfortable silence, the kind they hadn't shared for a long time. It was almost midnight when they went inside.

"We're going to sleep in my parents' room," she said.

"Won't they be pissed?"

"No, I always sleep there when I'm here alone."

"But you're not alone."

"Trust me."

Her parents' room was on the beach side of the house. The bed sat up on foot-high wooden blocks. "What are those for?" Gene asked.

"Lie down."

He lay down on the bed.

"Look straight up at the ceiling," she said.

She went to the window, and he heard her draw back the curtains and pull up the blinds.

"Now roll your head to the side," she said.

When he turned, he could see right out the window. The surf was a series of white lines coursing across a black backdrop like thick bolts of chain lightning.

"You want the window open?"

"Yeah," he said.

She cracked the window, and the sound came through on a cool breeze.

"Daddy says that the first few nights after he leaves here and goes back to Jersey, he has a hard time falling asleep without the sound of the surf."

He closed his eyes and listened to the steady rhythm. He could feel it coursing through him. Just like Number Four. His eyes popped open, and he laughed aloud.

They slept with the windows open, and the frigid, salty air whipped over their heads. Gene thanked God for down comforters and body heat.

In the morning, they walked the beach. There were no swimmers or waders or Canadian bikinis, just a few people walking the beach, bundled up in bulky sweaters.

The Clam Shack, Staci's favorite place, was boarded up. It was a shack so tiny it couldn't have contained more than a refrigerator and deep fryer, but Staci assured him that the owner squeezed in, too.

"You'd love him. He's this huge guy from Quebec with thick, black hair. He wears Hawaiian shirts all the time, and there's curly black hair sticking out everywhere."

Hairiness wasn't the first quality Gene would have asked for in a food worker, but he didn't want to ruin her memory.

They talked about books as they walked the beach. It was good to find out that he could still keep up with her.

He called in sick that afternoon, sitting on the front porch in the Adirondack chair with Staci perched on the arm.

"This is Phil," Blair barked when he picked up the phone.

"Hey, Mr. Blair. This is Gene Wheeler."

"Mr. Wheeler. What's up?"

"Well, I'm not sure if I should be talking to you or Mr. Supry, but I'm not going to be able to make it to work today. I'm sick. I've got some kind of flu or something." Staci tossed a stone into a flock of gulls feeding in the dunes and beach grass, sending them shrieking into the sky.

Blair chuckled. Had he heard the birds? They were so close to the surf, he could probably hear that, too.

"You did right to call me," he said. "I'm still the one who makes out your time. Supry asks for you every week, so I think you're there to stay."

"That's great news, Mr. Blair."

"Sorry to hear you're under the weather, kid," he said. "I bet it's one of those twenty-four hour things."

"I guess so. It came on pretty fast."

"Do you think it will go just as fast?"

"Sir?" The gulls were back, and Staci bent down to pick up another stone. He covered her hand with his. She let him pull it into his lap. She slid off the arm of the chair and on top of him. He covered the mouthpiece with his hand.

"This bug will probably pass by tomorrow, don't you think, son?"

"I hope so."

"We shall see. Let me know for sure tomorrow."

"Yes, sir." Staci blew in his ear. He jumped but didn't make a sound.

"Take care, Wheeler, and allow me to officially welcome you. You are now a full-fledged employee of The Company."

"Sir?"

"I don't consider someone a real employee until they call in sick on a Saturday or a Monday. Until then, I figure they're just visiting. You did okay, though, son. You held out longer than most. Don't forget to call me tomorrow. If you feel better, of course."

"Okay."

He hung up the phone. He picked up a stone and scattered the gulls. They made a satisfying ruckus.

"That is one crazy old man," he said.

"Doesn't he believe that you're sick?"

"Not for a minute."

"Did I get you in trouble?" She grinned as if she liked the idea.

"No. He made a joke about it. He said I've only been visiting up until now."

She frowned, her victory turned sour.

"And that's the way we want to keep it," she said.

She dropped him off at work on Tuesday afternoon. They sat in the back row of the parking lot, and he pointed out everyone as they straggled in. The first one to arrive was Old Man Grenier, who came across the lot kicking up a storm of gravel, in animated conversation with himself. He had on a red-checkered hunting jacket and a bright red ski cap.

"Does he always talk to himself?"

"I didn't know he did. I always thought he was talking to Number Four."

Next came The Flamer, decked out in a white jumpsuit, a red sweater, and matching cowboy boots.

"That's quite the outfit," Staci observed. "He must be going out after work or something."

"Actually, he dresses like that every day."

"But he must tone things down in his work clothes."

He laughed and told her about the color-coordinated scarves and tank tops.

"He wears tank tops all winter?"

"It's always summer in the machine room," he said. "The place is hotter than hell."

Dub and Judson showed up together. Dub's left arm dragged under the weight of his basket.

Hawkins's Porsche slid into the space next to them. He got out and glanced their way, appraising Staci, then looked toward Gene. He smiled when he recognized him. Gene motioned for Staci to roll down the window.

"Welcome back, Wheeler," he said.

"Hey, Hawkins. This is Staci. She's up visiting from college."

His name registered with Staci, and she studied his face with renewed interest.

He saw the look on her face and smiled.

"You've been talking about me, Wheeler."

"All of it was good, of course," Staci said.

"You don't have to lie, Staci," he said. "We had our troubles, at first. I like to think of Wheeler as one of my success stories. He knew not to take my bullshit personally. He knew everything was about the work."

He turned back toward his car and slid the key into the lock. When he pulled it away, he noticed a leaf stuck to the paint by the keyhole and flicked it away.

"Most people can't separate work and personal stuff," Staci said.

"No, they can't. So, I guess you're already on Thanksgiving Break, Staci?"

"Sort of."

"That was one of the nice things about college," he said. "They were always so laid back about vacations."

"Hawkins went to college for a while," Gene explained to Staci.

"Oh. Why'd you quit?"

"I guess I always felt out of place," Hawkins said. "I didn't really know what I wanted to study. I figured I'd get out for a bit, and I just never went back."

Staci glanced at Gene. Hawkins caught the look and frowned. If he were Dub, he would have smacked himself on the forehead.

"Sorry about that," he said. "I know you don't want to hear that since Gene's out of school for a while."

"It's okay," she said. "I know he needs to do what's best for him."

His eyebrows shot up. Gene recognized the look. He'd seen it every time he'd surprised Hawkins in a good way.

"You need to hold on to this one, Wheeler." He glanced at his watch. "I'd better get inside. It was nice to meet you, Staci."

"Nice to meet you, too." She watched him walk away. "Do you need to go, too?"

"No, the guys higher up in the crew go in early sometimes to get the feel of things. I can wait."

"Good." She took his hand and squeezed it like she might never let go. "Hawkins seems really nice. I would have expected him to be a real jerk."

"He's okay. He's just so into the work that it makes him crazy sometimes. That's what you can't take personally."

Hood tore up the lot and swerved into a place by the front gate. He jumped out and ran in without a glance in their direction. "I'm just as glad he didn't see us," Staci admitted. "He seemed in a hurry, though. Are you sure I'm not making you late?"

"No. Somebody must have pushed Hood's alarm clock ahead, though. I've never seen him show up early."

The last to arrive were Ben, Devoid, and Jimmy, all wearing their Bone Crusher sweatshirts.

Staci began to snap her fingers and sing softly, and he turned to see that she managed to capture their Jets-and-Sharks strut without leaving her seat. She sighed. "It's hard to believe you used to hang out with that bunch."

"I know, but if Ben hadn't gotten weird on me, I'd be walking right beside them." He also wouldn't have gotten home until Monday morning from the championship celebration, and she'd have had a long wait in his bed. "I don't think I'd walk quite like that, though," he said and ran a fake shudder down his spine.

"It's like you've been living on another planet for the last few months." It was her turn to shudder, but he didn't think she was faking.

"Sometimes it seems that way."

"Has it been worth it?" She put her arms around him and buried her face in his chest.

"Yeah, it's been worth it. I feel better about things. I've had some hard times on this job, but I've gotten through them. And I suppose I know now that if I don't get into engineering, then there are other courses that would be okay for me. I won't choose them just because I screwed up in math. If I can make the best of this place, I should be able to make the best of anything."

"And you might be an English major?"

"I might," he said. "For now, though, I think I'll just stay here, read all the books, and get paid for it."

She pulled back and punched him in the chest. "But you don't read all the time. You said that sometimes you have to work really hard."

"Yeah, but I like that part, too."

"You're a sick man."

"I suppose."

"And what about us? Can you see us getting together once every six weeks?" She burrowed back into his chest. He rested his chin on the top of her head, savoring the familiar smell of her hair. He might miss that as much as the sex.

"You're worth waiting for," he said.

"You know, I always figured you didn't come to see me because you had some little high school girl stashed away up here."

For once, his body didn't give him away. Maybe Lisa had rubbed off on him. "No." Not any more. Not even if Lisa forgave him for standing her up on Saturday.

She sighed. "I'd better get going."

"Me, too." He kissed the top of her head. "When will I see you again?"

"It's your turn to surprise me."

"How about Sunday morning?"

"If you tell me when you're coming, then it isn't a surprise."

Judson and Dub were at the front of Number Four when he walked into the room. From the way Judson waved his arms around, Gene guessed that he was sharing more of his knowledge from Papermaking 101. Dub, of course, soaked it all up with a studious look on his face. Gene could see Old Man Grenier and The Flamer down at the far end of the machine. Even at this distance, he caught The Flamer's wild hand motions and the old man's colossal disgust. Hawkins leaned over the winder, checking the blades.

The Bone Crusher gang was in the smoking area, Ben intent on a cigarette, while Jimmy and Devoid sparred over his head.

He smiled, humming the tune that Staci had given him in the car.

Chapter Twenty-Five

He read all night when he got home from work. He walked onto the back lawn at six a.m. and watched the sun creep up over the mountains on the eastern border of town. He had seen a lot of sunrises in the last few months, but this one was different.

He remembered all the times he'd collapsed on this porch after nights out at The Bone or emptied his stomach into his mom's rose bushes as Ben held his head. He remembered the times he'd slept with Lisa on Mt. Page.

When he was back in school, he'd pulled a lot of all-nighters studying. That's what this felt like. It felt right.

It was as if he'd been away for a long time, and now he was home. He was happy he'd had those nights at The Bone and up the mountain, but those things were behind him now. There was no going back, and for the first time, that felt just fine.

He settled into his new routine. Outside work, he read and ran and worked out during the week. He and Staci didn't stick to the six-week rule very long. She came up a couple times a month. He visited her the other weeks. He took a trick from his co-workers and worked overtime whenever he could early in those weeks, so he could call in sick on Saturdays. Phil Blair didn't find it as amusing once it became a habit, but he didn't worry about that. He didn't have anything to prove anymore.

At work, they solidified into their private cold war, as clearly divided as the folks in East and West Berlin.

His crew focused on the work. They established records of efficiency that The Company had never seen. Hawkins said that if the bosses had any guts, they'd adjust the specs to reflect their standards, but Judson gently reminded him that even the best teams don't last forever, and what would the bosses do after they retired or died or just moved on? He always raised his eyebrows toward Gene when he said this.

By now, they had all figured out that he was just passing through. He would stay until the fall and start fresh in school. If he bombed out in math again, there were lots of other things that he could be good at.

Still, Old Man Grenier and Hawkins taught him everything they knew about the machine and the winder. Hawkins told Gene that teaching kept him sharp.

"You ask the right questions," he said. "You keep me on my toes."

Gene remembered that the first few days Hawkins had told him that he asked too many questions. They'd come a long way.

Between rolls and lessons about the machine, Gene's crew passed the time reading. Judson and Hawkins liked to debate city government and world issues, but that was the extent of conversation. Dub still ate three times his weight every night, but even he had taken to reading the newspaper from the front page to the back.

When Ben and his guys were at the table, they read the sports pages. They still hunted out the boxcars for loads of porn, but all the rituals that used to go along with it were gone. No one lined up to get a fix. Dub even stopped drooling when he saw them huddled around the table with a fresh batch. There was no trading and no performances by Ben.

Gene knew they still spent most of their times off work at The Bone. Broom hockey replaced flag football. Dub was no good at this sport, so the dividing line between them stayed solid. Gene wondered if they would even let Dub play for The Bone Crushers in the fall. It bothered him that he might have ruined that for Dub.

Just like in the Cold War, Ben and his guys acted as if Gene's team wasn't there, while everything they did was based on the knowledge that they were.

When Gene sat on the winder, he was close enough to hear the conversations at the table, an undercurrent to his reading. One more undercurrent, as ever-present as the vibrations of the machines up though his bones. Still, reading pulled him away from everything and everyone around him.

He would look up sometimes and it seemed as if he were looking at things through a veil. When he really got into his books, even the sounds were different; the voices and the noises from Number Four were distant, muffled. When the horn sounded, he'd have to shake his head to clear the veil away. He remembered the feeling that he'd had sitting up in the big chair. Insulated. Maybe that's why Ben resented him sitting up there, why he'd sicced Jimmy on him and toppled his throne. Gene wondered how Ben would feel if he knew that books did the same now. He was in his own world. He should have known that Ben would find a way to bring him back to his.

"Rape," Ben muttered angrily one night, the words cutting through the veil. "Now there's a good one."

Gene looked up. "A good one?" he said. The words were out before he could stop them.

"Well, well, welcome back, Big Wheel," Ben said. "You were so far off in bookland, I didn't think you'd ever come down." He held up one of the porno rags. RAPE FANTASIES, the headline blared above a picture of a woman bound and gagged, her legs spread wide open, each tied to a stake. Her face was mixed with terror and fascination. "You got some trouble with our conversation, here?" Ben asked.

Gene looked past them. No one from his crew was around. He saw Judson at the far end of the machine with Old Man Grenier. Hawkins and Dub had to be upstairs in the locker room. Even Hood was probably out attacking the vending machines. He knew he shouldn't have spoken up.

"I don't understand, that's all," Gene said, trying to backpedal. "What did you mean, 'rape's a good one'?"

"Rape's a foolish word," Ben said. "Everybody knows there's no such thing. Rape is supposed to be forcing yourself on a woman, but they're all dying for it." He held the paper up to Gene again as if the photo proved his point.

"That's bullshit, Ben," Gene said. Devoid raised his eyebrows and shook his head slightly as if to warn him off. Jimmy leaned forward in his seat.

Ben blushed but didn't say anything. Instead, he lifted the lid of Dub's lunch basket and rummaged around in it until he found Dub's misshapen coffee mug. "So, you think I'm bullshit, Big Wheel?" he said, finally.

"I think what you said is bullshit."

Ben shrugged. "I'm bullshit, what I say is bullshit. It's all the same to me. Of course, I never took psychology or stuff like that, so I could be missing something."

"Rape is about violence," Gene said evenly. "It's not even about sex."

Ben laughed and held out his stick.

"Take this," he said.

"Why?"

"Just take it."

The others watched Gene as he took the stick. Ben lifted the cup as if to take a drink, then turned its open mouth toward Gene. Gene had always laughed at the rough-edged lips. Why had he never noticed that the clay was more pink than brown?

"Take the stick," Ben said, "and put the tip of it in this cup."

The others grinned. Gene felt the blood inch up his neck.

"Fuck you, Ben," he said.

"What's the matter? Afraid to test your theory?"

Gene grabbed the stick and jabbed at the cup, but Ben jerked it away.

"All right," Jimmy crowed.

Gene tried again, but Ben eluded him easily, flashing a smug grin. Even Devoid couldn't hide a smirk.

Gene stood up, but so did Ben. They moved away from the table, and Ben responded to every thrust with a move of his own, an agile matador taunting a clumsy bull. He laughed out loud.

"Hey, Big Wheel," he said. "That crow you got stuck in your throat must taste real good, huh?"

Gene lunged, and Ben held off to the last minute, then coyly pulled away.

"Olé," Ben yelled and clapped his hands together above his head. Gene stopped, sweating, winded. Ben smiled.

"I rest my case." Ben held the cup out as if it were a trophy.

Passing Time

Gene lashed out, splitting the cup in two. A rough shard ripped into Ben's palm. He screamed in pain, then leaped at Gene, crushing him in his arms. He spun Gene around and pinned his arms behind him. He slammed Gene's face into the rough wood of the picnic table. Gene felt someone else on his shoulder.

"Now you've done it, Big Wheel," Jimmy crooned. Ben shifted his weight, driving it into Gene's buttocks. His voice was in Gene's ear.

"You smart-ass little motherfucker," he whispered. "You want to talk about rape? I'll give you rape."

Gene felt Ben's stick dig into his back as Ben tore at the waist of his jeans. Gene arched his back up off the table and drove his head back into Jimmy's face. Jimmy grunted but held on. Gene kicked but got nothing but air.

"Way to go, Ben," Jimmy crowed as he drove Gene's weight down harder. "Ride that little motherfucker."

"Jesus Christ, Ben," Devoid said.

"Shut up, Devo," Ben grunted as he slid Gene's jeans down. The underwear went next. His rough hands gripped Gene's skin.

"This ain't right, man," Devoid said.

The horn sounded, and the hands relaxed for an instant. Gene drove his elbow into Ben's face, wrenched the stick from his grasp, and clubbed Jimmy on the side of the head. Jimmy went down without a sound. Gene slashed at Ben, and he dove away, scrambling across the cement on all fours.

Devoid wrapped his arms around Ben.

"I'm going to kill that motherfucker," Ben said.

"Easy, man," Devoid said. "Let it go. For Christ's sake, Ben, let it go."

Gene waved the stick in their direction, pulled his pants back up, and tightened his belt.

He heard Jimmy struggle to his feet behind him. He wheeled toward him, and Jimmy threw himself back down on the concrete.

Devoid looked toward Gene. "Come on, Wheeler," he said. "Things got out of hand, that's all. Don't go fucking crazy on us."

"I'm crazy?" Gene screamed.

"Is there a problem, gentlemen?" Judson said just behind him.

"What's going on, Wheeler?" Hawkins asked. Gene studied their faces, and he knew they hadn't seen what happened. He didn't know whether to laugh or cry.

"The little fucker cut my hand," Ben said before Gene could speak. A thin line of blood formed in the cracks between his knuckles.

"I'm sure he had a good reason," Judson said. Hawkins stood at Gene's right shoulder. Hood and Dub moved in on the left. Ben eyed them uncomfortably.

"We'll settle this later, Big Wheel," Ben said finally. "When your gang's not around."

"We're not going anywhere, Ben." Judson said. He waved his hand toward Devoid and Jimmy. "And you should be the last one to talk about somebody having a gang."

"Why don't you mind your own business, Jud?" Ben growled.

"It's like I told you before, Ben," Judson said, his voice calm but his eyes murderous. "This mess is my business. I'm tired of it. It's gotten way out of hand."

That seemed to finish Ben. All the anger drained away. "Don't I know it," he said.

The horn sounded again, and they turned toward the machines. Number Four was doing fine, but Number Five flapped her sheet in the breeze. Ben headed toward her, but then he wheeled back toward Gene.

"I want my stick," he said.

Gene tightened his grip on it.

"Fuck you, Ben."

"Give me my fucking stick."

Gene gave him the finger instead.

"Use mine this time," Judson said as he pulled it from his back pocket and tossed it to Ben. Ben caught it, eyed Gene down the barrel, and then turned away.

Gene could see The Flamer on the wet end as he washed the screen down with the hose. He saw Gene and smiled, dropped the hose down to his waist, and stroked the neck lovingly. Had he seen everything? Gene watched him, as he played the stream across the back of the machine, and he wondered if The Flamer had caused this break to calm things down. Not much chance of that. Maybe it was Number Five, herself. If that was the case, who was she protecting, Gene or her boy Ben?

Gene flinched at the hand on his shoulder.

"Jesus, Wheeler," Hawkins said. "What the hell happened?"

Gene held his hand up between them and turned away. He walked to the table and grabbed his lunch pail, then went out the door.

"Hey, Wheeler!" Hawkins called after him. "There's still an hour in the shift!"

"Let him go," Judson said.

He plunged through the doorway and into the corridor as it stretched before him for what seemed like miles. Brick walls and machinery gave way to excess paper in the warehouse, rolls six feet in diameter and ten feet wide, stacked to the ceiling, canyon walls clear to the exit, where the lights from the parking lot glittered, promising safety and sanity and a dozen other things that he'd always taken for granted, that he'd always expected to be his very own.

He walked toward the light, holding himself back, trying not to run, dragging the stick along the wire-mesh that stood between him and the rolls. At first, he took comfort in the tiny jolts that ran through it and up his arm, but when he reached the first sign: BETTER SAFE THAN SORRY, these were not enough. He smashed his lunch box on the sign, splattering the remnants of his supper across the bright, orange metal.

And then he ran.

Signs flashed by him as he sprinted down the corridor. MORE CARE—LESS HASTE. HEAVY EQUIPMENT. He ran past a security guard who stuck out one hand as if to stop him, but then he seemed to think better of it and backed away.

At the first junction, he caught a flash of red out of the corner of his eye—MOVING VEHICLES—but plunged across the aisle, anyway. Propane filled his nostrils. A horn sounded, and he dodged out of the way as the forklift brushed against his leg. "Are you fucking crazy?" the driver screamed, but Gene left him far behind.

The PINCH AREA sign showed the stick man caught between two gears, but he couldn't read the last one, its thick, black letters blurred by his running and his tears. He remembered it, of course, the first one he'd seen on his first day: DANGER: MEN AT WORK. Back then, he'd thought the danger was in the WORK itself, but now he knew that it was in the MEN.

He ran all the way home, but when he reached the house, he sprinted past it, climbing the hill that stretched beyond, winding his way to the base of Mt. Page. He ran until his lungs heaved and his legs trembled, until the street branched off in two directions, as a rutted logging road continued up the ridge, as the pavement dove back down into the valley. He threw himself into the grass beside the road, rolled onto his back, and looked into the flat, black sky.

When he could breathe normally, he crawled to the edge of the embankment that fell sharply to the neighborhoods below. He pulled himself up onto a pile of rocks and looked out over the town.

The houses below him gave way to Main Street, with its shops and businesses, then the Cumberland cut down the heart of the valley. Sprawled across its eastern bank were the buildings of Great Northeastern Paper, The Company.

Where else would a Cumberland man go when he messed up in college? What better place to hide?

A place to hide. He hadn't even gotten that right. He couldn't just blend in with the others, collect his paycheck, and bide his time. Not that it mattered now. He'd run out in the middle of his shift, and nobody would give a damn why; they'd just fire him. No great loss. He was a fuck-up, a kid who ran whenever the going got tough.

He remembered how Staci had said from the beginning that he was running away from his problems, and he knew now that she was right. He should have stuck it out at school. Running away was a hard habit to break. He shook his head. Not that knowing this would help him keep his job. It was too late for that. Ben was another story, though. Gene sure as hell could make Ben pay for what he'd done to him.

Chapter Twenty-Six

He waited for Ben in the alley behind The Bone, huddled down behind a dumpster, knowing that he'd better get comfortable because this would take a while. A light drizzle fell, so he flipped the lid of the dumpster back and over his head. He heard the water on the metal above him, and soon a thin stream ran off the edge and formed a puddle at his feet. He gripped Ben's stick in his right hand and slapped it into his left palm. He leaned his head against the metal.

He must have dozed off because it seemed to be only a few minutes before he heard Ben and Devoid's voices.

They staggered out the back door carrying Jimmy between them, his arms draped over their shoulders. Jimmy's eyes were closed and his breath came evenly, as if he were asleep.

"Damn you, Jimmy," Ben said. "Help us out here." His words were slurred. Gene had never heard him do that. He'd always downed gallons of beer and whiskey without effect.

"He weighs a fucking ton," Devoid grumbled.

"We're almost there, Devo," Ben said and nodded toward his truck. He took a step toward it, but Devoid didn't follow. Jimmy's arms slipped from Ben's shoulder, and all the weight fell on Devoid. He tumbled to the ground. Jimmy's body came down on top of him, and he rolled it roughly to the pavement.

"Fucking asshole," Devoid said. Jimmy snored on the wet concrete.

"Christ, Devo," Ben said. "What's going on? We'll never get his sorry carcass off the pavement."

"So, we'll leave him there."

"We can't do our boy that way," Ben said. "You know we've got to put him in my car so I can get him home."

"I don't think so, Ben."

Gene had never heard Devoid contradict Ben. Devoid sat in the rain, staring at the puddle by Jimmy's head. He took his glasses off and wiped his eyes. He wasn't going anywhere.

"Spill it, Devo," Ben said. He pulled a wooden crate from a pile of trash against the wall and sat down. "What's on your mind? Let's all just sit here in the rain and get fucking pneumonia together." He nodded toward Jimmy, who rolled over on his side and slid his hands under his head.

"I don't think you should be driving Jimmy home," Devoid said. "I don't think you should be driving anybody. I want you to ride with me." He looked at Jimmy the whole time he spoke. He wouldn't look at Ben.

"You want to drive? What are you trying to say, Devo? I always drive. It's what I do. I watch over your sorry asses and make sure you don't end up in a ditch somewhere."

"You're fucked up, man," Devoid said, still looking at the puddle by Jimmy's head. "I've never seen you this way. Let me get everybody home this one time."

"I'm fucked up? Me? Have you looked in a fucking mirror, Devo? You're the poster boy for fucked up."

"Not tonight, Ben. I slowed down a couple hours ago. I've only had two beers since closing time. You started talking weird and staggering around like a fucking rookie, and I knew I'd better put the brakes on. You didn't even notice."

"A rookie? I'm acting like a fucking rookie? Why are you talking to me this way? How many years we been doing this, Devo?"

"Too many. And I've never seen you this fucked up, and I'm not just talking about being drunk."

"What are you talking about? For Christ's sake, spit it out." He leaned over, and the box creaked in protest. He poked at Devoid, but came up about a foot short. Of course, he didn't have his stick. The thing was an extension of his arm.

"I need to know what's going on with you, Ben," Devoid said. "You've been acting like a fucking nut case lately. I want you to tell me why."

Ben stared at Devoid, as if he couldn't believe what he was hearing.

At first, Gene thought Ben was going hit Devoid, but then his shoulders slumped.

"I don't know what's wrong with me, Devo," he said.

"You've been acting crazy ever since Wheeler showed up, man. What is it with you and that kid? He probably won't even be around in a year. He'll be back in college with his egghead friends getting high and talking about books and shit. What do we care if he works with us or with Blondie's fucking fanatics? Good riddance, I say."

"But I thought he was one of us, Devo," Ben said. "I thought he wanted to be with us. I never thought he'd knife me in the back."

Devoid shook his head. He nudged Jimmy with his foot. Jimmy swiped at him and rolled away, right into a puddle. Devoid looked at Ben. They stood without a word and each got an arm under Jimmy's shoulders. They dragged him to Devoid's car, and Ben didn't protest. There was more in that than all the words they'd uttered so far.

Devoid fished out his keys as Ben balanced Jimmy against him. Devoid got the door opened and they rolled Jimmy into the passenger side.

"Get in the back, man," Devoid said.

"No way. I'll let you take Jimmy, but that's where I draw the line."

"Come on, Ben."

Ben squeezed Devoid's shoulder. "I'll be all right, Devo. Thanks for everything. You know you're my man."

"Does that mean we get back to normal tomorrow?"

"I don't know, Devo. I hope so."

Ben watched Devoid drive away and turned toward his truck.

Gene tightened the grip on the stick and walked out from behind the dumpster into the rain, blocking Ben's way.

"Jesus Christ, Wheeler! You scared the shit out of me. You almost gave me a fucking heart attack."

"No great loss." Gene slammed the stick into Ben's shoulder.

"Jesus, kid!" Ben gasped and went down on one knee. Ben had always said he'd get Gene when his gang was gone. Who needed a gang now?

"I'm not a kid," Gene said. He hit Ben on the other arm.

"What the hell, Wheeler? Have you lost your goddamn mind?"

"What do you expect? You tried to rape me." He hit Ben again. "You made me lose my fucking job." He slammed the stick into Ben's gut.

Ben gasped and grabbed his stomach.

Gene raised the stick, aiming for Ben's head this time. Ben looked up, and their eyes met.

"Christ, no, Wheeler," Ben roared and leaped up. His shoulders smashed into Gene's chest. Ben screamed in pain, but kept coming, driving Gene to the wet pavement.

Ben was on top of Gene. Gene couldn't get his arms free. Ben pressed his weight against Gene like he'd done in the machine room. Gene kneed him in the groin. Ben grunted and pulled away, got just enough distance to extend his arm, and caught Gene on the jaw with a hard right hand.

Gene's head spun. He expected Ben to finish him off, but Ben lay on his left side with his shoulder in a puddle, gasping for breath. Gene felt on the ground until he found the stick. He sat up, his vision still blurry. He realized it was the rain, so he swiped his hand across his eyes. Let Ben come.

Ben sat up but didn't move. He just sat in the rain, rubbing his arms.

"You're not going to lose your job, Wheeler."

"Of course, I am. I ran out before my shift was over."

"They covered for you," Ben said. "Hood did your work, and when Supry showed his face, Judson lied for you, said you were in the can."

"Why didn't you tell Supry the truth?"

He shrugged. "None of my business, really. You're not on my fucking team."

"That never stopped you before."

Ben struggled back to his feet. "Well, Jud did say something about tearing me apart limb by limb if I opened my mouth." He shook his head. "What the hell do they see in you, Wheeler?"

"You should know, Ben. You used to see it yourself."

He sighed. "I know."

Gene dropped the stick down to his side, his anger spent. "What really happened with us, Ben?"

Ben shuffled toward the side of the alley. He leaned against the building, finding the shelter under the overhang. Gene slipped back under the lid of the dumpster. It was pouring now.

"You know what happened?" Ben said. "You sold me out."

Gene tightened his grip on the stick.

"I didn't sell you out, Ben. Why should you care that I got along with Hawkins and Judson and Old Man Grenier? What does it matter how I voted on the strike? I still wanted to be your friend."

"My friend," he said. "Big fucking deal."

"What do you want from me, Ben?"

Ben sighed, paused, came toward him.

"That's close enough," Gene said when he was three feet away.

Ben set his shoulders and looked into Gene's eyes for the first time.

"What you said about rape was true, Wheeler. It isn't about sex. It's about violence. I was out of my mind tonight, but it doesn't have to be like that, not between us, I mean." He reached out to ruffle Gene's hair, and for the first time, Gene saw the gesture for what it was. He jerked his head away.

"Oh, Jesus, Ben."

"What?"

"I'm not like that, Ben. I'm not into guys."

"And I am?" Ben pulled away as if Gene had hit him. "I've been married for fifteen years, Wheeler, and regardless of how little I talk about my old lady, she is a great lay. I never said I was into guys, I said I was into you. 'Into guys,'" he said, his face an angry mask. He spit into the puddle at his feet.

"Ben," Gene said.

Ben held his hand up, cutting him off. "I didn't ask you to walk in the door, Wheeler. I could have done without that, but you did, and now I'm fucked, and I know I won't be happy until you're gone again. Shit, who am I kidding? I won't be happy, then, either, but at least I won't have to look at your face every goddamn day. Do us both a favor, Wheeler, and go back to school. Get your life back and let me have mine back, too." He shook his head. "Jesus, listen to me. Am I a fucking mess, or what?"

Gene wanted to touch him, to comfort him, but he knew he couldn't.

"How the hell was I supposed to know any of this, Ben? I

thought we were friends. You helped me out so much. You were like a brother to me."

"A brother," Ben snorted. "Big fucking deal." He shook his head. "You were so sorry those first couple days, and then before I knew it, you didn't need me at all."

"That's the way it's supposed to be."

"With brothers, maybe." Ben glanced toward his truck and held his hand out past the overhang to gauge the rain, ready to make a run for it.

"So, what are we going to do now?" Gene asked.

"Are you going to go back to school?"

"I don't know if I can do that, Ben."

"It's where you belong."

"Maybe I belong here, too. At least for now."

"Then we're both screwed."

Gene waited for him to go on, but he just stared at the pavement. He wouldn't look at Gene. When he finally did, the old Ben was back.

"Don't worry, kid," he said. "I should have known better, but I had to try. I won't bother you again. Not like I did tonight. We'll just pretend this never happened. God knows I wish it hadn't. As for the rest of it, though, as far as you sticking around, we are back to square one. I asked you nice to leave, I even told you why, but if you won't go, I'll make your life a living hell, and I know just what to do."

He paused the way he did when he was up on the picnic table reciting porn and wanted them all to know that the next line was the key to everything that had come before.

"I'll fuck with your job, Wheeler. You think I made life miserable for Hood? That was kid's stuff. I know a million different ways to screw you, some of them little, some of them big, but all of them a hundred percent effective and a hundred percent impossible to trace. By the time I'm done, everybody will think that you're the worst fuck-up in The Company.

"That won't be the worst part, though. I'll fuck up your whole crew. How long do you suppose Blondie'll stick by you with his precious reputation on the line? You think you know who your friends are around here? You just haven't run the right tests, yet.

Old Man Grenier and Blondie will drop you in a heartbeat. Jud and Dub? They might stick by you for a little while, but when push comes to shove, it's the she-bitch and their reputations that they'll protect. You'll find out real quick who cares about you." A pained look came across his face. "Who cared about you," he corrected himself.

"Come on, Ben," Gene said. "It doesn't have to be like this."

Ben held his hand up. "You made your bed, kid. Now you have to sleep in it." He looked into Gene's eyes and smiled sadly. "Do you suppose I could get my stick back now, or do you still want to break it over my head? That actually might be the best thing for both of us."

"I'll bring it to work tomorrow."

"Fair enough," he said. "Ain't this a bitch, Geno?"

"Yeah, it is."

Ben sighed. "Welcome to the land of the living." He walked across the alley and got into his car. He drove away without looking back.

Chapter Twenty-Seven

When Gene got home, the yellow glint of the sun fringed the mountains to the east. Here he was again. How many different paths could a guy take and always find himself in the same place? He felt the same way he had the final few days at school: backed into a corner. Calculus had whipped him, and he didn't know which way to turn, so he ran away.

This was no different. He could stand up to Ben, or he could run away. The only difference was that he didn't want to run this time. He was tired of running.

But no matter how much Hawkins and the guys on the A-Team had come to respect him, there was no way they would stand by him if Ben made it look like their team was fucking up. Gene had no doubt that Ben could do what he said.

He had no choice. He had to run.

He turned his back to the sun and went to his room. He pulled the curtain tight, cutting off the light. He pulled a full bottle of whiskey from under his bed, a souvenir from his last trip up Mt. Page. Hood had wanted him to save it for the next time, but there wouldn't be a next time.

The alarm went off at two. He called Phil Blair and told him he was sick. He wasn't lying. His head throbbed. His stomach revolted when he stood up, and he broke for the bathroom.

He puked his guts out for twenty minutes. When he'd emptied his stomach, he lay with his head against the porcelain, and an image of Ben's face came into his mind. First, the sad grin as he'd brushed Gene's hair; next, the anger. Gene staggered back into the bedroom and fumbled for the bottle in the dark. He rinsed with whiskey, held it in his mouth even as his stomach screamed in protest. He walked to the bathroom and spit it out, a string of spit hanging from his lips. He brushed it away and took a long drink. This time, he didn't spit it out.

He woke up the next morning before dawn and walked out onto the porch, the whiskey bottle dangling from his hand. He sat on the steps and looked out across the valley. The sun edged past the mountains. Ben's face edged into his mind. Running away looked better by the minute. Wasn't that what he'd done yesterday, anyway? It was just a fluke that he even had a choice. Some choice. He put the bottle to his lips, but it was dry.

He went back downstairs and climbed into the shower. At first, the water tore at his skin like gnawing insects, but he stood his ground, and it became water once again.

When he got out of the shower, he felt almost human. He climbed the stairs and let himself into the kitchen. His father kept his liquor on the top shelf of the pantry. Crown Royal in a purple sack. Saucier's face came to his mind. The old drunk toasted Gene with his mangled right claw. Drink up kid, he seemed to say. It worked for me. Ben winked at Gene over Saucier's shoulder.

He took a swallow of whiskey but gagged and spit it into the sink. He put it back in the sack and slid it onto the shelf. He sniffed the vodka, and his stomach barely twitched. Vodka it was.

He awoke at two and called Phil Blair.

"Okay, kid," Blair said. "Remember, though, if you don't make it tomorrow, you'll need a note from a doctor to get back on the job on Friday."

"Why's that, Mr. Blair?"

"It's in the contract. I can't ask you a fucking thing for the first two days, but after that, it's my ball game." He chuckled.

"Okay, Mr. Blair." Gene hung up.

Why not? Maybe that was the best idea. Stay drunk for a couple more days. If he didn't make it to work tomorrow and didn't have a doctor's excuse, it would be out of his hands.

He fell back to sleep without the aid of vodka, so he woke up after a few hours. He climbed back out onto the porch.

Staci was sitting on the back steps.

"What the hell are you doing here?"

"I'm like a bad penny," she said.

"But what are you doing here today?"

"You're not going to believe this, but Hood called me."

"Hood? How did he know where to find you?"

She patted the concrete beside her. He sat down, and she leaned into him. "Apparently, your drugged-out buddy is more resourceful than we imagined. He's a regular Sherlock Holmes. He remembered my name from the day you introduced us. He remembered the name of our school."

"I don't even remember telling him."

"You did. He put two and two together, called the switchboard, and somehow managed to charm the operator into getting my room number." She shrugged. "Who knew the little weasel had a charming side?"

She took his hand and interlaced her fingers with his.

"But why did he call you?"

"He's really worried about you. He said you ran out of work the other night and haven't been back since."

"I just needed a few days off."

"I don't think so. Something happened."

"It was nothing. Why didn't he come check on me if he was so worried?"

"He's afraid that if he talks to you, you might come back to work. He wanted to make sure that didn't happen. He's commissioned me to make sure you never set foot in the place again."

"He's nuts."

"Tell me what happened, and I'll decide who's crazy."

He shrugged. Maybe they were right. Why was he torturing himself? Why not get this off his chest and get back to his real life? Here it was, staring him in the face. He reached for a strand of her hair, wrapped it around his finger, and inhaled.

"Okay," he said.

By the time Gene finished, Staci looked ready to kill.

"You can't let them get away with this. You have to call the police, get those bastards thrown into jail."

"What would I tell the cops?"

"Tell them? Tell them that they tried to rape you. Rape isn't just when guys force themselves on women, you know. It might seem that way sometimes, but it's not."

"Nothing happened."

"Only because they got distracted, because you fought them off. Why would you let them get away with this? They're a bunch of animals. I knew you never should have gone to work there. You might as well have spent the last few months in Attica."

"It's not that simple," he said. He told her about Ben in the alley behind The Bone.

"You're joking."

"No."

"And this makes it better because the guy says he's in love with you or something. So, it's not a prison rape, it's a date rape."

"Jesus, Stace, could you stop this rape shit."

"No," she said. "That's what it was."

"It wasn't anything. It's a wild place. Things got out of hand. I handled it."

"You handled it? Have you lost your mind?"

"No." Not yet, anyway.

She shook her head. "I don't understand. It's almost like you're defending the guy."

"He's really messed up. He's confused as hell."

"I think you're the one who's confused."

"Maybe."

He turned away from her, but she grabbed his arm and spun him back around. She grabbed his other arm and pulled his face inches away from hers.

"Hood said that he thought you'd called in sick the last few days to give yourself a chance to think," she said. "What's there to think about? You've got to get out of that nuthouse."

"I don't know if I can do that."

"Why not?"

"I can't let Ben run me off like that."

"Run you off? What kind of macho crap is that? It's just a job, Gene. Something you did to pass the time until you could get back to school. So what if you go back sooner than you planned? It isn't worth risking your life to make a point."

"I won't be risking my life," he said, but his shoulders sank, sagging in around her body like a shell. She lifted his chin and looked into his eyes.

"What am I going to do with you?" Her grip loosened on his arms. She slipped her arms behind his back and pulled him to her.

"I don't think he'll try to hurt me again, not that way," he said. "But he told me he was going to mess with my work and the guys I work with. That's what I'm thinking about now. I don't want to run, but if I stay, he'll destroy everything that's good about the place for me. I won't be able to do my work, and neither will the guys on my crew. I don't care if he messes with me, but he's going to drag Hawkins and Judson and Dub and Old Man Grenier down, too. I don't think I could stand that."

"But what choice do you have? You said your crews work side by side. It's not like you can stay away from the guy."

"No, I can't." And then it hit him. Ben had him just where he wanted him. The only thing that he could do was run. Of course, there was more than one direction he could go.

"Come on, Stace," he said.

"Where are we going?"

"You'll see."

They parked in the back row of the lot next to Hood's pick-up, waiting for him to get off. Gene worried that Ben would spot them, but he and Devoid went by without incident. Gene wondered what had happened to Jimmy, but Jenna's station wagon pulled up in front of Hood's truck. She and Lisa got out and sat on the hood. They both wore tight jeans and red ski jackets. Jenna had her cowboy hat, and Lisa wore a bright-red visor.

"Those are the two girls we saw with Hood that time at the clam place," Staci said.

"That's right," he said. He wanted to slide down under the dashboard so Lisa wouldn't see him, but he had to see Hood, and they were obviously waiting for him.

"I'm going to talk to them for a minute," he said. "Wait here, okay?"

"Okay. I don't think Hood's little chickie thinks too much of me anyway."

"She just doesn't trust Hood."

"Smart girl."

He opened his door and walked toward them. Lisa didn't notice him, at first, but as soon as Jenna did, she planted an elbow in Lisa's side and pointed him out. Lisa smiled, but then she quickly took it back.

"Hello, ladies," he said.

"Hi, Geno," Lisa said. Jenna just nodded.

"You guys waiting for Hood?"

"I am," Jenna grinned. "Lisa's waiting for Jimmy." She seemed happy to be the one to tell him.

"Why don't you wait for Hood over by the front gate, Jenna." Lisa said.

"Why should I do that?"

"Because I asked you to."

"Anything you have to say to this creep you can say in front of me," Jenna said.

"Just go," Lisa said.

"Oh, all right." Jenna slid down to the ground, heading across the lot with her hips swaying in those jeans. Gene watched her in spite of himself. When he looked back at Lisa, he realized that she was looking into Staci's car, that she had seen her.

"Is that your college girl?"

"Yeah."

"She on vacation or something?"

"No. She knows I'm in kind of a jam, so she came to see if I was all right."

"What about her classes?"

"She blew them off."

"Good for her," she said. She waved at Staci. Staci returned it cautiously. Lisa looked back to Gene.

"Hood said something weird was going on with you. He seemed worried." She shook her head. "That asshole never worries about anybody but himself. You must be in a world of trouble."

"I guess you could say that. That's why I came to talk to Hood. I think he can help me out of it."

"Like I said. He's worried about you. I guess a lot of the guys are."

"I don't suppose Jimmy's one of those guys."

"Don't push your luck," she said. "Jimmy doesn't like you much. He likes you even less because he knows we made it together."

"I'm sorry I blew you off that last time," he said.

"It's okay," she said. "I always knew you were just passing through." She nodded toward the car. "I don't suppose she knows about you and me."

"No."

"Good," she said. She stuck out her hand. They shook.

Hood and Jimmy came out the front gate together. Talk about strange bedfellows. Lisa seemed to read his mind.

"Jimmy's okay when you get him away from his boys," she said. "Actually, I like the way this works. We get together once a week, and the rest of the time I'm on my own. You taught me how cool that could be. Thanks."

"So being with me wasn't a total loss?"

"Of course not," she said. "I'd better go get Jimmy before he sees you, though. I'll see you around." She paused. "Or maybe I won't. You going back to school?"

"That depends on Hood."

"Like I said, I think he'll help you out."

She ran to Jimmy and threw herself into his arms, wrapping her arms around his neck and her legs around his hips. Gene felt a pang of regret. When she finally slid down, she leaned over and whispered something in Jenna's ear, took Jimmy by the hand, and led him in the other direction. He seemed confused, so did Hood, but Jenna soon had him in tow and dragged him Gene's way. Hood grinned when he saw Gene leaning on the hood of his truck. Gene heard a door open behind him, and then Staci put her arm through his.

"Jesus Christ, Geno," Hood said when he reached them. "What the hell is going on? You ran out like a crazy man the other night, and then you call in sick for two days. You know, if you call in sick tomorrow, you'll need a doctor's note, or they can fire your sorry ass."

Hood felt Gene's forehead.

"I'm not sick," Gene said.

"No shit, Sherlock. What's with you, man?"

Hood studied Gene's face. He hadn't even glanced at Staci. Maybe Lisa was right. Maybe this would work.

"I've got a favor to ask you, man," Gene said.

"Shoot."

"Switch slots with me. Let me have my job back on Number Five."

"Your job back? You must be out of your mind, man. None of us knows exactly what's going on with you, but we know it's about Ben. Why the hell would you want to get back on the same crew with him?"

"You're right about one thing," Gene said. "My problems are with Ben. Thing is, he said that if I didn't quit and go back to school, then he was going to start fucking with my work."

"Tell me about it, Wheeler. I'm the one he perfected that routine on."

"Not exactly," Gene said. "He fucked with you. This time he's going to mess with my crew."

"He's fucking lost it, man," Hood said. "Why the hell do you want to give him a clear shot at you?"

"You don't understand. If I stay on Number Four, he's not just going to mess with me, but with everybody. He'll screw up our runs, make sure we never meet specs. He'll make everybody I work with look bad. I can't live with that, man."

"I don't know, Geno. The stuff he pulled on me was harmless, but if he messes with other people's runs, he might get himself fired. No offense, but I don't think he hates you bad enough to fuck up his own life. What the hell is going on with you guys, anyway?"

"I can't explain," Gene said. "All I can say is that he hates me bad enough."

"But he'll eat you alive, man."

"Maybe, but if I'm on his crew, he can't do anything but make me look bad. The other things he talked about, the things that would mess up the runs, he won't be able to do those without screwing himself."

"And Devoid and Jimmy, too," Hood said.

"You're the one who told me that he cares about teamwork," Gene said. "He might be able to mess with me or get himself fired, but I don't think he'd mess with his boys. And if he does, I can't get too worked up about it."

"I just don't get it," Hood said. "I mean I'll do it. It'll be worth it just see the look on Ben's face when he figures out the way you got around him, but I still don't get it. I wouldn't want to be in your shoes, either, man. He's going to make your life a living hell."

"Maybe."

"Besides," Hood said, "we all know you're going to go back to school before too long. Why whip Ben into a frenzy? What's the point? Go back to school now, man."

"I can't let him run me off. I've been running from things for too long. It has to stop." Staci squeezed his arm. He looked at her, and she smiled. Hood finally focused on her.

"So, Staci, what are we going to do with this guy? Can't you twist his arm and drag him back to school? It would save us all a lot of trouble."

She shook her head. "I've already tried that." She squeezed his arm again. "I don't understand any of this."

"Me, either." Hood flipped his hair out of his eyes and winked at Gene. "But I guess we aren't the ones who have to, are we?"

Chapter Twenty-Eight

When Gene walked into the room the next day, both crews were gathered at the picnic table, and Supry stood at the winder. Gene remembered the first time they'd had this kind of meeting, the time Supry talked about the first shake-up in the crews. He'd been nervous then. He didn't look nervous this time. He looked pissed. When Gene had called Supry that morning and asked about the changes, he'd insisted that Hood and Gene come to a meeting in Phil Blair's office. They'd grilled them about their reasons for the change. Blair didn't seem to care much one way or the other, but Supry hadn't seemed happy with the lies they gave him.

Everyone turned toward Gene as he walked up to the table. Even Riendeau was still there. Gene was his mate, but when he waved to him to go, he didn't budge.

"Well, well," Ben said. "Look who came back from the dead."

Hawkins and Judson stood up and walked over to Gene. Hawkins stuck out his hand.

"Welcome back, Wheeler," he said.

Judson put an arm on his shoulder and whispered in his ear. "Ignore Ben. If he gives you any trouble, I'll break him in two."

Gene nodded his thanks. They escorted him to the table and sat across from Ben and his boys. Devoid wouldn't look at him. Jimmy smirked. Dub and Hood sat on the winder. Hood winked. Dub gave Gene a thumbs up.

"All right," Supry said. "Since we're all here, I have an announcement to make." He waited until everyone looked at him.

"I'm tired of the game of musical chairs that's been going on around here," he said. "Ben wanted me to give him his own, hand-picked crew. Hood wasn't a part of that crew, even though he had more seniority, but I went along with the idea. After a few weeks, Hood decided that he did want to work with Ben. Ben got pissed off and harassed the shit out of Hood."

"Now look, Dale," Ben said. "If Hood told you I was harassing him, he's a lying sack of shit."

"Hood didn't tell me anything, Ben," Supry said. He glared at Ben. "What makes you think people have to tell me things? You think I'm blind? You think I'm stupid? Just because I'm not down here every minute you think I don't know what's going on in my own house. Sometimes, I just let things ride. I believed that you were a paper-maker, and that sooner or later, you'd stop fucking around because somebody hurt your feelings, but I was wrong."

"Now, you wait just a minute," Ben said.

"No, Ben," Supry said as he slammed his hand down on the control panel. "You wait a minute. Hood and Wheeler came to me this morning. Hood wants back on Number Four, Wheeler wants back on Number Five. They won't really tell me why, but I know it's got something to do with you, and like I said, I'm tired of this shit."

"What are you in my face for?" Ben said. "The Hood started all this when he wanted to get away from Blondie. I don't see you chewing them out."

"That's right," Supry said. "Because Hood is a kid, and Hawkins is a professional. I used to think that you were a professional, too, Ben, but now I'm not so sure. What I am sure about, though, is that the next change I make in the crews will be to boot your sorry ass out the door if you don't straighten up. Is that clear?"

Ben shrugged. Gene looked around the table and saw nothing but stunned faces. He hadn't thought that Supry had this in him. He remembered what Hawkins had said about Supry. *He was a hell of a paper-maker before they booted him upstairs.* Gene could see how he'd managed to keep all his fingers.

Supry looked around the table.

"I don't want any more musical chairs," he said. "I want everyone in specs. I don't want any more bullshit." He turned and walked out the door.

They sat for a moment, but then one by one, the others began to slip away. Riendeau was the first to go, then Devoid, Hawkins, Judson, and Dub. Jimmy was the last. He tried to get Ben's attention, but Ben just stared at the table.

Passing Time

Finally, it was just Ben and Gene. Ben looked at him and shook his head.

"I guess you're not such a little fuck-up, after all, are you, Wheeler? You're the one I should have been watching out for all along. Never mind this bullshit Supry's tossing around. I'm not afraid of him. Shit, the union won't let him touch me. Your getting back on my crew, though, it's perfect. You're giving me the thing I wanted most, but for all the wrong reasons. Don't think I can't see what this is about. You'll put yourself right under my thumb, just to protect your pals over there. You'll come back to me, but you're doing it for them." He stood and walked away, shaking his head.

Gene sat for a moment, felt one weight lifted from him as another took its place. Dub, Judson, Hawkins, and Hood talked by the front of the machine. They stopped when Ben approached. He glared at them, and they all looked at the floor, even Hawkins. After Ben passed, they looked back up and watched him as he walked away. One by one, they shook their heads. Gene realized they felt sorry for him. He knew that confused the hell out of them.

Gene knew just how they felt. They were his team, and he was glad that he'd saved them from Ben's plan. Still, they weren't the ones to help him through his first days here. Ben was right about one thing: If it hadn't been for him, Gene wouldn't have survived long enough to earn the respect of the A-Team.

Ben kept walking until he got to the front of Number Five. Gene expected him to measure his roll, but he just stood there, staring down at the paper as it surged from the front of the machine and wrapped itself around the roll. The stick hung in his hands. Devoid sat in the smoking area, staring at the floor. Jimmy stood halfway between them. He looked confused, as well. Now, it was unanimous.

Gene was proud that he'd stood up to Ben, that he hadn't run away this time. He had passed the test. So, why did he feel so lousy? Maybe this wasn't about running anymore. Maybe he was past that. Maybe this was about repaying someone who had been there for him at the start. Now that he knew that he had it in him to stay, the best thing he could do was walk away.

He looked over toward Number Four. Judson and Hawkins were

debating something. Now that the contract was settled, they were probably back on world affairs. Maybe they were still talking about Ben. Dub hung on every word. He munched on a hot dog, of course, but he still listened. Even Hood listened, though he fingered the paperback in his pocket.

He looked back toward the front of Number Four. Ben was watching him, his face blank. No anger, no love, nothing. An image flashed in Gene's mind: Ben standing on the picnic table, performing his favorite porn.

Gene stood, and though none of the others saw him, he saluted them. He turned back to Ben and nodded. A smile played with the corner of Ben's lips. He nodded back. Gene grabbed his lunch pail and slipped out into the corridor.

He caught up with Riendeau just where the first warning signs trumpeted their messages. PINCH AREA. Not anymore, Gene thought. "Riendeau," he yelled. Riendeau turned and frowned at him.

"What's up, Wheeler?"

"You want to work a double?"

"A double? There aren't any shifts open tonight."

"Mine is," Gene said. "I quit."

"You quit? Why the fuck do you want to do that?"

"Because I can," Gene said. "Because I don't have to."

Riendeau studied Gene's face.

"Because you don't have to?"

"That's right."

Riendeau nodded slowly.

"Fucking A," he said. He ran his fingers through his hair. "I don't want to work a double, but I sure as hell want to see the look on everybody's faces when I tell them about this. I have to hand it to you, man. First you saved Saucier, then you stood up to Ben, now this. It's going to be a long time before we stop talking about you. You'll be a fucking legend."

"I guess it depends on who tells the story," Gene said.

"Don't worry," Riendeau said. "I'll do you proud."

Gene started back down the corridor, following the signs, but he took a detour before MEN AT WORK. He wanted one last look at the loading dock. That and a NO HUMPING sign for his room at school. He walked through the rows of paper. Here, no fences separated him from the rolls, and he ran his hands along the surface. There were a hundred rolls of Duralon, the soft stuff that had been so comfortable in his throne. There were several hundred rolls of the thick, brown stuff that had almost killed Saucier. There were thousands more in a dozen different shades of white, and he could tell the difference in every one.

He smelled propane and stood back just as a forklift burst around the corner, tore across the dock, and humped its bale of pulp into a boxcar. He walked out onto the dock and smelled pot. Sure enough, a thin cloud rose from the door of a different car. He thought of all the nights he'd spent out here with Hood, of the night that Hawkins sat out here with him and Riendeau, and Gene realized for the first time that they were alike. He remembered warning Hood when Ben brought Supry out here to bust him. So many memories, and this was just stuff that had happened when he was on break. Maybe the old timers were right: The things he'd done to pass the time were just as important as the work itself.

He slipped into one of the boxcars and found the sign. NO HUMPING. He folded it carefully and slipped it under his shirt.

He walked back to the main corridor, took one last look toward the machine room, and turned the other way. When he came through the door at the far end of the mill, the sun glared in his face, and he took a step back. He'd never come through this door in daylight.

A horn sounded in the distance, and he turned, thinking it was one of the machines, but then he realized it was coming from the wrong direction, that it was just a train. Too bad. He wished he could have heard the ladies' voices one last time.

Ron Roy grew up in Northern New England in the shadow of the Presidential Range and the Brown Paper Company. He graduated from St. Michael's College in Winooski, Vermont, with a degree in literature. After a brief stint at The Company, he made his living in the healthcare industry, primarily in the operating room and sterile processing. He lived in Dallas, Texas, for twenty-five years and recently returned to New Hampshire, where he has driven cars for an automobile dealership and flagged traffic for a construction crew. He is the proud father of a son, Joshua, and a daughter, Coco, and the proud grandfather of Charlie Roy and Mattheus Reinhart. *Passing Time* is his first novel.